NONE OF THE ABOVE

HEIR AGREEMENT BOOK ONE

WILLOW SANDERS

Edited by
BRIGGS CONSULTING, LLC

Cover Design By
COVER ME DARLING

Copyright © 2025 by Willow Sanders

All rights reserved.

No part of this book may be reproduced in any form or by any electronic or mechanical means, including information storage and retrieval systems, without written permission from the author, except for the use of brief quotations in a book review.

Characters in this book are figments of the authors imagination and in no way represent actual people. Any similarities to people living or dead is purely coincidental.

This book is intended for an adult audience (i.e. there is S -E-X in it).

❦ Formatted with Vellum

DEDICATION

To Taylor Swift and Chinchilla,
Your rage songs were my gasoline.

1

THE INVISIBLE MAN

ELLIS

While being called into the boardroom by my father, Nathan, wasn't too out of character; being summoned at seven forty-five on a Monday morning certainly was. These days, the leader of Hawthorne Media Group tended to rule his kingdom from his suburban home instead of the concrete tower of our corporate offices. Over the last few years, he'd taken on a more consultative role. The day to day minutiae didn't appeal to him. Instead, he left those responsibilities to me and my brothers.

That suited me just fine. Considering his progeny were all raised with an absolute and unchallengeable knowledge we'd all ascend the throne and rule over his kingdom one day, as the oldest I knew the legacy began with me. I was ready for it. Prepared, I guess. One foot on the proverbial ascendant stones with a resigned sense of duty than actual enthusiasm for the role.

"What could possibly be so important that he'd put out an all-call first thing on a Monday morning?" My youngest brother Dash, leaned against one of the many flashy sports cars in his collection, holding two cups of what I assumed was Kopi Luwak.

He was a walking dichotomy. He'd drone on for hours about toxins in food, microplastics, hormones and other body disruptors. He'd passionately lament about ethical sourcing, plastics in the ocean, and any other number of granola, daisy chain, love the earth kind of foci; but then drove cars that burned more fuel in one ride than the average suburban family's minivan trip from Chicago to Disney World.

"Are we all in this meeting?" I asked, sipping from the proffered mug. His damn coffee cost more per cup than a normal family's weekly grocery bill. I wouldn't deny just how amazing the shit was, though. It took hyper-focusing to a level I couldn't experience with any other legal substance.

The elevator shot us up to the top floor of our Chicago-Loop offices. It contained our four offices, Father's office-though he rarely used it, and private conference rooms. The senior press core also held space up on the top floor, opposite us, with their own sets of conference rooms and media spaces.

"It appears so." Dash strut from the elevator first, pointing toward our other two brothers and father, already getting situated in the C-Suite meeting space.

"Anything that brings Dash downtown before the actual workday begins has got to be nuclear fallout level shit." My second youngest brother, Keats, whistled long and low while pulling out his laptop.

Dash flopped into the seat next to Keats, flipping him off as he did.

"Hey Ell, remind me, *who* was it on the phone with the AP—London at three in the fuckin' morning renegotiating our international broadcast contracts?"

"Gentleman." My father's age-roughened voice brought the bickering duo to heel with a single word.

"How did the meeting go?" Whit, the second oldest after me, asked simultaneous to my father calling the meeting to order.

"You can discuss the finer details of that meeting once I've concluded." My father ended the conversation between my two brothers before it could begin.

Nathan Hawthorne sat at the head of the conference table, his back to the expansive windows that looked out over Lake Michigan. Chicago was in that volatile time between winter and spring where the weather had no idea what to do with itself. It was perversely poetic—how gray and ominous the gathering clouds over the lake looked—given the news that our father was about to strike down.

"As you know, Hawthorne Media Group is a legacy." He began. We were all well versed in the history of HMG. We'd been force fed these stories for as long as I could remember.

"Built by my great-grandfather, Edmund Hawthorne who sought to elevate Midwestern journalism to east coast standards. He was the lightning rod; the purveyor of journalistic thought that pointed our familial compass true north. He was the one who developed Hawthorne Media Group into the bastion of information we are now."

Jesus. I had to hide my eye-roll and belabored breath behind the coffee mug Dash had given me. Directly across from me, he caught my eye and tossed me a knowing smirk and mirrored my belabored breath.

If I had a nickel for every time my father mentioned our legacy. By now, I'd have billions in a slush fund not tied to said "legacy" that could provide me with seed money for any number of secondary interests either me or my brothers would ever dream of.

He motioned to the oil painting of Edmund Hawthorne, which hung proudly beneath the HMG logo at the opposite side of the conference room. To be honest, when I was a kid, the painting freaked me out. Edmund was creepy. He'd been a wiry old codger with liver spots and stringy, receding hair. I'd always felt he gave off Mr. Burns vibes from *The Simpsons*.

My brothers and me used to scare one another by shutting off the lights in the office bathrooms as kids and calling the ghost of Edmund Hawthorne. Keats was the one who always fell for it. He got scared the most out of all of us brothers. He'd gone crying to my dad once, and instead of us getting a lecture about being nicer to our younger brother, we got multiple lectures on respecting our elders and were forced to write a report about Edmund Hawthorne and what he did for media. To better appreciate our *legacy*.

Based on the slouched positions of Keats and Dash, and my inability to spend more than a few seconds homed in on what Father said, Whit appeared to be the only one fully tuned in. Dash scrolled his phone. Keats doodled on his legal pad. Yet Whit, not only was staring right at our father, but taking notes on his tablet. He'd always been the brown noser.

My outlook chimed, signaling my first meeting of the day would begin at nine-fifteen. The old man needed to provide cliff notes post haste. Otherwise, Morgan, my executive assistant would be flitting in front of the conference room doors.

"Is there a point to this trip down memory lane?" Dash was the first to break.

"I have a nine-fifteen with our lawyers." I pointed at my

laptop, as if to remind him he too heard the meeting reminder chime.

"I want to retire." He waved his arm in the air as if clearing it of our protests. "Unfortunately leaving the legacy of HMG to your four is not a palatable option according to the focus groups."

He passed out the report findings I assumed someone from our PR team put together for him. They were dire, indeed. If the board saw them, there would be a power grab so fierce and focused, our employees would think it was a Black Friday sale at Walmart.

"I'm so glad I've been killing myself for the last seven years helping to streamline operations only for people to think I'm a silver spooned playboy wasting away on some Mediterranean island."

Dash tossed his report into the middle of the conference room table. He looked most like the Hawthorne side of the family with his jet-black hair, high cheekbones, and sharp, pointed chin. He had the same midnight-colored eyes as our father. Lucky for Dash, he benefited greatly from the wisdom of his eldest brother—me—showing him the ways of male grooming back during his pubescent years. Otherwise, he'd have the same bushy eyebrows and uncontrollably dense hair that Father did.

"That's what happens when you end up on the front page of the Italian tabloids with Miss Italy," Whit countered.

"We are both consenting adults," Dash replied. "What we do in our free time is not the business of any of these ninnies in Dad's focus group."

"You were both naked! On a yacht belonging to the Prime Minister, at what appeared to be a sex party. Not to mention Miss Italy wore a collar attached to a leash, with her face buried between your legs." Whit reminded him, his apoplectic tone causing his voice to raise an octave.

"What can I say, Miss Italy has very interesting tastes." He tossed his head in a half nod in my direction, raising his eyebrows at me as if we shared some kind of secret bond in our sexual proclivities.

"Don't involve me in this," I told him, raising my hands in defense. "I very specifically remember telling you what a terrible idea it was to go. The Prime Minister has a reputation."

"Speaking of not getting involved, why is Brontë never brought into these conversations? Surely her life is subject to the same evaluations based on public scrutiny?" Keats asked.

Barely giving Keats a second glance from whatever spreadsheet he worked on, Whit asked, "Does anyone even know where Brontë is? I haven't heard from her in at least a month."

"According to her YouTube channel, she's in Baja," Keats told us.

"What the hell is she doing in Baja?" I asked.

"Probably the same thing she was doing in Yosemite, Big Bend, and Joshua Tree." Dash leaned back in his leather chair, resting his head on his intertwined hands. "Staying the hell away from any adult responsibility and living the life of freedom that only the baby of the family could ever get away with."

Dash wasn't wrong. Other than trips that were wrapped around work, and the occasional weekend spent at our summer home in Wisconsin, I could count on my hand the number of times I'd fully gotten away from work. Meanwhile, Brontë graduated from college and had been living a free-spirited van life ever since.

"As I was saying," Father knocked on the table like a judge calling a trial back to order, "not a single one of you has any kind of positive public sentiment."

He named us off one by one. He pointed to us with the corner of his copy of the assessment his team put together. As if the judgment and condemnation in his demeanor wasn't enough, he summarized what they'd said about each of us.

"You, Ellison? Cold. Entitled. All polish, no presence. The kind of man who shakes your hand but makes you feel like he's already somewhere else. Just a suit in a chair he didn't earn. Lacks vision. Words like: puppet king. Iceman. Disconnected. They say you hide behind duty because it's safer than being seen."

What utter bullshit.

I was the face of Hawthorne. The king of connection. My shelves were lined with awards. My face had graced the covers of every major business magazine in the country—always paired with words like *visionary, trailblazer, modern magnate*. I had the soundbites, the press clippings, the gala speeches.

How could they say I have no presence. I was *everywhere*. I connected. I led.

Love? My family sure. The company, debatable. That had to count for something.

Love was as hard to hold on to as quick sand. Real, authentic connection was hard. Billion-dollar bank accounts tended to complicate things. But that was *personal* relationships. What did that have to do with standing at the helm of Hawthorne Media Group?

Legacy over love. What a crock of shit. As if I had the luxury of choosing. The floors of these offices were paved with all the times I'd bled for either—sometimes both at the same time.

The sword Father wielded burned. It felt too accurate and totally false concurrently. How did I put into words the contradiction of it all? I had a rebuttal but it was worthless. The truth was simply that the role was forced on me. It wasn't a passion; it truly was an obligation. One I dealt with the best I could.

"Whitman, the cold-blooded calculator in a designer suit. They say you treat people like numbers on a ledger—efficient, expendable, and easy to balance. Power hungry. Emotionless. More focused on profit margins than people."

Whit was not nearly as affected by his character assessment. He nodded along as my father spoke, though didn't indicate feeling any way toward what was said

"Keats, undisciplined, erratic, overly emotional, a chaotic liability." Father continued to strike with his sword, cutting pounds of flesh from each of us.

Keats reminded me of Brontë. They should have been twins. The pair of them matching flames that burned hot. He was all emotion. But that was what made him an amazing strategist. He saw things, felt things, that no one else in the room did. He was brilliant, albeit illogical most of the time.

"We already know what happened with Dash." Whit held up his hand to stop my father's tangent. "No need to rehash it. We know, he's the morally bankrupt playboy."

Dash didn't even blink. He leaned back in his chair, toying with the Graff watch on his wrist like he had all the time in the world.

"My morals may be bankrupt, but my deal with London just saved us about a hundred million dollars," Dash announced, boredom lacing his tone.

"You each have six months."

My father cut through the tension with all the subtlety of a guillotine. He didn't raise his voice. He didn't need to.

Whit's fingers froze mid keystroke. Keats blinked, his pen frozen on his note pad, looked up like he wasn't sure he'd heard right. Dash sighed so loud it echoed.

"Six months to do what?" I asked, re-reviewing the files he'd handed us trying to suss out what exactly could be done in such a short window of time.

"Six months to find your future wives and start dating them. It's time to settle down. The Hawthorne legacy can no longer afford to have its image tainted by four men who have sat on the 'Most Eligible Bachelors List' for far too long. Ellison you'll be forty in seven months. Whitman, eighteen months after that..."

"Yes, and Keats two years after that, and me right after him a year later. We know how old we are, Dad. I don't see how forcing us all into marriage solves anything." Dash cut him off with an impatient wave.

"Page three," Keats muttered.

I hadn't gotten that far yet. The bickering between my brothers had pulled my focus from digesting the full brief. I flipped to the tab marked *Heir Agreement* and skimmed the bolded paragraph. This had to be a joke. No one in their right mind would make these kinds of demands, would they?

"The board believes that the public has lost trust in us. The public, according to the board, feel the next generation of Hawthornes have created an air of instability," my father replied.

"So make Ellis get married. Why do the rest of us have to suffer? He's the one everyone expects to be CEO," Keats persisted.

I hadn't heard Keats whine this much since deciding where to go to college. He'd desperately wanted to go to the west coast. Pepperdine was his dream school. Knowing Pepperdine offered no palatable option for the family patriarch; he'd tried to negotiate for Stanford or USC. But like the rest of the Hawthornes, it was the Medill School of Journalism at Northwestern for him. So he could work while going to school, of course.

"We each hold a piece of the operation of this company. If one of us fails or is perceived to be failing it affects the entirety of the corporation." I told him.

The shock prevented me from absorbing what my father was saying. *Get married?* I didn't even date. Not really. There were women, ones with good family names and toothpaste ad smiles. Perfect for posing, great *optics*. It ended there though. They didn't come to my bed or in my life. At all.

Now, because of public decree I was supposed to open that door again? To let someone in? What a joke.

"I turn seventy in nine months." My father continued ignoring the cacophony of apoplexy around the table. "You'll all be engaged at the minimum by the time your mother throws me my combined birthday and retirement party."

Less than a year? In the span of time a woman grows a human being I had to find a woman, date her, and find her palatable enough that I'd put a Harry Winston on her finger? Not happening.

The image didn't even compute. I'd gone down that road already once. And even when I thought it was love, it was just another person desperate to take a pound of flesh out of the Hawthorne legacy. And now Father wanted me to open myself up to the butcher's knife for the rest of my life? What complete bullshit.

I hadn't let anyone in close enough to consider anything resembling permanence since—. I clenched my jaw, cutting the thought off before it could spiral. Letting someone in once had cost me more than I'd ever admit. I wouldn't make that mistake twice.

It wasn't just about the optics or public trust. My Father, the king of *don't let them get too close*, wanted me to give someone unfettered access to my world. He was the one who told me that the more people who had access to you, found ways to capitalize on your weaknesses. For someone like me, that wasn't just inconvenient. It was a massive risk.

I couldn't breathe. Words floated around me heard but unprocessed. Not until my brothers started grumbling again did the world reassemble itself again.

"Surely this isn't legal?" Whit turned to me for the answer. I don't know why he thought I'd know any better. Just because I had a meeting with the lawyers didn't mean I was one.

"By all means, challenge me." My father, pushed from the table and took a slow lap around the conference room, ominously pausing behind each of us. "If you don't want to abide by my stipulation, feel free to step down and walk away from Hawthorne for good."

He allowed the weight of that suggestion to hang in the air like an unwelcome guest. The implication to the statement was obvious to all of us. If we walked away, we'd also lose any inheritance that may be coming to us, along with the jobs that had sustained our lifestyles since college. Part of me briefly considered walking away. There was a freedom to that suggestion.

Media, unfortunately, was all I knew. We'd been groomed from diapers to understand print, radio, television, and eventually as the space expanded streaming and podcasts. HMG was everywhere. Not only in every facet of media but insinuated deep into the marrow of our bones. None of my brothers knew anything differently either. There wasn't a Plan B. We all waltzed to the same Hawthorne song and dance.

"As enlightening as this meeting has been, I still have to steer the ship." I collected my things and stalked toward the door. "It's always an interesting day at the office when you're around, Father."

As I sat at my desk, the view of Monroe Harbor just at my sightline over my computer, I felt like the vise around my chest loosened enough for a cleansing breath. I timed my breaths to the waves hitting the break walls out my window. The fury of the dreary morning's tide seemed to calm me somehow. The weight of my father's decree beat in rapid staccato with each inhale and exhale.

Engagement.

Marriage.

Optics.

Legacy.

None of it had anything to do with love. It was business. A performance. And if I had to perform, I'd need a script. A partner who knew how to help me find someone to play a part. I needed someone strategic. Sharp. Trusted. Someone who'd already survived the fire of being near the Hawthorne flame.

Rowan Sloane.

Her name landed as a punch to my solar plexus, sharp and sudden, followed by a wave of tender nostalgia. If anyone could handle impossible men with monumental expectations it would be her. Sharp. Trusted. The only person I knew who when pitched a curveball would swing for the fences with the accuracy of Babe Ruth.

I hoped she was still as precise and unflinching as I remembered. And that what I remembered of her was accurate and not colored by time and sentiment. When I knew Rowan Sloane, she was a woman who never asked for power but held it with confidence, like gravity. I hoped she still did. And that she'd take my call.

2

BATTLE ROYALE

Rowan

The first time Ellis Hawthorne called me, I assumed it was a mistake. It had been ages since I'd heard from him. Sure, we'd always promised to keep in touch, but once I'd left HMG my own life's ambitions carried me away.

That isn't to say that I didn't stalk his life like a trashy telenovela. The women of Chicago, hell the women of the United States, reported on Ellis Hawthorne, along with the rest of his brother's comings and goings as if they were the royal family. I knew he finally made it into the C-Suite. It was only a matter of time before that old codger Nathan Hawthorne stepped aside and gave Ellis the reins to HMG, fully.

Of all the Hawthorne brothers, Ellis was the most photographed. He had that all American look: the distinguished jaw, perfectly aligned and brilliantly white teeth, a smile that had its own heat index and made his cocoa-colored eyes crinkle along the joining of his eyelids. He and Keats—and Brontë, their elusive sister—had their mother's coloring. I'd never met her, but I knew the look. Auburn waves, wind-kissed cheekbones, and the kind of beauty that made you feel like you were in the presence of mythology.

Whit and Dash, the other Hawthorne brothers, had their father's dark countenance. Raven's wing hair and sharp, angular faces that only highlighted their unusual eyes. Green eye's like Whit's shouldn't look so cold. And the midnight blue of Dash's shouldn't belong on someone who made headlines for his sexual proclivities. And yet, the press loved Ellis best. Or hated him most. They called him The Iceman. Controlled, untouchable, forever alone.

The second time Ellis called, I watched his name scroll across my screen for long seconds before going to voicemail. That time his name ushered in a wave of memories. Late nights working on projects together. The weight of his stare, and the feeling of euphoria when I won a smile. The way he asked my opinion after everyone else had spoken. As if my opinion held the most weight.

I never felt like just an Admin with Ellis. He'd trusted me. Treated me as an equal despite our salary disparity. Maybe because there was only roughly four years separating us. Did he know, inherently, that I didn't belong in an admin's chair? That I'd always had my eyes on a higher prize?

The call finally went to voice mail. No message. I irrationally waited for one to load. No such luck.

By the third call, an hour later, I figured he must be desperate. I answered because curiosity is a dangerous thing for women who know better. And yet, I couldn't resist.

"Rowan," he said, his voice as precise as ever. Same clipped consonants. Same cool detachment. "I need your help."

No greeting. No pleasantries. No apology for losing touch, or inquiry into life's updates. I was certain he was far too busy and disinterested to stalk me on social media with as much intense focus I did him.

"Ellis Hawthorne," I replied, tucking my phone between shoulder and cheek as I sorted through onboarding materials for my newest client, "are you dying or just finally admitting to yourself I wasn't as replaceable as you thought?"

A pause. I could have driven a freight train through that pause. It coiled between us with long tendrils. Finally, just as I'd been about to say *are you still there,* he replied, "You should've never left. HMG needs people like you."

I snorted a laugh that I'd intended to be charmingly coy. "Aw, but you and I both knew I was never staying."

"You could've." His voice lowered into a quiet timbre. "You belonged here."

"No," I corrected, pulling a branded USB out of the stack. "The intent was always to get a few years of ironclad experience before moving on. Moving on, surprisingly, meant finally taking a leap and starting my own company. Which, by the way, is going exceptionally well, thanks for asking. Your congratulatory cookie basket must have gotten lost in the shuffle of all the well-wishers. Apologies for not sending a thank you note."

"Quit busting my balls, Sloane."

His laugh was loud and unexpected. A thrill went straight through my nervous system. The sound was rich, and achingly familiar. His laugh echoed through the phone like a memory I hadn't asked to remember. I pressed my palm flat against the desk, trying to ground myself against the sudden spike of heat. It wasn't until that exact moment I forgot what it was like to banter with Ellis. His intellect tickled all of my senses concurrently.

"Look, I get it. It must be difficult to fill my shoes. After all these years though, I worry how many congratulatory notes and flowers never made it to their designated recipients. If you're calling to ask me to return before you officially accept your crown and scepter, I'm going to have to decline."

I could picture the exact way he used to look at me across the expanse of his mahogany desk. He'd tip his chin slightly, a knowing smirk would dance across his lips. It was as if he already knew how I'd answer and anticipated the moment I impressed him.

"As incredible as the supposed offer would be," I continued, "I have my own company to deal with now."

My company. Pivot. It wasn't just a name on the door. It was proof of what I built. My fingerprints were on every inch of my company. Each process, pitch, and client were a result of digging deep and pushing ahead even when the naysayers didn't think I could succeed. But what they didn't know about me, was that working for HMG set a high bar. I learned how to lead from watching the best. I knew what it took to shape opinions and control narratives because working at HMG showed me every day how public opinion was created and formed.

Ellis had been a mentor. Whether intentional or not he set a bar and always encouraged me to reach above it. And I did. I rose. He'd created the pyre of ambition from which that first strike against flint billowed into fiery passion. And now, I had something to show for it. Pivot. My greatest source of pride.

"Morgan is top notch." Ellis pulled my focus back to the conversation at hand.

I imagined him in that sleek Scandinavian chair. He definitely was still on the top floor, only behind a new set of windows with a better view of the lake. His fingers were probably buried in his hair, making it look even more sexily disheveled without trying. He did that when he was tense. Or he did, when I'd worked for him. He'd run a hand through it, tugging just slightly at the back like he didn't realize it was his tell.

It had been ages since I thought about HMG, yet as I bathed in Ellis Hawthorne's voice, suddenly memories flowed into my consciousness from every direction. The playful way the brothers interacted with one another. Ellis hunched over his computer, sternly focused on whatever spreadsheet he needed to study and approve. The way he always ensured I was fed, hydrated, and rested.

I opened my mouth to respond. Perhaps I'd gone a touch too far and needed to apologize. But he beat me to it. Like always. He always moved first, and somehow, I'd fallen right back into that easy rhythm with him.

"...practically cloned yourself and left her on my doorstep. While you will always be irreplaceable, she runs a very tight second."

His tone was teasing, but the tension in his voice hinted that I'd struck a nerve. It was clear he deeply respected his assistant and didn't appreciate my slight. Even if it was innocent and teasing.

A beat passed. I realized I'd unintentionally taken a swipe at his assistant. It hadn't been my intention and just as I'd opened my mouth to apologize, Ellis responded.

"But I forgot—nothing stings quite like the suggestion that I've managed to move on without you."

My breath caught, though I couldn't wrap my head around why that comment affected me. I started at my screen saver, watching the colors bounce in slow arcs. I wouldn't flinch. Even if the line didn't quite feel like was entirely about Morgan.

Before I could respond, he chuckled and continued. "You know," the timbre of his voice warming, "going into business for yourself has really humbled you. I'm so relieved that your head hasn't gotten too big for your shoulders. It would be a shame for you to become a hunchback at thirty-six."

"Well," I volleyed back, "I had you as a personal case study on the effects of arrogance on cranial size. All of those coffee requests and meeting updates each morning. Given your head is still incredibly proportional to your body, according to the never-ending updates on your whereabouts across all avenues of media, I think I'll be okay."

It wasn't until I felt the ache in my cheeks, I realized I was grinning like a loon. It wasn't just memories. It was him. His voice, how precise and intentional he was with everything he said. The intense focus that caused something inside me to coil with warmth, like a cat wrapped around a dryer warmed blanket. Howdy I felt when he laughed at my jokes—as if I'd *earned* his delight.

We'd drifted into a soft silence. Not the uncomfortable kind. That pleasant space where both parties are kind of floating along memory lane.

"Besides," I reluctantly broke the genial bubble, "you knew I couldn't stay."

I wanted to. Considered it multiple times. The amount if pro/con lists I'd concocted on moving on or attaching myself to the rising Hawthorne were ridiculous. He never asked though. When I turned in my notice, he looked at me sad and resigned, told me he knew I was destined for better things. But he never asked me to stay.

"My cousin Hillary is in the C-Suite at Hursch Media. That would've created massive questions of either corporate espionage or collusion. I had to leave."

"I didn't like it," he said in that matter-of-fact tone I'd been all too familiar with when I'd worked with him. It was the stoic businessman voice. The one that revealed nothing. Emotionless and detached.

"I didn't ask you to." I replied.

He was the one calling *me*. Whatever the reason for calling, he needed something from me, not the other way around. And if he wanted to snap the thread of whatever warmth we'd found, I wasn't going to chase after it.

"I'm sure you're wondering why I'm calling." That same tone, The Iceman.

"Color me curious," I forced a smile hoping it would carry through the call.

"I need you." He stated simply.

"You know it's Mid-March, Groundhog Day already passed."

Paisley poked her head into my office with a lifted brow. My three o'clock. I waved her in, still clutching my phone. She tapped against her Apple Watch, impatiently signaling to me the time. Two fifty-six. As she gathered the materials from my desk, I couldn't miss the belabored look she threw me. I knew it all too well. If I wasn't on the phone, she'd pitch a fit about me doing work that could easily be delegated. But sometimes I liked doing busy work, it helped me clear my mind and focus.

"I don't follow," he said.

I'd been so wrapped up in tracking Paisley out of my office, I momentarily forgot I was still volleying with *the* Ellis Hawthorne.

"I just told you that working for you wasn't possible long term. Conflict of interest," I enunciated it slowly for emphasis. "I have a massive one. Besides, I have a job, Ellis. I own a company. With employees and W2s, unemployment taxes, and leases on office equipment- the whole nine yards. And I have a client who is sitting in my conference room waiting for me to arrive. So I'll need to let you go."

I let the last syllable hang. Part of me hoped he'd try to stop me. I wasn't ready to detach the tether. Our conversation had been...fun.

"Wait!" The command sounded almost pleading. Ellis Hawthorne did not plead. He didn't even ask most of the time. He demanded.

"I need to talk to you. Please. How does dinner sound?"

"Ellis..." I wasn't even sure what the source of my impertinence was. His name in my mouth felt strange. Familiar in the way a favorite song sneaks up on you after years of silence.

"Call it a consultation. Bill HMG double your standard rate. I'll have Morgan connect with your assistant and find a suitable time."

The line disconnected before I could even give him an answer. I guess I'd be meeting with Ellis Hawthorne and getting paid to do so. At double my normal rate, apparently. I guess if I had to "suffer" through dinner with him, getting paid double to do it wasn't too bad.

Morgan, Ellis's assistant booked us at the Signature Room. Some things never changed when it comes to Ellis. The restaurant sat atop the John Hancock building in the heart of the loop. The HMG offices were next door, sharing in those million-dollar views of the lakeshore and bustling metropolis. I missed those offices. My own tiny suite in a nondescript post war building looked directly into the building next door, which sold geriatric equipment. My views were anything but spectacular.

Being booked at the Signature Room was something Ellis reserved for important business. The restaurant's ambience led to quiet talks that could be guaranteed confidential given the many private rooms available for dining. It was his favorite place to bring people when negotiations were getting ugly, or he needed to curry favor to close a deal.

Knowing the hefty price tag on most of their menu, seeing the invite certainly raised my eyebrows. Clearly whatever he needed to talk to me about was important. Otherwise, his assistant would have suggested we meet for drinks at the gastropub on the first floor of their building. Despite a fairly open social calendar, unless one counts marathon watching *Gilmore Girls* for the nine hundredth time, I'd asked Paisley to make Ellis work a little to get on my calendar.

Not because I didn't want to see him. Jesus, it was ridiculous how much I *wanted* to see him. But I wanted him to respect me as a businesswoman, and businesswomen did not sit at home at night power watching old TV shows and eating take out nearly every night of the week.

Despite Ellis working exactly seventeen steps from the entrance to the Hancock building, I still managed to arrive first. I hadn't wanted to do. I wanted him to wait and squirm and wonder where I was. Not due to lack of respect, but because for once Ellis didn't have the upper hand. He needed something from me and deserved to squirm a little while he waited.

"Rowan."

The rich timbre of his voice behind me raised all the tiny hairs on the back of my neck. I'd just barely taken a seat at the bar when he approached from behind.

"She'll have a G & T. Botanist preferably, Hendricks if not. Light ice, with one lime and a cherry." He told the bartender as he placed a kiss against my cheek that lingered for the briefest, impossible moment.

"And for you sir?" The bartender asked as he chilled the glass that would hold my drink.

"French 95. Basil Hayden, not too sweet. Veuve to top."

Even his drink orders were elegant and refined. No need to flippantly signal his wealth with a rare and overpriced scotch. Ellis preferred the subtly of an aged bourbon with a sweet kiss of sought after champagne.

"Rowan." My name dripped from his lips like honey. It felt like the first rays of the summer sun, and the soothing warmth of a winter's fire all rolled into one. I'd wanted to stay on the high ground for the meeting. To show him I had my business chops, and I wasn't afraid to go toe to toe with one of the country's largest titans of industry. Instead, I simply melted when his fingers gently squeezed my shoulder and his lips brushed against my cheek.

"Ellis Hawthorne, owner of many luxury timepieces, yet unable to be on time even to a meeting he requested."

He took the seat next to me, a rare full watt smile playing on his lips. I still had the magic touch. Making him smile had always felt like summitting Everest.

"Rowan Sloane, still incapable of not busting my balls, even when she's making a small fortune off this dinner."

Maybe I fudged my consultation rate. I'd wanted to gauge just how important this meeting was to him. I almost felt guilty. But we weren't friends and this was business.

Even if he did kiss my cheek like we were old friends, and not his old administrative assistant.

"Call me crazy, but when you reach out looking for someone's assistance, typically you give even the slightest modicum of respect and show up on time."

I took a sip of my drink, watching him watch me. His smile dazzled me with little effort. Ellis wore his glasses tonight. A rare occurrence. I'd only ever seen him in glasses at a corporate retreat when he'd asked me to meet him in his suite to go over his presentation. And once when he contracted some kind of eye infection and wasn't allowed to wear contacts until it cleared. I liked them. They were just rounded enough to not be overtly rectangular. A cream colored tortoise shell that was striking against the honeyed color of his skin. How he managed to look so tan even in the first breath of spring was beyond me.

The Matre'd approached from Ellis's left to tell us our table was ready. He collected both of our drinks and signaled for me to follow the man to our private table on the second floor. Wealthy, powerful men like Ellis were the only ones allowed up the winding stairs and behind the velvet rope. It kept them out of sight of the average hoi polloi that dare celebrate their milestone occasions breathing the same air as Chicago's elite.

"You look lovely Rowan," Ellis opened the first volley of the evening's discussion. "Being your own boss suits you. You're practically glowing."

He didn't look so bad himself. Ever the restrained CEO in his black fitted cashmere turtleneck and whisper soft looking gray slacks. It was as if he'd stepped right out of the Brooks Brothers display case from the Water Tower shops down the road.

"The stress of the role certainly hasn't had any negative effects on you either, Mr. Ellison Hawthorne, CEO."

"CEO in name only." He chuckled, leaning back in his chair and crossing one leg over the other. "Nathan Hawthorne is surprisingly –or I guess not so surprisingly— having a hard time letting go."

I'd expected that. It wasn't surprising. The old man was a workhorse. Even when I'd been at HMG, his legacy was palpable. It pulsed through the halls, through the tone of every team meeting, through the pressure behind every pitch deck. It felt like everyone at HMG knew the history of the company. Could recite, from memory, the first newspaper ever produced, the first television station purchased, the first radio conglomerate and so on through all the various modernizations through history.

"Well, look at how much HMG has grown on his watch. When he took over from your grandfather HMG was newspapers and radio. Now it's a global conglomerate. There are a lot of personal sacrifices from him, specifically, in building it to what it is today."

Ellis tipped his head, eyes narrowing slightly — the kind of look he gave when he saw more than you meant to reveal. He never talked about the cold distance between him and Nathan, but it clung to him. Sat in his posture. Wove itself into every mention of duty, responsibility, or legacy. "I guess in five years I forgot how observant you are. I bet your consultancy business is immensely successful." He raised his glass in toast.

Did he know how much his pride affected me? Even if he was just buttering me up for whatever reason he "needed" me, that compliment swelled inside of me. Inside my head, a miniature version of myself spun and twirled in a shower of glitter and sunshine at his words.

"I love what I do." I replied, reluctant to tell him that my *tiny business that could* did *well enough*—I had a team of five that I was able to pay on time every two weeks—but every month was a rollercoaster of stress. Hoping clients paid, having to pull from my individual savings to cover payroll when they didn't. I still had too many start up loans than I was comfortable carrying. But I truly loved what I did. I loved that people looked to me as the expert in the room. That they showed me their fledgling businesses built on enthusiasm and dreams and asked me how to make them shine.

"I'd also really love to know why I'm here. The location isn't lost on me. This is where you take the big fish or have the big asks. So what's the ask?"

"For the record," He nodded at the waiter as he collected our menus as we finished placing our orders, "I would have brought you here even if it was just to ask you if you wanted to come to a Cubs game with me. The restaurant isn't about the ask. It's about the amount of esteem I hold my companion in. You, Rowan, would never be a drink at a local pub."

Ellis shifted in his seat, a rare flicker of uncertainty flashing across his features. For a man who spent his life mastering the art of negotiation, he suddenly looked like he didn't know quite where to begin. He reached for his drink, took a slow sip, and exhaled through his nose like it might brace him.

"You're right," he said finally, running a tired hand across his face. "There is an ask. And I won't sugarcoat it because you'd see through that anyway." He paused. "My father has decided to retire, but with one spectacularly *Hawthorne* condition."

Ellis took a slow sip of his drink and stared past me for a

long moment. The twinkling lights of a city morphing into night flickered like an afterthought in his eyes. When he finally looked at me, something had shifted. His smile was gone. But he didn't look mad, or even sad. The icy businessman wasn't present either. Ellis Hawthorne, ascendant heir of HMG, who could command the attention of an entire ballroom with a single clearing of his throat, looked *nervous*.

"It's going to sound" He gestured wildly, as if the air could provide the explanation he needed. "... insane."

"Try me." I tried to pull off coy, arching my brow and shooting him a wry smile, "I once had a client ask me to brand her llama farm into a wellness retreat and animal sanctuary."

"My father's retiring," he said, setting his glass down with a soft thud. "Nine months from now, my mom is throwing a combined birthday and retirement party for him. By then, he expects the four of us—me and my brothers—to be engaged."

They must have made my gin and tonic awfully strong. I had to have misheard him. There was no way, in this day and age, that even someone as controlling as Nathan Hawthorne would force something so ridiculous on his sons.

"Engaged?" I heard myself drawing out the word as if English wasn't my first language. I sounded asinine, yet I couldn't stop the apoplectic inquiry. "As in wedding rings and monogrammed towels engaged?"

"Well, I guess so, yes. It's optics more than anything. Falling in love and wanting to spend every second of the day skipping through flower fields is not a concern of Nathan Hawthorne." He replied, voice clipped. "Apparently the public doesn't trust a pack of rich, powerful bachelors to helm a global media empire. We're viewed as unstable. I believe the words untrustworthy and cold were also used."

He pulled a report out of his bag and handed it to me. I flipped through the massive report filled with pie charts and Likert scale responses amazed that anyone would do this level of research on their own kids. There were even pictured profiles of each son, along with callouts highlighting general opinions of each of them. Under Ellis's picture were words like "cold," "entitled," "lacks vision." It twisted my gut just reading them. This was not the Ellison Hawthorne I knew. Or the one his employees knew.

"And what does any of that have to do with me?" The question came out before I'd thought about how to form it with more finesse.

"I need help finding someone. The *right* someone. Someone the board and the media will believe. Someone polished enough to hold her own, smart enough to navigate the spin, and willing to play a role. Because this is *just* a role. A business arrangement. Two successful and driven people who understand the terms of the contract from the jump."

He leaned forward then, elbows on the table, his eyes practically boring into my soul with the intensity I saw there. "That's where you come in, Rowan. I need a strategist. Someone I can trust. Someone who already knows how the Hawthorne machinery works. I need you."

It was a lot to take in. Was he insane? Was I insane for immediately thinking of ways to help him get organized, while simultaneously doing a rapid vetting of the well-known women in is social circle?

"So let me get this straight: you want me to help you... cast a fiancée?"

"Technically a wife. But yes, fiancée first. Once the two of us determine the partnership is…palatable…we would move on to discussions of mergers." His mouth curved in a wry half-smile. I recognized that smile. It was the charming one that sent all the interns in a tizzy. It suggested shared jokes, common ground, equality when clearly given his role and stature was simply a fallacy.

I just stared. Mergers? Palatable? Who talked about marriage with such clinical detachment?

"Ellis," I leaned back in my chair, giving him the once over. "In looks alone you're A5 Wagyu prepared by a three star Michelin chef. Throw in the warmth and wit I know you're capable of, and you're…well, you're not exactly a hard sell. Why would you pick someone at random and throw a ring on her finger? It's unnatural."

He said nothing. That smirk was back. This time though it felt more like a mask than an attempt to charm.

"Are you sure about this? I've heard some wild pitches Ellis, but this one takes the cake."

He didn't blink. Just waited, calm as ever. I looked around the Signature Club, trying to convince myself that the ambient sounds of people conversing and eating were simply a richly illustrated hallucination. I'd shake my head any moment and find myself still on the phone with Ellis Hawthorne assembling pitch folders.

"This isn't a relationship," I said, hearing how flat my voice sounded. "It's optics. Simply optics with a shiny diamond ring to distract people's attention from the wool you're pulling over their eyes."

"Optics are the currency," he replied evenly. "You know that better than anyone."

God, he meant it. The stakes were high. So was the risk. It wasn't anything I could add to the roster on my website as a current project either. This would come with NDAs and promises to never speak of it.

"You want to engineer a relationship," I continued, baffled not only that he would willingly put himself through something like this, but also that I was the one he trusted to help him.

"Exactly!" he said, light flitting through the brindle color of his eyes, "I need a compelling narrative, with a clean execution. No emotion, just two people with similar goals, agreeing to align their lives for the optics. Certainly, there are busy career women out there that don't want the hassle of sorting through endless dates to find someone to get married and have a family with. It would be mutually beneficial. The fact that I'm a billionaire with unlimited resources certainly won't hurt."

I knew he didn't mean that. Ellis Hawthorne was grounded, caring, down to earth. When I worked for him, I forgot he was a billionaire most of the time. Ostentatious didn't even live in the same zip code as Ellis.

"You want a board approved, media safe, vetted relationship with a woman you don't love, but will love the way she photographs next to you, while enjoying the benefits of an unlimited bank account?"

How could he not see what he was asking for? I had confidence in my skills. I had zero doubt I could trot out dozens of vapid socialites for him to approve. But none of this jived with the Ellis I thought I knew. I couldn't imagine him being happy with something so empty.

"She doesn't have to love anything," he said. "She just has to agree to the terms."

There was something in that line of thinking that felt hollow and incredibly sad. He deserved more than an emotionless joining together of trust funds and asset sheets.

Certainly that wasn't what his dad intended when he'd given him the ultimatum. While I didn't know Nathan Hawthorne well, or his wife Clara, I assumed, given they'd been together for nearly forty-five years that he loved her. They had five kids—surely that couldn't just be wifely duties as her part of what she was contractually obligated to bring to the table.

"Are you sure this is what you want?" I asked. "What about love? The security of having someone who has your back. Celebrates your wins, comforts you when you stumble? This agreement you want to forge—it's cold Ellis. Detached. Is that really the life you want to live?"

The question caught him. Not visibly. But there was a shift — a blink too slow, a pause in his breath. Ellis didn't flinch. Didn't look away. But the silence stretched just long enough to make me wonder if I'd hit something real.

"Want isn't part of the equation," he said finally. "Not anymore. And given the strict deadline Father has provided, he clearly doesn't intend for any of us to find true love either. Who falls in love in less than a year?"

His voice was low, even. Practiced. But there was something underneath it — a tiredness, maybe. Or resignation. The man ran a multi-billion-dollar company. Solving problems was part of his daily responsibilities. How on earth was this the best solution to his father's ultimatum?

"Security?" he went on, rolling his drink across the crisp linen tablecloth. "That's an illusion. People stay until it no longer suits them. I've seen what happens when emotion becomes the metric. It's chaos. Unreliable. I don't need someone to hold my hand when I fall, Rowan. I need someone who won't let me fall in the first place."

The statement landed with a weight I wasn't prepared for. Words failed me. I could only gape like a fish desperate for air. I thought back to the years I'd worked alongside him. Sure he could be direct, dismissive even. But in between all of those phrenetic days of nonstop meetings, fires that needed putting out, and a constant parade of people needing decisions from him, there were peeks of a man and not just the executive. The one who looked up gratefully from his pile of papers when I'd bring a cup of coffee to him. Or who would say he "needed some air," but then would walk across town to pick up sandwiches from my favorite shop because he'd overheard me say to one of the other admins I was starving and hadn't had a moment for lunch. That man needed something more than cold indifference. He needed someone who would pour into him as much as he secretly liked to pour into others.

"So you'd rather be safe than loved?" I asked.

He didn't answer.

He didn't have to.

"And if this backfires?" I asked. "If your perfectly curated love story falls apart under scrutiny?"

There were so many potential pitfalls. Never mind the gossip or even people leaking this to the media. I was more concerned about long-term pitfalls. Sacrificing his heart to appease some stupid inheritance clause. I couldn't imagine how you could call that kind of cold, detached existence a life.

"Then I'll handle it," he said. "Like I always do."

There was a hollowness to that — the kind that echoed even in a place as luxe and manicured as this one. I pushed back from the table just enough to feel the shift in power.

"You're asking for a strategist," I said. "But what you really need is a shield."

Someone to protect him from himself. To help him see how dangerous it was to just jump into a relationship based on façade and negotiations. He looked up at me at that moment, his eyes deep pools of melted chocolate. I felt his focus shift, and it was as if he saw me, not as a resource, or his old assistant, but as a person who truly saw him for everything he was. Not just the billionaire, or the CEO, but a man who despite everything he laid out on the table, wanted to be seen and loved.

He looked at me then, for real this time. And not like I was a resource. Like I was the only person who'd seen through the armor and stayed.

"I need you," he said again. Quieter this time. Not a demand. Just truth. And damn it — I was already halfway to yes.

I stared at him, heart thudding. This wasn't a job. Not really. It wasn't media strategy or optics analysis or brand development. That was my wheelhouse. The place where I held my own against the best of them. This was a request to architect an illusion so convincing the public—and his father—would believe it was love.

He sat across from me in that perfectly tailored suit, so composed it almost masked the desperation pulsing beneath the surface. Almost.

"I know this isn't really what you do," he said softly, "but I also know no one else would be able to handle this. Not with the same care and discretion you would."

My fingers curled around the edge of the table, grounding me. Because it would be so easy to say yes. Too easy. I owed him nothing. But the ache in his voice, the vulnerability in the ask cracked something open I didn't expect.

And maybe it wasn't just about helping him. Perhaps I still felt the need to prove to him and myself that I could do this. That I wasn't the same naïve young girl who left HMG to forge her own path. Maybe in accepting, I could show him and all of those like him that people could be taken seriously in this city without a last name to open doors for you.

"I'll think about it," I said, standing. "*I'll* call *you* when I'm ready to discuss options and plans."

A voice in the back of my mind whispered something else entirely: *You're going to regret this.*

He didn't argue.

"Understood."

THE AIR OUTSIDE was colder than I expected. The wind off the lake stole my breath as it snuck between the open flaps of my jacket like it had every right to do so. It was such a contrast to the bubble of genial warmth I'd relished in sitting with Ellis. Even if that bubble also included a quandary of pretty lies.

My heels clicked against the sidewalk as I crossed Michigan Avenue. Despite the late hour, tourists still lined the streets, gazing at the display windows of all the stores closed for the evening. As I pressed on past couples, and between blaring cab horns, the city rolled out behind me and continued to glisten with its vibrant beauty, uncaring that Ellis Hawthorne, darling of Chicago, heir apparent to one of the largest media conglomerates in the country, had just asked me to fabricate his future.

I didn't go straight home. I couldn't. In fact, I'd already walked past my house, twice. I needed the walk. The movement helped the chaos in my brain. The cavernous night sky made my brain feel like it had more space than the claustrophobic weight of expectation sitting across from Ellis miming social niceties.

By the time I stepped into my house, my body was buzzing and my brain was on fire. I dropped my keys in the bowl on my kitchen counter, kicked off my shoes, and collapsed onto the couch without bothering to turn on the lights. The skyline blinked at me through the windows. I stared right back. I could hear music from the piano club down the street. Even its melodies sounded forlorn from where I sat.

"She doesn't have to love anything."

That line had kept echoing in my head the entire walk home. Cold. Precise. Like it had been rehearsed. But that wasn't what haunted me.

What haunted me was the flicker behind his eyes when I asked about love. That pause. That breath. The one that said he *had* thought about it — maybe once, maybe often — and decided it was a liability.

Ellis Hawthorne didn't want a partner. He wanted a firewall. And what scared me most? I understood it. I understood the temptation to control the narrative, to script the story so no one could hurt you with it. I'd done it. Still did it. Hell, it was the foundation of my career. But it felt different coming from him. I'd seen the man behind the glass. The one who remembered my drink order. Who wore glasses only when he forgot to guard himself.

He called me. *Me.* He said I was the only one who could help him. The man had an army of public relations and branding specialists at the ready. There were easily forty members of his staff that could have an entire selection and narrative drawn up before he walked in the door the next morning. But he called me, because he didn't trust anyone else.

God help me, a part of me wanted to say yes. Not because of the money, or the challenge. Because I wanted to be the person who *could* protect him. That terrified me. I exhaled slowly, letting my head fall back against the couch.

"You're an idiot," I whispered to the ceiling, wishing I had the stones to call Ellis and tell him instead of my ceiling. "A very well-dressed idiot with excellent bone structure, but still."

Still. I'd think about it. That's what I'd told him. What I hadn't said — what I couldn't say — was that I already was.

3

COLLATERAL

ELLIS

I DIDN'T GO BACK to the office despite promising Morgan I would. There was a battery of issues I'd left hanging that she'd left for me flagged red and urgent in my inbox. I just didn't have the mental energy to deal with anything else. Not after an evening floating in the phosphorescent orbit of Rowan Sloane.

The car picked me up from the Hancock and took me to Old Town. I loved this quaint little pocket of the city. Stately, reserved, historic. My house felt less cold and more austere on this side of the city. Something that felt synonymous with the four generations of wealth that provided me respite in this zip code.

Once this *merger* took root, I wondered if I'd have to leave my quaint hamlet. Would the person I ended up choosing prefer to live in the more prestigious zip codes. Perhaps demand one of those overpriced monstrosities in the suburbs.

The drink I poured didn't satisfy the ennui I no longer could ignore. I'd tried. The whole way home I forced myself to focus on what the lawyers had said to me about a merger we had taking place in Atlanta. When that didn't work, I forced my thoughts to the Middle East and the potential for a media foothold in the UAE. Even my pipe dreams couldn't distract me from the one thing I had insisted to myself we wouldn't focus on anymore tonight.

Rowan had said no. Not outright. Not yet. But I knew the shape of hesitation. Knew the curve of her skepticism. She was circling, like a hawk above an open field, waiting to see if this was a real opportunity or a trap. I couldn't blame her.

"So you'd rather be safe than loved?"

That question had no business hitting the way it did. She thought I didn't feel. That I'd grown cold in the years since she left HMG.

Maybe I had. Or maybe it was easier to play the part expected of me than admit the truth: love was a luxury people like me couldn't afford. Not when everything you built could be undone by scandal, a misunderstood turn of phrase, or unintended interpretation of intention.

Not to mention the potential of the person you love most, hurting you, intentionally in the avenue of public opinion. I'd seen how love could become ammunition. How the person who once swore they'd protect you would weaponize your worst moments for a headline. I'd seen the aftermath too many times—love turned lawsuit, intimacy weaponized for leverage. People made fools of themselves in love, and fools of each other in divorce. Love was a liability. And I'd spent my entire life learning how to mitigate those.

Rowan was right about one thing. I *was* strategic. Methodical. But she was wrong about what I wanted. I didn't want safety, I wanted *certainty*.

I needed the person beside me to be unflinching when the weight came crashing down. And it would. Many times.

Year after year, they'd have to shoulder the pitches and yaws of being the public face of a perception-driven empire.

I needed them to stay when it stopped being easy. They needed to choose me — not the title. Not the bank account, fancy cars, jewelry, or the designer clothes. I needed those things to mean nothing to them. They needed to know one should never believe the first story they heard. To understand that most stories, even the ones HMG presented as fact these days, were laced with bullshit to make people stay, to tune in longer, to react.

This person. The imaginary one I needed to find, needed to choose me over and again. Not the story, the illusion, or the social media sensation. *Me.* Just me. Ellis Hawthorne.

And I hated that the only person I'd ever thought might do that... walked away five years ago without looking back. Deep down I knew it was a career move. It made sense. Her cousin, Hillary Sloane, had an important place at Hursch Media. Her best friend Genevieve Hursch, daughter of Lucas Hursch, was a power house in this city. A one-woman hurricane whose company, much like ours, dabbled in all kinds of industries. Our companies *were* too similar. Rowan was a thousand percent correct. Her being at HMG would have made things untenable.

But the truth was, when Rowan Sloane left my company, it felt like something *ripped*. And now here she was. She'd sat across from me in her brilliant apple green dress, that fucking hair of hers looking like the wings of a Phoenix. Her sharp smile, and those intense amber colored eyes dissecting my life like a case study. She was still brilliant. Still maddening. Still the only person who ever made me feel like I wasn't pretending.

I'd told her, *I need you.*

I hadn't said *I miss you*. I hadn't said *you were the only part of this job that ever made it bearable*. Because that's not who I am. That's not who I'm allowed to be. Not anymore.

My phone buzzed from the coffee table where I'd tossed it alongside my keys and wallet. I didn't expect it to be her. She seemed like the kind of woman who needed at least forty-eight hours and a legal pad to make a decision. But there it was. Her name on my screen. Rowan Sloane.

> Rowan: Did a casual dive into your public dating history. 😊
>
> Rowan: My suggestion? A rescue dog and a hobby that doesn't involve mergers.
>
> Ellis: Astute observation, I'll take it into consideration. One question though.
>
> Ellis: Does the dog look good in a tuxedo?

HER RESPONSE WAS NEARLY INSTANTANEOUS.

> Rowan: Don't you mean the dog photographs well in a ballgown? 😊
>
> Rowan: Or did I totally misread what kind of partner you're looking for? You know what they say about assumptions... 😏😊

I stared at the screen, a chuckle surprising me as it ricocheted off the walls of my living room. She was teasing me, yes — but it wasn't careless. It was *precise*. She remembered exactly what I'd said, twisted it just enough to make it sting — then left it dangling, like bait in silk gloves. I caught myself smiling. God, I'd missed her brain. The kind that could dismantle your argument with one sentence and still make you want to say thank you.

> Ellis: Not ruling anything out. Tux, ballgown, emotional support alpaca — as long as the optics are clean

> Rowan: Excellent. I'll start a short list of emotionally stable mammals. I may even be able to get my client with the wellness retreat to give you one of her llamas. Do you prefer warm tones or neutrals in your engagement photos? I can have the buyer from Neiman's send over some wardrobe options as soon as Saturday.

This time, I laughed out loud. She hadn't said yes. Not officially. But I knew that tone. I knew that rhythm. Rowan Sloane didn't waste that level of sarcasm on jobs she wasn't already committing to. I didn't need a signed contract to know I had her.

KEATS HAD a habit of showing up uninvited. Usually when I least wanted company. Tonight was no exception. He'd been pacing around my living room, refusing to sit down, railing about our father and this ridiculous ultimatum.

"Why do you seem so calm?" he asked, heading to my bar and pulling the stopper to sniff what was in the leaded crystal decanter.

"Calm?" I felt anything but calm. I'd been climbing the walls wondering why Rowan hadn't reached out again. She'd been so cute with her texts on Friday, I'd been hoping for more. She was very specific with her desire to be left alone until she came to a decision, though. Abiding was proving difficult.

"Yeah," Keats flopped onto the chaise portion of my oversized sofa, barely managing to keep his bourbon in the glass. He raised it in toast toward me and sipping before continuing with his observation. "You're the oldest. The one at present with the most expectation on your shoulders. Without you taking over as CEO the rest of us really don't have a path to our required roles. We only work as a group. Yet you don't seem one bit concerned that you have to find a woman in three months and lock that shit down by the end of the year. Meanwhile I'm over here feeling like I'd being led to slaughter."

I checked my phone. Again. Still nothing. I needed to invent an app that prevented you from constantly doing things like this to avoid being a motherfucking fool. Maybe HMG should get into app development. It seemed to be a very lucrative income possibility.

> Me: Brother. App development. Thoughts?

Dash: We already have apps for every news outlet, streaming service, and podcast platform. Have you been drinking? They are outlined in the docs for the quarterly budget forecast Monday.

Dash: The ones you approved and signed off on Friday.

Whoops. Great. Now it really looked like I was the flippant CEO who didn't know his own businesses.

> Me: I meant like a focus app. I was looking for one and thought — why am I paying $8.99 when HMG could build it and brand it?

> Dash: * * Because the billions we earn every year aren't enough?
>
> Me: Just trying to innovate. Didn't realize brainstorming made me a heartless one percenter.
>
> Dash: Have you read any of the tabloids? I'm pretty sure your call sign is "Heartless One Percenter."
>
> Me: We employ over 16,000 people. We offer free healthcare, universal paid family leave, sabbatical programs, therapy, student loan help, full scholarships for employees' kids, plus mental health coaching—do I need to keep going?
>
> Me: We are the Forbes best place to work ten years running.
>
> Dash: JFC pull your panties out of your ass. It was a joke.
>
> Dash: Why are you bothering me on a Saturday night anyway? Go get your dick sucked. It will make you less of an asshole and please Father. T minus seventy-six days.

I must have made some kind of grunt because Keats was on me in a millisecond.

"Have you heard a single word I've been saying?"

"Of course. Poor you. Second youngest brother, middle child, the world owes you something, you shouldn't be forced to marry someone you don't even love just for a position and some respect."

I looked up and noted the shock widening his eyelids.

"I'm the CEO, Keats. Multitasking and listening to

multiple conversations at once is basically in my job description."

He leaned across me to grab the remote. "You know you shouldn't ignore me. It creates emotional trauma, makes me feel invalidated, and not an active part of your life. Causing me to question my role in our family dynamic."

I couldn't tell if he was joking or not. After dealing with the youngest brother, I didn't have the energy for the other *Tweedle*. Needing a break from his middle child spiral, I asked, "Have you talked to Rowan lately?"

Silence. My own words boomeranged back at me.

Keats blinked. "Rowan?" he repeated. "Wait. Why does that sound... familiar?"

"Forget it. I meant Brontë."

I could drive a Mac truck through Keats squinted, pregnant pause before he finally continued, sounding bored.

"Brontë is fine, as I said in our meeting with Father. I think she's in Mexico. You know her and these random road trips. She's always somewhere new. What does it matter anyway? She doesn't have to get married and step into the family legacy. It's daisy chains, and save the whales, living her best *Joseph Campbell* life."

After a beat, Keats leaned into my space like he was trying to read my mind.

"Brontë's a very boring topic. I want to know more about *Rowan*. Rowan," he repeated, tasting the name. "Damn. Feels familiar. Like I should know who she is."

"You shouldn't." I snatched the remote, flipping to a documentary about ketchup in Chicago. "Incredible." I pointed toward the television. "A ketchup conspiracy documentary. What a time to be alive."

"Actually, that's one of our affiliates," Keats said. "And

it's kind of fascinating. Meatpackers used to sell the scraps —lips, asses, whatever— as "high quality meat" and ketchup masked the taste. Mustard enhances it. That's why Chicago has such a no-ketchup stance. Being the center of the meat packing industry back in the day, selling ketchup on anything like hot dogs, implied they were trying to hide the subpar quality of meat beneath the taste. *The More You Know!*" He sang and wiggled his fingers in jazz hands.

"Great, I'll start prepping for *Jeopardy!*"

"Rowan!" He practically shouted, snapping his fingers. "Redhead. Old assistant. Wasn't there some big scene over a meeting scheduled at lunch?"

The kid had been maybe twenty-three when Rowan was my assistant. I was shocked he even remembered. He rarely spent any time with the junior executives or the C-Suite at that time, preferring to charm all the ladies down in Marketing and sleeping his way through the promotion team.

"It was the Editorial Review Board. Four-hour meeting on a good day. Rowan had to wait until it ended to eat. She'd been running all day with no break."

He rolled his eyes. "It's called DoorDash. She's smart. She could've figured it out."

"It hadn't been invented yet."

"Pizza delivery."

"The meeting was in the East Loop. No one delivers there."

"Still. It's legendary. Ellis Hawthorne, CEO, going to war over an assistant's missed lunch."

"It was an oversight," I said. "And I was still a junior executive. Besides, that meeting should've never been scheduled like that." I shifted. "Anyway. What does it matter?"

I checked the time. 9:45. Definitely the time. That's why I looked. Not because I was waiting for a message from a woman who clearly meant what she said about needing space.

"It obviously *does* matter," Keats said. "But what really has me curious is why her name's suddenly in your head—oh my god. Is she the choice? The one you're gonna get down on one knee for?"

I glanced around the room. Minimalist. Nothing to throw at him.

"No," I said it flatly. Hoping it would end there.

"Okay. Sure. If you say so. And yet you've been glued to your phone and texting someone with very little regard for your emotionally traumatized guest."

No such luck.

"Your brother." I held up my phone showing him the text stream between me and Dash that was open on my phone. "I don't think I can get down on my knee with him. That might not be legal and probably would be a little weird."

Keats eventually left. Muttering something about hot dogs and family trauma.

I stared at the unopened bourbon bottle on the counter. Then back at my phone.

Still nothing.

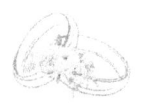

Four days.

That's how long it had been since Rowan's last text message. I'd respected her space. Silence was one thing. I knew how she was. She liked to mull things over, to give her intuition time to weigh in. But this? It felt like a power play. Images of her laughing with her assistant over having the great negotiator Ellis Hawthorne over a barrel and desperate for her call. The pictures my head painted for me were not pretty and affected me more than I cared to admit.

Putting a prospect on ice was a standard Ellis move. It was something I leaned on frequently when I didn't feel like I was getting the best option possible. People didn't like feeling like they were losing, and often times rushed to get things settled. Being on this side of the table was less than ideal. I didn't lose the upper hand. I always held the hand of power.

My focus was for shit. At one point the day prior I locked my phone in a desk drawer just so I would stop waking up the screen to see if I'd missed a text. Halfway through a budget forecast meeting the very last smidgeon of patience expired. I shot off a chat to Morgan.

> Me: Find out the name of Rowan Sloane's company and its address.
>
> Me: Today.
>
> Me: I want something on her desk within the hour.

Morgan had an answer in less than five minutes. According to her company website, *Pivot* "reimagined strategic storytelling for next-gen brands." Whatever the hell that meant. They did that reimagining from a nondescript building near the West Loop, tucked into some second-floor walk-up with exposed brick and start-up charm.

I sent flowers. I had the wherewithal to know she

despised the showy nature of roses and preferred the subtlety of peonies. I'd told Morgan to tell the florist to spare no expense. I didn't care that peonies weren't in season and were flown in from Israel. I sent them with a note that read: **"Patiently awaiting your input. These optics require an expert. — EH"**

And still nothing. No acknowledgment of the flowers. No email with a brief. I drove Morgan crazy with the constant inquiry into whether Paisley had reached out to put something on my calendar. Morgan was already well aware that Rowan took precedence to any meetings that weren't marked urgent or confidential. Thankfully Morgan came through as always.

> Morgan: The flowers were received and signed by Paisley. She also said that Rowan is having a crisis with one of her clients and isn't ignoring you.
>
> Me: Did she say when she plans to schedule a meeting? Time is of the essence.
>
> Morgan: No, Mr. Ellis. No mention of connecting calendars.

I was never impulsive. In the Hawthorne family, I'm the stalwart. And yet, I found myself standing in front of Rowan's West Loop office twenty minutes later with a bag full of sandwiches and various accompaniments from Ike's.

"You're lucky you're pretty." Paisley looked up from her desk, unimpressed.

"Is she busy?" I asked, ignoring her comment.

"Yes. And no, I'm not interrupting her meeting." She leaned back in her chair, crossing her arms in front of me as she shot me a long assessing gaze.

I'd been right about the pink. It was subtle, laced with apple green and cream, but it was a decidedly feminine space. Albeit a bit run down. Even with their attempts at luxurious cheer, the space felt dilapidated. I pictured them walking around with steaming cups and heavy wool cardigan sweaters in the bitter cold of winter.

"She's not responding."

Paisley clicked her pen with the calm of someone absolutely unfazed by someone like me standing across the desk from her. "She said she'd come to you when she was ready."

"I am aware." I tried to even my voice, to not allow too much impatience into its tone. I needed Paisley on my side. To help me through this uncharacteristic madness.

Paisley blinked. "Then you already know that pushing her won't work." She tilted her head, her uncharacteristically long, braided hair, flopping over her shoulder. Her gray eyes were steely, belying the polite tone. "Billionaires on deadlines don't get priority access simply because of who they are. We at Pivot are committed to treating *all* of our clients equally."

I opened my mouth. Closed it. Stonewall Paisley, ladies and gentlemen, apparent clone of Rowan Sloane.

"Please reach out to Morgan." I pretended to ignore the snide comment. "I'm needed in London and this needs to be settled before I leave."

Dash usually handled international emergencies in person. It was rare I needed to step in — unless something went completely FUBAR. And when I was needed, unless an absolute crisis, I typically participated virtually.

Paisley pointed the pen she'd been excessively clicking toward the door.

"When she has time, she will let me know to connect. Until then, go handle your own crisis."

The girl had moxie. She stared *through* me. I resisted the urge to ask her if she knew who I was. Of course she did. If I listened to the gossip, my face frequently featured on the celebrity rags. The only reason to ask that was to act superior as an intimidation tactic. And I needed her on my side. The key to success with CEOs, never piss off the admin who gate-keeps for them.

"There are two sandwiches in there," I said, pointing to the Ike's bag I set on her desk. "I figured you'd be just as hungry as she is if her day is hectic."

I didn't wait for her response. She could take or leave my offer, my day would continue just the same. I slid on my aviators and walked out the door.

4

BARGAINING IN GOOD FAITH

Rowan

I was elbow-deep in a rebranding crisis for a boutique fitness chain. Their CEO had been on a live podcast when she referred to someone's postpartum body as a "branding liability." It would take a walk through the Mojave, with bare, honey covered toes, and no water in the height of summer, to find our way out of this mess. It baffled me how many CEOs had no idea who their target audience was. Paisley practically stomped into my office. No knock. Never a good sign.

"Chicago's most beautiful billionaire just showed up with sandwiches," She held up the bag like evidence in a criminal trial.. "And an offensive vase of peonies got delivered. From him, obviously. They're still on my desk. I might throw my back out bringing them in here. Also, they're out of season. According to the sticker, they're Israeli imports, and I'm pretty sure he could feed an entire refugee family for what those cost."

The paper bag sat cradled between her legs as she made herself comfortable on my sofa, still ranting about the socioeconomic implications of imported peonies.

"Ellis was here?" Suddenly the crisis communication plan that had my sole focus for nearly an hour refused to hold my interest.

"Standing in this very office like a wet dream in a custom suit."

She hummed and shook her head, a sly smile on her face. Paisley and I were closer to friends than boss/employee. I'd recruited her right out of college, paid her well, and gave her the freedom to explore projects that interested her. Not only was she my executive assistant, but she also handled a lot of our social media, and concurrently media monitoring for our clientele.

Nearly every day I wished I could look as put together and stylishly eclectic as she did. Today's jumpsuit was a patchwork number that on anyone else would scream home economics project gone awry. But on her, it looked gloriously chic. Flower child meets in demand artist.

"I said I'd call him when I was ready."

I pinched the bridge of my nose. It had been a small motion to allay my building stress. Yet his cologne must have rubbed onto something I touched because my fingers smelled just like his *flying down the ski slopes into a forest of pine trees* aftershave.

"And yet he arrived like a man personally offended by the concept of patience."

I took a seat next to Paisley on my couch. She handed off the paper bag to me. Ike's. I recognized the logo immediately. The best sandwich shop in Chicago. Which, incidentally, was nowhere near my office, and certainly not "on the way" between his and mine. He had to intentionally go out of his way to get this for me. He'd even ordered me a Gonzo, which had always been my go-to when I worked with him. I pulled a pickle from my fried chicken wrapped in turkey sandwich. Just as I remembered, and still as messy.

The other sandwich was just a regular, grilled chicken sandwich. I'm sure it had a special name like mine. But I'd never ordered it. I wondered if he'd intended to eat the other sandwich with me, or if he really brought it for Paisley, who had already dug in and was chewing with gusto.

"He also brought another note, because the one attached the flowers apparently wasn't enough." Paisley added, wiping some kind of sauce from her mouth before drying her hands and reaching behind her. "Apparently it's 1873."

Heard you were busy. Some sustenance to provide you with enough energy to handle impatient billionaires.
-E.H.

WHY DID his handwriting have to be so elegant? Men like him, titans of industry, didn't have time to worry about every properly looped *p* and crossed t. It should have been chicken scratch scribbled on a Post-it Note, or the back of an Ike's take out menu. Not on a linen note card with his monogram embossed on it.

"He say anything else?" I put the card back in its matching envelope, placing it on the windowsill behind me, so as not to get stained by the bag of food on the coffee table.

"He said he's being 'pulled to London' and needs to get

this settled. He also tried very hard not to sound desperate. He failed."

I sighed and stared at my sandwich for a long moment. It was warm. Still fresh. Exactly how I would have ordered it — extra pickles, easy avocado, rainbow slaw on the side. *Of course* he remembered.

"Do you want me to call security next time?"

"No," I muttered. "If he's willing to bribe me with food just to get my attention then he's not a threat."

I gathered the sandwich and shuffled back to my desk, waking my computer screen. That same half-finished paragraph blinked back at me. Me and that cursor? Locked in a five-minute standoff before I caved.

"Paisley, can you reach out to Morgan?" I said with a heavy sigh.

"Scheduling the meeting?"

"Yes." The eyeroll happened unbidden. Ellis must just instinctively bring it out of me. "Tell her I'm free Wednesday at seven-thirty. His office. He wants strategy? He's going to get it."

Paisley didn't move, tapping her finger against her lips. "You sure you're ready for this?"

"I've negotiated with men more powerful than Ellis Hawthorne." I laughed, trying to sound confident. The truth was, Ellis Hawthorne was Goliath to my David. Aside from still feeling the same weird, desperate need to please him as I had back in my twenties, I also knew that the second even a whisper of me consulting for the great Ellis Hawthorne would have new work flooding in my direction. Which of course would be fantastic. There were so many capital improvements we needed to do on the office before I could even think about doubling up payments on my bank loans or upgrading our secondhand office equipment.

"Sure," she said. "But none of them were Ellis Hawthorne."

Damn her for being right, and him for being so charmingly persistent. And fuck me standing — already saying yes to his demanding charm before I even picked up the phone.

5

BUILD THE MASK, WEAR IT WELL

ELLIS

For seven-thirty at night there were still far too many people in our offices. I should have asked Morgan to select an alternate location away from prying eyes and ears. Even Keats was still in his office, a rarity at this hour. And of all the people I *didn't* want seeing Rowan to appear, it was him. He'd make it a much bigger deal than it was.

"I think we need to hold off on this sports contract." Whit walked into my office, not even glancing to see if I was busy or in a meeting. "Sure the revenue from all of these games across the network would be phenomenal but there are ten pages of secondary clauses in here that will string us up by the balls."

At that moment, I didn't care if we were offered the championship game. He needed to turn around on his fancy loafers and exit, stage left. If Rowan wasn't already riding the elevator up to our offices, she would be any minute.

"I have a meeting at seven-thirty. We can talk about this in the morning. Tell Morgan to bump my eight o'clock. Bring Dash in as well."

I was about to call Morgan into my office and tell her

myself, rather than have Whit relay the message, when she appeared. I knew exactly what she was going to announce.

"Dash is the one who sent the contract to me. He sent it to you too, around six. Look it over. I'm sure you'll agree."

"Morgan," I said a bit too enthusiastically. "Can you check my calendar tomorrow with Whit here and see when the three of us can discuss this contract. I can bump the eight o'clock editor's meeting, but I don't think Dash has a movable meeting at that time."

Thankfully, she knew my looks, and the insinuation that I needed her to get Whit out of my office.

"The representatives from Pivot have arrived," she told me, "and are setting up in Conference B."

The woman needed a raise. A raise and a vacation, paid for personally by me. Conference Room B was downstairs with the media team. Large, expansive, all kinds of fancy bells and whistles to allow them to give showy multimedia presentations with ease. Best of all, there were no windows, a do not disturb light, and far away from my brothers.

"Great. Let them know I'll be right down."

Whit tilted his head and looked at me, a question forming on his lips. I could see the wheels turning. He was trying to suss out what Pivot was. It wasn't a company that he'd be familiar with, unless of course Rowan had already sent in her consultation bill.

WMG headquarters spanned thirty-three floors. We owned the building. Back in the seventies, it had been owned by Hugh Hefner when *Playboy* magazine published in Chicago. When my grandfather retired and handed the reins to my father, it was right around the time that Hugh was packing up and heading to LA They were friends. Colleagues with common business interests. And Hugh was thrilled to hand the building over to someone else with a publishing legacy.

The studios for tv and radio that were local to Chicago were situated on street-facing floors and those directly above it. Most of the studios took up floors one through three because of the need for space in height for all the cameras and rigging needed. After that were the offices for the staff that supported the TV and radio stations, then podcasts, streaming services, and digital landscapes. Papers and magazines came next. Then all of the executive suites, from local managers, regional executives, and eventually the C-Suite on the top floor. Sometimes riding the elevator and thinking about all the people that existed just in this one building created both a sense of awe and a deep sense of pride. My family built this. My family built it and expanded it to what it was today, and now it was my legacy. Mine to build upon, to lead, and ensure it stayed successful.

The doors opened to the media floor. There was a hushed quiet despite the multitude of sound stages and air studios all with blinking *On the Air* lights of the evening shows. The multimedia conference room was at the end of the hall, closest to the employee elevators. My private elevator, while convenient in that I never had to wait for it, was situated in a hidden panel in the farthest corner of the building's footprint, which meant I hit my step goal every day without ever leaving the building.

I wasn't late," I said, pushing into Conference Room B. "The executive suite is in use, so Morgan had to make a last-minute pivot and this conference room is the complete opposite side of the building from my office."

Rowan sat at the head of the large conference table. Her laptop, notebook, pen, were all neatly aligned ready for use. The air smelled like her coffee — something warm, spiced, and vaguely sweet. I never remembered the name. Just that it was synonymous with ambition and too many deadlines.

"I guess I'll forgive the faux pas." She smiled genially before taking a sip from her cup.

Seven-thirty at night and she was plowing herself with caffeine. And not just a regular cup of java but some super complicated drink with extra shots and a pump of this and a foamy that.

"I've walked these halls, don't forget. I know just how far away from prying eyes this conference room is. Even if someone came looking for you, Morgan would be able to intervene with a warning text long before they arrived here."

A quirked lip and yet again a bust to the balls. Did she and Morgan have a little conversation on their way to conference room Siberia. Or was this yet again, something else the all too perceptive Rowan Sloane had sussed out.

"You're bringing out the big guns." I pointed to her coffee instead. "I don't know if I should be honored, nervous, or worried."

Every time Rowan laughed, something inside me shimmered — like some private part of me applauding for managing to entertain her. It was strange, but not unpleasant. It had been so long since we'd worked together, I couldn't remember if I'd felt this back then. Surely not. That would've been wildly inappropriate. She was my assistant. I was her boss. That was the boundary.

And yet.

"To quote a known, llama loving, cranial-proportioned, titan of industry, 'Fear is the sibling to ambition. One cannot exist without the other.'" She looked directly at me, flipping her pen between her forefinger and thumb. It was unnerving how direct her eye contact was. Had she always been like that? So straight forward and brimming with confidence.

I didn't remember ever using that quote. It sounded so wise. Written from someone who had their shit together.

"Do you know many titans of industry?" I asked. "Which titan exactly was this?"

I knew she meant me, but I hoped she jog my memory as to *when* I'd said it. It sounded too deep, far too wizened for my nearly forty years on this planet. She set her Cinnamon Dolce Latte down- thankfully with the name of the drink facing me—and huffed with impertinence.

"National Advertising Bureau Convention, Las Vegas. It was my first year working for you. You'd brought me with on the trip because you needed me to handle your insane schedule. I'd been petrified. Trying to juggle all the people, the places, who they were, where they were from, and what they wanted to meet with you about." She threw her hands in the air as if re-experiencing the frustration of that convention. "The amount of sleep I lost fretting over those five days."

She giggled. It was so un-Rowan-like. Not a laugh like she was entertained, but a nervous little giggle.

"They gave you an award on the first night. Don't ask me to recall what it was for. Probably just for converting oxygen into CO_2 while wearing a Brioni suit. I don't even know how you can make so many speeches and accept so many awards so graciously. How does that not get redundant? But that's not the point."

The further into the story she went, the faster she began talking. Was she *nervous*? Why on earth, of all the interactions would she be nervous over a story from a convention in Vegas?

"In the speech, you said that every one of us possesses

the power to direct the trajectory of our lives. That so many times, we let fear hold us back when we should embrace it. Because fear is the truest compass. And if we're afraid of it because it scares us into thinking we'll fail, that is exactly the thing we need to do. Because it's the sibling to ambition. I'd been toying with the idea, even back then, of running my own show. Being my own boss. I knew I wanted to do something in media but I didn't know what. But that speech, it watered the kernel that would eventually blossom into Pivot."

God help me, I didn't even remember the speech. But she did. She remembered it. Built a company on it. And now she was sitting across from me showing me a version of myself I didn't know I'd lost. Suddenly, this didn't feel like a business meeting anymore.

I'd selected Rowan because deep down I knew she knew me better than anyone else. She'd always been observant, intuitive. A female version of Radar O'Reilly from *M.A.S.H.* Those were the attributes that had made me think of her right away.

She'd find me the perfect partner because she'd *been* in that role before she spread her wings. But having her here, in my space, now? It felt like a surgery. Like I was about to step into a surgical theater, lay down on the table, and have her open and expose all of me, not just to a partner, but expose me *to* me. To remind me of versions of myself that didn't exist anymore.

I hadn't thought this through when I called her. I'd just *reacted*. As she connected her laptop to the multimedia display and called up her spreadsheet, I began to have serious doubts as to whether this had been a good idea. It was too late to run. Unfortunately, I was too far away to be rescued with a "work emergency."

"All right. Finding Mrs. Hawthorne, day one." She joked, as the name of her spreadsheet registered.

Not Real. Just Optics.

That's what she'd named the file.

"Catchy." I couldn't stop the smile as I pointed toward the screen.

"I thought it really drove home the project outcome," she said through a smirk. "Nothing real, just something that seems real. Selling the fantasy. Just like those reality shows your network seems to be obsessed with."

She looked at me then. Direct. Unapologetic. And for a moment, I didn't feel like the client. I felt like a brand being audited.

"Okay, so before we get to the list of your needs and wants, let's go through the research and data I've compiled." Panic had begun to bubble up my chest. Her laser focus as she studied the screens projecting her data, and the lullaby quiet of the room created a cocoon of nuclear silence that had become totally uncomfortable. "You can tell me what tracks and what was media spin, okay?"

I could only nod. This was going to hurt. I knew her direct look was supposed to gird my loins and prepare me for the uncolored look into my bachelorhood.

"I only did an audit on the last ten years. That is about the length of time that you've been on the radar of the gossip magazines, the *Most Eligible* lists, and people tracked your comings and goings and who you were... well... *coming* with."

I caught the entendre. Had she always been this teasing with me? When she smiled that sultry know-it-all smile, did I always feel such a strange delight when we volleyed back and forth? I heard people make sex jokes all the time, but

BUILD THE MASK, WEAR IT WELL

from little Ms. *Take Me Seriously* in her studious bun and custom-tailored pantsuit, the sex joke hit different.

"Low hanging fruit Ms. Sloane." I tried to sound bored and unaffected. "How about more substance, less cheek."

Her cheeks were a delightful shade of pink. I doubted it had anything to do with the warmth of her coffee. Though, it was possible. However I think she enjoyed the banter as much I did.

"Well, based on the pictures on the internet, there are an *abundance* of cheeks. The poor women you date can't seem to afford clothing that covers their whole ass. You're a billionaire Hawthorne. Surely you could have handed over that coveted black card and told them to buy themselves something pretty."

She'd put up a slide deck on the screen, the present page showing pictures of me and Savannah Albright. The event planner. I didn't even remember how we met. Though, my mother despised her from the jump. I believe she called her a *'high-heeled interloper'* after a disastrous charity brunch.

"Savannah really loved her *assets*." I joked.

"Well, no offense intended, but those assets are about all she has. Or even had back then. There is a myriad of reasons why this relationship would have never worked, but I assume this was one of those *sowing your oats* kind of relationships. The one you know is totally wrong but in the best way."

It sounded to be like Little Miss Proper had some experience with sowing your oats kind of relationships herself. The question formed on my tongue. I tried to ignore the need to know who Rowan had sowed her oats with and why he was totally wrong in the best way.

"So, who was he?" I usually had far more self-control.

There was zero need for me to needling into her life. Probably a defense mechanism. Since she was boring so deep into mine, I needed to feel like I wasn't off-kilter by balancing the scales a bit. That's what I told myself anyway.

"I'm sorry?" The signature Rowan head tilt. God she was so easy to read. But also very good at sidestepping questions she didn't want to answer.

"The one who sowed your oats who was wrong for you in the best way?"

"Except we're here to talk about you, not me. And who says I have anyone that fits that bill?" She played with the top of her coffee cup, flicking her thumbnail against the opening of the lid while she regarded me with. The look she gave me wasn't angry, but it definitely wasn't jovial or sassy as she'd been moments ago.

"Let's call it a friendly trade. You're breaking me open with a pair of rib spreaders on the operating table. The term you used sounds as if you have personal experience with a sow your wild oats adventure. I don't need to know the whole *True Hollywood* expose on the relationship but I'm curious when you've had time to have that kind of relationship."

"How about we just focus on you for right now. I believe we were talking about Ms. Assets." She pointed up to the screen where Savannah's picture was still displayed.

Rowan wasn't wrong. Savannah was amazing in bed. Thanks to her, I learned you *can* actually pull a muscle in your groin from too much sex. She'd loved being on top.

"Hello?" Rowan snapped her fingers, "I don't know where you went but that smile is more creepy serial killer than charming megalomanic billionaire."

Rather than encourage more of that tête-à-tête I circled my finger in the air, the universal sign for move along.

"After Savannah, there was Celeste St. Sebastian, daughter of a shipping magnate. Oxford educated, ran a foundation that upcycles clothing going to landfills and transforms them into designer wear. She simultaneously offers job opportunities to young girls in the Middle East by teaching them to design and sew. On paper, she checks every box for the perfect billionaire wife, especially since she had her own money."

"She was fucking boring." I told her. "Dinners with her were torture. All she wanted to talk about was global socioeconomics. It's one thing for you to be passionate about something. It's another thing entirely when it's your whole world. And the *judgment*. My god I couldn't even watch the Bears without a lecture on corporate greed, overconsumption, and the ills of consumerism."

I scrubbed a hand down my face; the memory of Celeste's relentless righteousness still left a chalky residue behind.

"She was brilliant," I added, because it felt like the kind of thing you say when someone's heart was in the right place. "But everything had an agenda. Even small talk felt like a seminar in geopolitics."

Rowan offered a small nod, her eyes back on the screen. "Okay," she said, voice measured. "Then let's move on to someone who wasn't arm candy or an activist."

The *click* of the slide deck felt weighted, as if it reverberated throughout the sound dampened room. The next slide bloomed onto the display.

Talia Brindley.

The shift in the air was instant.

The photo was cropped from an HMG sponsored awards gala, her arm around my waist. Talia always wore a specific shade of lipstick, red to match the sole of her

Louboutins, which stood out against the brilliance of her smile. Talia's style trended minimalist in all things. The navy gown in the photo encapsulated everything she was; elegant, understated, but packed a punch when needed. She was tucked into my side like she belonged there. She probably did.

Rowan didn't say anything at first. She just tapped her pen against her notes once. Twice. Finally, she said, "Impressive resume. I forgot she'd been up for the Pulitzer."

"She withdrew her nomination," I said, trying to keep my voice as steady. Talia was a skeleton I preferred gather dust in some forgotten room. Just the few minutes we'd discussed her felt like the rending of stitches on an almost healed wound.

"Why?"

I shrugged like it didn't matter. "The story unraveled."

It *technically* was true. And too complicated to unpack tonight. Especially with Rowan sitting across from me, looking more real than anything I'd ever fabricated with Talia.

"She looks... polished," Rowan added, voice tight around the edges. "You two photographed well."

"She was ambitious," I replied. "And smart. Too smart. She knew exactly how to navigate a room."

"She was different," Rowan said, voice thinner than before. She arched a brow in my direction, as by action she could get me to give her more. I couldn't though." Talia didn't seem to be your usual arm candy. More curated."

I paused. Talia wasn't a fling. She'd been someone who'd gotten close — but not close enough.

"She wanted a byline more than a relationship," I said finally. "We were mismatched. Eventually, I started to feel like the story instead of a partner."

Rowan glanced at the screen again. "Did you end it?"

I didn't flinch. Didn't pause. "Yes."

She nodded. But she didn't look convinced. She continued to tap her pen against the table, mulling over something. I waited. Sometimes she liked to process internally before she spoke. From previous experience, interruption of her process was not worth the price of impatience.

"So," she said, brisk again, like nothing weighty had just passed between us, "we find the perfect balance somewhere within these three."

She clicked her trackpad. Savannah vanished. Celeste followed. Talia lingered half a beat too long before disappearing too.

"A woman with presence," she continued, "but not the need to dominate a room. Beautiful, but comfortable in something with hemline that doesn't require a modesty panel when she bends over. Educated, but not looking to lecture you on late-stage capitalism over filet mignon."

"That seems like a reasonable ask," I muttered, sitting back. "You know. For a unicorn."

"Luckily, I have a knack for hunting the rare, and usually with much less impressive resources."

She opened a new tab in the spreadsheet labeled *Candidate Criteria* and began typing.

"You should really try to smile more." I joked. "I worry that experiencing such displeasure while doing this work risks you dropping the assignment for lack of enjoyment."

She grinned wildly at my teasing while she referenced as she typed.

"I don't think I could enjoy this more if I tried," she said, "Now, let's talk deal breakers."

I stood, removing my coat and hanging it on the hook on

the door. For a media company that I owned, the dress code was constrictive on a good day. Right now, when I felt like I was being examined under the glaring lights of an interrogation room, I was immensely uncomfortable. The tie came next, followed by the cufflinks, which I tucked in my coat pocket before rolling up my sleeves. When I turned to sit back down, I noticed Rowan staring, pen leaning sensually against her mouth. I wanted to say something flirtatious and biting as she did with me, but my brain chose that moment to flatline.

"Okay. Ideal woman. Close your eyes and tell me what you see when you picture your perfect partner."

I closed my eyes, but the only thing I could see was Rowan. That pen. Her saucy look while we'd bantered back and forth. Her earnest amber colored eyes softening with pride when she told me about her company's origin story.

"You messed me up." I whined. "All I see is you and all your questions tonight. Give me something to focus on."

"Good grief," she said from across the table. "I'm certain a man in your position needs to come up with creative ideas *of his own* based on *his own imagination and thoughts* all day, every day. Why do you need me to give you a jumping off point? Think about these three girlfriends, pull what you liked about them what you didn't and start from there."

They weren't girlfriends. Girlfriend implies seriousness. Suggested commitment. These were flings. Some with more longevity than others, but flings, nonetheless.

"No society women." I started. "I just can't imagine having a single, genuine interest or feeling with someone who schedules in sex like it's a reminder to schedule her annual women's exam. Not to mention treating blow jobs like special occasions. I like having my cock sucked far too much for it just to be a birthday or anniversary thing. And the obsession with keeping up with the Joneses it just something I have zero interest in. I don't give a shit whether people think our house, car, vacation to Mykonos, or where little Bobby and Misty are going to preschool measures up."

"Bobby and Misty?" Her voice dripped with judgment. She'd frozen in position, fingers hovering above her keyboard, her face glued in confused dismay. "Have you honestly thought about this and *that* is what you want to name your kids? Mr. *Family Legacy* and *Hawthorne Honor?* Surely your pretend kids will be named something in line with that legacy—something like Langston and Harper Lee."

While it didn't take a Rhodes scholar to connect the dots, most people never understood the connection to our names. Not even some of my closest friends *got* it. With a name weighted in literary history like Hawthorne, my mom wanted to keep in tradition given Father's name was Nathan, similar in style to Nathanial. Each of us was named after a literary great. Me, Ralph Ellison, Whit after Walt Whitman, Keats for John Keats, and Dash for Samuel Dashiel – and Brontë, the most obvious because Mom got to name the girl. She couldn't choose between Charlotte or Emily, because she loved them equally, so she went with Brontë, their last name.

"That was an error on my part. I should have *pivoted* considering who my audience is and how much she adores collecting various editions of *Jane Eyre*." I couldn't hide the fondness in my voice that even I recognized as such.

Rowan didn't laugh this time. Didn't throw it back with a smirk or another jab. She just looked at me. Not amused. Not judgmental. Just... considering. Then, calmly, she reached for her laptop and clicked open a new tab in the spreadsheet.

"Got it," she said, typing. "No performance. No status climbing. No sex-as-reward systems. Needs to be real. Consistent. Unscheduled."

Her fingers stilled for a beat. "Do you want that written into the contract? Or just... implied?"

I didn't answer right away. Because I didn't know. She didn't wait for me to answer. Just clicked back to her original spreadsheet tab and cleared her throat like she hadn't just dissected my psyche in six keystrokes.

"Okay," she said, her tone rehoming to a controlled and efficient businesswoman. "So far, we've eliminated: society women, performative partners, and anyone who names children like an afternoon cartoon. Let's keep going."

I leaned back in my chair, watching her reset.

"You're not going to ask about looks?" I said. "No model clause? No preference for leg length or cup size?"

"We're getting there." She smirked without looking up. "But unlike most men who lead with that, I figured you'd want to pretend you have depth first."

"Depth? Me?" I leaned back, forcing a smirk. "You said you read the gossip magazines. Ten years' worth, right? I've been called the Ice Man for at least that long. Ice doesn't have depth, sweets. It's just water—exposed to cold long enough that it forgets how to move."

She looked up at that. Her quiet, assessing gaze felt too powerful. As if she'd seen all the way down to my marrow. There wasn't a biting comment forming on her pouty lips. The spreadsheet glowed on-screen, momentarily forgotten. The two of us just existed in the silence. The silence felt *different*. Not uncomfortable, weird, or weighed down by unwelcomed revelations. Comfortable almost, like having coffee and sharing a newspaper on a Sunday morning. After a moment, Rowan cleared her throat, ran her fingers across the keyboard, her painted fingernails clicky quietly against the keys.

"Okay, noted. Prefer someone who doesn't need thawing instructions."

I knew it was a joke, but it didn't land for some reason.

"What else?" she asked, fingers at the ready.

"No sorority girls."

"Well, last I checked we were looking for *women* not college co-eds."

"No one who was part of a sorority. Even later in life, those sororities are part of their personalities."

"How so?" she asked, looking genuinely confused.

"It's manufactured. Paying for friends and then obsessing over them once college has ended. You get together with Bunny, Kennedy, and MarieClaire and hug and screech and uncontrollably cackle over *that time at Kappa Lamda, don't you remember?* Hard. Pass. It's insufferable."

"That Shakespearean monologue speaks longingly of inclusion dear prince. Did that big bank account of yours scare away the bros at Delta Kappa Epsilon? Did you lose your chance at rubbing elbows with the next George Washington? Must have stung to be rejected by the elites."

Her tone dripped with saccharine. If she wasn't smiling maniacally as she sat there, I'd almost be offended. With a man like Nathan Hawthorne as your father, anything social at college was absolutely forbidden. We were there to learn. To have the very best education money could buy. Apologies to the Ivies—Nathan Hawthorne turned his nose up at those. Northwestern was elite and supposedly working class, concurrently. The pick yourself up by your bootstraps and push forward in the name of education. And, that is what we all did. Except for Brontë...but she was raised in a completely different solar system than the rest of us.

"I wasn't interested in popped collars, waiting lists for British Racing Green Jags, or learning how to do keg stands." I meant it as a deflection. But the room felt different, too still for a joke that should've landed. She didn't laugh. Just looked at me again, like she saw something I hadn't realized I'd revealed.

Rowan clicked her pen, refocused on the spreadsheet, and said, "Okay. No screeching, no Greek letters. Definitely no popped collars or fans of Kappa Lambda. Got it."

"Oh and no tattoos." I add almost as an afterthought.

"Tattoos? That's a strange thing to have a hang up over." Rowan tilted her head, regarding me for long moments.

"They're trashy."

Wasn't that the general accepted belief on tattoos? Rowan lifted her wrist, shifting aside the tinkling bangle bracelet that hung on her wrist. She pointed to the tiniest piece of skin that was just slightly off color.

"Two strikes in one sitting," she said with a smile, holding out her wrist toward me so I could see her tiny, flesh colored tattoo. "Delta Gamma, guess I'll recuse myself from consideration."

Color me surprised. Little miss poised and perfect had a wild side.

"When did you get that?" I asked.

"Freshman year of college. Just after bid day. I was a big chicken shit though, so I got it in a flesh tone so my parents wouldn't notice it. They hold the same opinion as you on the matter of marking one's body with ink."

"I would have thought you attended Smith or Wellsley. Somewhere that turned their nose up at sororities and pointed toward a deeper sisterhood that only an all-girls education could provide."

"Ugh." She lifted her arm, the bracelet sliding back into place. "No way. I went to Iowa."

That also surprised me.

"Wait, if you went to Iowa, and you're thirty-six…you went to school with Beckett Murray?"

"He loved flip flops, even in the winter, and always smelled like chlorine. He kind of reminds me of you in a way."

"I don't think I've ever even owned a pair of flip flops and I can't remember the last time I was in a pool," I said, unreasonably annoyed by the comparison. Aside from being an arrogant prick—not that I knew him personally, but I knew him by reputation—he was also too contrived. Like he knew how attractive he was and capitalized on it at every turn.

"No his personality. Charming, but knows it. Witty. Owns every room he walks into. But also, he's really cool when he's not in *Beckett Murray, Olympian* mode."

"You *dated?*" I couldn't hide my shock, or the unexpected jealousy that she knew someone like *Beckett Murray* on an intimate level.

"No way. He loved himself too much and was too hyper-focused on the Olympics to care about anything other than swimming. But we were friends. Are still friends. His brother is a podcaster on my cousin's network."

It was too much information to process. Minutiae I

didn't care about. This meeting kept derailing and losing focus.

"All right, let's get back to putting a list together." I made a show of looking at my watch, as if this meeting had gone past my scheduled time. Despite it being held after hours, and I had no other commitments. "What do you need from me to expedite this?"

"Okay," she pivoted with grace, "So far, your ideal woman needs to wear respectable clothing, doesn't name her kids like Disney Channel extras, doesn't have Greek letters in her Instagram bio, believes in year-round oral reciprocity, and doesn't judge you for eating steak and indulging in splurges. What else should we add?"

I didn't know why I suddenly felt so impatient. I'd been happily following along her bantery trail, piecemealing my likes and dislikes. Then, it felt as if I was slowly being suffocated by a grocery store plastic bag. I needed out of the room.

"I just want someone normal." I spat out.

"Normal?" she asked her voice rising at the end in question. "Define normal."

"I don't know. Like a teacher or a vet. Someone who doesn't know why Vassar is a separate college but also part of Harvard, has never heard of the *Guards Invitational*, and doesn't care about the fish fork!"

"Are you sure about that Ellis? This kind of girl will get chewed up in your circle."

"No, she wouldn't." I practically growled. "Because she'd be real, and I'd make sure no one touched her. Not the media, not the snooty elite, not even my *mother*."

Suddenly this whole thing felt off, wrong. The room felt too small, the lights too bright, and Rowan's line of questioning too grating.

"It's getting late." Rowan pointed to the clock on the wall. Ten thirty? How did that happen? We'd been at this for two hours, yet it felt as if she'd just arrived at my offices.

"You've given me a lot to work with here." She shut her laptop with speedy efficiency. "By the time you make it back from London, I should have narrowed down a shortlist and we can move on to implementation."

"London?" I asked. Even I heard the question in my tone.

"The urgent meeting that you've been called to and the reason why I had to skip my meeting with the Green Tie Ball Planning Committee to come here."

"Oh gosh. Tomorrow is already Thursday. I need to get home actually; I still have to pack. I'll be back next week. Have Paisley connect with Morgan and we can regroup."

She stood, slipping her laptop into her bag and slinging it over her shoulder in one fluid motion. "All right then, good luck in *London*. I'll make sure Paisley and Morgan have something on the calendar before you return so we can hit the ground running."

I felt the weight of her London comment. As if it had an asterisk. Like even the air in the room knew London was bullshit for *I couldn't wait to see you for some inexplicable reason tied to anxiety and impatience*. Before I started back peddling and making an even larger ass of myself, my brain took hold of the tiniest detail. One that had me regrouping faster than a school of fish in a hurricane.

"Gateway Green must be really anxious to get started on the thirtieth anniversary plans. Usually, the committee meetings recess until after the spring vacation season. You know, all those school vacation schedules the committee need to work around for meetings."

Rowan didn't flinch. She just smiled, unbothered. "It is

the thirtieth anniversary after all. People are anxious to get started."

Then she left, the subtle *swish* of her elegant suit the only sound as she exited. I waited until the door latched behind her before dragging a hand across my face. We were both full of shit. But somehow, sitting across from her tonight, it hadn't felt like it.

6

THE EVIDENCE OF THINGS SEEN

Rowan

IT WOULD'VE BEEN EASIER if he'd just lied. If Ellis had looked me in the eye and admitted he wanted to manipulate public opinion, impress his father, or trick the board into thinking he was palatable; I could've worked with that. Those kinds of optics I was used to, I thrived in them. Manufactured authenticity with neat soundbites and flattering lighting was my bread and butter.

But no.

He sat across from me, earnestly trying to appear casual in his luxe, custom suit, and said he wanted someone *real*. Someone normal. And worst of all, he meant it.

The man who built an empire on perception was outsourcing intimacy. How did he fail to see the irony? That truth rattled me. It made me feel complicit, like I was forging something counterfeit and trying to convince everyone, even him, it was connection. This wasn't just doomed. It was destined to destroy.

He'd caught my lie. The one I'd told about the Green Tie Ball. I tossed out the reference so casually. It was a white lie. Something to make me seem busy and successful.

Because for some inane reason I wanted him to see me as a social equal.

By the time I reached my car, I realized no one at Hawthorne had asked me to sign an NDA. Ellis was too sharp for that to be oversight. This was trust, handed to me with a weight no signature could match. Which made the lie sit heavier than it should.

He was a job. A well-paid job. Period.

But he was also a human being. He carried so much pressure on his shoulders that he needed to fake a love life for the sake of someone he respected. I wanted to help him. Needed to ensure someone was looking out for him. My biggest fear in doing so, however, was that it might fracture the parts inside of him that made him most attractive. His goodness. Not many got to see the soft part of Ellis, and I feared that this kind of glass house he wanted to build wouldn't just shatter, but it would gut him from the inside out.

THE TABLE at Raze was already covered in half-empty cocktail glasses, mismatched appetizer plates, and a nearly toppled votive candle. We'd been coming to the same bar for nearly a decade. When my friends and I chose Raze it was because of proximity to our offices and cheap booze. Now the once trendy turned hole in the wall bar felt comfortable, like an old sweater.

Lyris got overly enthusiastic retelling a story about her mishap learning how to make focaccia for a new piece she was working on. The alcohol probably hadn't helped with her hand-eye coordination either.

Lyris had a byline for *Bites,* an online magazine and educational cooking platform. She and I went to college together. As we ascended the corporate ladder and our lives became insane, we created a standing, monthly girls' night for drinks and gossip.

"Okay," Greer said, sliding her glasses back up her nose and lifting her drink like a gavel. "Let's do this before I get another mezcal paloma and forget who I hate most this week. Catch of the month. Who landed the whale?"

Greer also worked in media. She joined last. Our other college friend, Hollis, moved to Chicago to take a job a few months before I met Greer. Hollis was out of town reporting on a segment and hadn't been able to join our monthly girl's night, dubbed *Pitchfest.* Because who doesn't love a good pun?

Somewhere along the lines of our professional ascensions we'd started a friendly competition called "bag the whale." Each month we celebrated our wins by disclosing our largest "get." The group decided on the collective "win," and their check was paid for by the others.

"That would be *me*," Lyris grinned, tossing a lone cheddar cube from our appetizer platter into her mouth with the flourish of a magician. "I got an exclusive with Gemini Tate before her cookbook drops."

The words got faster the more information she gave us. Her eyes sparkled with an excitement I hadn't seen from her in ages. Journalism can be a drag sometimes; it steals your light. But this trip had been great for her.

"The company flew me out to Barren Hill, and I visited her gastropub *The Tuckaway Tavern.* She let me *cook with her*. One of her business partners, Emmett, only has one arm. But he's amazing! Him and Gemini's fiancée—the other partner, Finn, have a YouTube channel. They teach adaptive cooking methods. I'm still blown away, a full week later."

More seriously she tells us, "She won the James Beard. There are rumblings of a Michelin Star."

Greer made a face. "So much information dumped into such a tiny span of space. Did you even breathe?"

"I can't help it!" Lyris laughed before downing the rest of her bourbon—Lakshmi—she'd informed us when she ordered it that *Chef Tate* had introduced it to her when she was in Barren Hill. Magically, it was on the menu at our monthly haunt. She'd nearly broken the wineglasses over the bar with the shriek when she made at the discovery.

Greer turned to me, "Good luck following up after that."

I reached for my G & T to bide time and think about what I could offer up. I didn't have any whales. I was in the ocean without a life raft at the moment. Deep sea fishing was not even on my radar.

"Well, I've been so heads-down on a corporate reputation salvage job. You know. CEOs, podcasts, stupid fucking comments, and foot-in-mouth syndrome."

"Sure," Lyris said, drawing out the word.

"I don't follow?" I told her, not understanding the sing-song sarcasm in her voice.

"Someone was checking in at the security desk of HMG last night."

"You were at HMG?" I asked. HMG had no holdings in Chicago that were cooking related. Their reality television arm was in Los Angeles and none of those executives had offices here.

"I was across the street at WGN. Walked out right as

you were chatting up security. So why the late-night meeting at Hawthorne group, babe?" Lyris leaned forward, smiling.

My mind spun. What the hell did I tell them? I couldn't tell them I was working with Ellis. This was a secret project, and he'd entrusted me to be discreet.

Greer's gaze sharpened. "Wait. You're working for Hawthorne?"

"It's complicated." I told them both, sipping my G & T and trying desperately not to look called out and panicky.

Greer and Lyris exchanged a look. Greer smirked. "That sounds suspiciously like a win you don't want to count. Why wouldn't you want it to count, Rowan? Are you back working for old *Most Eligible Bachelor* boss?"

"Look I can't give you any details other than to say, Ellis's father is doing some legacy planning and Ellis asked if they could meet with me for a temperature check. But it's not a get. It was an hour's worth of listening and suggesting."

"And *yet*," Lyris sing-songed, "Ellis Hawthorne."

The two of them made swoony faces at me and started to fan themselves. Jesus. It was Ellis Hawthorne, not a fucking Hollywood celebrity. My laugh came too fast, too brittle. I adjusted my blazer sleeves like that could somehow pull me back into the version of myself who wasn't unraveling every time Ellis Hawthorne smirked at me.

"Honestly," Greer added, sipping her drink, "even if you don't bill a dollar, just being in his orbit qualifies you for the leaderboard."

I rolled my eyes. Of all the times to be spotted. In all my life I have never noticed someone in another building checking into security.

"And you?" I asked, desperate to turn the focus to someone else.

"Meh, a city council member, a dinner the mayor held, and a blurry shot of the former president coming out of a library planning meeting. I got nothing." Greer worked in political news. She was what they called in the industry a double threat with a law degree and broadcasting chops. Her knowledge of constitutional law rivaled Supreme Court employees.

"It looks like Lyris is the clear winner then, with the James Beard award winning chef." I pulled out my wallet and throw a hundred-dollar bill on the table.

"Oh come on. Don't rush the goal just because you don't want us asking anymore questions about your secret whale." Greer pushed my money toward my side of the table.

"You've been hanging out with Hollis too much. In all my years I've know you, Ms. Pulse of America's politics, I've never heard you make a sports analogy."

Greer shrugged, smiling, "Don't change the subject. We aren't going to let go of this Hawthorne development."

Somehow, I felt like Ellis Hawthorne's name would be called up like an incantation at every Pitch Fest going forward.

IT HAD BEEN five days since Ellis left for "London." Complete radio silence since then. No follow up emails. Not even a passing one that shot off some random idea he may have had. His assistant hadn't even reached out to Paisley to schedule our next meeting.

I existed in a vacuum of replaying our last conversation, fretting over whether he knew I'd caught him in his London lie and was rethinking the whole partnership, and wondering if he had gotten cold feet and decided *not* to abide by his father's request and allowed things to happen naturally. Long enough for me to wonder if I'd imagined the look on his face when I mentioned the Green Tie Ball.

He hadn't called my bluff. Not directly, anyway. But the brief flicker in his expression before he regrouped had told me he'd caught the lie and pocketed it like a secret. One we were both now carrying.

Morgan finally reached out a full week later, she'd given Paisley a date and time to meet at The University Club not at Hawthorne Media Group. Part of me was relieved. I didn't need my friends finding me there again and asking for another explanation. The location though, also would prove impossible to explain if we were to be seen. Sure, the club was private, unmistakably curated, with scads of elite members who belonged because of the club's adherence to discretion and privacy, but it was also *private*. The kind of place that would raise eyebrows.

It felt like a choice. Something about it said: *This is where I meet serious people for serious conversations.* Which meant I'd need to be polished. Strategic. Detached. Instead, I felt like I was walking into a performance I hadn't rehearsed for. One that tugged at my heart over its fetid authenticity. Could I really do this? Helping Ellis find a fake fiancée suddenly felt like dooming him to a marionette's life. Living on strings his father attached, never being released from the performance.

In my bag was a folder with four curated candidates—

each meeting the criteria Ellis had given me: smart, stylish, accomplished, running the gamut of *elite* to his definition of *normal*. All *technically* real. Though, also crafted with care. The irony wasn't lost on me. I'd created a shortlist of real women to fulfill a fake relationship request for a man who claimed to want something authentic.

And the worst part? Part of me hoped none of them would measure up.

7

PRESENTATION DAY

ELLIS

She was late. I'd tripled check my iCal just to make sure *again* \ I had the right time on the right day. Six thirty, exactly as Morgan had scheduled. It was almost six-forty-five and still no sign of Rowan. Tardiness was not like her. In a brief moment of panic, I wondered if she wouldn't come because she knew I'd caught her in a lie.

To: Sweenie VanMeter
Re: Green Tie Ball

Sweenie,
Ran into an old friend recently who has a rare knack for positioning and storytelling. Thought she might be exactly what the 30th Anniversary Gala needs to sing. I've looped in Morgan to coordinate a meeting. I heard Thatcher announced his retirement. Congratulations you both. The newfound time is well earned for both of you! Let me know if you'd like to use the London house, I'm sure Winston and Maeve would be over the moon to have a guest to fuss over. —E.

. . .

I DIDN'T KNOW whether Sweenie was her actual name or a nickname. I'd never bothered to ask. It sounded like a nickname gone wrong. As if someone had drunkenly tried to call her sweetie and their words slurred. Regardless, the woman had chaired Gateway Green for twenty-five of its thirty years in existence. She and my mother were quite close. We all frequented the same events when our calendars aligned and we were in the city concurrently.

Six forty-five. Fully fifteen minutes late now. Was this a power play? A blow off? Or was she hurt somewhere and unable to get a hold of me.

> Me: Morgan, Ms. Sloane's assistant confirmed, correct?

> Morgan: She did. Twice. And reached out this morning for specifics on where Ms. Sloane should meet you.

> Me: Third floor executive's study?

> Morgan: Yes, sir. Has she not arrived?

> Me: Not yet.

> Morgan: I'll reach out to Paisley and see if Ms. Sloane's availability changed.

> Me: Not yet. Give her a few more minutes.

I DIDN'T WANT to seem like I was watching the clock with intense focus. I was Ellis Hawthorne, CEO for god's sake. I had plenty of people waiting for me. Emails to return, meetings to attend, responses to proposals, drafts, and contracts to sort through. All of those things could firmly hold my attention while Ms. Sloane continued her attempts to make me squirm.

"I'm so sorry!" Her heels clacked staccato across the quiet, marbled interior. "There's an accident on Lake Shore Drive. I finally gave up and just walked the rest of the way."

She looked at me with wide, panicked eyes. Other than the concern I saw in them, everything else about her screamed elegant businesswoman, despite the potentially mile walk depending on where she gave up and canceled her ride with the car service. She wore camel colored, ankle boots with an impressive heel. Rushing down a packed rush-hour sidewalk in those had to have been a herculean task. An apprising glance up her shapely calves to her smart herringboned checked dress and I all but forgot why I was annoyed.

"You look lovely, even after running down the street to get here."

There was a slight flush on her cheeks not tied to the breathless apology. She ran a smoothing palm down her dress after removing her coat and handing it to one of the staff. As she caught her breath, she took a seat and pulled a sleek folder bearing Pivot's logo.

"I took the liberty of ordering a drink for you." I felt a need to fill the silence. "If you're hungry we can eat here, now, or grab something downstairs when we're finished."

"I'm good for now." There was still that pleased half-smile on her lips, "Let's find you a fiancée."

She pulled four glossy dossiers from the folder and set them across the wide table between us.

"Based on immediate first impressions, is there someone you'd like me to give a rundown first?"

Two blondes, one brunette, and a redhead. All generally similar heights. Tall, five seven to five nine, in heels we'd be close to the same height. *Photographs*. It meant we'd pair better, present equal, aligned, visually symmetrical. Constance, Noeme, Simone, and Trinidad (Trina for short), they were similar in age, the oldest (Noeme) thirty-eight, the youngest (Trina) at thirty-six.

She'd expect me to pick a blond first, Simone or Constance. Not one of them stuck out over the others. Despite their difference in aesthetics, they all felt gray. The weight of this reality made me fairly agnostic to any sense of choice. Sitting there, staring at the four women with their toothpaste ad smiles, I felt like just closing my eyes and picking whichever my finger landed on.

"The way you are tracking my every move, I feel like you have a favorite. How about we start with that one."

The subtle copper shade of her nail polish caught my eye as she collected the four sheets. She chewed her lip while considering the options. There were so many tiny details I couldn't help but notice about her. Whether it was the shade of polish, the barely there shade of lipstick on her lips, or her hot as hell ankle boots, suddenly I was a sponge for Rowan's idiosyncrasies. It had been a while since we'd seen one another. Assumedly that was the reason for the unending catalogue of Rowanisms.

"Constance Ashcroft," she said, placing one of the blondes in front of me.

The woman pictured stood leaning against a desk, laughing with two posed colleagues, a well-appointed office unfocused in the background. She wore a berry-colored dress that played beautifully against her honey-colored hair and sun kissed skin tone. Clearly an executive. Those were professional headshots for the corporate masthead.

"Director of Global Philanthropy for Privé, an international fashion house with six clothing lines beneath it. Ivy league educated: Columbia undergrad, Wharton MBA. She checks a lot of boxes, Ellis. Independent and successful, has a packed calendar between work and social responsibilities, she sits on multiple boards for nonprofits, is poised and elegant, and given her social stature would easily win over anyone at HMG, the press, and your parents."

There was enough there to make her interesting. I assumed based on her education, background, and work that she'd be a decent conversationalist. It was worth a meeting.

"Good," I nodded, taking her picture and putting it aside. I knew Rowan put a lot of work into researching all of these women. It was the only reason I sat here and let her present them. This whole meeting had gone from feeling important to empty and the less time we spent talking about them the better. "Next?" I pointed to the other blond.

If my brusque pace annoyed her, she hid it well. Not missing a beat as she pushed forward the next option.

"Simone Adler." She began. I skimmed the sheet as she put in front of me. "Documentarian focusing on cultural think pieces, she recently has broken into culture and food documentaries having recently returned from Asia. Her documentary will focus on the subtle differences in cuisine between cultures, within the countries, and related to others in the area."

She seemed a bit too bohemian for my taste.

"Simone would definitely hold your interest. She has a myriad of interests and passions, she's very active on social media, and would piss the hell out of your parents. They'd probably be mortified. However, she is exceptionally popular with the charity circuit and despite her chaos she is very press aware and delivers fantastic sound bites when needed. Plus she would fit really well on the business side of HMG."

If Rowan thought she'd be a good fit I'd entertain an evening with her. Simone seemed a better fit for Dash. That was the kind of chaos he lived for.

"Okay. I'll trust you on that one. Next."

It sounded as if she was sucking air through a straw, though she didn't argue, push back, or express any opinion.

"Who is the redhead?" I asked, trying to slow my pace at least a bit. The last thing I wanted Rowan to think was that I wasn't impressed with her efforts.

"That is Noeme Castillo. Forbes *Thirty Under Thirty*, made her first million at thirty-two. She created an investment app that teaches women how to be stock market savvy. She got her start in podcasting: Deconstructing Wall Street. Gained notoriety with a Ted Talk at South by Southwest and was approached by Vention to develop an app using the training and education she breaks down in her podcast. Then, boom! Meteoric rise to fame and fortune. You wouldn't have to worry about her being interested in you just for money. She has her own. But she is decidedly middle class. Went to Northern Illinois University. Her father works for Vanguard as an investment fund manager; her mother stayed at home with her and her brother. Dad helped her get a chair at the Chicago Board of Trade and she elbowed her way up."

"She sounds a lot like you."

Had I meant to say that? Was it a compliment or an observation. Sure, they both had red hair but their jobs were so vastly different. What had been the common denominator.

"I don't see it." She turned the picture this way and that.

While Noeme was a bit lankier than Rowans meatier and more curvaceous frame, Noeme by description alone sounded like she had moxie. Something Rowan had in spades.

"Yes to this one as well."

"Okay and last but not least Trina, formal name Trinidad. She is decidedly normal. A former teacher at the Math and Science Academy—which is a magnet school near Museum Campus—she now is the education adviser to the Governor's office. She lives in a quaint townhouse in Printers Row that she bought for one hundred and ninety thousand dollars seven years ago. According to her Instagram she just bought a new Mazda SUV that she named Felix, and has a golden retriever named Molly. Other than small bureaucratic circles, she will have zero idea about anyone in yours. More than likely, she'll confuse the fish fork with the pastry fork and will wear an off-the-rack poly blend dress she got on sale at Macy's for whatever fundraiser you attend. She is truly your unicorn if you meant what you said."

Had I though? I looked at her picture. She was gorgeous, long chestnut-colored hair and matching eyes, a warm smile that immediately said of course *I own a golden retriever*. She wore jeans and a simple blouse in her picture, her arm loving wrapped around *Molly*.

"You've clearly done your homework," I told her. "These women are impressive."

I meant it. But I didn't feel it. "I approve. Set up meetings with them. Go over expectations and arrange for them to meet me here next week. I'll have Morgan set aside two nights next week and two nights the following to meet each of them."

"Um, I'm sorry." Rowan held up her hand to stop my

directives. "Set these up? Go over expectations? You have an assistant Ellis, and she's not me, remember? CEO with my *own* assistant who has plenty on her plate from me already."

As if I could have Morgan handle any of this. The entirety of this charade was about discretion. Selecting those we were confident would value the benefit without getting caught up on emotion.

"That was why you were hired, Rowan. *Discretion.* These women need to be prepped, told the reasoning behind it, given their NDAs and brought up to speed on expectations. That's not a responsibility for my admin. That is what I pay my *adviser* to handle. Once that is complete, then you may ask *Morgan* to coordinate the women's calendars with my own."

Rowan didn't flinch. Though I saw the shield come down in her eyes. They'd been bright and engaged, now despite the warm shade they felt cold and detached.

"Right," she said, gathering the dossiers and stuffing them back into the folder. "Because nothing says, 'authentic connection' like briefing women on how to fake it for press photos and family dinners."

The folder snapped shut with a finality that made my jaw tighten. I hadn't meant to be curt. But I also hadn't meant to feel so conflicted either.

"You're right," I said after a pause, dragging a hand down my jaw. "It's a lot to ask."

"Ellis," she said, her voice softening just enough to register, "it's not the workload. It's the weight of it. You keep saying you want someone real. But nothing about this is real." She tilted her head signaling around the expanse of the table.

A silence stretched between us for a long moment. I

could feel the heaviness. Like a gathering storm that weighs down the atmosphere with anticipation. She stood and signaled to the host for her coat.

"Not even this meeting."

Both of our coats were delivered with efficiency. I signaled to the man to hand over Rowan's coat and held it open for her to step into. The collar smelled delicate, just like her. Subtly floral, mysterious, like a rare orchid that bloomed once a year.

"I'll set up the meetings. You'll get a full summary report and candidate briefings in forty-eight hours."

"And after that?"

Her eyes flicked up to mine. "Then we test the theory."

I ruminated on that statement as I followed her out the front door, standing with her while we waited for a hired car.

"Thank you for all of your work so far on this," I leaned in and placed a kiss on her cheek, pulling her briefly against my chest before helping her into her car. "You continue to impress me Rowan Sloane. I am so proud to have you in my corner."

Before she could reply, I closed her door and signaled for the driver to take her home.

8

A THEORY WORTH TESTING

Rowan

I SHOULDN'T BE THINKING about it. That kiss. I broke my brain, officially. That kiss, albeit brief and entirely platonic, truly the most parochial goodbye brush of the lips in existence, still lived in a Newtonian loop inside my head. My body vibrated with awareness. At a frequency that a blushing eighteen-year-old virgin probably felt at her first suggestive, flirting interaction. But I was far from eighteen and hadn't been a virgin in two decades.

Yet, even as I floated in a bubble bath that evening, surrounded by the warm smells of water and bath oil, I could still recall that snowy pine smell of his. I felt his warm palm still resting on the small of my back, and the abrasive scratch of his five o'clock shadow on my cheek. In my head, time had slowed down at the moment his lips brushed my face. On replay behind my eyelids, that kiss had been whisper soft and lingering.

Ellis Hawthorne was my client. A powerful, strategic, emotionally armored client with a press problem, a family inheritance clause, and a borderline obsession with authenticity despite outsourcing every ounce of emotional connection. He was off-limits. Even if I hadn't just hand-picked four very successful options for him to date, it would be wildly inappropriate to entertain any kind of relationship. He'd been my boss for fuck's sake.

And yet.

My fingers had hovered over my phone more than once that night. I vacillated between wanting to send him a neutral and efficient message, just to continue to feel a connection. And also wanted to ask if that kiss felt *different* for him too. I didn't do either. I was a professional. He had hired me to build a lie, and whether the kiss's meaning was real or imagined, it didn't matter. Ellis Hawthorne was not mine to claim. So instead, I focused on the task ahead.

Four women. They'd been carefully vetted and checked every box Ellis had given me. My job wasn't to analyze his kiss; it was to execute his plan. The following morning I'd hit the ground running connecting with them, checking for interest, and briefing them on the expectations. But that night, before the decisions became final, I luxuriated in the fantasy of his kiss.

CONSTANCE ASHCROFT WAS the first on the list. She sat in my conference room, dividing her attention between two phones each pinging nonstop. Paisley had shown her into my conference room five minutes previous. She'd arrived fifteen minutes early.

Did I have a meeting? No. Could I technically honor her early arrival. Absolutely. But something made me set my position in concrete. She could wait until two o'clock as scheduled.

She'd been Ellis's first choice of the four, but I don't think he'd truly thought that through. Constance was exactly what a billionaire like Ellis should want to marry. But he'd insisted he wanted exactly the opposite of that. He'd wished for real, down to earth, not a society woman. Yet here we were.

While I futzed around on my computer pretending to look busy, an email dropped into my inbox I'd never in a million years expected to receive.

To: Rowan Sloan
From: Sweenie VanMeter
Re: Green Tie Ball 30th Anniversary

Hi Rowan,
Ellis and I were speaking recently, and he mentioned what amazing work you do helping companies define their voice. I think you might be manna from heaven in making our thirtieth year one for the books. Are you by chance available sometime this week? I'd love for you to meet with the rest of the committee and start bouncing ideas around before planning season kicks into full gear after everyone returns from their spring break holidays (We usually kick things into full swing Mid-April to Early May).
If you'd prefer I work with your executive assistant, feel free to loop her in and she and I can find a convenient time on your calendar.
I'm looking forward to working with you!
Best,
Sweenie

. . .

Sweenie VanMeter emailed me. The proverbial Queen of Gateway Green sent me an email and asked me to join the planning committee. The level of visibility that came alongside working with those women. They were the wives of the most elite businessmen in Chicago, alongside a few sports wives.

Sweenie VanMeter. My brain could not compute. I read and reread the email at least fifteen times and it still didn't seem real. Finally the most obvious detail stuck out. Ellis. He'd mentioned me to Sweenie. Despite my white lie, and him obviously knowing what a total Pinocchio I'd been in that moment, rather than call my bluff, he made it a reality.

Ellis Hawthorne, not such an Ice Man after all. That man needed someone who would love him the way he *deserved*—wholly, authentically, without a spotlight or a boardroom watching. He needed someone to pour into him the same way he poured into others. I was determined to find someone who would. Unfortunately, Constance was first on my list for meetings and I got the feeling she paid people to pour for her.

"Constance, Rowan Sloane, it's a pleasure to meet you."

I'd worn my favorite dress to meet all of Ellis's potentials. I'd done my nails, put on a full face of makeup, with lip plumper, foundation primer, and brightening serum. Why did I care how pretty I felt next to these women? None of them paid a lick of attention to me.

"I was starting to wonder if I got the day wrong." Constance smiled through a front of fake charm. "I guess that secretary of yours neglected to tell you that I'd arrived."

I hated people like her: condescending, superior, fake.

She wore her shoulder length, honey-colored hair pony straight and sleek, pushed back off her face with a wide bowed headband that would look juvenile on anyone else. Seeing her pull it off had me yearning to run to Target and grab one in every style and color. Her sea-foam green blazer paired with a gingham check pedal pant was sharper than my best strategy pitch. I'd seen confidence before, but Constance wore hers like a pair of worn in jeans and an old college sweatshirt. It was effortless.

"Before I continue, I want to confirm that this NDA my assistant handed me was signed by you, and you had the option to have your own attorney look it over before signing it and having it notarized."

"Yes, yes. To the point. I have a conference call in an hour." She waived her manicured hand in my direction with a flippant twirl.

"In plain language this is basically what the NDA covered. You agree not to share, publish or profit from anything I disclose from this point forward. That includes any personal details, business operations and things heard in passing from now until five years after the arrangement ends. This includes disclosure of any of the above verbally, in written documentation, on social media or via text. If it's not public knowledge, it's off-limits to discuss. You may speak with a doctor, lawyer, or therapist as they maintain confidentiality with their clients. Any breach of contract will be subject to damages including legal fees, valuation of harm done to reputation, and financial losses. Depending on the nature that could be seven to eight figures. Any content, ideas, or insight remain the sole property of Mr. Ellis Hawthorne and Hawthorne Media Group."

"I said yes," Constance snapped with barely veiled impatience. "Can we just get to the point of why I'm here."

"I'm just doing my job, and the nature of this meeting requires the pinnacle of discretion. No recording, I see you have two phones there, I'll need to collect those, along with your laptop and any other electronic devices you have and give them to my assistant Paisley for the duration of this meeting to ensure confidentiality. If the relationship ends for any reason, you are still bound by the rules of this NDA, as I said previously for five years from the date the relationship terminates."

Constance flipped her hair over her shoulder, an impatient frown bending her lips.

"I have too many projects I'm working on, I can't give you my phones."

"Then this is where our meeting terminates."

I would admit that having the upper hand with her gave me great joy. She handed over her very heavy Louis Vuitton Bag, both of her phones and her Apple Watch tossed inside, with an arrogant huff.

"Let's get a move on then. I'm expecting calls I can't afford to miss."

Once Paisley had collected the purse and closed the door again, I continued.

"From this point forward, you are prohibited by law from discussing anything from the rest of this meeting."

I waited a beat, and she didn't respond other than a roll of her eyes and an impatient smirk. Maybe I was overdoing the checks and cross checks, but you never knew with these rich people. They were always looking for loopholes in everything.

"As we said on the phone, Ellis Hawthorne would like us to arrange a meeting with him to examine the potential compatibility between the two of you. Based on our extensive vetting, we—and he—believe that you are one of the top candidates for a marriage partnership with Ellis.

"You of course are welcome to say no and leave now, remembering of course your binding NDA. However if you agree to meet Ellis and you both agree a marriage would be beneficial to both parties, he has a contract being finalized with his lawyers that discusses your freedom and autonomy in the marriage. Bonus trusts every five years you remain together, luxury houses, vacations, monthly allowance if you choose not to work and elect to raise your children. He is very open to any arrangement that is mutually beneficial."

I handed her the draft copy that the attorneys had asked to present.

"That stays in this office," I told her. "Until of course, you come to a mutual decision to begin dating."

"I'm assuming discussions of modifications to this would be between our lawyers?" she asked, holding the document up between her forefinger and thumb as if covered in Ebola.

"Yes, that would be a discussion for Ellis and eventually the lawyers. He'd like your first meeting to be this week. Here is the contact information for Morgan, Ellis's admin she will take care of scheduling your date."

THE MEETING with Constance went better than I'd expected, and the rest did as well, I thought. When I presented Simone with the information, she asked me if it was a "social experiment" that she could spinoff into a podcast. I couldn't wait to hear the update from that date with Ellis. Noeme asked the right questions, was skeptical in the right places, and somehow managed to make "market disruption in gendered finance" sound flirty. Ellis would be on his toes on their date for sure. I wished that hers had been the first date scheduled. Noeme was definitely more intense in person than her background profiling gave off. Unfortunately, if I didn't go through with her meeting Ellis, I feared the constraints of the NDA wouldn't be able to be upheld. And finally, there was Trina. The woman was too sweet. Like I feared a cavity just from interacting with her. She was Midwestern to a T. Her entire personality was genuine. Dressed in a sweet pink dress with a peter pan collar and a pair of ballet flats, the woman had come bearing gifts. Banana Bread and chocolate chip cookies, because she "figured I'd be hungry after such a long workday" –we'd met at four thirty after she got off work. I hoped Ellis would be kind to her. Trina's light felt like sunshine, and I would hate if her phosphorescence pushed him into a wall of discomfort that would trigger Ice Man CEO.

> Me: All four dossiers briefed and debriefed. NDAs signed. Expectations aligned.
>
> Me: You're officially scheduled to charm your way through four women.
>
> Me: Try not to ruin them. Remember the optics.
>
> Ellis: Define "ruin," because the chances of me fucking them after one date are nil 😒
>
> Me: My my aren't we brimming with bravado 😏
>
> Ellis: It's not bravado if it's been fact checked and verified.

Ellis: They don't call me tripod because I like to take pictures.

Me: Tripod?

Me: Please tell me that's a nickname you gave yourself and not one bestowed upon you by some poor woman who signed an NDA afterward.

Ellis: It was college. Things stick.

Me: So do rumors.

Me: Especially ones whispered by board members trying to figure out why their heir apparent needs a relationship consultant.

Ellis: Tell them I'm performance testing. Thoroughly.

Me: You're incorrigible.

Ellis: And yet, you still haven't quit.

Me: Because you're paying me double my rate

Me: Mama needs a new office. Preferably before winter.

Me: Old buildings are cute and charming until it's minus twenty outside

Ellis: If a heated sidewalk and better insulation keep you in my orbit longer, I'll happily sponsor the Rowan Sloane Office Renovation Fund.

Me: Flirt less. Focus more. You've got dates to impress. Four of them.

Ellis: Only four?

Me: Unless staring at yourself in the mirror counts too. Then five.

Ellis: Out of curiosity... if the roles were reversed—if you were the one picking from the four—who would've made your shortlist?

Me: Easy. None of the above.

Ellis: None?

Me: They're brilliant. Beautiful. Polished. But not my type.

Ellis: And what is your type, exactly?

Me: Emotionally unavailable men with control issues, clearly. Now go charm someone. I've got invoices to send and an office renovation to fund.

9

THE ECHO IN THE SILENCE

ELLIS

"None of the above." Rowan said. She'd tossed it off like a joke. It would be on never-ending repeat and taunt me for days after. If she wouldn't choose any of them, why was I?

I needed to talk to someone. Rowan clearly had her stance; she wasn't an option. I ran through my list of brothers...Dash? No. Too serious and too emotionally stunted to understand nuance. Keats? Too *follow your bliss* to provide unbiased opinions. Brontë even if I could get a hold of her in the middle of nowhere couldn't care less about family, legacy, or responsibility, and would tell me to marry who I want and fuck the duty to family. So that left Whit.

"It's nearly midnight," Whit said in place of a greeting. "If this is about the proxy vote, you'll survive."

Of course Whit's mind was on work. When was it not. Though, up until this *thing* with Rowan, thanks to Father, my mind would usually be on work at this time also.

"I've been thinking about the requirement." I confessed, wishing I'd have steadied myself with a drink before calling him. Of all my brothers, Whit could be concise and belabor a point concurrently. And where a phone call with either one of the younger two would last all of fifteen minutes, Whit's calls could go upward an hour.

"Which one?" He sighed heavily into the phone. Given the time, it was natural to be tired, however he sounded weary. Weighed down by the world. "The one that says we inherit a billion-dollar empire only if we pair off like it's a Regency-era marriage mart?"

"That would be the one." I replied, heading downstairs in the dark, in search of something strong and bitter to match my mood.

"And here I thought you loved a good power play." Usually, his witty commentary landed with force, accompanied by an arched eyebrow or laser sharp precision. But tonight, the joke fell flat like it was half deflated already when he lobbed it.

"I don't mind structure." I confessed, "But this feels off. I don't like being Father's puppet."

"You're just now realizing that Father likes to make puppets?"

The answer was no. We'd been the Hawthorne son marionettes as long as I had memories. I remembered when Whit and I were enrolled in prep school and taken out of the local grade school around the corner from our house. *Hawthorne's needed foundation building education.* He'd said to my mother despite her protests over the importance of friends, especially ones in the neighborhood. But Father didn't care about Jamie DeMario or Sunil Patel. Not that we weren't allowed to be friends with them anymore, he'd never issue ultimatums like that. But he knew that once we moved to the prep school the rigorous expectations of a school like that made it nearly impossible to socialize with our neighborhood friends. We kept in touch of course, but

Jamie and Sunil deepened their friendships with other kids at the local schools and though we've always been *friendly* we were no longer *friends*. Not like we'd been.

"You seem to be handling it." I volleyed.

"I'm faking it." Whit replied, shocking me with the admission.

"To whom?"

"Mostly to myself."

He huffed sardonically, before I heard the telltale tinkle of ice in a glass. It looked like Nathan Hawthorne had pushed all of us into nighttime confessions and imbibing in liquid salve. I didn't have a response. Mainly because he and I seemed to be embracing the same coping mechanisms. Yet layered within the fold of the night's confessions, one person's voice could still be heard.

I would choose none of the above.

But why? Hadn't I paid her to pick women perfect for me? So wouldn't she have a choice too? She knew me better than anyone, yet she would abstain from the most important decision of my life?

"Are you considering not following through?" Whit's voice was incredulous, suddenly sharper than it had been.

"I honestly wish I could." I admitted. "I don't want any of this."

Whit took another deep breath, letting it out slower than before. "You don't have to want it," he said finally, the pitch of his voice had lost the bitterness, and sounded almost gentle. "But you do have to face it. If you don't do the work to figure out who fits, someone else will make that decision for you."

Another beat passed.

"I don't think I'm built for this." I admitted. "Going through the theater of dating just to have a loveless relationship under contract and NDA. It feels like sentencing myself to an entire life of non-existence. Theater. Performance. Dooming us to this deadline ensures none of us find real love." I confessed.

"Is that the route you chose? Just randomly selecting someone who sort of holds your interest and treating it like a company merger? I don't think that is Father's intention. There is no rule that says you can't find someone you're interested in, Ellis. You have time. Why not pick a handful of women and just see where things go? Maybe you'll surprise yourself and actually enjoy someone's company."

I let the suggestion hang. I didn't mention Rowan; I didn't need to. The weight of her name sat between every line.

"Also," Whit chuckled, "Not to be a gossip, but Dash has already called dibs on easily ten women. So you better move fast before he turns this into a game show."

Soon after we hung up. It seemed like both Whit and Dash were further along than me. As the oldest, it was assumed I'd jump first and be the standard bearer. Being forced to walk the proverbial plank was not high on my list. But Whit was right. If I didn't want "none of the above," then I needed to figure out who was worth everything.

Constance Ashcroft was every bit her resume. Styled, smart, and socially fluent; the kind of woman you could drop into any room and she'd walk out having bagged the keynote speech at the next event, a massive donation, and a write-up in *The New York Times, Page Six*, and a personal feature in a women's magazine like *Marie Claire*. It was clear from the second she extended her ostensibly manicured hand with the perfect amount of jewelry, that she knew the exact right amount of eye contact to make to appear interested but not too interested. Controlled flirtation, calculated warmth, curated elegance.

I hated how much of it felt like a job interview I hadn't asked to sit for. We were barely through cocktails when she brought up the setup. "So, this mysterious secretary of yours," she began, swirling her Negroni, "Regan?"

"Rowan," I corrected about to further explain who she was, except Constance had the floor and refused to cede it.

"The redhead with the off-the-rack "power suit." She used air quotes and winked at me, "With the bottle version of red hair that screamed *JC Penney on a lunch break?*"

She laughed like she expected me to join in. I didn't. I stayed quiet because I wanted to give her plenty of rope to string herself with.

Constance recovered quickly, flashing a smile like a politician spinning a gaffe. "Forgive me if you feel protective of your subordinate. I just was surprised she is from HMG. Someone working for a Hawthorne heir should put a little more effort in. You know, take a little pride in her appearance. Optics are everything these days, don't you think?"

I took a long sip of my Barolo and let the silence stretch just long enough to let her feel it. "I trust Rowan's judgment more than most."

She blinked, surprised.

"Funny you mention optics." I continued, "Rowan, who is a CEO by the way, and does incredibly well for herself, runs a Fortune 500 consulting firm. *She* is the one doing *me* a favor, handling this incredibly delicate situation."

Rather than acknowledge her potential faux pas she pivoted smoothly back to the subject of her work with Privé's global philanthropy arm. "It's so exhausting being invited to a never-ending parade of galas and committee chairmanships. People are always asking me to lend my name," she said, "I must be so selective. Your name is your most valuable asset, I'm sure you agree. It can't just be bandied about for anyone to use."

That earned the thinnest curl of my lip. She mistook it for amusement. I nodded along, let her talk, and even asked questions when necessary. But, throughout the night, all I could hear in the back of my mind was Rowan's voice, and the conversations we'd had. *"Nothing says authentic connection like briefing women on how to fake it for press photos and family dinners."* She'd told me. As I sat there, getting tipsier than usual on a five-hundred-dollar bottle of wine, half listening to Constance drone on, I wondered if I could really do it.

I tried to picture Constance and me together with my family at the holidays. Sure, she'd probably convince us all to take a picture sporting her luxury brand, designer pajamas. And not the subtle ones, but the tacky, status signaling ones with garish logos on them that screamed "I can afford these designer pajamas, and I wanted you to know it so I put them on our Christmas card." I was certain once the holiday celebrations were over she'd want to jet off to Switzerland where she'd post a never-ending stream of photos starting from the flight in the HMG jet, shots of whatever outrageous hotel she booked us in, photos of us skiing, at dinner, and whatever other #blessed condescending, status signaling she could do while wrapping it into some well-crafted message about how doing good for others also meant doing good for oneself because you can't pour from an empty cup, or something equally trite.

When Constance reached for her phone to show me photos of her *Hamptons-for-a-week pop-up fundraiser*, I fully checked out mentally. That Hamptons "fundraiser" photos struck far too close to the mental image of our pretend family holiday.

She was everything my parents would love. Everything the board would eat up with a sterling appetizer fork. And I couldn't wait to be done with her.

ROWAN WAS ALREADY at the University Club when I arrived. She sat at the bar in a smart tweed skirt and an innocent gray blouse with a cute, rounded collar and pearls. Her hair was braided into an intricate pattern that shimmered beneath the drop lights above the bar.

The bartender had been pulled into Rowan's orbit, exchanging pleasantries with her while she sipped from her Gin & Tonic. The pair of them nudged at something inside me. Grated even. I felt myself irrationally annoyed that she was drinking her signature drink. As if she didn't know how to order it herself. But I'd wanted to. Because I loved the way she raised her eyebrow but blushed just slightly when I did it. It quietly thrilled her that I remembered. And I lived for the moments when I could show her how much of her habits I had logged.

"Hey, you're late. Again." She called to me as I walked nearer her orbit. "Sam here is just about finished with your French 95."

I took the seat next to her, hanging my jacket on the one next to me. The club's main bar was uncharacteristically slow for a Tuesday night. Up close, Rowan looked even more stunning. From the slight flush on her cheeks, she must have been incredibly early, which only highlighted my tardiness even more.

"I guess that makes us even." I brushed my lips across her forehead, seemingly on autopilot. "I'm so sorry. Whit and I got stuck in a meeting about our sports contracts. They've been giving us a headache for a week now and nothing seems to help." She'd leaned into it, like it was the most familiar thing in the world. As if we were a couple, and the bar was our usual haunt.

Reality hit us nearly at the same time. We both froze. I desperately tried to recover.

"You weren't kidding about the traffic on Lake Shore Drive," I said, "I eventually gave up and had Uri dump off around Chestnut and take side streets."

"That's why I left thirty minutes early." She admitted, "I was so paranoid of being late again!"

"Have you eaten?" I asked, glancing at the restaurant across the foyer. "It doesn't look terribly crowded. I bet we could get in right now without a reservation."

"Morgan reserved one of the Executive studies upstairs?" Her voice raised in question as she signaled toward the grand staircase.

I didn't give a shit if Morgan reserved one. That's what they were for. And if executives decided not to use them or came later than expected, no one batted an eye. Because they were for *executives* with insane schedules and thousands of last-minute pivots every day.

Aside from housing executive offices, conference rooms, and meeting spaces, the place may as well be a hotel.

Between the full gym, pool, hot tub and steam rooms, along with the various ball courts—it also served as a full service hotel. Anyone who was a member of the multitude of University Clubs across the country could stay and have access to all the amenities along with its four restaurants The space was incredibly convenient. I met with each of my four dates there, though we'd been upstairs in its more private restaurant. The one typically used for business meetings or negotiations couched as working meals.

The main floor restaurant was for enjoyment. To feast among those who cared about the status of being *seen*. And the chef's menu was exquisite. The host ushered us to a private booth in the back corner. Tucked in a quiet corner, it was perfect for both enjoying the ambience while also carrying on a conversation away from nosey ears and the din of post-work diners.

Rowan smiled sweetly as the host pushed in her chair, graciously accepting her menu while offering a quiet thanks. She hadn't come armed to the teeth with laptops, folders, and neatly arranged dossiers. Just a notebook and pen, sitting on the chair to her left.

"I didn't realize that our meetings now came with a dinner kicker," she said with a lazy smile.

"Given that your smile is awfully loose, I'd say those two G&Ts were consumed on an empty stomach. Dinner is probably a necessity at this point before we dive in to my "love life."

Her faced snapped into a businesslike frown in an instant. No more adorable, toothy smile.

"I am not drunk. I'm a professional Ellis."

"I know that." I fought the urge to push away the strand of hair coming undone at her forehead. "You're just a little more mellow than you usually are. Adorably so."

"I'm fine," she insisted, donning a mask of passive businesswoman. "I skipped lunch, and Sam down there has a generous pour. A glass of water and a few bites of one of these rolls and I'll be completely capable of collecting feedback from your dates."

"Mm hmm," I mused, buttering a roll for her without asking. "If I'm hearing you correctly, you're both hangry and tipsy. A dangerous cocktail."

She narrowed her eyes. "Says the man who's already two minutes into trying to distract me with carbs and charm."

I pushed the plate toward her with theatrical innocence. "Distract you? Never. I'm merely ensuring the strategist responsible for my romantic future doesn't faint at the table."

She tore off a corner of the roll and popped it in her mouth. "Deflection."

"Managing expectations." I threw back with a smile, scanning the starters and weighing which could be produced quickly.

"Same thing."

"And yet, is that the roll I buttered and offered to you hanging between your fingers?"

Her lips quirked before she managed to rein them in. "You're starting to sound dangerously like someone trying to be charming."

I gaped at her in mock offense, "I'm *always* charming."

"Really, Mr. Ice Man? Charming? Is that what they call indifferent and unflappable these days? No, you're powerful. People just pretend they can't tell the difference."

"Around you, all my ice melts." I told her honestly.

Rowan blinked, caught off guard. "That's a line."

I shrugged, trying to deflect. "I try to feed you and you accuse me of false charm. I try to explain and it's a line."

Her lips pinched and twitched. I could sense her discomfort. Her unsurety that she'd somehow stepped over a line and put her foot in her mouth. She finally said, "It was a good line."

Rather than reply I signaled to the waiter, ordering our starters, before deferring to Rowan for her salad and dinner selection. With that out of the way, and a few grounding sips of water, Rowan regained her footing and lost that sweet shimmer she'd glowed with when I arrived. I wanted to assure her I loved when she loosened up as much as when she kept me on my toes. But Rowan was back to showing me how smart and capable she was.

And Christ, she was both. Everything. The kind of woman who could disarm a boardroom and then dismantle your ego with nothing but a well-placed sentence. She was the rarest kind of threat. The kind that quietly infiltrated and elicited surrender before you realized you'd raised your white flag. Not because you had to, but because you wanted to. Because she made you want to be better.

"Okay, let's start with Constance." Her notebook was at her fifteen, pen held at the ready.

I didn't want to talk about Constance. Or Simone, Noeme, or Trina. I wanted to rewind to when I'd innocently called out her tipsiness and bask in that warm glow instead of cutting it short and forcing her into CEO mode.

"Society women are an absolute no. They're mean, catty even." I told her.

She didn't say anything. Didn't write anything down or even raise an eyebrow at my declaration.

"Why aren't you arguing with me?"

"Are you seriously surprised?" she asked me? "Ellis, women in your circle are Tuesdays with a capital T."

"I don't follow," I said, sliding my hand off the table to allow the server to plate my salad.

"A Tuesday? As in C-U Next?"

It took a minute. Well, many minutes honestly. I'd never heard something so filthy from Rowan before.

"Jesus, you can't just go around calling women that!"

"I didn't. I called your circle that. Collectively. Besides, you've never used the word?"

"Of course not," I couldn't hide the mortification from my voice. "It's the most offensive word you can call a woman."

She shrugged. As if I'd told her I preferred vanilla ice cream and hers was mint chip. It stunned me silent. Though the thought of her saying the word, in other contexts, had heat collecting in my groin.

"For a man to say it, maybe. From a woman? It's a step above calling someone a bitch. Context matters."

"Still. It's crude."

Rowan leaned back in her chair and smiled like she knew exactly what I was thinking. Which was problematic. Because my imaginings involved her saying that word again, only this time while straddling my cock, her rising Phoenix colored hair, hanging wildly down her back, her breasts, pink from exertion and pressed against my chest while she demanded I abuse her cunt with a passion rasped voice.

I had to stop. She was a professional. And so was I. I tried to be as subtle as I could while I adjusted myself beneath the table.

"So unsurprisingly Constance is a no." She wrote something in her efficient little notebook.

"Unsurprisingly?" I couldn't hide the note of

incredulity. "Why would you have me go on a date if you thought it would fail? I don't have time to waste, Rowan."

"Unsurprising because even though you keep insisting you want fake and façade—your words say the exact opposite. And Constance is nothing but façade."

"And judgment and condescension." I didn't mean to say it, but seeing Rowan sitting across from me in a very professional and not cheap looking, Diane Von Furstenberg outfit pushed forward that same protectiveness I'd felt when Constance tried to call her cheap. Rowan loved Diane's designs. Her dresses were Rowan's go to; she'd worn them often when we worked together. While not flashy, it was *prete a porter*—off-the-rack—but not in a horrible or offensive way as Constance implied. My mother similarly loved Diane Von Furstenberg, calling her a staple for every businesswoman.

"Got it. Constance and all society women going forward, off the list!" She made a show of aggressively crossing something from her notebook. "What about the other three?"

Ugh. The other three. They were no better, but not for the same reason. Each one was pleasant enough. But they each were missing *something*.

"Simone was too...*much* for lack of a better word. She referred to my family as late-stage capitalism and said that elitism was on its last dying breath. During dinner she tried to earnestly convince me that we should "be like Harry and Meg and walk away from it all and start a charitable foundation and podcast."

Rowan tried unsuccessfully to keep her sip of wine in her mouth. I passed her my napkin, chuckling as I did.

"I'm sorry, I didn't realize you were taking a sip. And until now it hadn't even felt all that funny."

"I just can't." Rowan laughed, folding my napkin into a discreet square she left on the corner of the table, and passing me hers. "I thought she had just the *right* amount of chaos to keep you on your toes. Not try to derail the entire plan. So another one bites the dust."

Her cheeks had pinkened again. Not the same way the gin had affected her, she wasn't soft and glowy, but the rod that straightened her spine had definitely disappeared.

"Innocent Trina." I sighed. "The wolves would tear her to shreds. Her and sweet, little Molly. You were right. Our lives are too different. Sadly, she reminded me of why my dad told me it would be hard for us to be friends with the neighborhood kids. It wasn't meant to be the slight I always thought it was. It was a reality. Our worlds were so different. And she would be violently ripped from everything she loved and found comfort in and thrown into a world of façade and disingenuous friendships."

Rowan nodded, continuing to take notes. I couldn't stop watching the varying facial expressions she made as she catalogued my dates. Not that I expected anything less from Rowan Sloane, but she took this so seriously. Every word, turn of phrase, and observation as noted and catalogued in various columns.

As if feeling me observing her, she looked up, pen at the ready, eyebrows lifted encouraging me to continue.

"Which was the polar opposite of Noeme." I continued. "You were right about her. On paper she was my dark horse. Polished and witty, I had an enjoyable evening with her. Our discussions ran the gamut from little known Chicago bands to esoteric topics like the influence of AI and how it is poisoning accurate history on the internet."

"That sounds, like a successful night then." Rowan

tapped her pen against the full bow of her bottom lip. "Where was the problem?"

I wanted to say *she wasn't you*. It was wildly inappropriate, I knew. But as I'd sat with Noeme, I kept expecting her to be like Rowan. I wanted the banter, the subtle jabs, that quick, circular intelligence that always had me on my toes. The way Rowan spun me in circles wondering where her next playful jab would come from.

"She was *too* aware of optics. It felt like I was the one being interviewed. Like she wanted to see what benefit I could provide her."

"Isn't that sort of the point?" Rowan asked, clearing the bottle of wine between our two glasses. "You're using each other for mutual benefit, right? Certainly you didn't expect this to be one-sided. She deserves to benefit as much as you."

I was never the one whose words failed me. I didn't like this feeling, the inability to not mean exactly what came out of my mouth.

"Of course not. I know this isn't one-sided but I didn't expect to feel like a commodity. I thought, or I guess my misguided assumption was that I'd find someone who at least would look past my last name and see a person. Someone compatible enough, who would be treated well, and maybe eventually develop some form of love. People have had arranged marriages for centuries."

She leaned back and crossed her arms, her head tilting while I continued to talk. Eventually, she said, "What I think I'm hearing is that you don't like being the one getting appraised. Judgment doesn't feel so great when the spotlight is on you, does it?"

"Ouch." That struck with the precision of a surgeon's scalpel. "I thought if I found someone else whose name was in lights, it wouldn't matter to them if mine was. But even she—" I stopped myself before I vomited too many feels across the pristine white tablecloth.

"Even she what?" Rowan pressed.

"Made me feel like a means to an end. Just an empty commodity. But you knew this was going to happen, didn't you?"

She took her time taking a long, appreciative sip of her cappuccino while I waited for her answer. Finally, after what seemed like an eternity, she said, "I suspected, but you needed to see it yourself."

I huffed a quiet laugh and handed our bill back to the waiter. Once returned, I stood and helped her to stand. The hum of low conversation and clinking glassware faded behind us as we stepped out into the cool evening air. My SUV idled, driver at the ready to take me home.

Rowan opened up her ride-share app to hire a driver.

"I can take you home." I pointed toward the Navigator waiting for me to approach. "It's not that far out of my way."

"Ellis," she laughed, placing her hand on my chest as she tried to pivot in the opposite direction, "I live in the Ukrainian Village, that is the complete opposite way from Old Town. We may as well be in different states."

I moved a step closer. The strange pull that had distracted me all evening, thrumming with even more insistence. "Still. I could make the detour."

"You want to make your poor driver sit for endless minutes in the cattle drive known as the Kennedy, when I could just as easily hop in an Uber and we can both go on our merry way, a million times more efficiently."

Her body shifted so we were nearly perfectly aligned. Just a subtle shift from either one of us and we'd be toe to toe, nose to nose. I was so close in fact, I caught the subtle, bright notes of her perfume. The scent, reminding me of apples just beginning to blossom.

"I want to make sure you get home safe." I pursued.

The air between us shifted. It felt as if time became gelatinous. Her mouth, open and poised to give another excuse became too tempting. I leaned in, with intent. There'd be no mistaking it this time. No cheek, and no pretense of polite farewells. My lips just grazed hers at first, just a taste. I hovered for a breath, allowing her the opportunity to back away. To say how wildly inappropriate this was. That we were supposed to be business partners and I was paying her to find me a wife.

My lips met hers again. This time I took my time exploring their weight, the softness of her lush mouth against mine. I savored the bitter taste of espresso on her tongue, mingled with the subtle crème and hint of cinnamon. I went to pull away, and she pressed on. Her arms looping around my neck, her head tilting just slightly to give me better access.

I felt her warm body meld against mine. Heard the subtle moaned sigh as it vibrated between us. Slowly, the pair of us separated, trying to steady our breath. I stepped back, slowly. Watching her eyes search mine like she was trying to recalibrate the rules.

"If you won't allow me to drive you home, then please let Uri take you." I opened the door to my car and helped her into the backseat.

"Uri," I asked, "if you could please take care of getting this precious cargo back to Ukrainian Village I would appreciate it."

"I can't steal your ride!" She tried to push back out of the car. "Ellis, I swear I'm fine waiting for a Lyft."

"Are you saying you prefer the driving of a total stranger

to riding in the car for twenty minutes with me? You're old friend? I'm heartbroken Rowan. After all those warm croissants you would save for me."

That halted her exit.

"Oh Uri!" She laughed, "I'm more worried about you and that long drive back in all that traffic."

"It's no bother Rowan. I would feel better knowing you're home safe too. A beautiful woman in this city can never be too careful."

Not that Rowan wasn't absolutely gorgeous, but Uri laid it on awfully thick. Anything to get her to agree though. Which she did, with little protest after that.

"Let me know when you get home." I asked, pressing one last kiss to her forehead before I closed the door and Uri drove off.

10

HEAT AND ILLUMINATION

Rowan

THANKFULLY, even on a Tuesday night getting from the loop to Ukrainian Village was an exercise in patience. Which worked in my favor. It gave me time to process.

I *kissed* Ellis Hawthorne. Well, technically *he* kissed *me*. But I definitely kissed him back. Enthusiastically so. Jesus I was so fucked.

This was supposed to be *find the fiancée* not *seduce the strategist*.

For the last ten minutes, the only thing I could think about was how good Ellis smelled, how devastatingly well he kissed, and how tenderly he'd held me. Like I was the most cherished being in his orbit. It had been magic. It was so wrong. My bank account overflowed from the first payment for our initial meeting. The contracts for the women I was *paid to introduce him to*, still sat in my phone's inbox, top of the screen.

Sure, we'd talked business but the dinner hadn't *felt* like business. Not entirely.

Maybe it was the gin and tonic, but the whole night had

felt different. Warmer. Like a gravity had shifted between us. Not quite romantic, not exactly platonic—but circling something dangerous. Like we'd been skimming the edges of curiosity for weeks, and tonight, we finally fell in.

"It'll be different in the morning." I mumbled to my reflection in the car window.

Once the booze wore off, and we both slept on it, tomorrow morning we'd wake up, have an *Oh Shit* moment, and then we'd figure out how to navigate around the awkwardness.

I should've pulled away. I should've said something clever, something to reestablish the boundary we'd been toeing for weeks. Instead, I tilted my head, leaned in, and let him kiss me like I was the destination, not a detour.

And now here I was, staring out the window of his chauffeured SUV like a woman who had absolutely no idea what game she'd just agreed to play.

THE PING CAME BEFORE SUNRISE. I saw it through the haze of half-sleep, blue light washing over my bedroom ceiling. My phone buzzed again, then again. Each vibration stacking unease in my chest like bricks. I reached for it, still groggy and half asleep, my eyes squinting as I tapped open the first notification.

Chicagossip:

> BREAKING: HAWTHORNE HEIR CAUGHT IN RARE DISPLAY OF AFFECTION—WHO IS THE MYSTERY WOMAN?
>
> *Chicago's most elusive bachelor was spotted exiting University Club last night—an eyebrow-raising location for what appears to have been a decidedly intimate evening.*
>
> *Our photographers captured Ellis Hawthorne kissing a red-haired beauty in what can only be described as a very not-platonic display before helping her into a waiting car. Sources say the mystery woman is not a known fixture on the Chicago social circuit. Is the Ice Man finally melting? Is this just a fling—or something far more headline-worthy? More to come.*

I STARED AT THE BLURRY, flash-lit photo. Ellis's mouth unmistakably close to mine. His hand at my lower back, my fingers curled into the lapel of his coat. The city glittering like scandal behind us. My face was partially turned, but still—there was enough. Too much. The arch of my body toward his. The way my hand clung. My stunned, swooning, *what-am-I-doing* expression. Maybe we could play it off as a platonic goodbye kiss. The picture caught us right after we'd pulled apart. Not the full lip lock, thank god for small miracles. It could easily be written off as sensationalism at its finest.

There was plenty to speculate on. Enough to fuel a thousand guesses. More than enough to unravel everything.

The next alert was from *Page Six Midwest*. Then *The*

Real Print. By the time I made it into the shower, the group chat had lit up:

> Lyris: ROWAN. WAKE UP.
>
> Greer: Are you on every tabloid's homepage or did someone leak a deleted Hallmark movie?
>
> Hollis: Please tell me this is an elaborate PR stunt because I am OBSESSED.
>
> Lyris: Also? We knew something was up. Remember Pitch Fest?? You said it wasn't a get. WELL??

I didn't respond. Not right away. Instead, I sat on the edge of my bed, phone resting on my knee, the damp towel wrapped tight around me like armor, as water dripped from my still soaking hair. The photo stared back from my screen. I could practically *hear* the click of the shutter now, feel the warmth of Ellis's palm on my back.

The meeting was strictly professional. I didn't even make any cheeky jokes or use innuendo. There was absolutely no warning. He hadn't hesitated.

I'd been so stunned. There were so many ways I could have responded if my brain would have functioned properly. I could have laughed it off and pushed back. Staying cool would have been fantastic. But I hadn't done any of those. I'd just *felt*.

That was the most dangerous thing of all. Because Ellis Hawthorne wasn't supposed to make me *feel* anything. He was a job. A client. A well-compensated crisis in a sharply tailored coat. And yet, last night, standing outside one of the most exclusive clubs in Chicago, I hadn't felt like an adviser. I'd felt chosen. Not for the hired role, or my previous one as his assistant. This was something else. Undefined. And I hated that part of me who loved how true it felt.

Another ping. This time, from

BuzzSociety:
"EXCLUSIVE: Who's the Redhead With Ellis Hawthorne? Our Sources Say She's *Not* a Regular Fixture in the Hawthorne Inner Circle... But She Might Be Now."

Beneath it was a super clear image, zoomed in and unmistakably me. God help me, it would only be a matter of time before they figured out who I was, and shortly after that before someone produced a picture of us actually in the act of kissing. And I knew, once they printed that picture, there was no way we'd be able to deflect.

> Greer: Rowan Anastasia Sloane Do NOT ghost this chat.
>
> Lyris: Ew seriously Greer? Cringe. SO cringe.
>
> Lyris: Rowan, we're super worried...
>
> Lyris: But also nosy.
>
> Hollis: I am like four steps behind this whole development and suddenly hella jella that I missed an apparently very important Pitch Fest!! Girls, fill me tf in.

I finally replied, fingers moving fast, tone firm.

> Me: Guys, I already told you—Nathan is working on succession planning. Of course that naturally would meld into discussions with the future CEO. Nothing has changed. Some idiot caught a friendly goodbye and is making a huge deal out of nothing. I need to call Ellis and get ahead of this scandal.

I didn't wait for their responses. My fingers were already dialing. Fucking voicemail. Of course!

"Hi, it's me," I said after the tone. "I'm assuming your phone is imploding or you're already in an optics meeting or maybe both."

I could hear myself leaving that voicemail. I sounded panicked, teetering on unhinged.

"Someone got a photo of us last night and it's everywhere. I'll craft a preliminary narrative. Succession planning optics, strategic advisory, clean and professional. I'd used it on my friends at Pitch Fest and it seemed to work just fine. So hopefully this will all blow over by this afternoon. Regardless, I'll meet you at your office at 8 a.m. sharp. We need to coordinate response before it snowballs. Call me if you get this."

I fired off a text for good measure.

> Me: Caught early media coverage of the photo. I've got it handled. Will run with standard optics around succession planning—nothing romantic. Meeting you at your office at 8 sharp.

Then I dropped the phone on the bed, exhaled, and finally let myself *feel* the way my stomach had dropped when his voicemail kicked in. This wasn't just a hiccup in narrative control. This was the moment the story started writing *us*.

11

ACT NATURAL, THEY'RE WATCHING

ELLIS

I'd barely taken a sip of my coffee when the security notification buzzed on my phone.

ROWAN SLOANE CHECKED IN – GUEST PASS 1 – 7:56 A.M.

She was early. Of course she was. Morgan hadn't even arrived yet. Which meant I had exactly three minutes to brace for whatever storm was about to come through my door. Rowan in a tailored coat, walking fast and furious down the HMG corridor? A force of nature with the punch of a hurricane.

I'd barely slept. Not because of the unending questions from my PR team. We'd navigated scandals before. I knew exactly what to expect from them. What I hadn't expected was for that photo to feel so intimate. I'd reviewed it at least a dozen times, trying to convince myself it was just good lighting. Just a flattering angle. But no, it was there, every single time. I looked... happy. Open. And that was never part of the plan.

The photo wasn't scandalous, not really. The tenderness of my expression might raise an eyebrow but that could easily be written off as congenial. We were "old friends" after all. I needed to stop romanticizing the way her hair caught the light like something out of a film still. Even if the tabloids certainly had. *"Mystery Redhead Spotted with Ellis Hawthorne in Exclusive After-Hours Rendezvous"* The headlines grew progressively worse.

But it wasn't the story spinning out of control that had me in knots. It was that I didn't look angry. Or cold. Or calculated. There was no "Ice Man" present. I genuinely looked at peace, and it shocked me that a camera could capture that part of me. The part that I'd learned only surfaced around her.

When the knock came, it wasn't tentative. It was confident. Controlled. The sound of someone who'd already written the statement in her head.

"Come in."

Rowan entered with a leather portfolio tucked under one arm and her chin lifted in challenge. She didn't sit, not right away anyway. She just stared with measured silence. I couldn't tell if the controlled look on her face, with that pouty frown and wrinkle between her eyebrows was fear, concern, or disappointment.

"You saw the coverage?" she asked, like it wasn't rhetorical.

A small part of me felt a pang of disappointment that her concern over optics was the top of mind. I'd hoped she come in and smile, maybe blush in remembrance of how wonderful that kiss had been. Did she regret it? Because I sure didn't. Even if this fall became nuclear, all I wanted as a result of that kiss was more. Of everything. Of anything that had to do with her.

I nodded. "They're relentless."

"Yep. But we'll get ahead of it. My story is completely feasible. It makes absolute sense."

She dropped into the chair across from me and opened the folder with a crisp flick of her wrist. "Standard language. Succession planning. Strategic alignment discussions. It made more sense to meet offsite; we didn't want anyone internally to get wind and worry about the future. I'll take the heat on the optics. We'll say I arranged this meeting and chose the location for the aforementioned reason. The kiss was a genial goodbye between friends. I have yet to see a photo of the actual kiss. Every news outlet has the moment just after it."

"That's not the truth though." I watched her as she scribbled notes furiously on her notepad, turning over her phone with each new buzz that sounded off.

She paused, eyes flicking up to meet mine. "It does the least damage."

I hated how right she was. But even worse was the fact that I had no words to stop her. Not because I disagreed. But because a part of me—the dangerous, impulsive part—liked that they thought she was mine. Even if she wasn't.

Before I could respond, the door opened without zero knocking.

Whit walked in first, tie loose, phone in hand. He looked like a modern version of a fifties era expectant father pacing the halls, waiting on news of his wife's delivery. Dash sauntered in next, all sunglasses and swagger. And then Keats with an obnoxious *cat ate the canary* smile splitting his mug.

Of course, it would be Keats. The man was a bloodhound when it came to juicy gossip that didn't involve or concern him. The know-it-all smirk on his face, as if he already knew a secret, was far too grating this early in the day.

"You're trending," Whit said, barely looking up.

Dash tossed a gossip rag onto the desk with a thud. "And not for the reason I thought. I was betting on another 'unapproachable Hawthorne' think piece. But this? Redheaded mystery woman? Intimate late-night meeting? Delicious. Please tell me you were in the overnight accommodations, and an enterprising young reception desk clerk is going to leak your credit card receipt to the media soon."

"I don't recall inviting anyone to this meeting," I muttered, straightening in my chair. "And don't be crass in front of guests."

Dash dropped into the seat next to Rowan without hesitation. "And miss the PR crisis of the quarter? Come on, we all got the alert. Board's already sniffing around."

Rowan, to her credit, didn't flinch. Just folded her hands neatly and met their scrutiny head-on.

"Ms. Sloane and I were in the middle of discussing the official response," I said, slow and measured. "It will fall under strategic consultation during succession planning."

Keats ignored me completely and turned his full attention to Rowan, leaning on the end of my desk, facing her, leg dangling. "Succession planning, huh?"

There was a gleam in his eye. The kind that suggested he was poking at the truth like a loose tooth. I hated that she was surrounded by my brothers and what felt like light years away from me, even if I did sit on the other side of my desk. From where I observed, she was trapped beneath the glaring spotlight of three Hawthorne brothers. I wanted to collect her and bring her to my side of the desk, away from prying eyes and inquiries.

"I don't buy it," he said, smiling like they were old friends. "No offense. But you don't drag someone to the University Club for a professional chat unless you want it to look unprofessional."

"None taken." Rowan quirked a brow. "I didn't realize you're an expert on optics now. Funny I thought that's why Ellis reached out to me."

Keats leaned back, unbothered. "I pay attention," he said, cradling his head and resting his foot on the arm of her chair. "You've been in the building a lot lately. Bit odd for a former assistant turned CEO, don't you think?"

Whit, who'd been quietly reading something on his phone, finally looked up. "Are we seriously doing this right now? Gossip hour with Keats? Or are we fixing this before it turns into a full-blown boardroom referendum?"

Rowan turned to me then, totally unfazed by Whit's chippy attitude. Her expression when she looked at me was all business. "You said discretion was everything. That's off the table now. I'm not intending to be punny here, but we're going to need to pivot."

"I don't get the pun." Keats said just as Dash weighed in.

"Pivot? To what?" Dash asked, twirling his sunglasses in his fingers. "You two pretending to date? It's not the worst idea."

"Pivot is the name of Rowan's company, Keats. She handles crisis communication and corporate imaging."

"You know people love a good, reformed man story." Dash continued. "We serve it up like a reality show, feed small things to the press. Reformed billionaire falls for the girl next door? It's as close to a royal family type of story that you can get. Rowan can be America's version of Princess Catherine."

"It's not a romance novel, Dash," I snapped.

"Could've fooled me," Keats murmured, still watching Rowan like she was a puzzle he was halfway through solving.

I turned back to her, lowering my voice. "You said we needed to test the theory. I think the theory just got an accidental head start."

Rowan nodded once, eyes steady. "I guess it's time to shape the story before someone else does."

Whit crossed his arms and stared at both of us, humorless and stoic. "Let's *actually* talk strategy for a second. What's the message? I guarantee the board will be asking by noon."

He thankfully took a seat on my couch, crossing a leg over the other, holding it at his ankle. "Are you leaning into the succession planning narrative and keeping this under the radar—or are you going public?"

I opened my mouth to respond, but he cut in.

"Don't wing this, Ellis. This isn't just a gossip column item anymore. It's narrative now. If you two met at the University Club to reconnect after years apart, then you're dating. If it was a business meeting, we better get quotes in three reputable outlets by end of day. You can't have it both ways."

"There is nothing to go public on," I explained. "This was truly just a meeting between friends."

Rowan didn't flinch. We hadn't exactly discussed what the story would be to our inner circle. I didn't care if my brothers knew I hired her to find me a fake wife, but I also didn't want to lose her trust or her friendship. There'd been no discussion on this. Whether she even wanted to be involved in the fake date narrative. We'd simply had proverbial bags thrown over our heads and were being forced into the spotlight.

"What would you recommend?" she asked, exiting the chair she'd occupied and positioning herself across from Whit in the high back armchair kitty corner to where he sat.

Whit turned to her. "Soft open. We hold the line on the succession planning story. You two will release joint statements. It will be along the lines of Ellis enlisted the help of Pivot for succession planning for Nathan Hawthorne. With him planning to retire, the two of you wanted to ensure a plan could be put into place with minimal emotional impact to the team at HMG. Pivot's CEO, Rowan Sloane, was concerned for the well-being of employees some who have been here over thirty years would take the news that Nathan planned to retire from someone other than them. Rowan is familiar with Hawthorne and our legacy because she got her start here, and naturally she and Ellis had developed a bonded trust working together for so long."

"That story *is* the truth though it's not spin," I said, though the words tasted stale.

"No, Ellis," Whit said, calm but firm. "That's a *version* of the truth. One that buys us time. But it also makes you look like you're hiding something. Which only invites more questions."

"Which brings us back to the dating angle," Dash added, grinning. "There's no shame in having history with someone. Everyone loves a slow burn romance. Old flame reignited, timing never worked, he was her boss, it never felt appropriate blah blah blah."

Keats chimed in, still annoyingly fixated on Rowan. "You two ever actually date before? Or is this going to be the media-friendly version of emotional improv?"

Rowan glanced at me. I couldn't read her expression, but it was controlled. Measured. Exactly what Whit wanted from a PR angle. And the opposite of how I felt.

"Let's say we go that route," Whit pressed. "What's the emotional logic? Why now? Why her? Why you? We need the dots to connect so we can feed them slowly. A quote here. A soft launch there. Build enough credibility that when the board starts poking, they'll find roots."

There was a long pause. Then Rowan, ever composed, said simply, "We let them assume. We release nothing but a holding statement about succession planning. If the story has legs, the public will do the work for us. Rumors are often stronger than confirmation. And if we do our jobs right, we can give the illusion of inevitability."

Dash let out a low whistle. "Damn. That's almost hot."

"Thank you," Rowan said dryly. "I think."

Whit still looked unconvinced. "This will buy you a few days, max. But work with Keats, we need a five-point message map by the end of day. If this gets legs and starts influencing HMG stock or board cohesion, we'll need contingency language. What happens if the story flips? If she becomes the distraction?"

Rowan arched a brow. "Then we pivot again."

Everyone turned to me. As if my opinion were the final word. But the truth was—I didn't have one yet. Not one I could speak out loud.

So I settled for: "Let's start with the truth we can shape. Succession planning. Strategic consultation. And, like Rowan suggested, we let the rest... build slowly."

Rowan nodded. "Then I'll work on a calendar of quiet, believable touch-points. Places we can be seen without being *seen*."

"And we monitor the fallout," Whit added, finally sitting. "Every. Single. Day."

12

WEAR THE MASK

Rowan

The moment I pushed through the glass doors of HMG out onto the street I let out a breath I hadn't realized I was holding. HMG's offices were glossy, full of glass, oozing legacy from every corner. They'd designed it to impress and intimidate.

For most of the time we'd sat in that executive war room I'd held my own. I went toe to toe with three Hawthorne brothers and stared down Ellis like it hadn't meant anything when he kissed me as if I was his future and the fallout all in one.

Now though? The mid-morning lake air bit through my coat, reminding me spring never arrived on time, I shook. From the insides of my bones. I vibrated on an entirely new frequency sure to disrupt every radio and television station in the area. My portfolio felt slippery in my grip. My breath fogged into the air in bursts, erratic and unsteady—nothing about me suggested calm or control.

The performance was over. I'd worn the heels, donned the respectable business suit, delivered my bullet points, arguments, and counter arguments with stone faced neutrality, even when Dash and Keats tried to pin me to the wall like a captured butterfly.

Not Pivot. Not the HMG succession line. Me.

Another breeze whipped through the buildings sluicing beneath my coat and rattling my bones until they shook out the lie I'd been telling myself since last night. That this was temporary and controllable. I couldn't stop seeing the warmth in Ellis's gaze when he said, "Let's start with the truth we can shape."

That was not a comment born from strategy. It was personal. Ellis wanted proximity not practicality, and that is what scared me the most. Because somewhere between the briefings, the dossier of potential love interests, the recap meeting and the taste of cinnamon on his mouth and the tender way he held me, I believed the illusion too.

My phone chimed, pulling me out of my panicked mental spin.

> Greer: Saw the photos. Where are you?
> CALL ME.

She answered before it even rang on my end.

"Please don't say anything cheeky." I told her before she could even say hello. "I'm about one sentence away from a total emotional breakdown."

"Rowan! You kissed him in front of a camera. Is there even anything clever enough that covers the infinite universe of complication you find yourself in?"

Not helpful. Like at all. My spiral squeezed my chest like a vise, refusing to allow breath to pass.

"It wasn't supposed to happen." I choked out, barely.

Suddenly it seemed impossible to stand for two more seconds in the heels, feeling the wind trying to knock me down, standing as I was on Michigan Avenue. I half leaned/half sat on one of the planters in front of their building.

"I was just trying to get home." I told her. "He was worried about me hiring a service to take me there, and insisted I ride in his car. I refuse to be *that girl* and blame it on the gin and tonic but I did have two without eating."

"Babe," Greer's voice softened. "Booze isn't going to make you do anything you aren't already hoping it would happen. It may soften your inhibitions a bit, but it's not a robot. When you drink, someone else doesn't take the reins."

She was right, of course. And, by the time we left my buzz was long gone. This happened. And it happened because despite myself and my ridiculous attempt to stay professional, I couldn't help falling, piece by piece, for Ellis Hawthorne.

"This has all the workings of a Shakespearean tragedy," I said.

"Where are you?" Greer asked.

"I just left Hawthorne. I need to call Paisley and tell her I'm heading home. I need to work on controlling the narrative, but I don't think I'd be able to do it at the office."

"All right Ophelia," Greer joked. "Call me later."

BY THE TIME four o'clock rolled around, I was exhausted. My little walk up in the Ukrainian Village wasn't large by any accounts, but it was charming and had amazing light. On an average day, my house is warm and cluttered. Not enough to qualify me for *Hoarders* but I definitely would need to have an "oh shit!" room if Home and Garden called telling me they'd be there in ten minutes to photograph.

It was well lived in, and I accepted that. Books stacked on side tables. Dishes in the sink that I told myself on Saturday I'd get to on Sunday –and yet it was Wednesday. There were throw pillows scattered about as if I'd taken their names literally.

If I didn't have company, I didn't bother to really clean in the OCD top to bottom *make it shine like the top of the Chrysler Building* kind of way. I didn't have a baker's dozen of singing orphans to keep it militaristically clean.

Now that my entire life felt like I was experiencing the most epic level of tumult, my living room mirrored how I felt. Chaotic, spiraling, trying to find up in both my professional and emotional vortex. There were papers scattered across my living room. Because why bother to use the office where the desk and the folders, and the aesthetically pleasing décor was? The couch, with the TV in the background tuned in to the celebrity gossip channel seemed the most appropriate place to hunker down. Coffee mugs laid down and forgotten about only to be replaced with a new one. Notepads on various surfaces holding whatever random thought that had surfaced at the time I walked past it.

My group text had been chiming incessantly most of the day. Ninety percent of it ignored. I scanned every so often, *ha ha'd* or *thumbs upped* a stray comment or question if I was doing okay.

> Lyris: @Rowan there is a Zoom in 10. No exceptions. I've already poured my own Sav Blanc so feel free to come armed.

> Greer: Hollis will be a few mins late. Apparently other news is happening today. I guess some people care more about sports ball than poor Rowan's existential crisis.
>
> Hollis: I'll be there soon. But did anyone save the photo? I think it needs to be framed. And scrapbooked into the "Rowan and Ellis Origin Story: The Beginning" album.
>
> Me: 😌
>
> Greer: Oh good! You're here. We'll see you online in ten. Go get a drink. Being drunk with us will be the best way to spend your evening.

My laptop booted slowly, like even it knew the madness that was about to ensue and it was bracing for impact. When the screen finally blinked to life and I was able to connect to the video conference three familiar faces in variations from smug, curious, and concerned, greeted me.

"Rowan Anastasia Sloane." Greer began, her hair already thrown up into a lazy knot. "What exactly is happening between you and the Ice Man?"

"Has he cometh?" Lyris winked at me over a sip from a wine glass as large as her face.

"Boo." Hollis pressed both of her thumbs downward. "Low hanging fruit Lyris. Like grabbed as it was rotting on the ground."

"I thought that was quite clever, actually." She laughed, giving Hollis the middle finger.

"I'm going to seriously kill each of you. Slowly." I replied, reaching for the throw draped across the back of the couch.

"Well now that you have a billionaire boyfriend, our deaths wouldn't even be avenged. You probably wouldn't even see jail time." Greer giggled as well, reaching for her own glass.

"Seriously though." Hollis asked. "Are you sleeping with him?"

"Hollis! He's a *client*."

"If that's how you treat all of your clients, I have every confidence your business is going to be booming." Lyris cut in, barely able to spit the words out while she cackled at her own joke.

"At this point you're picking the fruit out of the garbage Lyris." Hollis winked. "Let's aim higher."

"In all seriousness." Lyris, somehow able to recompose herself began. "You want to though. I recognize that look Rowan. The one you're wearing now, and the one from that picture. That man hangs the stars for you."

"It wasn't supposed to be like that." I whined, carrying my computer with me to the kitchen. I was starving and at that place where I didn't want to wait to cook anything. Unfortunately, working from home the whole day, I somehow managed to consume all of my snacks. "He kissed me like he believed he *did* hang the stars for me Lyris."

"Oh." Hollis said softly.

"Shit." Echoed Greer, stopping mid-sip.

Silence fell over the entire call. No one said a word. As if we were all prostrating at the altar of what might have been or should be—who knows. But the silence was reverent. All in the name of Ellis Hawthorne, the man with the lazy, hard-earned smile and an earnest desperation to be seen.

"This wasn't supposed to happen." I continued, just to fill the silence. That felt too heavy. Uncomfortable. It held a mirror to my face and forced me to examine things I'd been trying to avoid all day. "I'm being paid guys. A truly irresponsible amount of money to help him find someone *else*. That's the secret. Not succession planning but helping Ellis find a wife. Per his father's orders. And instead, I allowed him to kiss me like I mattered."

Greer leaned forward, as if doing so she could actually gain a closer look at me.

"Roe, did you kiss him because you panicked in the moment. Or did you kiss him because you hoped his kiss meant something more?"

My phone chimed with an incoming text.

> Ellis: Are you home?

> Me: Yes...Why?

> Ellis: Because I'm standing outside your door.

I had to reread the text four times. It refused to compute. I slowly stood, crossed to the bay window and peeked out. Sure enough, there he was, in a charcoal overcoat, holding a paper bag with a look I couldn't read from that far up.

"Girls, I have to go," I said turning back to the Zoom.

The each of the four began to protest in chorus.

"What? No!" Came from Lyris. "What just happened? We deserve to know."

"Pitch Fest rules!" Greer cried. "Disclosure first. Then you can go."

"OH MY GOD!" from Hollis. "He's there isn't he?"

"ADD HIM TO THE ZOOM!" Cried Lyris. "We can all figure this out together."

As I made to shut my laptop closed, I heard Greer call "I swear to god if you hang up this—"

I shut down my computer and padded barefoot to my door. There stood Ellis, in my doorway, with the sweetest smile and a bag full of something hot that smelled amazing.

"I figured you probably hadn't eaten all day." He held up the bag like a white flag. "But if I came and suggested we go out or order in, you'd pretend otherwise. So, I brought it to you."

Close up, I recognized the bag. The Fat Shallot. Comfort food to the nth degree, gooey cheese, delicious bread, nothing could warm you and fill you concurrently like their grown up versions of grilled cheese and some of the best fries in the city.

I stepped aside and let him into my house. The moment he brushed past, I once again caught his scent and was transported back to that muscle melting, brain scrambling, earth tilting kiss. I was so fucked.

"I reserve the right to question your motives once we've digested our comfort carbs."

"I figured The Fat Shallot was a safe bet. It seemed like something to placate you enough that you didn't yell at me."

"Jury's still out, Hawthorne."

It was so weird having Ellis in my house. Pause. Ellis was in my freaking house. The one that looked like nuclear fallout had occurred. The one where I currently stood, facing him, in yoga pants and a *very old* and *wildly inappropriate* Hawkeyes shirt.

I was torn as to which would be more mortifying for

him to notice, the mess of a house that spread out behind me or my sweatshirt. Guess which one won?

"Anchors down, legs up?" Ellis raised a brow, lips twitching. "DGAF but... DTF?"

Oh god. He was reading the sweatshirt.

"It was for a river float trip," I blurted. "Delta Gamma As Fuck. Down to *Float*. Not..." I waved my hand.

"Not what it sounds like." I groaned, relieving him of the bag.

"I'm going to the kitchen. You can hang up your coat or run. Dealer's choice." I tried to keep my voice casual despite my heart not being anywhere in the universe of normality.

News flash. He didn't run. Alert the press. Of course he hadn't. Ellis does everything with exacting authority, calculated and quiet.

I heard the soft scrape of the coat hanger sliding across the entry way closet rod then his focused steps, slow and unhurried, as he made his way into the kitchen. It felt normal. Like he'd done it a million times, though he'd never come to my home. Like, ever.

I unpacked the bag, setting up each of our meals on a plate, arranging the sandwich, fries, and special *Fat Shallot* sauce on each. My hands shook just enough to give me away if he looked close enough. I felt him watching me. Long before I felt brave enough to glance over to where he stood, I felt his presence on me. Like the summer sun baking me in wooziness by the side of a pool.

I crossed to the table, set a plate at two chairs across from one another. He took the one closest to where he stood. He didn't speak until I returned with two cans of pop, and glasses filled with ice.

"Do you always take care of people like this?" he asked, pushing up the sleeves of his cashmere sweater to the elbows before unbuttoning the custom shirt beneath it and folding it up until it rested on the sweater.

"Like what?" I asked, passing him a few napkins from the holder in the middle of the table.

"As if they're the most important person in the room. All of the details, down to the placement of the special sauce and the napkins, everything is arranged to loudly proclaim their welcome, even if the panicked look in your eyes might make someone second guess that emotion."

I took a breath, feeling his words settle around me like a blanket. This was too surreal. What was my life right now? Between the kiss, the PR crisis, and Ellis fucking Hawthorne sitting in my house, in my tiny kitchen with my Pottery Barn kitchen table and the living room mess he'd yet to see. This wasn't my reality.

"You're here," I said more to myself than out loud. "In my house. My house on the total opposite side of the city. I'm sitting here, looking like this." I waved my hand down my raunchy sweatshirt that would be burned in a bonfire the moment the final piles of snow melted in my backyard. "And you look like that, and my brain is just having a really hard time melding all of this together. Between last night, and the kiss, and the press, and your brothers—I just. Is this real life? Did someone surreptitiously slip me some Ayahuasca. Is this one deep, convincing trip?"

Ellis let out a soft laugh and leaned back in his chair. It wasn't the smug or self-satisfied laugh he sometimes had. It just sounded sincere. Almost as if he too felt the same off-kilter feeling as I did. I watched him as he took in what I said, rolling his glass along the table as he processed.

"Well, if it is Ayahuasca, I hope it doesn't end yet."

My stomach flipped. The food I'd just been ravaging because it was so good suddenly paled in palatability against the warm admission from Ellis. He took a sip from his glass, yanking my focus to the way his throat worked to swallow it down.

"I do think we need to talk." He wiped his mouth of whatever condensation he imagined there was. "You know messaging. For the public...and for us."

That tiny pause before *and for us* hit like a spark in a drought roughened forest.

"Absolutely." I agreed, setting down my French fry and wiping the grease from my hands. Business topics. Those were safe. I could find level ground on that territory. "Whit's right. The longer we stay vague the more we invite speculation. I think the best play is a controlled roll out. A few quiet sightings. Me coming into WMG. Us at the country club. Maybe a trip to Los Angeles to meet with the TV Execs. Alongside that, a carefully worded joint quote that confirms nothing and denies nothing."

"Okay, play it out further." Ellis gazed at me, his head tilted in consideration while we continued to discuss. "What is this carefully worded quote? What does it say?"

I grabbed my drink, giving myself a few seconds to collect my thoughts. "We say what I suggested before. It makes the most sense and has the largest change of believability. Given our past working relationship, you reached out to Pivot to assist HMG with succession planning. Your father has indicated he'd like to retire soon, and the four of you need to align the brands to figure out the best path forward for the next generation. Our relationship is rooted in long-standing trust and shared professional values. Period."

He gathered my plate and placed it on top of his. "You make it sound so clinical."

"It's PR Ellis, not poetry." I stood alongside him, grabbing the glasses and the trash to finish cleanup.

"You're good at both," he said, so quiet I almost missed it. "You always have been."

The compliment surprised me as much as it tickled me. He looked at me with soft, unguarded eyes that would have made me believe the earth wouldn't implode as we felt the violent heat of the asteroid zooming past.

"Maybe this whole thing is temporary," he said, brushing past me to put the dishes in the sink. "But when I'm with you like this? It doesn't feel that way."

The tension that had roped around us the night before, returned. I couldn't blame the booze this time. It was alive, I could feel it raise the hair on my arms, and make my lips tingle.

"We're business partners." My argument felt weak even on my lips. "We shouldn't confuse this with something it's not."

He leaned in, pressing me against the sink. "What if it *is* something though?" he asked, holding my gaze like a hostage. "What if, this something is more than we think, and we're only pretending otherwise so we don't have to admit that somewhere in the trajectory of our history we crossed a line."

Alarm bells rung with the incessancy of a five-alarm fire in the heart of the loop. Backup firetrucks were screaming down every side street, desperate to warn us of the impending implosion. I couldn't look away. Not when his chocolate brown eyes melted into something even softer. The lines that usually creased his forehead and his mouth in stress had smoothed into something resembling peace.

"This is supposed to be fake." I swallowed hard, barely able to keep an even tone to my voice.

"It was supposed to be." His reply was quick. Reactionary. As if the admission fell from his lips too quickly. "But nothing about last night felt fake. And nothing tonight, with you so close to me in your adorably dirty sweatshirt, and your haphazard bun, and your emotional freak out feel fake."

I couldn't breathe. I needed oxygen. A mask that one of those firefighters would have strapped to their backs would do.

"We don't need to define anything. There doesn't need to be thesis level research on the implications of leaning into a feeling we're both experiencing. But maybe, in this moment, let's be real in the moments where it feels like it is."

This time, I was the one who kissed him. I fell first. I blinked and my hands were in his hair, feeling the silken curls slip through my fingers. I luxuriated in the heady moans against my mouth, and the warm hands desperately digging beneath my sweatshirt and running along my back, hot skin to hot skin.

I felt the length of him press between my legs. It was a subtle movement. It didn't appear intentional. But my body took whatever form it could get its intent and rolled up to my toes and opened my hips enough for him to press between them.

"I'm serious Ellis. If we do this..." My voice trailed off, I pulled my lip between my teeth to stop me from saying anything too needy something weird that would burst the bubble we existed in.

I pulled back for half a breath, my fingers skimming along his cheek. His expression was so open, so vulnerable, I almost couldn't look at him.

He didn't flinch. Didn't argue. Just kissed the space

beneath my jaw like it was sacred. Made a map of my skin as if storing it away for later. Somewhere in the folds of my heart, I admitted the thing I wasn't ready to say out loud: *Maybe I always knew it would be him.*

    I didn't stop him as he kissed his way along my skin. I didn't overthink the way his hands framed me like a prayer. I didn't reach for logic or contracts or conditions. I followed his lead, willing to go wherever he led. I'd subject myself to the fall if it meant feeling real, without conditions.

13

ALL THE WAYS I LET YOU IN

ELLIS

I KNEW WHAT SHE MEANT. Doing this changed everything. There's no rewind, no reset. No coming back from it once we give in to the fall. I saw all the road signs, every blinking warning screaming caution. And still, I pressed the gas.

"I know." I ran my thumb gently beneath the hem of her t-shirt where her skin was softest. "Maybe our lives could use a little disruption."

She locked eyes with mine. I hope mine reflected the same earnest belief that hers did. She searched mine for something. The truth of us, maybe. Of what this meant. Of who we were in this moment together. Or maybe what it would mean that we broke the rules, together.

However, she didn't stop me. Not when I bent down and fused my mouth with hers. I kissed her long and slow, tasting every question on her lips, and answering them as best I could. She didn't stop me when I gathered her legs and affixed them against my hips, turning toward her darkened bedroom. And when I placed her on her bed, gathering her sweatshirt in my hands, not only did she not stop me, she lifted her arms to help me remove it.

She pulled back for half a breath. Her fingers skimmed along my cheek, her expression open and unreadable. "This was never my intention." Soft fingernails causing gooseflesh to rise where she tickled just beneath the collar of my shirt.

"The story I built—the one where this was about a job, a contract. You weren't supposed to be the part that mattered."

I nuzzled her jaw, just at the soft expanse where her hairline met her jaw.

"I know."

I placed a kiss there, more than one, actually. Her skin, the soft, clean smell of it combined with the seductive floral of her hair, I couldn't pull away.

"Maybe all along," I admitted. "Somewhere deep down, I knew it would be you."

And then, I kissed her neck, her lips, her eyelids, her breasts. Every inch of skin I could mark with my mouth I did. I wanted to rewrite the words of our contract, except strike business from relationship, and the replace the paper it was written on with her pale pinkened skin. No need for pens when my lips pressed against it, hearing her soft sighs, feeling her nimble fingers threading through my hair was everything I needed.

I forced myself to go slow. To linger, anticipate, and enjoy every moment I had in this space with Rowan. Who knew if we'd ever be in this situation again. And if I was going to burn in the flames of her passion, I'd throw gasoline on it and revel in the suffering.

"Ellis..." the s came out serpentine, her voice tinged with need.

My body responded to her plea, my back arching and

my hips pressing between her legging covered legs without warning or conscious intent.

"I know." I assured her, tracing my lips down the tendon of her neck, "I've got you."

It was a promise, and a reminder to myself once again to take my time. Her mouth parted in a soft sigh that I collected in my own mouth. She tasted like surrender. Everywhere my lips imprinted, she'd wiggle, rock, or call my name on a plea. I'd barely gotten the most innocent taste, and Rowan was already a pliant ball of bliss.

That Rowan had opened herself to me, trusting what existed between the two of us was real, was a gift I wouldn't take for granted. I gathered her leggings in my hand, rolling them down over her ass, past her thighs and off her flexing toes.

She wore plain cotton underwear. No expensive lingerie. Just practical, cotton, blue striped panties that rode high on her hips and did little to hide how badly she wanted me. Those practical undergarments undid me in a way the sexiest piece of La Perla never had. She wasn't performing. There was no attempt to seduce with a piece of satin. This was authentic Rowan, real with no performative polish.

I placed my nose between her thighs, inhaling her sweet scent. The moment I touched the sensitive inner skin, her fingers were back in my hair. Her caress sent a lightning bolt of pleasure so intense, I could only groan and arch into her fingernails like a greedy kitten.

My lips traced a path along her cotton gusset, exploring that wet strip of cotton with the tip of my tongue, casually swiping at the sensitive nub that sat just beneath. I wanted to worship her. To lay, prostrate at the altar of her need and overwhelm her with pleasure. I craved her fall and fought the battle within me to force a quick orgasm from her and take my time with the second, or string her out until she was begging and the thought of any other man that had been between her thighs before me was banished forever to the black hole of her forgotten memories.

"You're shaking." I murmured against her warm skin. "Do you want me to stop?"

I pushed back, away from her sweet mound, fighting against my desperate need to fuck and claim. I held her generous hips between my hands, the top of her panties gathered beneath my hands. She leaned up on her elbows. I felt her gaze roll over me like a break of sun on a cloudy day.

"So are you," she finally said.

She wasn't wrong. My hands didn't feel steady. Nothing about me felt steady. Not with the weight of what we were about to do pressing on my shoulders, and the scent of how badly she wanted it making me dizzy with need. I stole another kiss from her. Luxuriating in the silken feel of her lips. And committing to memory every second of how blissfully she surrendered to sensation.

"You can stop me," I said, dragging my mouth to her ear. I needed her to know. Even if my cock throbbed against my pants and howled at the thought of not being let out to luxuriate in her silken heat. I was already so far gone. "Tell me to stop, and I will."

She shook her head, biting her lip concurrently. "Don't stop. I want more."

Those had to be the best words I'd heard up to that point in my life. I ripped her panties from her hips, Rowan's surprised squeal bouncing off the walls. It only made me even more desperate to plunder between her legs.

My tongue parted her, slow and sweet. It drew a sound from her so raw it nearly sounded animalistic. I anchored her hips down as she tried to arch them upward pressed into my face, my own restraint beginning to fray.

"Fuck, Ellis." Her fingernails scratched at my scalp. Her ass wiggled against the sheets, legs bent at the knee, desperately trying to press her ass off the bed and create more friction. My tongue lashed at her clit. I drowned in the pool of desire that flowed like the first spouts of Mount Vesuvius.

It was rare that Rowan swore. So rare in fact that hearing her scream it, with that sex shattered voice and for only my ears to hear was a memory that would forever be burned in my mind. The smell of her desire, how wet I'd made her, the feel of her firm ass in my hands as I brought her closer to my mouth to drink from her.

Rowan Sloane was imprinting on my soul in a way I'd never expected. I didn't want just one orgasm from her. I wanted a million of them. I wanted to gift her so many that her reaction to me would be Pavlovian every time I walked into a room. That pussy of hers would be so attuned to the pleasure I gave it; it would weep any time it sensed me in proximity.

"Give it to me Rowan." I thrust my fingers inside, twisting them until her g-spot presented itself for my manipulation. "You have exactly five seconds, and that come is mine."

"Ellis, dear god, I'm about to." She never got to finish the sentence. Between my lips sucking the life from her clit and my fingers massaging and manipulating her g-spot Rowan soared into the solar system with my name on her lips.

I'd never removed a single item of clothes. My sweater, shirt, pants, hell even my shoes were all still on. While Rowan floated back down to earth, I made short work of stripping down, hoping like hell one of us had protection.

"Sweetheart?" I asked, kissing her back to consciousness. "Do you have any condoms?"

She nodded pointing to her nightstand. Her drawer offered a couple different options, size and preference dependent. I tried to ignore the meaning behind having those. That other men who had been there. Had seen her come apart, had tasted between her legs and felt the snug heat of the place I was about to enter.

I wasn't naïve. I'd bedded my fair share of women too. But this with Rowan felt different. Special. The last thing I wanted was the specter of past boyfriends to infiltrate our moment.

I tore the foil open with shaking hands. Not from nerves, but from the staggering weight of how much I wanted her. I needed this to mean something more than just friction and release. I rolled the condom on, glancing at her sprawled across the pillows.

She lay back; one arm curved over her head. That riotous waterfall of autumn leaf colored hair sprawled behind her like the crown of Demeter. Across her lips was a lazy smile, her fingers drawing lazy circles across her stomach. Her chest still rose and fell in the uneven rhythm of aftershock. She looked like she'd been made for this moment—for me.

"Are you sure?" I asked, quieter than before.

Rather than speak an answer, she gave me a slow, deliberate nod, spreading her soft, milk white thighs in welcome. I moved between them, bracing myself on my elbows and caging body beneath mine. I kissed her again, slower this time. I savored the tremble of her mouth against mine.

We weren't going to rush. It became a mantra in my head. The only way it seemed I'd keep from blowing too soon.

"Tell me how good it feels." I asked her, pressing the tip just past her fluttering entrance. "I want to know you're as twisted inside out as I am."

Her hips moved in circular patterns, trying to control the pace and speed that my cock impaled her. I wouldn't let her push me in to the hilt. I craved the stretch. The inch-by-inch intrusion as I felt each flutter while I pressed home.

"Ellis." She pulled me down against her mouth, plundering inside, sucking my tongue out and tucking it into hers. Her fingers traced down my ribs before gathering my ass in her palms and trying to push me harder against her. "I can't take it anymore. Please. I need you."

The first inch stole my air. She was hot, impossibly tight, and slick with need.

"Jesus," I breathed, my forehead pressed to hers, our noses brushing. "You feel like heaven."

Her nails dug into my ass, anchoring me, tethering me to the moment.

I eased forward, inch by glacial inch, until I was fully seated inside her. The moment I felt the full welcome of her heated core I know. Rowan Sloane had absolutely ruined me for anyone else. We stilled, breathing each other in like oxygen was only possible in close proximity.

She wrapped her legs around me and I almost lost it right there.

"Move," she whispered, hips tilting up in invitation. "Please move."

That word again—*please*—a weapon when she wielded it like that.

I set a rhythm, deliberate and deep, grinding our bodies

together in a cadence that had nothing to do with performance. I wanted her to remember every thrust. Not for what it did to her body—but what it did to her soul.

She felt so good it bordered on unbearable. My control frayed at the edges, but I held on, just barely. I gripped her hip with one hand, the other cradling her cheek like she was too precious to be left untouched.

"You let me in," I rasped, pressing kisses to the curve of her jaw. "All the way. Do you feel that?"

She nodded. I thought I saw tears shining in her eyes, but in the darkness, it was hard to tell.

"Are you okay?" I asked. "Did I hurt you? Should I stop?"

"God no. Don't stop now." Her heels kicked at my back like I was the odds on favorite to win the Derby and I'd lost some gas along the back half. "It's so good. Too good almost."

I wasn't rough. We weren't rushing. I worshipped her with reverence. I laid claim. Pushed my flag in and declared Rowan Sloane's body would forever be mine. Every kiss, whisper, smile, and come. They all belonged to me.

She started to tighten around me, her breath coming faster, head tipping back.

"Ellis." She moaned in warning.

"I've got you," I assured her, anchoring my forehead to hers, pistoning into her as we chased the fall together.

When she shattered for the second time, I followed close behind, exploding with an orgasm pulled from the deepest part of me like a promise I hadn't known I was keeping.

14

WHAT THE SILENCE REVEALS

Rowan

My bedroom was too warm. That was the first thing that stirred me awake. I rarely set my heat too high; I actually loved sleeping in a cold bedroom. Somewhere in another room I heard my phone pinging, repeatedly. Then, in a convergence of stimuli I realized the heat I felt was centralized along my back, which nestled against the downy chest hair of Ellis Hawthorne. His breath was slow and even, stirring the hair at the back of my neck. One of his fingers twitched, brushing the underside of my breast with an unconscious possessiveness that nearly broke me open. My body felt frozen in place. Not because I was afraid of him. I didn't trust what would happen when my movement woke him up.

I'd slept with my boss.

My. Boss.

Well, former boss. Client was the more appropriate word. The client who was paying me *new offices in the loop* level money to help him find a fiancé. And I'd slept with him.

Hadn't we just agreed the night before that we were going to stick with the paid adviser story? Did I imagine the entire dinner where we'd gone over the strategy? So how did we get from that, to here.

You weren't supposed to be the part that mattered.

Memories from the night before tormented me. A convergence of feelings: satisfaction obviously. But I hadn't expected to feel so safe and cherished.

Here we were, limbs tangled, my heart trying to scream over the cacophony of reason. The story I'd written was slowly being rewritten. I couldn't catch my bearings as feelings and waged war with one another.

"Maybe all along... I knew it would be you."

He'd said that with his lips on my skin. Did he know how deep his words would burrow? How they would insinuate into the marrow of my existence. He had to know. But if he knew, there was an equally great chance that he meant it.

The taste of his kisses still lingered in my mouth. Achingly tender but confident and possessive. Just the remembrance of them made me want things logically I should ignore. Those weren't the kind of kisses you gave someone you planned to forget, though.

"I can hear your mind whirring at a million miles an hour. It's not even six thirty in the morning."

The mattress dipped behind me as Ellis turned enough to wrap his arm tighter around my waist and run his nose along the slope of my neck. My traitorous body didn't care that I was *being paid to be a professional*. No. It threw down it's metaphoric AMEX to purchase an unlimited, annual pass to the Ellis Hawthorne fun machine.

Morning light always carried the truth of what was

done in the cover of darkness. But last night wasn't strategy. It wasn't optics or messaging or what was best for the company. It felt honest. Personal even, and so incredibly real.

My throat tightened. I tried to find anything to bide my time, even for a few minutes until I could centralize my thoughts and figure out a game plan. There was a feeling in my chest—well actually lots of feelings in my chest: fear, anxiety, panic, guilt. The one I hadn't been expecting though, was hope. And it bloomed like it had been exposed to the first warm rays of spring.

"I've got a conference call in an hour." I lied.

I hated myself for doing it. The discomfort of it slid past my tongue and lodged in my chest. I couldn't be next to him, wrapped in his warmth when everything in my body scream *liar!*

"Coffee?" I asked, pushing out of bed before he could call me on my strange behavior.

He followed me a few minutes later, rumpled, shirtless, just in his thigh hugging boxer briefs. Somehow, despite the whirlwind of emotions swirling inside me, he seemed utterly composed. Ever the astute businessman, even nearly naked.

"No fancy elusive coffee brands here." I tried a joke to lighten the heaviness I felt, "Just some grocery store Dunkin."

"I'll have to get Dash to share his supplier with you." Ellis rumbled close to my ear, leaning in to brush a kiss against the top of my head.

"Good morning." I felt him smile against the crown of my head, "I believe we skipped that part of the morning wake-up ritual."

The two of us stood silent sentry on either side of the

coffee machine, waiting, cups in hand for it to deliver its thinking juice.

"We should probably talk about last night." I tried to sound casual as I filled his cup.

"I'm always open to dialoguing on how to make it better for next time." He smirked before taking a tentative sip.

"That's right." I played along, "Blowjobs aren't just for special occasions."

"There's always next time." He laughed, grabbing the creamer from my fridge and pouring it into the cup I held but had yet to sip from.

Next time. There it was. The cavernous segue opportunity. Except I was a chicken shit. I couldn't sit there drinking coffee in robes and underwear, talking about how sticking to the optics plan.

"We're meeting today at two, right?" I asked.

The tilt of his head caused his eyes to catch the small beam of light from my kitchen window, making his eyes look witchlike and otherworldly. As if the amber gleam signaled some kind of magic spell that allowed him to look past my words and see the hesitation buried beneath.

"I believe it was changed to nine," he said, taking a deeper cup of coffee as he glanced at my stove clock. "Whit wants a follow up to yesterday's release out this morning."

"Oh no!" I set my mug in the sink. "What happened to my conference call then?"

And the Oscar went to me, in the category of believable bullshit to push forward with a poorly executed lie. I shuffled to my mess of a living room in search of my phone. It's never-ending beeping and vibrating cluing me in to its location beneath the throw I'd be using during the girl's zoom last night.

> Greer: We expect a full report of the dick down tomorrow.
>
> Hollis: You should have brought him on the Zoom
>
> Greer: Let her have a little fun. It's been ages since anyone visited her lady garden.
>
> Lyris: JFC Lady Garden? Okay Bridgerton.

THE TEXTS from them went on for ages. With multiple inquiries into the remainder of my evening and whether I'd actually taken the "Big D" from Ellis. With follow up debates on whether Ellis actually in fact possessed a Big D.

I was less concerned about them discussing, based on photos on the internet, the size of my boyfriend's cock than I was about Paisley trying to contact me about upcoming meetings.

Wait. Full fucking stop.

Ellis Hawthorne was *not* my boyfriend. Nor would he ever be. Sleeping together did not equate to a relationship. Period. I was his booty call. End of story.

> Paisley: Are you working from home again today?
>
> Paisley: Not sure if you saw the meeting invite, but you're wanted at HMG first thing.
>
> Me: Ellis called me already, twice, to make sure I'd seen the last-minute add.

> Paisley: Are you planning to work from their offices, come back to Pivot, or work from home today? Just LMK and I'll make arrangements to your schedule once I get in.

Out of the corner of my eye I saw Ellis, leaning casually against the archway to my living room. He continued to sip from the coffee cup, a strange, inquisitive look furrowing his eyebrows just slightly, and making soft frown lines appear around his mouth.

"Paisley." I held my phone up in explanation. "Trying to rearrange my calendar."

The taffy like silence pulled and warped as we both left too many things unsaid. He hadn't put any more clothes on. Still stood sentry in just a pair of navy blue briefs, my *Oxford Comma* mug in his hand.

"I need to get ready. I rescheduled my morning call to this afternoon, but if we're going to make it to HMG in a respectable amount of time we'll need to leave soon."

He nodded, turned to the kitchen where I heard him set the mug in the sink.

"There are clean towels and everything you need in the guest bathroom." I pointed in the direction opposite my bedroom. "I'll try to get ready quickly. Give me maybe thirty minutes?"

I didn't wait for a reply, just turned and marched into my bathroom. Did he also feel awkward? Or was it just me? I'd become so obsessed with the never-ending spin in my own brain I hadn't heard the bathroom door open or the gentle snick of the shower door unlatching.

Through the shampoo threatening to burn out my eyes, I saw him. Standing just out of the stream, naked, a saucy smile on his lips.

"I figured this would save time."

"Ellis." I couldn't tell if his name coming from my mouth was said in relief or warning.

He turned me around so my hair was directly underneath the stream. He gently pressed my head back so the shower head rinsed the shampoo from the crown of my head down, making fast but sensual work of it.

"You have the most gorgeous hair," he said, grabbing my conditioner and gently directing me back to face the stream while he gathered my hair in his hands. After applying the conditioner, he wrapped my hair in a bun on top of my head "to absorb" he'd murmured while taking my sponge and sudsing it up with my soap.

Each sensual pass against my skin was the aphrodisiac I'd been resisting all morning. His wet thighs pressed against my ass, his roving hands and their focused attention to my breasts and nipples, and his mouth, running lazy patterns along the slope of my neck.

I heard the telltale crinkle more than I saw it. Though it surprised me that he somehow managed to smuggle a condom into my shower without me seeing it.

"Just a few more minutes in heaven before the bubble bursts," he whispered in my ear before taking it between his teeth.

He pressed against my shoulder until I leaned, bracing against the glass.

"We need to talk. To figure things out," I said, trying to slow the freight train of sensation already barreling toward me.

His fingers gently slipped between my legs, caressing my aching clit. I floated in the bliss he gifted me for long moments before he finally pushed in, setting a focused pace.

"Ellis," I groaned, lost to the sea, the haze of my

impending orgasm threatening to steal away my sense with the tide. "We need to figure things out."

He placed his hand on my shoulder, pushing me onto his thrusting cock with erratic, nonsensical motions.

"You don't have to know where this is going, Rowan. Not everything needs a slide deck and twenty hours of qualitative research to tell you how to feel."

"Ellis..." I don't know what I planned to say, but it didn't matter. Ellis's large hand came down across my mouth, stymying my words before they could exit. I gasped against his palm, as he shattered what was left of my control. I gripped the glass, letting him take the reins. Just this once. He swung his hips up, landing a bullseye shot to my g-spot that had me moaning against his hand and calling to the stars that appeared behind my eyes.

"No lies." He grunted, "Lie in the boardroom. Lie to my brothers, or the public. But not in here. Not with me."

In less time it took to nod, he had us both sling-shotting over the edge with no map telling where we'd fall. The moment had been intense, but not lacking in emotion, and I didn't know how to process it.

I'd willingly done it again. This was not good. Our professional lines blurred more intensely by the minute.

We both gasped for air, our faces pressed against the subway tile wall, waiting for the running water to bring both of us back to reality. Steam clung to the glass, dotted our skin, and amplified the silence of words we refused to speak.

Ellis surfaced first. I heard him remove his condom before grabbing my soap and rinsing himself off. I stayed frozen for a moment, forehead against the tile, the sound of the water pounding above us as loud as the question in my chest: *What now?*

Ellis kissed the spot just beneath my ear. Not rushed. Not triumphant. Just gentle.

"I'll be in the car," he murmured, before stepping out and grabbing a towel without fanfare. "Nine o'clock meeting. You've got twenty minutes."

He left me there, blinking through the spray, stunned that somehow, he'd given me everything I needed, and still I had questions I was afraid to know the answers to.

15

THE PUBLIC FACE

ELLIS

My body buzzed with latent satisfaction. Sleeping with Rowan, both literally and figuratively, had settled something in me. Waking up with her pressed into me, that seductive apple ass of hers pressed into my groin—it was so incredibly real. Something millions of people across the world did every day. Top that with a shared pot of coffee and then that shower. The shower had been unexpected. But there was a weird energy I couldn't put my finger on.

Sure, we'd said we were going to be professional and stick with a narrative and then we said *fuck it* and did exactly that.

Except, with Rowan it wasn't fucking. The act wasn't just an exercise in mutual satisfaction. It had been different. *More.*

"Where are you going?" I asked her as she made a beeline for the SUV revealed as her garage door rolled up.

"We have to get to the office," she said, pointing at her car as if the most obvious notion in the world.

"Yes. And here is my car, to take us to the office."

Rowan looked at me as if I had three heads. She stood

sentry next to her car, her oversized tote bag slung over her shoulder, key in hand, confused look not leaving her face.

"I have meetings I need to handle." She persisted.

"And once the meeting at HMG is over, someone can take you to work, me, one of my brothers, Uri. Hell I'll give you Uri for the day. Wherever you need to go. But right now, T Minus twenty-two minutes and we're seventeen from the office on a good day."

I didn't mention that once we got to said office, I'd need to sneak into mine unnoticed to change out of the clothes I presently wore. There was an emergency suit in my closet. I kept it there in case I had a red-eye, or I spilled something on my suit. In all the years at HMG I'd never needed to use it. But I was grateful for being too paranoid to not be prepared for this exact moment. If anyone would notice a walk of shame outfit, it was Keats. That asshole didn't need any more reasons to start yarning on about our "relationship."

Finally, Rowan approached my car with the motivation of a pack mule traversing the Grand Canyon.

"What will people say when they see us pulling in together?" she asked. "Ironic that we're heading to an emergency meeting about optics where the center of the optics crisis is us, and yet we're about to roll up in your car, with you wearing yesterday's clothes."

During her monologue, she'd walked around the passenger side of the car, gotten in, arranged her water jug, travel mug of coffee, and cell phones in my console. Her tote was arranged neatly on the floor next to her, and she'd managed to strap in all in a span of mere seconds.

My car purred to life, my stereo rolling right into the next song on my playlist as soon as the car turned on.

"I wouldn't have taken you for an Avett Brothers fan."

Rowan watched me back down her short driveway and turn toward the office, a soft smile gracing her lips. "I would have thought you were an NPR man through and through."

I hated talk radio. It drove me to distraction. I heard people giving opinions all day long. The last thing I needed while I drove was more of the same.

"*If It's the Beaches.*" She identified the name of the song right away. "Beautiful song. Though The Gleam wasn't my favorite of their albums."

Shocked. How did I never know that she, too, was a fan? I'd know her for years. Had I never heard any music playing at her desk as I walked past.

"Dash and I were in Charlotte years ago." I told her, suddenly needing to show her just how long Dash and my fandom stretched. "We had a few friends with us, checking out the bar scene in NoDA and stumbled into a bar called The Evening Muse. Avett was playing, and they hooked me on the spot. I bought a copy of their self-titled album *The Avett Brothers* and listened to it nonstop during our week in Charlotte. Followed their trajectory as they rose to fame."

"I can see that," she said, running her hand along the matte dashboard, seemingly deep in thought. "They are quiet, reflective, deeply layered. A lot like you."

I glanced at her as the harmony swelled. "Didn't realize you were a fan."

She shrugged, still watching the road. "Didn't realize you were either."

We didn't speak for a few blocks. But the song played on, and so did whatever was quietly unfolding between us.

"What kind of car is this?" Her question broke the quiet reflection we'd existed in.

"This is a Polestar 1. Swedish. Fast. There was a very

limited production. Quietly powerful with nothing to prove."

I watched the merge lane as every crazy kamikaze driver tried to take us out while they tried to exit and we tried to enter the expressway. As if on cue I needed to accelerate fast to get us flowing with traffic in order to safely merge. The car shot to life with a quiet purr and seat melting torque.

"Wait. Why does Polestar sound so familiar?" she asked. Though she didn't give me an opportunity to reply. "Wait. This is that car that when it came out the price tag was insane and then a year later it's resale was like in the low thirties, right? It was a huge PR nightmare. I remember thinking '*man whomever does their crisis communication has got to be wishing for any other job right now*'"

I chanced a glance in her direction. Her hair was still a little damp from the shower, curling as it dried. She smelled faintly of her rainstorm and eucalyptus body wash. It reminded me of her shower. Of all the addictive ways she'd handed me her trust. She was both the best distraction and the one I couldn't afford, concurrently.

"They only got flak from people who bought the for the wrong reasons."

She raised an eyebrow. "Which would be?"

"Status. Flash. Investment." I let the words sit between us like a judgment. "It's not a car for people who want to be seen. It's for people who want to *know*. The ones who recognize worth without needing it to shout."

She went quiet at that. But I could feel her thinking. With Rowan, silence didn't mean disinterest, it was the quiet before the interrogation storm. I liked that about her more than I should.

"I didn't buy this car to make a statement." I continued.

"I bought it because it does exactly what it promised, without compromise. Fools measure worth by resale value. They toss things away when the glitter doesn't shimmer brilliantly enough for them. Me? I know that glitter is just a cheap distraction and it's what's inside, under the hood, and the reliability by which it performs that matters most."

She didn't answer. Just looked out the window and tucked a loose strand of damp hair behind her ear. But something about the set of her shoulders made me think the message had landed exactly where I hadn't meant to aim it.

16

THE FACE YOU SHOW THE WORLD

Rowan

By the time we pulled into the executive garage beneath HMG, my pulse had smoothed into something manageable. Not calm. Never that. But composed enough to step back into the game.

Ellis exited first, every movement already calibrated for control. He circled the car and opened my door with intent. Like every move this morning was a statement in subtle punctuation.

"Private elevator," he said. "Obviously."

Obviously. The alternative was the main lobby and a potential parade of witnesses. And Ellis Hawthorne didn't believe in coincidence. Not when it came to image and risk.

The elevator opened directly into the top floor. We stepped inside. I stood to his left but didn't touch him, didn't even glance his way. My hair was still slightly damp, my lipstick reapplied twice. I told myself I looked like I'd worked out early. Like I'd showered and dressed and arrived with intention.

"Go on ahead to the boardroom," Ellis said, the moment

the doors opened. "It's probably better if we don't walk in together."

I nodded once. No argument. I understood this game, we'd built the rules together. But that didn't stop the sting from registering. He turned toward his office, already pulling his sweater over his head. There was a backup suit in his closet. Probably the same one I'd seen when I actually was his assistant. He kept it on hand for emergencies. Like today. The man was always ten moves ahead.

I headed to the boardroom.

Dash was already inside, lounging like the meeting had interrupted a nap. Whit looked crisp, caffeinated, and already three bullet points deep in his tablet.

I didn't sit at the head of the table. That was Ellis's seat. I took the spot two down from it, far enough not to send any kind of subliminal message, but close enough to catch any body language that said I needed to step in.

The door opened behind me, and Ellis strode in. Fully changed. Crisp suit. New tie. Even his cufflinks were different. But something was off. His energy was different.

"Nice of you to join us," Whit offered dryly. "Should we have rescheduled? You know I hate to inconvenience you."

Keats and Dash snickered, Ellis didn't even entertain the comment, just pulled out his chair and opened his laptop.

"You smell weird," Keats told him.

"Thanks for the vote of confidence," Ellis replied.

"I didn't say you smelled, like BO smelled. You smell like a chick. Like you took a shower with *someone else's* soap."

I refused to look at Ellis. I didn't know where to place my focus because it felt like every option would expose us.

The silence that followed felt charged. Not hostile. But heavy.

Ellis didn't blink. "The showers at the gym didn't specify their soap was called *smells like a chick* but I'll be sure to pass along the feedback."

I kept my gaze on the screen. Didn't flinch. Didn't breathe too deeply.

Keats hummed. A noncommittal sound that said *sure, for now*.

I cleared my throat. "Let's focus on the purpose of the meeting. The objective is containment. Strategic narrative development, consistent talking points, and a timeline for soft rollout. Ellis and I have aligned on a messaging framework that begins today."

Keats smirked again but didn't speak. Though the twinkle in his eye and the smirk playing across his lips told me that if I stayed a single second past the end of this meeting I'd be under the spotlight of interrogation.

The meeting was as expected. Toe the line. Stick with the talking points. Pivot and by extension me, were only associated with Hawthorne as advisers on how best to transition. I provided the best unbiased insight because I used to be an assistant to the C-Suite. Of course I would understand the dynamic because I witnessed it first-hand every day for five years.

Everyone agreed. Ellis and I would proceed as usual but planned to make appearances at various Ellis holdings to further reinforce that message. Clean, professional, no emotional complications.

Except, Ellis and I knew we were carefully crafting a Fabergé egg atop a barrel of TNT and praying it wouldn't explode.

Dash and Whit were the first to leave the room, tablets

tucked into their chests, phones in hand, off to handle whatever was next on their list of tasks. Keats lingered. The smiled at the two of us, taking pointed sips from his to go coffee cup.

"I know," he said.

Ellis stared at him with such blank impassivity that I nearly believed he had no idea what Keats was talking about.

"She comes in here with damp hair looking like she's going to expire at the first unexpected sound in the room, and you walk ten minutes later nearly to the second smelling not like your soap and wearing the suit that's been hanging in your office closet for the last god knows how many years."

He stood, slinging his messenger bag over his shoulder, collecting his laptop and his coffee, "Don't worry. I'll keep your secret. But just know I one hundred percent am here for this."

Keats didn't wait for either of us to say anything. He simply pulled open the glass door and sauntered out. But not before pointing at his brother from the other side of the glass wall and thrusting his hips in the most juvenile display of suggestive sex.

"We should talk." I finally said once Keats had cleared the visual space of the glass enclosure.

"About how Keats is far too young and immature to be forced to marry anyone? I agree. But we should probably have that conversation with more than just you and me." Ellis's smile though appearing naturally, lacked the full warmth of his real one.

"Tempting." I laughed, also not fully real but to cut the tension that built faster than a summer thunderstorm, "No. About us. Or, what kind of us there should be."

Ellis stepped back to the table, gathered his laptop, closed it with a soft finality. "Walk with me."

We walked down the hall side by side. A path so familiar given the years I worked by his side, that it felt achingly familiar. So much had changed. Since then, and even in a handful of days. I nodded at Morgan as we passed by her desk and walked into Ellis's office after he opened the door and gestured me in first.

Once inside, he didn't sit. He strode to his bank of windows and gazed out at the few brave sailboats dotting the lake. His hands in his suit pockets, his posture, stoic set of his lips, and seemingly unfocused gaze gave nothing away.

"I think we need to keep things clean." I began to fill the silence. "Same as I said in the boardroom. We need to stick with the narrative. It's believable if we all lean into it."

He didn't react, but I felt the air charge with his slight change in posture.

"Professional," I added, watching him turn toward me, arms crossed as he leaned against his window. "Businesslike. What we planned."

"You mean before..." he started but didn't finish the thought.

I nodded once. "Exactly. Before."

"And last night?" His toe kicked into the lush pile of his carpet, barely making a sound but the action felt to me like it topped the Richter scale.

I swallowed. "Last night was last night. It was real. So real." I couldn't help the shake in my voice when I admitted it. It was a stupid slip up but holding on to my mask of businesslike professionalism was a tenuous hold at best. "That doesn't mean it was wise."

"Right." I saw a muscle in his jaw twitch. He checked

his watch, adjusted the face, before placing it back in his pocket. "And you believe the wise thing to do now is to pretend it didn't happen?"

"No." I tried to push back gently.

I didn't want this to become an argument or anything unpleasant. The last thing I wanted to do was hurt him. But surely, he had to see how dangerous it was building a fantasy for public consumption with feelings that, at least for me, felt too real.

"We're protecting what *could* happen if we don't light it on fire trying to pretend we know what we're doing."

That registered, given how the way he looked at me shifted from stony to warm. Though his gaze had changed, his voice had not. It remained cold and impassive. "We act like nothing's changed?"

"We act like we're professionals with a job to do." I tried to smile, but the muscles in my mouth gave up halfway through the effort. "Isn't that what you hired me for?"

He didn't answer at first. Just stared at me like he was trying to figure out whether to call my bluff or fold.

Finally, he said, "Fine. Then let's get to work."

But his voice was quiet. Not clipped. Not cold. Resigned. And that felt worse than anything else.

17

THE QUIET BENEATH THE NOISE

ELLIS

Rowan's exit wasn't dramatic, but when the door clicked shut, it might as well have been a slam. Deliberate. Final. The kind of message only someone fluent in the language of silence could deliver.

I watched her retreat through the smoked glass panels lining either side of the door. She never looked back. Not even once. It was better this way. Cleaner.

We still had work to do. Optics. The word was beginning to grate on my last nerve. Everything was fucking optics. I didn't want performative anymore. After getting the taste of something real, I couldn't stomach the thought of anything less.

I was frozen, both physically and metaphorically. I had work that needed to be done. A tidal wave of emails I needed to reply to. Yet my feet stayed cemented in place, my attention pulled once again to those sailboats dancing gracefully across the lake like their freedom was something we should all aspire to. To live a life unbound, free to follow where the tide took us. I'd envied a lot of things in my life: power, clarity, even the damned ease with which Keats could charm a room. Today, however, I envied those damn sailboats.

I had anchors in abundance. Each one cementing me into a place I didn't want to be. Whether that was the expectations of my father, the weight of the Hawthorne legacy, the responsibility as CEO. But also, Rowan's weighted words threatened to expedite me to the bottom of the lake with no hope of air.

"Isn't that what you hired me for?"

To control the narrative. Spin my life for the masses. It was exactly what I'd hired her for. But everything *changed*. Somewhere along the line, she became the standard by which everything else got measured. Yet just now she hadn't given me even the slightest indication that she was anything different. Rowan Sloane was the epitome of professional, strategic, and controlled.

Except…

None of that applied to when she lay beneath me, naked. Those words had no welcome in the space where she trembled when I touched her. Or how she moaned my name like it was the most delightful treat against her tongue. Worse still, how she looked at me when she fell apart. As if I were more. Something other than legacy or leverage.

Until I wasn't.

I finally returned to my desk, shaking my computer screen awake. My work responsibilities should be the last thing that annoyed or bothered me. They'd been my constant. I should have been grateful for the distraction. However, all I could think about as I replied, gave approval for, or questioned decisions of those seeking my insight, was how this is what robbed me of the one thing that felt real.

She told me last night was real. That last night mattered. But apparently, it mattered in the way lightning matters to thunder. Bright, fleeting, tearing apart your reality and demanding silence in its wake. The two together better admired from a safe distance.

Maybe I could live with that. I'd lived with less. Except my time with Rowan had planted something far too dangerous. Hope.

For men like me hope was a dangerous currency. It created value where none was promised. Inflated the tiniest sentences or inflections with those insistent grains. Hope tricked you into believing the coal you held were diamonds and left you bankrupt when the varnish washed away.

I thought she was different. Convinced myself it was. God help me, I still hoped she was. But we all needed to ignore the truth. Because *optics* forced us all to invest in the lie.

I buried myself in my inbox. Work had always been the answer. My calendar was stacked with strategic reviews, investor notes, a proposed acquisition needing legal review. Morgan thankfully color coded everything. Red was only used for urgent meetings. Thankfully nothing was red. I didn't have the bandwidth to handle external emergencies when internally I felt like nuclear fallout.

I clicked on the calendar invite for the meeting we'd just left and opened the attached document. The strategy Rowan and I had built together. Every line was crisp, pristine even.

The annotations she'd begun to insert were brusque, organized, and soulless in the way only professionals trained in political messaging could manage. But I saw the seams. The faint indicators of her heartbeat.

A misaligned text box. A half-deleted note she'd rewritten three times. The typo she corrected and forgot to hide in track changes.

It was stupid. Insignificant. But it said what she wouldn't: this hurt her too.

I kept reading. Cross-referencing her site visit proposal against the investor call timeline. My eyes passed over every line, but my focus didn't hold. It kept catching—tripping over one name embedded in her logistics document like a hook:

Pivot.

Not Rowan. Not something vanilla and benign like Sloane Strategies.

Pivot.

Clean. Distant. Professional. Exactly what she'd asked for.

I sat back in my chair. Ran a hand over my jaw. I hadn't even shaved this morning, and my skin was starting to itch with the weight of it all.

I should've been sending emails. Whit had a budget restructure that I was supposed to approve. And Dash had been on my ass for a week and a half to look at his new proposal for acquisitions in the Middle East.

Instead, I clicked open Rowan's original proposal file. The first one she ever sent me. The one she titled *"Proposal: Pivot x Hawthorne"* with a smiley face in the metadata like she dared me to notice it and comment on her whimsy.

I noticed but never commented. Back then I thought it was just something to throw me off my game. Some way for her to fish for a response so she could fire back something witty that made me feel defenseless.

Back when I saw her as all polish and ambition. Fire in a silk blouse. I hadn't realized that she was also the first person in years who saw the weight I carried and didn't flinch.

Now, she could barely look at me.

My phone buzzed with a calendar alert—reminder: **Review new ad placement mockups.**

I dismissed it.

Then another. **Prep packet for candidate media training – Rowan to lead.**

That had crashed and burned. *None of the above*, she'd said when I asked her which was the one she would pick. In the end, the same went for me. But for different reasons. None of the above because no one could measure up to the one person who had it all but didn't want to share it.

I chatted Morgan:

> Me: Please move the media training to next week. Inform Rowan that we'll need to "pivot" from the original need for this meeting to align with the new goals.

> Me: Also, please send her flowers from all four of us. Nothing flashy. Something classic and elegant. No peonies.

> Me: Note: Thank you for always knowing where the lines are

> Me: Also no orchids. That's Whit's thing and honestly, they're expectedly ostentatious

> Me: ...and boring

18

WHERE THE CRACKS BEGIN

Rowan

I TOLD myself I'd done the right thing. That drawing a line would keep things clean. Safe. But even as I walked away from the HMG building, coffee cup in hand and a bullet point list of follow-ups in my inbox, I felt like I'd swallowed glass.

I wasn't afraid of losing the contract. I was afraid of what I'd lose if I let myself believe Ellis Hawthorne truly wanted me. Not some last-minute Hail Mary crafted to ensure he pleased his father and maintained the Hawthorne legacy.

I'd spent my whole life trying to prove I was worth something. First my parents, who seemingly spent most of my growing years constantly disappointed in my "wasted potential." Friends, boyfriends, former colleagues, my twenties were squandered bouncing from one taker to the next. I grew exhausted from chasing other people's approval. I turned myself into a one-woman circus desperate for anyone to be impressed with the many talents I could juggle concurrently.

When people broke me, I filled the cracks, like the

Japanese and their Kintsukuroi. Where I'd broken was filled with gold, so I remembered every day my value was my own. Just like the Japanese, I honored those wounds and made them beautiful.

I built Pivot so I would finally *matter* on my own terms. Without suited men with titles patting me on the head and manipulating the oxygen valve that dispensed praise and recognition.

If Ellis said last night mattered and then changed his mind, I wouldn't just lose the contract—I'd lose the part of me that finally started to believe in myself. The once barren garden of my self-worth had finally bloomed with the seeds I'd sowed and tended to. But those flowers were always leery of impending frost. Because deep down, those flowers were tenuously rooted at best.

A new floral arrangement arrived before I'd even finished skimming the flood of meeting requests in my inbox. Paisley set them down on my desk like she was delivering a verdict. "Company card," she said. "Standard verbiage, I'm sure. Definitely not worth your tears."

They were beautiful. Elegant in a quiet, expensive way that meant someone didn't just throw money at a florist. They understood restraint. Ivory ranunculus, soft green hellebores, a little flowering oregano for depth. Classic and grounded, hand curated versus an online order.

The card was simple. Cream with indigo ink, HMG logo embossed in the top middle with forest green foil surrounds. No personal monogram this time but definitely written in his handwriting.

Thank you for always knowing where the lines are.

He hadn't signed it. He didn't need to. I tucked it into my drawer like it burned. Paisley didn't comment. Just topped off my coffee and wordlessly rescheduled two nonessential calls before slipping back to her desk like the rockstar she was.

I turned back to my screen. Twelve new invites. One media training. Three site visits. Five photo ops. One trip to the West Coast HMG office marked *mandatory attendance*. I clicked.

HMG Los Angeles
Internal Transition Strategy Visit
7AM Monday – 6PM Thursday
A car will pick you up at 6AM
Drop Off at FBO Terminal, O'Hare

Sure. Because nothing said 'clean and professional' like a public-facing visit to the most optics-heavy division of the company. That sounded like a stellar idea just days after our faces hit every media feed in the country.

He was controlling the fallout. It was the plan we'd all agreed on. My role was to help solidify the narrative. To preserve it, just like I promised I would. So why did it feel like I was the one getting rewritten?

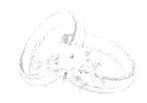

By the time I got to Raze, the girls were already at least a glass and a half in and mid-analysis.

"I'm just saying," Hollis was saying, "if the kiss was that good from ten feet away on a long lens, I can only imagine—oh hey Rowan."

She drew out the hey in the way that made it obvious they'd all been discussing me at *length*. The rest of my friends all suddenly became super invested in their menus, despite there being nearly full drinks in front of them and a selection of appetizers scattered across the horseshoe booth.

Greer slid a menu toward me. "You missed most of the 'getting everyone up to speed and on the same page.' Now that you're here, we're officially moving on to moral support."

"And, probably some judgment." Hollis warned, giggling into her margarita.

Lyris scowled in her direction before raising her glass. "To surviving the fallout."

"To *managing* the fallout," I corrected, settling into the booth. "Let's not pretend I didn't orchestrate this."

"You didn't orchestrate getting caught looking at each other like that," Greer said. "That wasn't spin. That was some *I choose you in every lifetime* energy."

Lyris and Hollis leaned into one another, making juvenile air kisses toward one another. I didn't respond. I folded my napkin, repeatedly, until I felt satisfied with how it laid on my lap. That had provided enough time for my G & T to arrive from our server.

They let the silence sit, like good friends do when they know you'll fill it eventually.

"So...you bailed on the Zoom when he showed up at your house?" Hollis gently inquired. "Obviously something happened. We're not here to grill you, but..."

"... some of us have very inquiring minds and dirty imaginations." Lyris added, earning her a smack against her shoulder from Greer.

"What Lyris *meant* to say was that we just want to know how to show up." Greer clarified, always the intermediary. "And without something—a direction, an emotion—we're kind of stumbling around blind."

I pressed my lips together. "We had to *make a decision* about the narrative. It couldn't be nothing. So now it's something. Publicly, it's professional. Strategic. Clean."

"And privately?" Lyris asked.

I looked down at my hands.

"It's complicated. I told him we needed to protect the story. That we should focus on the work. That what happened..." I shook my head. "It doesn't matter if it was real. If it doesn't serve the outcome, it's a risk."

Greer's eyes softened, she reached her hand out across the table, lacing it with my fingers just as Hollis put her arm around me. "But it *did* matter... to you."

"Yeah," I whispered. "That's the problem."

They didn't push. They didn't say "I told you so." Didn't offer solutions. They just sat with me while I tried to figure out how to find up again. Hollis signaled to our server for another round. For a while the conversation flattened, updates on family, complaints about annoying siblings. They all carried the conversation and allowed me to just sit in the ache of the things left unsaid between Ellis and me.

Eventually, I asked, "Is it possible to want something you can't trust?"

Greer pushed out of the booth and scooted around to my side, so she and Hollis bookended me. Her arm went around my shoulders, her head resting against mine. "Ro—sometimes the lesson is in allowing yourself *to* trust. Maybe your lesson here, is that not everything can be controlled. Not everything has a perfect narrative with zero blind spots and a ten bullet point list to prepare for every pitfall. Sometimes you just have to drop into the mud pit and figure it out. Whether you end up being used, using someone else, or discover an in-between that blissfully serves you both."

Except, Ellis hadn't used me. That I think was the worst part of all. He'd meant every word. I'd felt his soul in every touch.

Maybe Greer was right. Perhaps *I* was the one trying to repurpose something real into something safe. My friends knew me too well and they'd already seen too much. They knew that photo meant more than what we'd said. They were the ones that told me it was obvious from the way he looked at me that he was already rewriting his future. But believing in something so tenuous was far too dangerous.

19
WHAT WASN'T SAID STILL ECHOES

ELLIS

Keats stood beside me on the tarmac like a man being punished. Spring was taking its sweet damn time. The wind cut hard, blowing our coats open like it had a grudge. The cold shears tearing every last shred of warmth from our bones spoke directly to that fact.

"Remind me again why I'm being dragged to LA like it's a mandatory team-building retreat?"

Jesus, he exhausted me. Ever since the calendar invite popped up on his iPhone, he'd been incessant with his whining. How the person responsible for *Strategy and Public Relations* at Hawthorne failed to see the importance of his presence in an exercise in *optics* was beyond my capacity of understanding.

"Hmm, I can't imagine anything the Chief *Strategy Officer* has to do this week would be more important than *driving the strategy* for this sham of a publicity tour. Besides at least its fucking warm in LA You should be thanking me."

I handed my suitcase off to the co-pilot before taking the stairs into the cabin.

"Dash would have been much better in LA" Keats

persisted, "He's the one that handles TV and Networks. We'll have to have a *second* optics tour after I say something fucked up that somehow causes the trust from our West Coast partners to collapse. You know I suck speaking off the cuff. I'm much better when I have time to think and prepare." He followed at my elbow like a lost puppy and not like an almost thirty-six-year-old man with an executive's salary and responsibility.

"Dash is needed in Dubai. He wants us to strike while the iron is hot partnering with providers in the Middle East. This was the only time all of the players could all come together for discussions."

"What about Mr. Pocket Protector? He's fantastic at staying on his toes and staying on message."

"Keats, I swear to god. You would exhaust a nun."

He smirked at me and raised his eyebrow pointing a finger gun my way and pulling the trigger.

"Keats," I could feel my blood pressure raising. "Do we need to reconsider your role at HMG? If the thought of having to speak with someone without the benefit of a focus group and A/B testing, freaks you out, then perhaps we should put you somewhere else. I'm sure Engineering would love to have you. Just make sure not to wear those fancy loafers you're sporting when you're three thousand feet in the air. I wouldn't want you to slip."

I checked my phone. Still nothing. Not an update from Uri and not a peep from Rowan since last night's emails about my speech to senior leaders this afternoon.

"I can see it already." Keats continued, rifling through the snack basket that the flight attendants typically waited until we were in the air to start passing around. "You're going to have me battling it out with the press, answering the hard questions, while you take the redhead for photo ops at fucking Disney World."

"Land," I said, too exhausted to even try to follow his litany of complaints.

"What?"

"Disney *Land* is in California. Anaheim. Not exactly close to *Los Angeles* where we will be. Second, what hard hitting, journalistic questions do you think you'll be responding to with a site tour and a company fucking picnic?"

"Nice dance around the subject there. You and Rowan have been like the north and south pole lately. What gives?"

I didn't answer. Mostly because I didn't have one. Not one I was willing to say aloud.

"How does she go from coming to a meeting glowing like a Christmas Tree, to practically tripping over how far back she ran to distance herself from us?"

"Glowing?" Even I heard the sardonic tone to my question.

"Come on. Just stop with the tap dancing. I know you spent the night at her house. You two both smelled exactly the same."

"When did you become part bloodhound?"

"Should I pull up a spritely tune on my phone for you? I hate for you to keep dancing with no music playing."

Where the hell was she? The sooner she got here, the sooner we'd be up in the air. Then we could all focus on our work and not on idle chit chat.

> Me: Uri the instructions were 7am takeoff. What is your ETA?

Uri replied back almost instantaneously.

> Uri: Traffic on the Eisenhower. ETA fifteen minutes.

Great, in addition to Keats giving me a headache, Chicago O'Hare would slap me with a fifteen thousand dollar fine for delayed takeoff. We should have taken off on Sunday night or after the morning rush. Those assholes in Air Traffic Control hated private jets like ours. Especially when we messed up their perfectly aligned timelines.

"Sophie, please tell the pilot that one of our colleagues is running late and we'll need to push back our assigned take off time."

The passing flight attendant nodded and hustled toward the captain.

Keats sighed. "I thought this trip was about meeting with the West Coast division heads, not throwing a press-friendly Olympics gala."

"We're attending the gala, not throwing it. The City of Los Angeles is throwing it, in honor of the upcoming Summer Olympics."

"You hate galas," he pushed. "You always make me go to them."

"Wow, and look at that," I said, lacing my voice with saccharine and grasping my cheeks *Home Alone* style. "Conveniently, here you are. On a trip *to the location* where the gala is planned. Lightbulb!"

"This is about her, isn't it?" he pursued.

Keats needed to come with an off switch. I looked down the runway. The jet engines hummed like tension beneath my skin. "It's about the company."

Keats made a low noise in his throat that said *bullshit* without forcing me to respond. He didn't look convinced. I glanced at my phone. Nothing else from Uri.

Keats tossed his phone onto the tray table and stretched his long legs into the aisle like we weren't about to be joined by other staffers, as well as Rowan.

"You're not fooling anyone, you know," he said lightly, but there was weight in the center of his gaze. "Least of all her."

I rubbed a hand over my jaw. Despite being freshly shaven, I could still feel the stubble from *that* night. When I hadn't meant to fall asleep tangled in her sheets.

"She made herself very clear, Keats. So let's drop the damn subject since she'll be here any minute."

"No," Keats said, reclining his chair and adjusting it *just so*. "She made herself *safe*. That's different."

I didn't look up. What could I say in response to that. She didn't feel safe with me. Despite everything, all the ways I thought I'd shown her how invested in *us* I was.

"Anyway," he added with a shrug, "you know who else lives in LA?"

I narrowed my eyes. In the breath between his sentences, I felt tension coil. I didn't want to know who lived in LA Because if it was a friend or long-lost family member, I'd know. Which meant whatever name came out of his mouth was an enemy.

"Talia."

My attention snapped to him, hard. Not who I expected. I never bothered keeping tabs on her. She wasn't important enough for me to care.

"She doesn't matter."

I heard the quiet squeal of tires turning to align with the carpet. The opening and closing of multiple doors and feet climbing up the stairs. First our two junior executives boarded smiling their good mornings before pushing toward the back of the plane. And finally, Rowan appeared.

She stepped inside, all clean lines and strategic restraint. Her camel trench coat and black slacks, was elegant but stunning concurrently. She'd braided her hair, which hung loosely over her shoulder. Cinnamon and eucalyptus followed behind her as she took the seat across from us, facing the front of the plane—directly across the aisle from me. It had to be a strategic selection. Near enough to feel. But not to face, unless she chose to. The expression she'd worn as she boarded was unreadable. There was a smile on her lips, but her gaze lingered just one beat too long on me before noticing Keats seated with me.

I couldn't tell if she'd heard us talking. But the flicker in her eyes suggested as such. It had created just the smallest crack in the mask.

Keats stood, all easy charm and wrapped her in a hug.

"Look who finally decided to join us! I was starting to think I'd have to suffer through this PR parade without you."

Rowan's smile didn't quite reach her eyes. "You and a PR parade by yourself would be a disaster." She joked with him, her eyes finally getting some light in them. "Though I guess if I wanted to ensure that Pivot and Hawthorne remained contracted, I should have let you go alone so I could guarantee myself enough work through the end of the year."

She removed her jacket and handed it off to the attendant, who rushed her into getting situated and belted in seat could taxi and takeoff. Once seated, she focused on her laptop, not even chancing a glance in my direction. I felt her though. She had a gravity all her own. One that reset the laws of physics.

Keats decided to abandon me in favor of a flight filled with laughter and quippy banter. Which was fine. He'd already drained my tolerance capacity for obnoxious conversations. Though, the way they dipped their heads together as if best friends at a slumber party, winnowed between my ribs like the most brilliant shade of envy.

"Should I know who *she* is?" I heard her ask Keats.

He didn't miss a beat. "No one to worry about. Just a ghost of exes past."

"A threat?" she asked, her fingers hovering above her laptop as if she was about to compile an entire dossier on my ex-girlfriend.

"Definitely not. Not anymore," he said.

She didn't reply. Just refocused her attention to her laptop, seamlessly slipping into work mode like it was armor. But her posture changed. Just enough that I felt the space between us stretch wider.

I told myself it was better this way. Cleaner. Safer. And yet, I hated it.

20

OPTICS ARE ILLUSIONS

Rowan

I TRIED to float along on the genial current Keats created. The entire ride to the airport I'd told myself, repeatedly, that surviving the week meant keeping it light. Pining wasn't for jet setting to LA. That town was nothing but curated reality.

"So Rowan." Keats leaned onto the table that separated us, his cognac colored eyes twinkling with conspiratorial glee. "I know you have single friends. Give em up. We all have the same requirements as Mr. Sulky Suits over there. Which one could use a nice strong dicking and the Cinderella treatment of an Amex Black Card?"

What was it with the Hawthorne men and their obsession with their dicks? First Ellis and his blowjobs aren't just for birthdays and now this one with his discussions of dicking down random girls. Were Whit and Dash similar to these two? The only interactions I'd had with Whit and Dash were purely professional. And mostly through email.

"My friends have excellent taste, an elite sense of self-preservation, and zero need for a prince's silver spoon. They make their own money and live by their own rules."

Keats faked a hit to the chest, falling dramatically back into his seat. Even Ellis turned to look at what the commotion was, grunting and rolling his eyes when he realized it was just Keats being Keats.

"Rowan, you wound me. Are you saying that I'm not a catch? Have you met me? I feel like I'm the total package. Smart, well educated, so much more fun than any of my brothers. And I can never say no to a woman's frivolous requests for presents. You want a Louis? How about one for every season. Baby needs a vacation—off to the Hamptons we go. Dinner at Alinea? Done. We don't even need to wait weeks on the reservation list. I'll get you in there tonight."

"I didn't say you aren't a catch. Just one with a very inflated sense of self, and probably a need for a regular regimen of antibiotics."

Keats made a mock gasp, clutching his invisible pearls. "Low blow, strategist."

That's when Ellis laughed. Not a chuff, a chuckle, or a chortle. A laugh. Loud and surprised, like I'd caught him off guard in his eavesdropping.

Keats grinned at me like I won a prize. "There it is! The elusive Ellis Hawthorne chuckle. I was starting to think you'd left your personality back in Chicago."

"I'm just enjoying the show," Ellis said smoothly, his tone dipping into dry amusement. "Though if we're keeping score, I've seen Rowan dismantle bigger egos with less material."

I glanced over at him. The smirk was there—soft, subtle. The same one he wore when he was quietly impressed but didn't want anyone to know it. It hit me in the solar plexus with unsettling precision.

Keats caught the shift instantly. "God, the tension in here is delicious. I should've brought popcorn."

"Yet you remembered a protein shake, an egg white spinach wrap, two books, and your iPad." I pointed at his spread taking up nearly all the real estate on our shared table.

"I thought this was a work trip." He volleyed, his smile stretching the expanse of his lips, "not a new telenovela called *Pride and Press Releases*."

Damn. That comeback was fire. Even I couldn't hold back an appreciative giggle. Ellis caught my eye, something unspoken hanging in the air between us. In a second, it was gone, and Ellis's focus was back on the scenery outside his window.

"For the record." Keats pulled my attention back to him. "Dash is the walking STD with James Dean energy."

"Except *Mr. Sustainability* would never be caught dead in a leather jacket." I volleyed back.

"No just assless chaps and a flogger," Ellis quipped from across the aisle.

I nearly expired.

"Miss Italy," Keats whispered, calling up the tabloid story on his iPad. "One of the Prime Minister's crazy sex parties."

"Jesus." I needed to bleach my eyes. "At this rate, you four are going to keep Pivot flush for decades."

"Just be sure you name the conference room after your deep pocketed, though slightly scandal prone, benefactors."

The rest of the flight passed in a blur of stories and jabs that melted some of the frost that had been lingering. No one said anything real, not in the way that counted. The undercurrent, however, had shifted. For the first time in days, I wasn't holding my breath at each interaction. It finally felt real again, like we weren't pretending.

Thanks to the two hour time difference, we landed in LA just as their day began. The HMG team was hustled into SUVs like talent being shuttled to a press junket. The four-day whirlwind was packed the gills. There'd be zero time to focus on anything but my job and the tasks at hand.

THE NEXT FEW days passed in a blur of coordinated chaos. Morning briefings, curated photo ops, impromptu fireside chats with division leads wanting face time with Ellis. We toured studios, oohed and aahed at building upgrades and renovations, sat in on live tapings, visited innovation labs that promised to "revolutionize West Coast vertical integration." It was a whirlwind. Exhausting in the way only relentless charm and high-stakes performance could be. I didn't know how the Hawthorne brothers pulled off cool, collected, and accessible all at once. The introvert in me wanted to hide in my room and binge bad hotel room movie offerings with a side of room service.

Our suite at the Pendry Hotel downtown had three rooms and a shared living area. It felt comfortable. Too comfortable, maybe. Every night we drifted back into our rooms like ships awkwardly passing one another in the night —or in our case a very elaborate foyer.

On our last night something shifted. By the time we returned from the company picnic, we were sun-flushed, windblown, and drunk on the kind of good mood that felt too rare to trust. The picnic hadn't just been a photo op, but actual fun. The kind you forget about as you get lost in the grind of corporate existence. I'd kicked off my heels at some point during the photo session and never put them back on.

There'd been carnival games and amazing food, the craziest contests for some incredible prizes and of course Keats being Keats. He was a hit with everyone we met. For all his insecurities at not being good in front of crowds the man could charm the skin off an alligator and make himself a new pair of boots.

I entered my room, and there it was. Hanging against the wardrobe: a deep emerald silk gown with off-the-shoulder draping and subtle beading at the waist. Beside it, a pair of heels—elegant, sharp, clearly tailored to my taste.

A note sat on the dresser, written in his handwriting:

Apparently, Morgan forgot to loop Paisley in. I hope this suits you. The gala is black tie.

No signature. No flourish. Just Ellis—quietly moving mountains while pretending they were pebbles. I changed slowly, unsure what I was walking into. When I stepped out, Ellis was waiting in the shared suite. He stood at the window, hands in his pockets, silhouetted against the skyline. When he turned, something unguarded flickered across his face.

"You look..." He cleared his throat, gaze raking over me once, then again more slowly. "Perfect."

"Smooth recovery," I said, adjusting one of the earrings that had been placed just to the right of the note. The *Cartier* label wasn't overlooked. "Is this the part where you tell me we're attending a royal ball or where you offer me the red box with the jewels that snaps shut on my gloved hand when I go to reach for it?"

His confused smile was charmingly vulnerable.

"Pretty Woman." I provided, assuming he didn't catch the reference.

He cracked a smile. A real one.

"We are attending a gala celebrating Olympic media partnerships. I'm sorry to spring it on you last minute. I hope the dress suits."

The dress more than suited. It was picked as if had been made just for me by a bunch of musical mice. I felt elegant and beautiful. The tear drop amethyst earrings were such a stunning contrast.

"Not because you aren't deserving of diamonds." Ellis took one of the earrings between his fingers, "but because you are far too unique to wear something so expected."

He took the air out of the room. The familiar smell of his *Après Ski* fresh snow and pine scent, the way he wore the *shit* out of that custom tux with its deep midnight accents had already been enough to make it hard for me to breathe. Then he goes and says things like that? I wouldn't survive the evening.

"Keats is meeting us there." He held out his arm, and without thought I looped mine through his. "While I have to assume almost four full days of the Laurel and Hardy show must be exhausting, I didn't want you to worry you wouldn't have your comedic entourage with you tonight."

A laugh escaped me before I could stop it. The elevator chimed at the end of the hall, but I barely registered it. "I'll be sure to keep an eye on the punch bowl." I joked, practically floating toward the elevator.

"And here I thought you'd abandoned your good girl days." His gaze dipped, briefly, to my neckline, and the corner of his mouth tugged like he'd caught himself. Under the influence of the Keats Hawthorne magic, I was certain you'd charm USA Gymnastics into a cartwheel contest."

The warmth pooling in my chest had nothing to do with the champagne I'd already promised myself at the gala. I tilted my head, smiling up at him. "The night is still young Hawthorne, and we do have those press photos to think about."

His arm tightened ever so slightly against mine, a move that was protective, or possessive, or maybe both. For the first time all week, we stepped out together. Not boss and consultant. Not client and strategist. Something riskier. Toeing the line of optics and the danger zone. And maybe, finding the balance for the one thing we weren't ready to name.

21

THE QUIET COLLAPSE

ELLIS

THE MOMENT we stepped onto the ballroom floor, I regretted everything. The emerald, green dress Rowan wore had looked innocent and graceful on the hanger. Yet once she'd stepped in to it, it was silk made for sinning. Every step she took, that gorgeous ass of hers was kissed by the soft drape of the fabric. Each gesture, whether it was to extend a hand in greeting, or accept a glass of champagne created a symphony of sound that reminded me of satin bedsheets and her seductive mouth calling out in apogee.

She'd swept her hair into a sleek updo that exposed the graceful slope of her neck. And that delectable piece of skin became the most distracting thing in the room. With Keats running a close second.

It felt as if she laughed at everything Keats said. Her hand repeatedly brushed against his arm, her lips parted just slightly in amusement. She glowed beneath his spotlight. *His.* None of it was for me.

I knew the rules. We'd agreed to them. Professional. Polished. Controlled. And yet I found myself reaching for the small of her back to pull her in close. More than once.

I'd had to force my hands into my pockets as a preventive measure.

"Rowan? Oh my god! What are you doing here?"

An exceptionally tall woman with waist-length hair ran, rapidly approached us from our left.

"Hollis? What the hell are you doing here?" Rowan pulled the young woman in for a hug so fierce, she nearly pushed the woman's strapless gold ballgown clear off her back.

"Um? Hello? Sports broadcaster." She pointed at herself with sarcasm lifting her burgundy painted lips. "I'm supposed to be here. My network carries like eighty percent of the Olympics. The question is what the hell are *you* doing here?"

She asked Rowan but looked directly at me.

"Holy shit." I saw recognition light her eyes before the sentence was even finished. "You two are here *together*? Like together, together?"

"And how do you two know each other?" I asked, feeling as if I were simply an observer and not the reason we were attending this gala in the first place.

"Even I know the answer." Keats knocked against my shoulder. "Once a month Rowan meets with her friends. Hollis and Rowan went to college together. Lyris—a food critic and blogger—and also one of their other college friends moved to Chicago with Rowan. They were the original two. Then came Greer, who is a political editor. Finally, Hollis, arrived in Chicago and rounded out the group. They named their little group *Pitchfest* because they're all in the industry, and it plays off a bitchfest where people get together to complain about the general annoyances of life.

Why did *Keats* get to know something so deeply

personal about Rowan. I'd known her for years and didn't know that detail. And fucking Keats answering like he's her damn best friend?

"She's been doing it for years." Keats offered, "All the way back to when she still worked at HMG. She goes to Raze, you know down off State Street—we've run into one another a few times."

I'd never once heard her mention Pitchfest. Not in five years working together. But apparently Keats knew the whole history. Even the damn spot they went for drinks.

Before Rowan could explain further, Beckett Fucking Murray sauntered up. The man owned the space like the planets worshipped the sun. The whole room just gaped in his direction. Sure he was good looking in that *all American* kind of way. But the guy pissed in a fucking fountain and got himself not only kicked out of Rio but USA Swimming entirely.

"Beckett?" Rowan practically screeched, "You too? Why are you here?"

"Hollis and I are color commentary for all the swimming events," he explained, leaning in to place a kiss on her cheek before pulling her in for a hug.

"Beckett Murray," he extended his hand to me in greeting as the women went off on some tangent about dresses, designers, and who they'd gotten to meet. "I have heard a lot of good things about you and HMG."

"Beckett is also from Chicago," Rowan added. "But him and *his wife and daughter* live in San Diego now."

The emphasis on wife and daughter were not lost on me. "Daughters, plural in about three months." He laughed. "I thought I'd get a son the second time around, but apparently the fates have decided that with four Murray brothers, the next generation needs to be filled with little, redheaded, X chromosomes instead."

"Priscilla and Presley?" Rowan gasped, grabbing his forearm in the animated way she always did when truly excited, like she'd forgotten anyone else existed. It was a forearm. A forearm in an Armani tux, attached to fingers that bore a tungsten wedding ring. Yet, her hand on *his body* twisted something inside of me.

It wasn't flirtation. It was ease. History. She laughed like someone who didn't have to watch herself, who didn't feel like she was under surveillance. And that killed me most of all.

"Ella," Beckett nodded, waking up his phone and scrolling through his photos, "though Harris jokingly called her Bitsy and the nickname kind of stuck. Much to Presley's chagrin."

The trio of friends continued on chattering over one another. As if sensing I awkwardly stood on the outskirts of their conversation, Keats returned to the orbit of commotion between the three friends, dismissing whomever he'd been casually chatting with. He and I stood together quietly standing sentry to their interactions. Rowan excused herself to the powder room, promising to return quickly. I'd been perfectly happy babysitting my bourbon when a comment caught my attention.

"I saw Danny Trizinski over near the photo-booth," Beckett mentioned to the group, pointing his beer in the director over his shoulder. "Talk about a total blast from the past."

Hollis slapped his shoulder with a loud *thunk*. "What the fuck Beck? Why would you bring that up?"

"I didn't realize talking about someone who is ancient history would be verboten."

"Thank god Rowan isn't here to hear you say that." Hollis continued. "Forget you saw him and certainly don't tell Rowan."

"Who is Danny Trizinski?" I asked. The question was directed at Beckett but neither him nor Hollis seemed to clock my question. Of course, fucking Keats had the answer.

"He plays baseball," Keats answered. "Milwaukee."

"He went to college with us." Hollis further explained.

"Why is it such a big deal then?" I asked, sensing there was more to the story.

"They were engaged." Hollis continued. She may have said more but the world suddenly became a nuclear fallout. *Engaged?* How had I not known this.

"It was more like a promise ring." Keats offered. How the fuck did Keats know any of it?

"Did you go to Iowa too? Funny I could have sworn the degree hanging in your office said Northwestern like the rest of us."

"Don't you remember the summer that Rowan disappeared for like two weeks and you had to hire that temp?

Any moment spent with Rowan should be burned into my memory. Unfortunately there was only so much room in my brain to hold historic knowledge, and professional information. Knowing I'd ignored a significant piece of Rowan Sloane history, dwarfed me in shame. How many opportunities had I missed? Maybe she'd left HMG because I made her feel unseen. That thought ate at me.

I made an excuse and exited out of the conversation. Keats took off in directions unknown and I tried to distract my spiraling thoughts with banal chatter. Wherever I went in the ballroom though, Rowan's laugh was a siren's song. I heard it everywhere. She caught me watching her. Just once. Eyes soft, mouth slightly parted, like she might say something across the space between us. But then Beckett cracked another joke and the moment vanished. And each time she laughed at something he said, it twisted the knife in my gut tighter. Envy raged inside, shaking its fists at injustice of having to compete for her attention.

Keats clocked me from across the room, arched a brow, and a smile that said he knew exactly why I felt so unhinged. He mouthed, 'not yours,' before turning back to his own conversation.

I needed air. He was right but so incredibly wrong at the same time. Publicly, yes, she wasn't mine. Hell even privately I had no claim. But motherfuck I wanted it more than air. I wanted her laughs and inside jokes. I wanted to keep working the room, with her on my arm, and that razor sharp wit tickling not just me but whomever we deigned to speak with. And I wanted them to know she was with *me*.

Unfortunately exiting one emotionally trying conversation and escaping to the balcony had me stumbling into the single person I absolutely wanted to avoid that evening.

"Ellis?"

Fuck. I turned slowly. I already knew, like cows can sense impending slaughter.

Talia Brindley.

Keats had warned me. I knew logically she'd be floating around. In my mind though I figured with as many people were invited to this thing, we'd never see one another.

I used to love that chill in her voice. Thought it meant she was sharp. Now I knew better. Cold only cuts when there's nothing left to burn.

Of course she would look stunning. Her black hair was still razor-straight, her lipstick still calculated, her eyes still impossibly cold beneath the warmth she performed for a crowd. A media darling in her own right, Olympic media partnerships were naturally in her wheelhouse.

"I didn't think you'd show," she said lightly, leaning in to stain my cheek with the blood of her painted lips. "I thought you hated these kinds of things."

"I do." My voice was flat. "So is the life of a CEO. I was here visiting the offices and got roped into attending"

She tilted her head. "Oh yes, I heard. Succession planning right? The narrative spin and control are impressive, even for you."

I didn't respond.

She let the silence stretch just long enough to remind me who she used to be. Who I used to be with her.

"And that?" she asked, chin tipping slightly toward Rowan. "The one from the photo, right? Is she the spin or just another social climber who hasn't yet realized how the story of the two of you ends."

I stepped closer. Not enough to start a scene. But enough that she'd hear me clearly.

"You don't get to talk about her." I told her. "That woman has more integrity, is vastly more intelligent, and far too classy to be swimming in the cesspool of LA Press, that's for sure."

Her smile was all snark. "I touched a nerve."

"No," I said. "Corpses don't have nerves. And that's what I am, all that's left."

I walked away before she could reply.

22

A LIE THAT LOOKS LIKE TRUTH

Rowan

Ellis was like a firefly, one minute illuminated, the next lost in the fray. He'd been acting strange. While I'd never *attended* a gala with him, I'd observed him at plenty of functions to know he was usually charming and gregarious. Tonight though, impatient and disinterested were putting his attitude nicely.

Then I felt it like an impending thunderstorm. The full weight of Ellis the CEO was both awe inspiring and a bit intimidating. The tiny hairs on the back of my neck stood at attention, as if even they knew the power approaching me from behind.

"Come with me." His clipped directive didn't just suggest but demanded compliance with no argument—which had been on my tongue.

The two of us walked side by side, shuffling through the masses until we found ourselves pushing through to the entrance of the hotel. Ellis paused, smiling at those calling his name, looking this way and that in search of something.

"Who are we looking for?" I asked him. "Your brother is

over by the bar, chatting it up with a few of the women from the tennis team."

Instead of answering, he grunted, low and impatient, like civility was hanging by a thread. He took hold of my hand and lead me down a quiet hallway. My heels clattered against the marble floor as I tried to keep pace with his wild, nonsensical searching.

"Ellis, I'm in heels. Heels that *you* bought me. This floor is slippery."

He stopped mid-step, turned around and looked down at my feet. I lifted my foot just a touch so he could see the stilts he'd given me to balance on.

"Gorgeous." He muttered. "Better than I could even imagine them looking."

Rather than clarify, he tried a door to our right and pulled us into it when he discovered it was unlocked. The moment he clocked that the room was empty save for a few benches and chairs inside, he had me up against the wall, hands in my hair.

"I can't stand it." His lips came down against mine with possessive force. It was rough, wet lips, demanding and possessive. "It's too much. More than I thought it would be."

There was a strain in his voice that I'd never experienced before. He leaned his forehead against mine, massaging the back of my neck. The amber ring around his chocolate eyes shimmered in the atmospheric light, telegraphing far too many emotions than I ever thought I'd see in Ellis Hawthorne's gaze.

"You're *mine* Rowan." The way he said it. Brusque, commanding, possessive, it triggered a switch, buried soul deep that thrummed with insistence. "You have been from the second you answered my phone call."

His hands tilted my face and his lips reunited with mine, less urgent than before but equally as claiming.

"This fucking dress." His palms were hot against the soft, cool satin. Every place he touched on my body caught fire beneath their heat. Electricity sang through my bloodstream, my erratic heartbeat and the breath stealing kisses made me lightheaded, but I couldn't stop.

We were thieves, stealing pieces of one another with each frenetic pass of our lips. It wasn't enough. Balancing against the weight of my overwhelming desire was causing my legs to go weak, and my feet to teeter. Ellis flipped me around, face to the wall, hands braced on the doorframe.

"I'm about to take what's mine, Rowan." His hands gathered my dress, collecting it in one hand as the other gentled as it massaged up my thigh toward my cotton covered mound. "Tell me now. Say no, and this stops. Otherwise, be prepared to have every other man who has enjoyed being in this position, getting fucked clear out of your memory."

"Is this about Beckett?" I could barely speak. My words were stilted while I panted, desperate to catch my breath. "He's *married*. And we're just friends, Ellis. We've only ever been friends."

He spanked my between my legs, the jolt cracked like lightning over my clit and sent a strong current of desire firebombing through my nervous system. There was an orgasm orbiting just past the horizon. I watched it, a fireball of energy gathering, spinning, compounding in size and threatening to overtake me.

Ellis gently thumbed over my clit, the action in total dichotomy to fierceness of his words and action only seconds ago.

"Tell me, Rowan. Yes or no. Do you want this? Do you need me as much I need you? Are you out of your head every second of the day, fighting back words you know you shouldn't say? Because I am. And I can't do it anymore Rowan. I'm tired of fighting what's right in front of me."

"Yes." The word fell effortlessly from my mouth.

"Yes, you want me to fuck you? Or yes, you're as turned inside out as I am."

"Both," I told him.

In the milliseconds it took for me to answer him, I heard the descending zipper, the crinkle of the wrapper. Ellis's hand, hot, possessive, but also soft and gentle rest on my shoulder. He pressed down, wordlessly commanding me to bend further.

I felt the cool breeze against my thighs as he gathered my dress and rest it up above my hips.

"Home." Ellis replied. "This, here, with you. This is my home. The only place I ever feel as if the world is quiet."

He said it like a benediction. Like the words weren't meant for me, but for the parts of him still trying to believe this wasn't real. He'd anchored me. Possessed me in a whirlwind of heated action and heart-rending words. Yet still, it was that single word—home—that totally unraveled me.

He pushed in with such focused effort, with such a bruising pace, I was halfway up the summit before my brain caught up.

"Rowan," He groaned, canting his hips against my thighs. The sound of our skin slapping against one another was near pornographic. I could only imagine what someone would think if they walked in right now. Ellis's tuxedo pants at his ankles, my elegant dress practically draping over my head, and the two of us fucking against one another as if the world was about to end.

With each deep thrust his name slipped from my lips like an incantation and a curse. My sweat dampened fingers slipped against the doorframe. Even in the low light I could see the white of my knuckles as my body melted with each punishing, pleasurable inch of him.

I wasn't prepared for this. The entirety of the rise and set of the evening, and certainly not for how he fucked me like it meant something. Like I was the answer to something long-unsaid.

"I'm the last one." He insisted. "No one else gets in here but me."

"Ellis..." I tried to form a sentence, but all that came out was a breathy moan as my orgasm threatened to crest. He slammed back into me, and the words died in my throat. My brain could no longer conjure thought. I simply existed in the white-hot pleasure of this man and his possession. No, this wasn't just possession. It was devotion wearing the mask of dominance. A declaration dressed as sin.

His fingers trailed up my stomach, pulling down the satin of my dress and pushing down the cup of my bra. My breast sang against the tendrils of pleasure his fingers brought. All too soon his hand was searching higher, capturing my face and turning it toward his own.

I sought out his mouth, desperate to ground myself, needing to feel every piece of me connected in some way to him.

"Rowan," he said again, panting my name like a precious secret. "You are everything I never dared believe I could have."

The orgasm came like tsunami: violent, unrelenting,

and all consuming. My knees buckled, the only thing keeping me in place was Ellis's thighs pressed against mine. His name, torn from my throat, sounded nothing like fear and everything like surrender. Surrender, and the smallest hint of the one word neither of us dared to speak.

23

THE UNSPOKEN PLACE

ELLIS

I HADN'T PLANNED to take Rowan in an overflow room in the midst of some theater of status gala. Between that smiling maw of a *friend* Beckett Murray and then getting sucker punched by the reappearance of Talia, I needed to feel something real. I was bone tired. Not physically. In fact my body hummed with a satisfaction I hadn't experienced in ages.

Mentally, emotionally I was tired. I hated how *fake* I'd had to be over the last three weeks since the kiss that broke the internet. Even more so, I despised that I'd had to put on a cool exterior with the one woman who heated me to my core. I didn't want to pretend. Despite thinking I could spend a lifetime married to pretense, doing it with Rowan made me hate myself a little more with every practiced smile and carefully crafted omission.

As hard as I tried not to ruin Rowan's elegant dress and hair, we'd lost control the moment we surrendered to what we clearly both wanted. We snuck out of the party the second the two of us looked decently presentable and dashed back up to our hotel room. Once there, we spent hours reacquainting ourselves in every position imaginable.

Keats had sent me a message around midnight instructing me not to wait up. He'd yet to come back. We were scheduled to take off for Chicago around one p.m. Though, Keats had unwittingly given me an idea for the day.

The water sluiced across my back and along my shoulders, deepening the wave of satisfaction I already luxuriated in as I reflected on Rowan's lush body, the trusting look in her eyes, and the way she hung on to me for dear life. It felt like I was her life preserver as she floated, unmoored, through uncharted territory. Except, I was the uncharted territory. My love for her was an unknown island, lush, over grown, but not yet discovered. Yet, it was me she clung to. I was the person she wanted holding her when she faced something she was unsure about.

I heard the snick of the door and the soft padding of her footsteps. She stepped in behind me, her palm pressed to my back, a warmth I could feel even through the water. An unexpected familiarity. As if she and I had done this very thing a hundred times before. For a moment, we stood like that, with her touch feeling like an anchor that held me in the moment.

Then her arms came around my waist. I closed my eyes. Of all the ways I'd imagined this morning might go, *soft and intimate* wasn't on my list. I expected awkwardness. Prepared for it even. I thought she'd wake up and the room would be full of tension and regret, like last time. Rowan pressing her face between my shoulder blades like I was something solid? I wouldn't have ever dared to even dream it.

"I couldn't sleep," she murmured. Her lips brushed the

space between my shoulder blades. "Every time I closed my eyes, I kept thinking you were a dream I was going to wake up from."

I turned slowly, steam curling between us, hands sliding to her hips like they belonged there. Because they did. I'd waited a lifetime to have this—*her*—in my arms with no one watching, no performance required.

"You're not dreaming," I said softly. "If anyone is dreaming it's me, and if Keats wakes me up, I'll beat the motherfucker like he's still six."

She searched my face, her brows drawing tight like she didn't quite believe it, her lips finally quirking up in a smile. I reached up and cupped her jaw. Held her gaze, ran my thumb across her lips.

"Last night wasn't performance." I assured her, "And it wasn't just sex. It was the first time I've ever touched someone and felt like I was *home*."

Her breath hitched. "Home," she whispered. "There's that word again."

I leaned in, rested my forehead to hers. Let the silence stretch, heavy with promise.

"We don't have to figure it all out today," I added. "But when we go downstairs, it's not a lie anymore. We're not hiding. Not from anyone."

She swallowed. "You sure?"

"I'd stake my whole fortune on that truth."

I pulled her in for a kiss, pouring every word I'd ever wanted to say, anything we'd left unsaid, and every word I'd speak in the future, into that kiss.

She pushed against my chest, ending the kiss far sooner than I would have preferred. There'd been a question forming on my lips, but it died when I saw her slowly go to her knees.

"Your birthday is in October. HMG was founded in November; I don't think anyone is having a birthday or an anniversary today."

Her hand went around my cock and I saw stars. The moment she welcomed me into the wet warmth of her mouth, she owned me—completely and forever. The strong pull of her mouth didn't just titillate me, it unmoored something in me. Dislodged my soul and handed it to her like she was the only one I'd ever trust to keep it safe.

"Rowan, sweetheart."

My toes curled as the edges of my eyes went black. I tried to keep a firm lock on my control, but it quickly unraveled with each seductive swirl of her tongue. The moment her dainty fingernails caressed up my thighs to cup my sack, I was a goner. I usually had far better staying power. Especially considering the three orgasms we'd shared the evening previous.

"Rowan, pull off. I'm sorry! Rowan... You're so fucking good at th—" She didn't, choosing instead to take everything I had to give. For the first time in a long time, however, I didn't feel empty at her thievery. I felt overfull, like I could give for the rest of my life and still want to give some more.

***

"Hey stranger!" Rowan's sweet voice carried down the hall into my bedroom, where I'd been packing. "Where did run off to last night?"

I heard Keats's chuckle and heavy footfalls as he walked into the hotel suite.

"A few of the ladies from the tennis team." I heard him say.

"Please tell me whatever you took out of your pants ended up far away from cameras and paparazzi," she called back. "I don't have the bandwidth for a full-blown PR scandal today."

Rowan joked, as she moved back and forth between the living room and her bedroom. I assumed collecting whatever she needed to get packed.

"Well I can imagine you would be exhausted after an entire night of the two of you playing hide and seek with your feelings for one another." Keats replied, glancing at her before noticing me.

I poked my head around the corner and found the two of them perched at the bar, coffees in hand like this was any other morning.

"Change of plans," I said. "The jet is still scheduled to take off at one, but I told the HMG team they could join the rest of the media at ESPN's Disneyland takeover. Since you're the one who suggested Rowan and I play hooky, Keats, I figured we could all go. Unless you've got pressing matters at HQ."

Two pairs of wide eyes stared back at me like I'd announced a nuclear de-escalation summit with North Korea.

"Rowan, sweetheart, did you bring anything casual enough for Anaheim? Or should we swing through The Grove?"

Her head tilted slightly at the endearment, but she didn't say a word—just shook her head once, a subtle smile tugging at her lips. Keats caught the sweetheart. He made a sound somewhere between a cough and a laugh. His neck snapped toward me so fast I was surprised it didn't dislocate.

"Keats?" I repeated, "You coming with us or heading to the jet?"

In the end, we all made the trip to Disneyland, with a brief stop for theme park appropriate clothing.

"I've never stayed in a Disney resort!" Rowan practically skipped to the tram that would take us to the park. "I always wanted to as kids, but they were way out of the Sloane family budget."

My brothers and I begged our parents to take us to Disney *World* multiple times when we were younger. Especially after hearing about how cool it was from our friends who'd vacation there. Hawthornes didn't vacation like commoners. That was the standard Nathan Hawthorne decree. Our summers were spent in Switzerland or touring Anne Franke's house in Amsterdam. Three months off from school meant doing nothing fun unless it was educational or sandwiched into a business trip.

"I don't know how well this would go over with the old CEO, but I think I like the new CEO's style." Keats's smile was as bright as Rowan's. He knocked my shoulder before taking off in a run to catch the boarding tram.

"Do you think we'll see him again today?" Rowan asked, following my gaze, tracking Keats's to his seat where he waved wildly to both of us before the tram driver double honked and took off toward the park.

"Doubtful. But he probably doesn't want to be a third wheel, either."

I watched her chatting with some random family as we boarded. Her laughter was unguarded and glowing, her hair swept up in a knot that had already started to unravel. The midday sun caught the amber in her eyes and turned it gold.

While in business today would be a "nothing day," it was everything to me.

For once, I wasn't calculating angles or forecasting outcomes. I wasn't navigating board dynamics or legacy pressure. I was in the moment. With her. And if anyone asked what made me believe this wasn't just optics anymore, I'd point to this exact second and say: *her. This. Us.* Love looked exactly like this moment unscripted, full of unfettered joy, and utterly impossible to fake.

24

A PICTURE OF THE FEELING

Rowan

"Before the day gets crazy," Ellis gently tugged my hand, pulling my focus from the Main Street Map. "One more picture?"

His eyes were wide and unguarded; the lopsided smile was childlike in its innocence. How could I say no when he looked so endearing?

"Really Hawthorne? An optics photo here? In the happiest place on earth?"

"Not optics." He insisted, tugging me toward Cinderella's castle, "I'm immortalizing the day. So that sometime in the future, when you're wearing the white dress and I'm looking dashing in my custom tux made for the occasion, we can have this picture on the thank you cards gracing each table."

The spring sun cast a golden hue on the whole of Main Street. As if they too had just heard Ellis's heartfelt fantasy and wanted to match the warmth of the moment with some mood lighting. The park was filled to the brim with spring breakers and all the LA Olympic invitees. But the world went still. I couldn't hear a thing as Ellis positioned me directly in front of Cinderella's castle, his smile so wide and so full of hope, it was contagious.

"Ellis—" His name was my anchor. But before I could finish my sentence, to tell him how much he meant to me, and how glad I was we were done hiding from our feelings —he dipped me—fully. Once I was nearly horizontal, he kissed me with breath stealing passion. Like I was the star of my own Disney movie.

My fingers curled into his Polo shirt, kissing him back with as much emotion as he poured into the act. We were a hurricane, stealing the air from everyone around us, gathering strength as we went on. And then we heard the camera shutters clicking.

"Mr. Hawthorne!" Someone called, "Is there a headline you'd like us to use with that shot?"

He didn't even hesitate. Looking straight at me, smiling like he'd just snuck candy into church he answered, *"From business partnership to fairy tale: The Iceman finally thaws."*

More pictures, more members of the press calling our names. I felt my face heat that had nothing to do with a potential sunburn. We were here, and *out*. Official. A couple. No more optics. No more lies.

Ellis took my hand, kissing it before waving at all the people, and turning toward Adventureland. Just as we crossed under the sign announcing the location, I heard someone calling my name.

"Hey! Rowan! Long time!" A pixie of a woman with wild, strawberry blond hair and a very obvious baby bump came shuffling toward me.

"Lane, hi! It's been a while. I think the last time I saw you was at your wedding. And now look at you! Baby number two."

"Baby two!" She laughed, rubbing her belly.

"Where's baby number one?" I looked around her, there was no stroller in sight.

"Marin is with Beckett. *Someone* convinced her Daddy that she needed *yet another* ear-splitting toy that she'll lose interest in by the end of the day."

"What's the purpose of having all this money if we can't use it to make people's lives better?" Beckett approached from our left, Marin on his shoulders. "Especially the life of *this* little monkey!"

"Beckett." Ellis nodded in his direction.

"Smooth, Ellis. Loved the headline. Real subtle." Beckett smirked and tipped his chin toward me. "Can't wait to see how *The Times* spins that one."

"Well, you know the Hawthornes," I said, stealing the line before Ellis could. "Quiet, restrained, never one to draw attention."

Ellis didn't argue. He just reached for my hand again, threading his fingers between mine as if they'd always belonged there.

My phone chimed with a text to the Pitchfest group:

> Hollis: Hear ye, hear ye 🎤📰
>
> Hollis: [Image Attached] — Rowan sucking face with Ellis Hawthorne in the happiest place on earth 😘✨
>
> Hollis: Ellis Hawthorne is officially off the market. RIP to my hot rich fantasy leagues. Long live Queen Rowan
>
> Lyris: Wait—has it always been him? Like, slow burn office tension? Or fake dating gone real?

> Greer: Is this an enemies-to-lovers situation or friends-to-lovers with benefits on top?
>
> Hollis: Or was it the "we work together and one night everything exploded" kind of thing? Because that is my personal catnip.
>
> Lyris: If you don't tell us soon, I'm going to write an entire narrative with unauthorized artistic liberties.

I grinned and typed back one line:

> Me: None of the above. 😏

> Greer: You're insufferable.
>
> Lyris: …and yet, iconic.
>
> Hollis: I knew it. The Rowan Sloane Origin Love Story is going to break me.

I bit my lip to keep from laughing. Ellis caught the expression and leaned down, brows lifting.

"Do I want to know?"

"Probably not," I said, quickly texting back:

> Me: Where are you? I thought you were supposed to be at the park today as part of media day

> Hollis: I am. I'm on the train. Where are you?

> Me: Adventureland, we just found Beckett, Lane, and Marin

> Lyris: This back and forth is absolutely fascinating. Don't mind us over here doing our boring jobs while you two carry on in the group chat.

"I'm right here!" Hollis called, skipping down the train platform. "Where's Keats?" she asked.

We all collectively shrugged.

"COOKING SHOWS ARE ALL the rage right now." Beckett held court while we sat together on the patio of the Grand Californian. The group of us enjoyed the last remaining minutes of daylight. Marin slept peacefully on her mom's shoulder, one of many stuffed animals acquired from the day tucked protectively in her elbow.

"He's not wrong," Keats agreed, rubbing at his chin—something I noticed all the Hawthorne brothers did while they considered business things. "And we have an arm of our network that basically creates reality shows."

"I think though you could do something better than just a battle royale style cook-off., I told them. "Beckett's sister-in-law is super popular in College Town, Texas."

"Bourbon City," Beckett corrected me.

"My point was that it's a small town supported by the colleges nearby not that it is actually named college town. Geez, keep up." I winked at him, barely able to contain my laugh.

"And Lyris won't shut up about this chef she profiled, Gemini James." Hollis added, her eyes shining as the momentum of the conversation grew. "She is also a small town, stick to her roots, kind of chef."

"The *former* Chef James, now Gemini *Tate* is from Chicago." Beckett said, the timbre of his voice triumphant that he is more in the know about this chef than either of us were. "She was chef de cuisine for Chef Tobin Laurent. Who incidentally has now opened a restaurant in Austin, near my brother and sister-in-law. But she's not just some small-town diner owner. She just won the James Beard, and I hear she might be up for a Michelin Star."

"Are you and Lyris secretly friends?" Hollis laughed. "Are you in cahoots to get this off the ground? Because she practically spoke from the same talking points."

"We'd need to market test and focus group, obviously," Ellis chimed in. But I like the idea of these amazing women tucked away in various parts of the country, having some kind of chef's table where the rest of the group, let's say maybe eight of them, all come and sample one another's food. It's not necessarily reality, more of a cooking documentary with some lighthearted appeal."

I watched Ellis as he spoke—fluid, focused, entirely in his element. He wasn't appeasing shareholders or worrying about legacy. He was investing his brain power into a dream, without hesitation.

The sun dipped below the horizon, and I was struck by how ordinary the moment seemed. Marin shifted on her mother's shoulder, starting to stir in her half-sleep haze. Hollis playfully snagged the last stuffed mushroom from Beckett's plate. Keats and Beckett volleyed names of chefs while sketching out concepts on an iPad like two kids building a treehouse. And Ellis? Ellis looked at me like I was the only person on the entire damn patio.

How ironic that what felt like a fairy tale day unfolded in the one place devoted to fairy tales.

And when everyone stood and stretched and hugged their goodbyes, it was my own prince charming—hair mussed, hand warm in mine—who pulled me close and whispered, "Come on, sweetheart. Let's go home."

Even if it was just to a hotel room.

25

THE UNFORGIVING MIRROR

ELLIS

Rowan fell asleep practically as soon as we took off and stayed that way through touch down at O'Hare. Not that I minded. There was something deeply peaceful about having the woman you love, curled up against your body, placing her trust in you while she lay defenseless. Even if it was a private jet appointed with every luxury one could need or want.

The woman I *loved*. I said it. Hopefully I showed it enough to convince her how real we were. That I'd come to the realization early on in that ridiculous circus act of Elizabethan marital arrangements, she was the only one who settled and challenged me. Thinking about years spanning out ahead of me, with her by my side, didn't choke me in anxiety or freeze me into a nihilistic pantomime of existence.

While Keats droned on about wanting to jump right into this chef project, I made a visual catalogue of Rowan's delicate features. The soft pink of her cheeks, both from days spent in the sun, and from the cozy blanket I'd asked the flight attendant for. She'd worn her hair braided all day, though the wind, and her sleep had pulled strands loose, those kinked pieces shot out every which way like a crown of copper colored bramble.

Rowan roused just as we touched down, walking herself to our waiting car before dozing off again, face against the coolness of the window. She didn't wake up when we exited the highway to the bustling streets of Old Town, or when Uri pulled into my driveway and the door open chime and interior lights came to life.

"Where are we?" she asked, as I gathered her in my arms.

"We're home." I told her. "My home."

I didn't like the clarification. We'd been in this magical existence for the week, sharing space, and eventually a bed. Now we were back to Chicago where multiple zip codes and one very obnoxious highway separated us. It marked the beginning of the time where we would need to figure out where we went from here. How we navigated a relationship between two busy, working executives. Adding commutes and separate homes into the mix was an annoyance I wanted to eradicate.

"I can walk." Rowan tried to sit up more fully, kicking her legs in my arms in an attempt to slide down out of my arms and to the concrete.

"I know you can. But I like you like this, and I don't want to let you go just yet."

"Okay." She whispered, her lips fluttering against my neck as she tucked herself beneath my chin, arms wrapped protectively around me, as if I'd ever think of dropping her.

Uri opened my front door for me, signaling me inside while he went to collect our luggage. I nodded my thanks at him and continued up the stairs to my bedroom. A place up until that moment, I'd never thought much about. I walked in there every night, sorted my things, lay in my bed and went to sleep in a routine. A pantomime of actually living a full and satisfying life. With her sliding out of her shorts and pulling off her bra beneath the Disney Princess t-shirt she'd purchased at one of the gift shops, watching someone climb beneath the covers in a bed meant to be shared, shifted something that until that very moment I wasn't aware was misaligned.

"I don't know why I'm so tired." She yawned, snuggling beneath the covers and adjusting her head on the pillow. "Mmm, so comfy."

That was the last thing she said before she was out again, a soft smile playing across her lips.

THE FOLLOWING MORNING, I woke up and reached over to an empty bed. Of course, she'd be up early given she'd probably slept for a solid ten hours between the plane, car, and bed. I found her standing at the kitchen counter. Her ridiculous princess shirt stopped at her waist, showing off her cock stiffening pair of cheeky panties. I'd been about to rub said stiff cock against her, when I saw what she was reading over her shoulder. She sensed me behind her, and when she turned to look at me, I saw two amber pools overflowing with empathy.

"I didn't know you ran into her."

She placed her phone on the counter so I could see the grainy picture of Talia and me coming in from the patio. The headline read

"Lover's Quarrel?"

with a subheading that read:

Tensions ran high at the Olympic Media Gala, where exes-turned-industry-rivals Talia Brindley and Ellis Hawthorne appeared to exchange pointed words on the rooftop patio.

"I didn't think I would. Hoped I wouldn't, actually. I've done a pretty good job lately of avoiding industry parties I know she'd be invited to." I smiled but it wasn't really a smile. Sardonic, laced with the same anguish I felt standing in front of her out on that patio. It may have been years since Talia and I broke up, but it hurt like it was yesterday.

"I'm so sorry." Rowan turned and wrapped her arms around me, settling her head on my shoulder. "I guess when we talked about her and you were so quick to write her off, I hadn't realized—" She stopped mid thought. The end of the sentence felt like a noose tightening around my neck.

I moved to stand in front of her, hands on the counter, bracing. "Talia wasn't just an ex. And, while I may have been the one to end it, learning there was never an 'it' to begin with, cut the deepest."

Air rattled in my lungs with the sharp, cleansing breath I needed to get through this story. It had to be done. Half of it was here, flayed, bleeding on my marble counter. I may as well drive the killing blow to it. Maybe then I'd finally be able to exorcise the demon and be at peace.

"She was a journalist," I told Rowan. "You already know that part. We'd met casually, both bored to tears at yet another sailing regatta, a WASPy activity Chicagoans can't get enough of during the summer months."

Talia was a monsoon. Powerful, sharp, sometimes choking, in how fast she could absolutely decimate those who challenged her. But she was also endearing. No one could say no to her smile, especially because it was such a rare occurrence when she was hyper focused and in journalist mode.

"We started dating. Father seemed thrilled, especially because the magazines just loved us. We photographed well and they would write such glowing things about the two of us. What I hadn't realized is that while I was considering whether a solitaire emerald cut suggested the right balance of elegant and understated, she'd been authoring an exposé."

"The Pulitzer?" Rowan took a breath in as she said it, as if the story pieced itself together in her head faster than I could tell it.

I nodded. The words began to feel like jagged glass. I knew I needed to get them out before they cut me so deep, I bled out, but the act of eliminating them began to hurt too much to bear.

"It had started as genuine interest. The more time we spent with my family, the more exposed she was to Father droning on about family legacy and our social responsibility as truth sayers with journalistic integrity given we were one of the first. Her question and the start of her research had been to examine *how* the Hawthornes had been able to become such a global powerhouse starting just a few generations prior as a humble newspaper on the East Coast. The hunt, digging through history, learning the patrilineage had been an adventure for both of us. For me, I became deeply enamored with the *push up your shirtsleeves* work ethic that appeared to be a trait passed through our DNA in the Hawthorne family.

"For her, something changed. The project for Talia went from quiet awe at what we had established, to an exposé on classism, domination of markets, and an *eat the rich* lightning rod. Unfortunately, as her opinions changed, so did her view on our relationship. I was no longer just Ellis the man who loved her. I was Ellis Hawthorne, next in line to inherit an unearned legacy. "

Rowan was raptly attentive. She hadn't so much as taken a sip from her coffee as I extricated the history from the depths of me. I expected her to be put off, to roll her eyes at privileged Ellison Hawthorne, family over all. Instead, when I paused to take a cleansing breath she put her hand on mine, warm and assuring.

"Our relationship crashed and burned in a glorious way." I continued, relieved to be nearly finished. "Most of it stayed out of the papers, because Talia was as invested in public image as the Hawthornes were. But she walked away with battle scars too. Unfortunately for her, too. The Pulitzer committee decimated her story. They found too many gaping holes between fact and emotional fueled supposition. If they had published their review of her story, it would have ended her career. Instead, they offered her the option to withdraw. She blamed me of course. Of the length of reach Hawthornes have.

"But in taking down the family legacy, what she really took apart, was me. The symbol of all she wanted dismantled, even if she had to do it personally with my heart instead of my wallet. She claimed to be in love with me, all the while collecting a Pulitzer package filled with half-truths and cherry picked quotes."

Rowan stood still. Too still. Then she nodded like she understood. As if that one story was the burning bush that provided her with all the information she sought.

"The arm's length, contracted marriage makes so much sense now," she said almost to herself. "I was so sad for you. That you were throwing yourself on a sacrificial pyre just for your father's approval. But contracts you know. They keep you safe. They spell everything out in triplicate. No one can use you or get too close."

I met her gaze, shocked at how close a bullseye she'd struck. "And that is why this, between us, terrifies me."

Was it a mistake to be that honest? Possibly. The shock that reddened her cheeks and puckered her lips told me I'd swung too hard and in the wrong direction.

"You think I'm *using* you?" Her words were half shock, half unabashed affront at the very thought.

"Not actively, no." I tried to pull her in for a hug, but she leaned back, planted her ankles into the tile floor, crossing her arms and staring me down. "But being this real with anyone...it opens me up to the risk *of being* used. Of someone else just wanting me for what I could do for them, then throwing me away when I'm not useful anymore."

It was the most honest and vulnerable I'd ever been in a relationship. I wanted Rowan to know, needed her to know how much power she wielded, especially given how risk averse I was. More than anything though, I wanted her to see that in exposing my fears, I was showing her how real I wanted us to be.

She stared at me for a long beat. Then her voice came, small but sure. "I know what that's like."

I blinked. "What?"

"To be used. To be useful, until I wasn't anymore."

That wasn't the response I'd been preparing myself for. Any number of heart-rending possibilities had fluttered through my mind. Her knowing that apprehension and responding in kind? Wasn't in my mental list of scenarios and outcomes.

She reached for her phone and opened a different tab. A headline about Danny Truzinski, the baseball player from Milwaukee. Mr. *No one mention to Rowan that he's here.*

"He was mine," she said softly.

"Did he say something to you at the gala? If he did, I promise you his career will end much sooner than he anticipated."

"He was at the gala?" Her face paled, and momentarily she swayed as if she were about to faint.

Once she was settled into one of the chairs tucked beneath my kitchen island, I explained what I knew.

"When you went to the restroom at the gala, Beckett mentioned he'd seen Danny at one of the photobooths. He and Hollis got into a very heated discussion about disclosure of that fact."

She simply nodded, barely acknowledging the comment. Her hands gripped her coffee mug, her thumbs tapping out some unheard beat against the side.

"All through college." Rowan eventually continued, "After graduation, I helped manage his press. When I could, I got him press coverage, helped him land a profile with *Sports Illustrated*. HMG didn't know I was dating him. But all the stories I fed to outlets were above board. I never abused my connections. The instant they brought him up from the farm league and he signed with the team's PR agency, he ghosted me. Took everything I gave him—access, visibility, contacts—and handed it to someone who promised him the world. I became footnote in his origin story."

Somewhere between tucking her in last night and now, she'd taken the braids out of her hair. It rested on her shoulders like wavy ribbons. It felt like silk running through my fingers, a feeling I couldn't resist repeating while we continued to talk.

"I'm sorry that I never knew about him. About whatever it is that he did to you. It kills me that Keats knows more about you that I do."

"It's okay," she said in that dismissive way someone does when they don't know what else to say. But I didn't want to be dismissed. You did that to people that didn't mean anything. I wanted her to be mad at me. To rail at me for leaving her alone to navigate through that heartbreak while I stormed in every day, too wrapped in my own shit and insisted she do any number of benign things I probably could have handled myself.

"Love is just another word for leverage." The sad, resigned look in her eyes broke me. I pulled her against my chest, kissing the top of her head, and tightening my hold on her as if I could squeeze out the heartbreak and replace it with my love.

"You hold it until the other person gets what they want." She continued, "and then, they leave."

It felt like the air had been punched out of the room. Her words echoed in my head "the person gets what they want and then they leave." Over and again, in her grief-tinged voice, distant and detached. I wanted to promise her the world. To take the little plastic tie that sat on my counter from the coffee bag and tie it around her finger. To promise her I'd never leave. Tell her she's never been leverage. I wanted to lay my entire world at her feet and tell her to take her pick of things she might want. We were way too new, though. And to Rowan that stuff didn't matter. I learned one thing about her over the years. An observation that probably even Keats never made. Rowan was a giver. Almost to a fault. She gave of herself so much that she poured herself empty. And the way to show a giver they were safe, wasn't to shower them in gifts, but to pour into them the non-tangibles: support, pride, love. And that couldn't be done overnight. It had to be built slowly.

"Maybe we're both just scared," I said. "But if I had to choose someone to be scared with, I'd choose you."

She leaned in slowly, forehead resting against mine. Her words alone were a salve I wanted to bottle and protect like a discovery more precious than the rarest stone.

"I don't want to be scared anymore," she whispered.

"I can't say we won't ever be scared." I promised, "But whenever you are, I'll be right here to help you through it."

Tomorrow, I'd begin to show her what permanence looked like. But today? Today was for safety. For softness. To let her know without a single doubt, that she was mine, and I would choose her every day. This was our last day in the bubble, and I wanted us to revel in every second before the real world came knocking.

26

THE SHAPE OF SAFETY

Rowan

Can you even say the last week of your life felt like a fairytale if the week ended in the place that monetizes fairytales? Because that's what it had been. Not the jet or the fancy parties. Not even when Ellis went and bought me a *dress* and Cartier earrings. The fairytale wasn't in the tangibles.

Sure the moment in front of Cinderella's castle was full of magic. Ellis's genuine smile, that kiss that made my knees weak, and the whispered suggestion of white dresses; all of it made my pulse race. But even in the reality of the moment was the silent, ever-present specter of *optics*. I was paid for optics. Built an entire business around them. But I'd come to despise the word.

What was most magical though, wasn't any of the flashy stuff. It was in the quiet day with Ellis at his house. Waking up next to him. Seeing his beautiful face at total peace as he laid next to me. Even more magical still, was knowing that I was cherished exactly as I was, no need for evaluation sheets or scoring metrics.

"Did you just get this meeting invite too?" I asked Ellis

as he drove us to work. "There's a meeting at *your* offices in a half hour. I guess we can just head straight there and Uri can take me to Pivot after."

I'd been monitoring our developing "story" all weekend. After the story about Talia, I'd been afraid it would snowball. So far, I'd seen nothing. But if we had a last-minute meeting with everyone first thing on Monday morning—there was some story breaking I hadn't heard yet.

"Whatever is it, we'll figure it out." His warm smile set off a riot of flutters deep in my chest. I'd thought the weekend at his house would be weird. It was the first time I'd ever been there.

An actual *house* in Old Town was not what I expected from Mr. Efficient and Predictable. Given his offices were steps from the Hancock I thought for sure he owned a condo in there, or even in nearby Marina Towers with all the other titans of industry, and the occasional sports celebrity. But no. Ellis owned a house. A warm, welcoming house full of rich woods, oversized furniture in soothing autumnal shades, and a back patio with to die for views.

"What's your middle name?" he asked randomly, pulling me from my remembrances.

"That's a strange and random question." I laughed at the tangent of inquiry. We'd gone from discussing a morning meeting to my middle name.

"I was thinking about it last night. You know mine because of all the things you handled for me over the years. But I never had a reason to ask about yours. And since *Keats* seems to know so much about you...much more than I do."

Ellis Hawthorne, communications powerhouse, billionaire who knows how many times over, pouted. Not frowned, not smirked, but *pouted*.

"I can't believe you're jealous of your brother." I laid my

hand on his cheek, gently swiping at his downturned mouth and furrowed eyebrows.

"Not jealous." He replied, "Annoyed that I wasted all these opportunities to get to know you. Instead of gluttonously soaking up every detail like Keats apparently did, I buried my head in a pile of work and never came up for air."

At the next stoplight, he placed his hand on my thigh. His thumb rubbed circular patterns into my thigh, just below where my skirt ended. My body, ever the traitor, primed itself for something tawdry. But the gesture was anything but sexual. It was quietly intimate. A blend of comfort and familiarity. It whispered *I choose you*.

"It's Anastasia." I told him.

"What? Oh, your middle name. Rowan Anastasia Sloane. Fittingly regal. Just as beautiful as the owner of the name."

He squeezed my thigh gently as punctuation to the claim. Ellis turned his car into the HMG garage and slid it into the very first spot closest to the elevator. There was no fancy sign that said *Reserved for the CEO* or *Property of Ellison Hawthorne*, but the move alone spoke of his hierarchal power. Based on the empty spots to the left of his, either his brothers were running late or they'd all chosen to have their drivers bring them in.

Ellis came around to my door, opened it and leaned in, placing a kiss at my temple.

"Keep an open mind," he said, extending his hand. "And try not to freak out."

"With a preface like that why would I be anything but serenely calm?"

He took my hand and led me to the elevators. Not his private elevator that would take us up to the executive floor, but the general use elevator. I watched him press the starred L for lobby, winking at me as he did.

"Is that a wise idea? What if there is press hanging around the lobby? Oh god this isn't *another* optics photo, is it? The cute couple heading in to work together? I would have insisted I go home and get a better suit to wear instead of the semi-casual dress I brought with me to Los Angeles."

He turned, pressing me against the side of the elevator. With my face cradled between his palms, he skated his lips over mine, teasing me with a gentle, pulse fluttering kiss.

"Did I say to trust me and not freak out? I think you missed the day in school when they taught you what a freak out was."

The elevator dinged and the doors slid open, depositing us directly into the lobby. Milo, the building's longtime security guard, greeted us with a grin that could have powered the entire lobby.

"That picture, Mr. Hawthorne—woo lawd! I think I got a sunburn just looking at it."

Who knew that our Disneyland adventure made it all the way to whatever social media site a middle-aged man scrolled through. Ellis, however, blushed clear up to his ears. A sight I never thought I'd see from "The Iceman."

Ellis took both of my hands and walked backward toward a dark-glass storefront just off the lobby, directly across from Milo the security guard, and across the way from a flower shop.

"Wait here for one second." He requested. "And remember, you promised to trust me."

He dashed off before I could say a word, disappearing around the corner, down toward the west-facing street entrance and the hallway leading to the ground floor production studios and warehouse. Before I could even wonder what he was up to, the offices in front of me lit up and Ellis unlocked and pushed through the glass door.

Those two small details would be barely a blip on the radar of an ordinary day if the glass door wasn't embossed with a peony pink Pivot logo.

"Paisley has been working non-stop since we left for Los Angeles to bring your vision to life." Ellis said, pointing toward a nervous looking Paisley waving and smiling as she approached.

"What happened to *our* office?" I asked her. "Did that pipe burst again?"

I couldn't take it all in. There were so many details. Warm, muted sunlight flooded in from the street view windows. Mahogany colored wood floors glistened throughout the space. Beyond the curtains and the black out shades, Michigan Avenue bustled with commuters bustling to work in any number of the surrounding skyscrapers.

I had a new office. He built me a new office! It was modern but incredibly warm and welcoming at the same time. Most of our furniture had been brought over: my apple green sofas with the shades of pink throw pillows. The space was huge. Easily double the size of our current offices. We had small nooks dotting the space with whiteboards and oversized chairs for when the team wanted to congregate. The sleek, glass conference room sat to the right of Paisley's new office space, outfit with every modern convenience I could ever dream of needing.

"You bought me an office?" I asked, running my hand along the antique executive's desk. Behind the desk, floating bookshelves that ran the wide expanse of the wall. They were already dotted with personal effects: a few plants, books, the picture of me and the Pitchfest girls, reframed to match the new aesthetic. And a new photo sat on my desk, sitting in a quiet, Tiffany frame, of Ellis and me in front of Cinderella's castle.

"No, Sweetheart." He wrapped his arms around me and placed a kiss on my head, "You bought yourself an office. I just sourced the location and negotiated your contract. Only a hundred and fifty dollars more than your current rent. And this space is managed by a leasing company—not Hawthorne. So, it's yours, free and clear, with no strings or obligations."

He looked like a man bracing for disappointment. A man waiting for another shoe to drop. But I wouldn't be the next one.

"I'm not running," I said quietly. "Unless it's straight into your arms—to thank you for seeing me."

Given that Ellis stood nearly six feet tall, it was hard to describe him as "melting" into anyone. But that's what it felt like. He melted—emotionally and physically—into me the second those words left my lips.

He pulled me into a kiss worthy of its own fairy tale ending. Thankfully, that kiss was just for the two of us. And, well... Paisley.

"Plus," he added, squeezing my ass and giving it a soft pat, "it's in a prime location."

"I'm not sure how many walk-ins I'll get," I said, turning to survey the street-facing door. "But I can't beat the view."

"No," Ellis chuckled, stepping up beside me, his gaze sweeping over the city. "I meant you're just a private elevator ride away from me."

27

IN THE LIGHT OF ORDINARY JOY

ELLIS

THREE WEEKS since that magical day at Disneyland. The photo of us sat on my desktop, its match I knew was down on the first floor. Having that office space open had felt practically fated. And now, nearly every day, I managed to find a few minutes to sneak down just so I could see Rowan smile when she looked up and saw me standing in her doorway. I lived for moments like that.

Given how addicted I was to controlling every narrative —with her—I didn't care what the press printed about us. Luckily, they loved us. Loved *her*. She was meant for a spotlight. Her quick, quippy wit had every picture snapper eating out of her hand each time we stepped out and they asked her a question.

With her the whole word went quiet. My pulse lowered, I could breathe and exist without a never-ending check list of to-dos. I found myself able to eat dinner, watch a tv show, walk around the block eating ice cream and not have the compulsive need to check my phone and respond to emails. Rowan had shifted me from pantomiming an existence to living life.

"What do you guys think?" Keats asked the group. "The initial focus groups seem to really like this idea."

The idea for this cooking documentary-con-reality show had grown legs fast. Since it became less a competition show and more a cozy profile on inspiring women chefs—we couldn't get the inquires to stop. Not just from small-town chefs either. Heavy hitters with multiple restaurants and network TV shows wanted in.

"Did you put together cost projections?" Whit asked flipping through Keats's prospectus.

"Who is going to lead?" Dash asked, immediately looking panicked. "I can't go to Los Angeles right now, Ellis. You know I'm needed for this UAE deal."

"Keats is going to run point."

It had been a surprise to me that he not only suggested the need for someone to relocate to Los Angeles for launch and initial season but enthusiastically offered to be the one to do it.

"Beckett Murray, huh?" Whit said. "Kid's got star power right now. The networks love him. I've never seen one athlete's face on so many network gigs."

"Careful Whit," Keats joked, tossing a foam basketball my way. "Ellis still isn't convinced that Murray didn't take his girlfriend to pound town."

"They're just friends." I rolled my eyes before whipping the basketball back toward him. He reacted a second too late and it landed with a satisfying smack right against his chin. "Fuck man—that hurt!"

I pretended to feel bad. Even help my hands up in mock apology. That didn't stop him from seeking retribution with a fireball of his own. Unfortunately for him, I expected it and batted it away with ease.

"Girlfriend, huh?" Dash smirked at me before making

juvenile kissing noises. "Father will be thrilled that Mr. Obedient Lap Dog locked it down in record time. Maybe that will take the heat off the rest of us."

Lap dog. The little shit.

"Easy to exist in glass houses when you're not the one responsible for sitting at the helm of the ship." I tossed back, not wanting our executive meeting to denigrate into a pissing contest.

"Am I interrupting?" Rowan's sweet voice carried through the crack in my door, her knuckles gently rapping on it before entering.

"See that, Dash." Keats knocked against Dash's knee with his foot. "If you find yourself a girlfriend, maybe *she* can come up for a little afternoon delight too."

"I'm out." Whit stood and gathered his laptop and assorted papers. "Keats you're coming with me; we need to figure out a timeline for this project before I bring it to the board. Dash—go do whatever it is you do."

Whitman Hawthorne, ladies and gentlemen, the best wingman I had. He knew that any suggestion of Dash not working as hard as the rest of us would have him sprinting out of my office to go and prove he was just as busy as the rest of us.

"Pitchfest tonight?" Keats asked, kissing Rowan on the cheek as he walked past. It wasn't lost on me that he said it just to get under my skin. I wouldn't give him the satisfaction.

"Stop." Rowan playfully smacked at his chest. "You're just trying to start something. Pitchfest the first *Wednesday* of the month, not Tuesday. Between that and your afternoon delight comment, you have lost out on the contents of this bag I picked up just for you guys."

"Do I smell Theo's?" Whit poked his head back around the side of the door.

"Can I have lunch with my girlfriend please?" I shot Whit a dirty look before turning Keats around by the shoulder and escorting him out as well.

With my brothers gone and the door to my office closed, I could finally focus on the ravishing beauty casually leaning against my desk with a bag from Theo's for lunch. The diner was legendary for Chicago locals. It was nearly impossible to find, unless you walked there. Navigating Lower Wacker in a car was not a fate most would wish on their worst enemy.

"Did you walk all the way to Theo's in this?" I asked, running my hand from the hem of her far too sexy, summer dress down to a pair of strappy heels with the tiniest heel I'd ever seen. Chicago was in the midst of a surprise heat wave. Winter got tired of wintering, spring never showed, and the city vaulted straight into summer."

"I did." She smiled, cradling the bag against her chest. "I was downstairs, staring at a picture that is strikingly similar to that one." She nodded her head in the direction of my picture, "Thinking what an amazing man I have and how incredibly lucky I am. And I saw the time, checked your calendar, and figured you must be famished given all your meetings today."

I pulled her between my legs, loving the feel of her silken skin and the soft cotton of her deceptively sweet sundress. Her usually milk white skin still held on to the last remnants of the tan she'd gotten in Los Angeles. The white dress with sweet yellow flowers patterned across it, made her look like as innocent as a schoolgirl skipping to town with a basket and ribboned hat.

"You're right about one thing." I swiveled my chair,

positioning myself so she stood directly between my open legs. "I am absolutely famished."

"Ellis! Morgan is *right there!*" She gestured to the other side of my office door, where I knew that Morgan was listening to an Audiobook through AirPods she thought her long, dark hair hid.

"I guess that means you'll just have to be extra quiet." I skated my hands up her thighs, beneath her dress, pressing her into my desk as I did.

"Miss Sloane!" Even I heard the surprise in my voice. "You come in here feigning sweet innocence and yet you walk in here, lean against my desk *with no panties on.*"

My hands were on her hips and maneuvering her onto the desk in a nanosecond. Theo's was a distant memory given I was staring straight at my girlfriend's gorgeous pussy, ready to be devoured.

"Put the bag on the desk, Miss Sloane." I told her, as I pressed her legs open, and folded her innocent fucking dress up over her hips. If I didn't get my mouth on her in the next sixty seconds, I was going to combust. Lunch could wait. She couldn't.

"Oh but Mister Hawthorne," she pulled her voice up super high and whispery. "I need to get back to my desk otherwise my boss is going to so mad at me. I'm not supposed to be up here on the executive's floor."

"You tell me who your boss is, Miss Sloane. I'll make sure he knows what an incredibly good girl you are."

I dipped my head and ghosted my lips across her thigh. She startled with the first press of my mouth, accidentally opening herself even further to my exploration. Her giggle was mischief coated in temptation. She leaned back on a bliss-filled sigh, allowing me to position her thighs over my shoulders.

"This will definitely be frowned upon by HR." She told me on a quiet moan as my tongue swept through her damp slit. "There's definitely verbiage in the handbook about fraternization."

"My sweet little sorority girl should love fraternizing." I nibbled at her thigh trying to control my wide smile.

"Worst joke." Her voice was whisper quiet, but it shook with the tense control of someone trying desperately not to get any louder.

"Then I guess you can lean back and rest easy knowing that I am the one that rewrote the handbook last quarter," I said, before directing my tongue through her sweet slit a second time, earning me a barely controlled whine.

"Oh?" she said, her voice tense as she continued to attempt to control her volume. "And you added a clause about laying your girlfriend on your desk and eating her within an inch of her life?"

"Oh Sweetheart, I haven't even gotten started. If you're already hopping on the bus to the great thereafter, I have not been tending to you very well. We may need to go home right now so that I can spend all day convincing you the difference between light play and soul searing pleasure."

I loved how her ass wiggled across my desk. Her desperation continued to wind tight. Rather than give her what her hips were begging for, I blew across her damp pussy, loving how out of her head she was becoming. All for me.

"Section 4.2." I told her, knowing she'd long forgotten we were in the midst of bantering about pretend HR codes. "I remember very specifically adding a paragraph about exceptional personnel being rewarded, on-site."

Her laughter filled my being with sunshine. As much as I wanted to relish in that feeing, I had more important things to tend to. The moment I flattened my tongue and doubled down on showing Rowan what heaven looked like, that laugh broke into a *not quiet* languorous moan.

"The Hawthorne attorneys may have a different interpretation of on-site rewards." She panted, lifting her hips and bringing them as close to my mouth as she was able to given my hand had them imprisoned.

"Well, sweetheart, I always keep copies of everything I sign or revise. In triplicate. One for legal, one for compliance, and one to keep in my desk for moments like this. Now show me what a good girl you are. Open wide and get ready to scream."

"Just so we're clear." I told her as we gathered up the remnants of our actual lunch. "That was an appetizer. The main course will be served tonight, my place. Multiple courses are promised. I'll come down and collect you, just tell me what time."

"Can't." She stood, smoothing down her dress, checking the back in the reflection from the window. "The Gateway Green committee is finally back from spring break. It's my first meeting on the planning committee for Green Tie Ball."

Being with her was effortless. I spent every day trying to find ways to see and be near her. The days we couldn't because of our insane schedules, I pined for her like a lonely puppy. I'd sailed far beyond smitten with Rowan Sloane and fell headfirst into love.

"Wow, the Green Tie Ball Planning Committee. What

an honor. You know people wait years to be tapped by Sweenie VanMeter." I wiped some errant lipstick from the side of her lip, pressing a gentle kiss to mouth before patting her lovely—albeit pantyless—ass.

"You know I was thinking the *exact same thing*." Rowan wrapped her arms around my neck, her hair swishing behind her back in long, copper colored ringlets. "One day, out of the blue, comes an invite from Sweenie. Never met the lady but suddenly she tells me that one of her very generous benefactors mentioned in passing that she needed someone like me to help her plan the 30th Anniversary. And like that—" she snapped her fingers, her smile dialed up to full wattage, "I have an invite."

"That benefactor sounds *very* generous. He's probably super smart and dashingly handsome."

"Mmhmm," Rowan whispered solemnly, "Though I hear he is a repeat offender with HR violations."

"Go on and take that ass out of here before you make me violate them again."

I pulled her in for a last kiss before releasing her. She grabbed the lunch bag and brought it with her, I assumed to go disburse her "gifts" to my undeserving brothers. Unfortunately, I had three back-to-back meetings to round out the rest of my afternoon.

> Rowan: Ellison Orwell Hawthorne! Morgan was BEET RED when I came out. She couldn't even make eye contact with me.

Ellis: 🙄 🙈 😌

> Rowan: Ellis Hawthorne, CEO , Medill graduate, loquacious public speaker who texts like a thirteen-year-old boy.

> Rowan: This is the best you've got? Seriously?

Ellis: I save the good stuff for when I'm trying to get in your pants. 😏 And since you're not wearing any, and I'm still wearing the evidence of you coming against my tongue, clearly you don't need my "A" game right now.

Ellis: Now stop sending me flirty texts or I'll have to report you to HR. Section 4.2 does not cover sexual advances made via internal messaging.

> Rowan: Good to know. Remind me tonight to redraft Section 4.3 "Retaliation." I'll be sure to give you a preview of the statutes and limitations tonight. 😉

LIT FROM THE WRONG ANGLE

Rowan

It was my first meeting with the Gateway Green and I hadn't heard a single word Sweenie VanMeter said. There I sat, in the opulence of The Astor Club, one of Chicago's most exclusive members only clubs—even more so than Ellis's membership at University Club—and my mind was on the dirty fucking texts coming from Mr. Ellis Hawthorne himself. If I were to be distracted at all it should be with my surroundings. Or with the committee members themselves. Ellis hadn't been joking—these women were married to the city's most powerful men. Politicians, old money steel and rail families, dot com "new money" wives, I couldn't wrap my head around it. These were the people in Ellis's social circle. Meanwhile I'm shocked they didn't run a credit check just for me to walk through the door with a "guest" placard pinned to my dress.

> Ellis: Sitting at home, trying to watch TV but I can barely see anything with this getting in my way
>
> Ellis: [Image Attached]

It was a picture of his hard fucking cock—hidden beneath a pair of basketball shorts thank god.

> Ellis: If you're wondering if I'm thinking about you in that sweetly sexy dress with no panties on I am.

I felt the flush creep clear up to the tips of my ears. I had to turn my Apple Watch into my wrist so no one could read his dirty messages.

> Me: Did you know they meet at The Astor Club? This place is insane. Everyone is looking at me like they know I'm way too poor to have a membership here.

> Ellis: Only because Kennedy Walker is a member there and she's married to Sweenie's nephew. On her side, not her husbands.

> Ellis: Sweenie's sister, Bunny, has VanMeter money but her husband didn't come from legacy money and has blown through most of Bunny's. But their son, Philip, was lucky and invested in the ground floor of some of the more famous tech companies. He has money, but it's new. Not legacy.

> Me: Jesus. Okay Dallas. Let me know when you find out who shot JR.

> Ellis: Probably more Dynasty than Dallas. Dallas was all about oil—and new money oil, not old money oil barons. And you're way too young to be throwing out 'Who Shot J.R.' references. What's next, Murder, She Wrote and early bird specials?

> Rowan: You make my eyes cross.

> Ellis: Tell me something I don't know 😉 I make your legs shake too.
>
> > Rowan: Oh geez 😳 I walked right into that one 🙈
>
> Ellis: Just like you did this afternoon, except hopefully you're wearing panties now. Otherwise, we may need to have a talk about acceptable attire to be gallivanting around town in when you still have the memory of my tongue on your pussy. 😈
>
> > Rowan: 😒 I am trying to pay attention. It's bad enough they think I'm an interloper who is only here because of Ellis Hawthorne money. I don't want to also appear like I can't even be bothered to pay attention.
>
> Ellis: You want to be a member there?

He texted after a beat. I tried not to outwardly show the level of shock I felt that he could so casually suggest membership at a club he deemed too "new money" for anyone to take seriously. Just to make his girlfriend comfortable.

> Ellis: I can have Morgan send over the paperwork in the morning.
>
> > Rowan: Ellis! Be serious. The initiation fee here is more than I make in a year. And that's just the initiation fee! I can't imagine what monthly dues are.

> Ellis: Surprisingly they're only about $500 a month. The people who belong to clubs like Astor are the ones who care about others knowing how wealthy they are.
>
> Ellis: If I were you I wouldn't give a shit what any of those assholes think about you.
>
> Ellis: But… I have it on good authority though that your boyfriend would send over the initiation fee and a lifetime membership in a heartbeat if you really wanted to join.

I was about to text him that he was crazy and no freaking way did I want to join, especially for not that kind of coin when another message came through.

> Ellis: And…if you're a really good girl and ask nicely. 😉

"What do you think Rowan?" Someone—I think her name was Miriam—snapped my attention back to the meeting.

"I'm so sorry." I held up my phone as proof, "Crisis with one of my clients. What were we discussing?"

"Change of venue for the thirtieth. We've always loved being at Navy Pier but given it's a pretty big event and with Sweenie stepping down, we just feel like it needs to be somewhere grand."

My watch buzzed in concert with my phone lighting up. Ellis. Again.

> Ellis: Are you sitting there with a huge smile on your face thinking about my tongue in you this afternoon? Because I can still taste you. So warm and tasty. The way you call my name just before you come. It's heaven against my mouth and in my ears.

"A change of venue is definitely a great idea." I agree. "Will the change of venue impact the budget?"

"Well," Sweenie winked at me. "That depends on our what our legacy benefactor donates this year."

The rest of the women snickered like they were in on a joke I missed.

> Me: Who is the legacy benefactor of Gateway Green?

I send the text to Ellis, though I was ninety percent sure I already knew the answer. Well, a fifty/fifty guess anyway.

> Ellis: Your poor sex addled brain.
>
> Ellis: You already know who the legacy benefactor is.
>
> Ellis: Aside from mentioning it just recently, I'm certain you were the one that had to send over all those gift bags for the ball when you worked for me.
>
> Me: Of COURSE you are. That explains why Sweenie fell over herself to get me on her board
>
> Ellis: You deserve to be on that board regardless. They need new blood with fresh ideas.

"I'll be sure to check with that benefactor and get back to you. I'm sure he'll be amenable to sourcing new locations." I told them, biting the inside of my cheek so as not to give away the dirty thoughts in my head on fun ways to entice him to be amendable.

Pitchfest Group Chat:

> Lyris: Uhhh, Rowan. You may want to check this out.
>
> Lyris dropped a link to a livestream that was happening at that very moment. Constance Ashcroft. That little society princess had the gall to be putting Ellis on blast via social media?

"And I'm not going to keep pretending I didn't see what I saw". Constance sat on her couch, wineglass in hand spinning her tale like she sat on a reality tv show casting couch. *"A few weeks ago, I was one of the women selected to date Ellis Hawthorne. Yes, that Ellis. The same Ellis who's now suddenly playing America's most eligible boyfriend on social media. Only, here's the thing—none of it was real. We were vetted and cast. An audition to be the wife of one of America's most eligible billionaires..."*

> Hollis: OMFG
>
> Greer: Sweet mother of Jesus • • Is this true?

> *"And the woman who orchestrated the whole thing? Surprise, surprise—it's the one he's now supposedly 'madly in love' with."* She air quoted her words, wineglass still in hand. *"'From business to fairy tale'? Please. They're selling you a story, and you're all inhaling it like a fat girl at a buffet."*

I needed to get home. To Ellis's house I meant, not my home. If this was exploding on social media, we'd need to figure out a pivot immediately.

> Greer: He was paying you to find him a fiancée?
>
> Lyrics: Damn…and he fell in love with you instead? Stop. 💀 I can't with you two.
>
> Hollis: This sounds bad Rowan. Are you okay?

"I'm so sorry to cut out early ladies." I announced to the room, "I just received a message from a client, and I am urgently needed to handle some crisis communication."

> *"Maybe we should be asking what kind of man needs to fake a relationship to look trustworthy enough to lead a company? And what kind of woman is willing to play along?"*

I didn't even wait to go through the theater of social graces with the fifteen-minute goodbye. I just grabbed my bag and dashed out the front door. Even waiting for the valet to bring my car around felt like torture.

She signed an NDA. That thought screamed louder than traffic all the way to Ellis's house. *How on earth could she do this?* She had to be insane. NDA's meant something, didn't they?

Ellis's front door was unlocked. He'd been expecting me to come over, so naturally it would be. I didn't have a key. But it should have connected a bit faster that the door was unlocked. He'd wanted me to come in without him needing to get up from wherever he was in his house, to answer the door.

"Ellis!" I could hear the panic in my voice as I threw open his front door and rushed toward the back of his house. "We've got a problem."

There were a million scenarios flying through my head. What to say, who to call first. Well, the lawyers, obviously. But after that, we needed to get ahead of the story. Surely being media magnates they had connections at the different outlets. Other than the gossip rags, I couldn't imagine any actual news stations would pick up the story.

Suddenly, the words died on my lips. Ellis Hawthorne, reclined, naked in one of the leather wingback chairs in his study, cock hard and at the ready.

"Miss Sloane." He drawled, lazily stroking his cock. "Did you rush here because the thought of sitting there for one more second droning on about coordinating cocktail napkins was too much to handle? We both know all you wanted was to come home and take a ride on this."

"Put your cock away."

I couldn't believe in my reality I had to say things like that.

"We have a big problem on our hands."

"Bigger than what's in mine?" He smirked, not caring that I'd basically sprinted into his office like a crazy woman.

"Ellis, I'm serious. Constance is live-streaming right now, blowing the whole search for a fiancée clear out of the water."

He looked surprised—less shaken than I was—but had at least stopped stroking himself, phone now taking priority over his erection.

"How could she be so stupidly naïve?" Ellis asked. I think it was a rhetorical question. I didn't reply. "Doesn't she know that NDA she signed is airtight?"

He stood, scrolling through his phone, evidently finding the desired contact, he strolled out of the library and took the stairs up to his bedroom two at a time.

"Mark? Ellis Hawthorne. I have a situation we need to get our arms around."

Mark? Surely, he didn't have the personal cell phone of *that* Mark. Did he?

29

DAMAGE CONTROL

ELLIS

Constance Ashcroft, *of course*. A woman who'd spent her entire adult life trying to curate proximity to power was never going to handle being benched with grace.

"She's live right now. It's already going viral," Rowan said breathlessly.

It would be taken care of. From every avenue. As soon as I got some pants on.

I dialed Mark first. Not *my lawyer*. Not PR. *Mark*. The CEO of the very platform Constance was streaming on.

"We've got an issue on your platform that needs to come down. Immediately." I continued as I paced the floor to my office. "Her creator ID ends in 6337. It's in violation of a legally binding NDA and slander adjacent." A beat passed. "You know I wouldn't call unless it was urgent. I'll expect confirmation in five."

I ended the call before he could argue. He wouldn't. Not with the kind of investment capital HMG injected into emerging verticals last quarter. Rowan followed behind me into my office, but I stopped and turned, gesturing for her to stay put.

"Get in touch with Paisley, we'll need her on strategy right away. And text Whit. Make sure both Paisley and Morgan are looped in with whatever discussions we have with Whit."

The call with my lawyer, Anthony, lasted all of twelve minutes. Eleven of those were spent identifying exactly which clauses Constance Ashcroft had just obliterated in her NDA. She hadn't just breached the contract—she detonated it. Live, with a wine glass in hand and a smug little smirk like she thought she was the victim in some dating reality show plot twist.

"She'll be receiving a cease and desist before the livestream is even archived," Anthony assured me. "We'll pursue financial penalties. Her trust fund can take the hit."

Good. I wanted her to feel it.

Rowan stood across the room, still tense from the drive over, arms folded, eyes wild with worry. I wanted to pull her into my arms and tell her I had it handled, that nothing—no entitled socialite with a bruised ego and a social media following—was going to shake what we had. But right now, she needed a strategist. Not a boyfriend.

"Sit," I told her, "Please." I added, trying to gentle my voice despite my annoyance at the situation. "I need twenty minutes to clean up the mess. Then we'll deal with the optics together."

I was getting so tired of dealing with optics. I hated the very word. I was such an idiot. I should have told my father to fuck right off when he suggested this whole stupid thing.

I had barely put my phone down when Whit and Keats walked in without knocking. Dash followed, slower, typing furiously on his phone as he walked.

"She's trending," Keats said, tossing his phone on my

coffee table. "#ConstanceSays is already over two hundred thousand tweets. Her story's gone viral."

"I'm aware."

"We need to get ahead of this," Whit said, tugging at the cuffs of his suit jacket. "Constance violated her NDA. That'll help with credibility, but we can't assume the other three won't start sniffing around for attention too."

"It will be wiped from social media in a matter of minutes. I've already spoken with Mark."

Rowan looked as if she'd just witnessed a major car accident on the expressway. Her normally creamy skin looked gaunt and tight. Her eyes still hadn't lost that wild eyed panic she'd had when she stormed through my front door.

This was not how I'd wanted out evening to go.

"They all signed ironclad NDAs," Whit said, but his tone said *but that didn't stop Constance*. He sat on the edge of my desk and crossed one ankle over his knee. "Let me handle the other women, just in case they get a case of *monkey see monkey do*. I'll send something direct—calm, but firm. A little reminder about the confidentiality clauses. And a quiet bullet point list of what happens when you break them."

"What will happen to Constance?" Rowan asked, moving into my arm when I opened it for her to snuggle in to.

"She'll be required to issue a retraction. She'll suffer financial penalties. The normal legal reprimands that come as a result of knowingly violating an NDA." Whit said smoothly, flicking his hand into the air with casual grace.

"What she isn't expecting is the social fall out." Ellis added, "She'll be uninvited from every single event Sweenie VanMeter or the rest of her group has ever touched. Her social life is already beginning to collapse. By Friday, she'll be a cautionary tale, not a headline."

Lucky for us, Constance had chosen a social network to post her livestream. One that had very long arms and corporate control over many of the feeder networks that those livestreams would sit on. That allowed us to take control of her narrative *very* quickly. It would cost me for sure. I could expect to have to write some *very* big checks relating to global sustainability research, and microcomputers.

By Friday the story was just a murmur. Whit had personally reminded the other women about their legally binding silence. Dash, the one who handled Father the best, managed to talk him off a cliff and not rail into me for my "stupidity." Despite him hating how I'd gone about satisfying his requirement, it still stood—and we were *all* expected to show up at his retirement party with a woman on our arm. One that wore a sparkling piece of jewelry on the fourth finger of their left hand.

"Hi stranger." Rowan floated into my office, the satisfaction of a successful pivot with very little firestorm glowed on her skin like Olympic victory.

"Yet another sundress." I pulled her on to my lap the moment she bent in close to give me a kiss. "I wonder what's underneath."

Her scandalized laughter was my drug. I'd take a hit from that needle every day for the rest of my life if she'd let me. There was nothing more I loved than making her blush or flush with desire while laughing concurrently.

"Rowan Anastasia Sloane!" My fingers gently stroked the soft hair between her legs. "Once could be written off as a walk on the wild side. A *throw caution to the wind* moment to surprise and titillate your boyfriend. But *twice?* Tell me what I should be thinking when you walk in here like this?"

She turned, throwing her leg over my hip, opening herself to me across my lap. My hands immediately went under her green cotton dress, up her thighs, to her exposed slit. She leaned over, sliding her lips across mine, taking her time to taste every inch of my mouth.

"You should be thinking that Morgan is on lunch, Whit is behind closed doors on some call, Keats is having lunch with Hollis to talk about that chef show, and who the hell knows where Dash is. But we have the executive wing all to ourselves. At least for the next thirty minutes.

I pulled her hair out of its graceful chignon, watching it fall in waves around her face and down her back.

"There are no words to describe how beautiful you are."

Truths fell out of me every time she was around. Telling her what I felt had become the most effortless thing I'd ever experienced. Being with her, loving her, was heaven on earth.

"There is a lot of talking going on for someone who missed out his grand finale on Tuesday. I'm pretty sure we pressed pause right around the time you surprised me, hard and ready."

She ground against me, her lips tickling down my neck while she whispered in my ear. When I didn't rally fast enough for her liking, her hand undid my belt, took down my zipper, and dipped inside my pants to work me to proper attention.

"Mm, now who is the one being good?" She purred with the heady confidence of Domme in leather boots with a riding crop. I didn't know where she suddenly found the inspiration, or the motivation to come *work out some tension*, but I dug it. I more than dug it. I was drawn up by my balls, and ready to beg for her to sheath me so I could pillage her like a pirate on a newly discovered island.

"There is a condom in my top drawer." I told her between heated kisses. "You have exactly thirty seconds to get it on, or I'm taking you bare."

It was an empty threat. I wouldn't do that without discussions. But if there was anyone I wanted to go bare with, it was her. The notion didn't even scare me. I'd spent every decade since my first sexual experience with Annie Templeton the summer before college, making sure I never went exploring without my rain slicker. That was something Father had drilled into our heads nonstop from the moment our voices started changing. As I'd gotten older, I understood why Father had been so obsessive. Some women would stop at nothing to bag a billionaire and lock him into eighteen years of easy money.

Rowan lowered herself on my covered cock, rocking her hips in seductive circles as she buried my length in her warm body.

"I'll never get used to this." She sighed, swaying against my pelvis. Her rhythm was both lazy and frenetic simultaneously. Each time she lifted off my body, her legs quivered as if the pleasure was too much to contain, and each slow, tortuous press back down, she groaned from somewhere deep in her chest. Her seduction was an experience in senses.

The light tickle of her fingers against my shirt, her muscular legs pressed against my thighs, the wet warmth that encircled my cock and dripped like heaven's manna making her motions more fluid with each push and pull. Her lips, swollen from our heated kisses, hung open, gasping for breath as we spirited up the summit like we were being chased.

"We'll take our time when we get home." She promised.

When we get home. We. Home. Words that meant so much more.

"Come with me Ellis. I'm almost there."

I lifted my hips, bouncing her on my cock as I tried to take over the pace.

"I'm right there with you sweetheart. Jump and I jump with you."

And we did. Every time we did, I fell harder, deeper in love with the one woman I'd never seen coming.

"Hey... Hollis just dropped a link about Danny Truzinski into our group chat."

After we cleaned up, she and I relaxed on the sofa in my office. I had a million things that needed to be handled, and my alerts told me I had an upcoming meeting in fifteen minutes. I was tempted to text one of my brothers and make them attend for me and take Rowan to lunch. I wasn't ready for her to leave just yet.

"Oh?" I asked, feigning ignorance. "The old flame?"

She rolled her eyes in my direction. "Oh yeah, him. As if you don't remember."

"What's the story about?" I asked, pulling her against my chest, seeing the headline on the story she read from her phone.

"Famed Short Stop Suspended on Suspicion of Gambling"

In order for *our* story to disappear off the radar of the news outlets, something needed to be fed in its place. If we gave it a little push to make sure our story got shouted over by something even bigger, what was the harm? Other than to the person the story was about. And that, I didn't feel bad about.

"You're telling me you had nothing to do with this?" She looked up at me, a questioning smirk compressing her lips and squinting her eyes. "Seems awfully coincidental, I tell you about us and suddenly here he is front and center in the press. Is the story at least true or are you ruining some man's career into the ground because of some caveman need to piss on me and mark your territory."

"I can't help it if *your* best friend happens to have a brother who is a world-famous poker player who *may* have seen him in Vegas hanging out in the sports betting section of an elite casino. I didn't report the story." I told her, trying to feign innocence. "I simply made it very easy for *other* people to find the story."

"Jesus Ellis." She tried to stand up, but I held her in place, kissing the fight off her mouth and hoping for the best. "Should I do a quick google of Andy Wilson too? Maybe there's something on him you may want to publish because god forbid, he hold your girlfriend's vCard."

This woman.

"Did he hurt you?" I asked.

"Who? Andy? No. God no. What the hell Ellis?"

"Then I don't care about needle dick Andy Wilson and

how he initiated you into sex with probably a three pump and dump experience. Danny though? Is a piece of shit. I won't apologize for defending my girlfriend against *anyone* who tries to hurt you. Past or present."

She stared at me for a long beat. There was a determined look she got when she was weighing options. It was strange in the sense that I'd never really homed in on women's facial expressions before her. But I knew the look. Recognized it. She was trying to decide whether she wanted to be mad at me or move past it.

"You're lucky you're rich," she joked. "If it wasn't for that private plane, and the top notch oral, you'd be toast Hawthorne."

I grinned. "Baby, I'm lucky you're mine. And I'll burn through every dollar I've got to make sure you always know it."

Her expression softened, those amber eyes getting misty around the edges. "I just want one week without someone coming for our throats. No drama. No PR crises. Just quiet."

"Then I'd suggest you not answer your phone or read your email." I murmured, pulling her closer. "Because I just received a request to increase funding so the Green Tie Ball can move to a new venue. Sweenie volunteered *you* to present it to the board."

"Of course she did." Her melodramatic groan was Oscar worthy. My laugh couldn't have been more genuine. For now, those stolen, quiet moments were enough.

30

THROUGH SOMEONE ELSE'S LENS

Rowan

IT WAS MORE an inconvenience than anything; this presentation for the Gateway Green to find a new location for Green Tie Ball. I wasn't sure why we needed to go through the theater of presenting anything when Ellis had basically opened his checkbook and asked, "how much?"

I learned, however, HMG wrote the checks. Ellis wasn't a *personal* benefactor, the company was. Because of that, the entirety of the board had to sign off on it. Which included Nathan Hawthorne, all the brothers, and the heads of some of the various arms of the company. Thirteen in total.

It was a formality, really. Ellis told me Whit already had the request entered and was just waiting on the official nod to cut the check. While volunteering with the charity was something that would help in the long run, my poor adrenal system couldn't handle another roller coaster week of juggling more things on fire while doing my own work, concurrently.

Mama needed a weekend at a spa. Somewhere warm, where they'd bring me bottomless mimosas and scoop my gelatinous form up from one treatment table and usher me into the next. I wondered off hand if Ellis had ever been to a spa. Given how uptight he was, I doubted he'd even enjoy the quiet.

"You nailed it!" Ellis led me by the hand into his office, shutting the door behind us. We'd left the board with Sweenie once we wrapped up the presentation and received the official nod from Nathan. Both of us excusing ourselves under the guise of work needing our attention.

"That was the longest I've ever seen Dash pay attention to anything," I said. "Trouble in paradise with Miss Italy perhaps?"

"You are the only woman I know who can confidently pitch legacy donors in four-inch heels while simultaneously wondering what scandalous things one of said board members is doing on his phone."

His lips graced across my knuckles before inching higher up my arm until he landed at my neck, sucking gently on my pulse point.

"What does your afternoon look like?" he asked, "Are you interested in having lunch with me?"

"Lunch as in actually going somewhere and eating?" I asked turning into his kiss, "Or the kind of lunch that has me spread on your desk and Morgan wishing she liked Death Metal?"

"Miss Sloane—you are absolutely insatiable. I'm beginning to think you only like me for my sexual talents."

Before I could come up with an equally witty rebuttal, Whit stormed it, not bothering to knock.

"Sorry," Whit said, waving a file folder in the air as he stepped inside. "I'll be quick, promise. I just have a weird charge that doesn't have a corresponding invoice and isn't making any sense."

Ellis stiffened, putting his body between me and Whit. I wasn't even in a compromising position. Sure, it may be inappropriate to be sitting on his desk, but I was fully dressed and wearing panties.

"Later, Whit. As you can see, I'm busy."

"It's literally one question. Don't be a drama queen." Whit dropped the folder on Ellis's desk. "George Brown is billing us for freelance hours on April fourteenth? There weren't any stories on the docket that day. But he's charging us for two hours of freelance photography. Editorial said they never hired him."

April 14th sounded so familiar the hair on my arms raised. I pulled out my phone, scrolling through my calendar as the two of them discussed the photographer. That was the day that Ellis and I had our meeting at the University Club. After he'd gone on his dates. When he kissed me.

No. It had to be a coincidence. The company had a million stories they worked simultaneously, and surely just as many photographers working on them. I looked over at Ellis and his face was an unreadable mask.

"Maybe the invoice should go to Marketing instead of Editorial. They use our freelance photographers for social media posts." Ellis dismissed Whit's inquiries with an impatient wave.

"Accounting already researched every avenue before it made it to my desk." Whit pulled out his phone and began dialing a number assumedly on the invoice. It rang once and a deep baritone voice answered.

"Hey George—its Whitman Hawthorne, HMG. Quick question. I have an invoice from you, number 04160312. My accounting team is having a hard time pairing this invoice with any work orders. Could you tell me where you were working for us that day?"

"Uh, sure. That was at the University Club," the photographer said easily. "You guys asked for a few discreet candids. Pretty sure I sent them to a Morgan Rosenthal after. Pictures were of a guy in a navy suit, woman with red hair. I think she was in like a light brown business suit. Good stuff—one of 'em kind of exploded online. I assumed you knew that."

The silence that followed felt like the quiet of a nuclear fallout. The absence of a single word spoken from anyone created a vacuum of silence that made my ears ring. Whit looked as if he'd accidentally run over someone's pet. While Ellis? His face had shifted from warm and flirty to ice cold in a nanosecond.

"Oh. That makes sense. Yes, that was a successful story. Thank you, George. Excellent work."

Whit disconnected, staring between Ellis and me. The tension kept twisting the three of us, the pressure threatening to bend us to the point of breaking.

"Ellis?" Whit asked.

He didn't say anything. He just shook his head, his eyes darkening from warm chocolate to stormy black.

No.

It couldn't be.

Ellis wouldn't do that to me, would he?

Suddenly my voice wouldn't work. My lungs wouldn't deliver air; my mouth had dried up to the point my tongue lay tacky and immobile against my teeth. I needed to get out of there.

"Rowan."

I held my hands up. I couldn't be around Ellis. The

room suddenly seemed freakishly long. Like a room reflected in one of those funhouse mirrors.

I stumbled toward the door, Whit catching me before I face planted right into the door.

"Please, Rowan. Say something." Ellis was at my side in one long stride.

"You *paid someone* to take pictures of us?" I spoke the words but they didn't make sense. My brain tried desperately to take the sounds coming out of my mouth and process them in a way that I could understand.

Ellis held me by the shoulders, his voice was measured but I saw true panic causing the iris in his eyes to narrow. "I didn't expect it to go viral. It was just supposed to be a backup. Something to buy us some time. I knew it was you," he said. "As soon as those dates were over. I knew there was just you. But I didn't know how long it would take you to see it too. I just wanted it in case my father pushed too hard on this stupid deadline. I didn't want to rush you. I wanted to woo you—"

I held up my hand, cutting him off. "So the photo wasn't an accident. It wasn't even about optics? You planned it?"

"Rowan, please. Just let me explain." He pressed.

"You know." Whit pressed gently against Ellis's chest. "Maybe let's press pause on this conversation. "Rowan looks pretty overwhelmed. Give her a minute to process."

I didn't need his stupid collusive brother to step in and be my intermediary. He was just as bad as Ellis was. The lot of them. Fucking optics. *Legacy*. Stupid, ridiculous rules declared with heavy handed patriarchal superiority.

I pushed past both of them and stormed to the elevator. Thankfully, whether because of Whit or his own good sense, no one followed me. No one followed me.

All this time, I thought we were the story. But I was just another headline.

***

IT HAD BEEN FOUR DAYS. Four long, quiet, terrible days since everything unraveled. I'd asked Ellis to give me some space, and he obliged. Of course he would. The man who built his life on legacy and toeing the line wouldn't break through someone's boundary just to prove a point.

I wished I still had my old office. The new one was beautiful, gorgeous even. Perfect in every way. It couldn't have more of my DNA in it if I'd come and built it myself from the ground up. It had warm light, a sitting area by the windows, open breezy spaces that felt effortless. It was a literal dream.

But dreams look different through tear swollen eyes. Every day I lived with the ghost of the man who moved mountains to make this office happen. His fingerprints were everywhere: in the finishes, the layout, the obscene convenience of being one elevator ride away from his domain. At least my old office had the entire expanse of the city as a buffer between me and that beautiful man and his damnable lies.

I couldn't even look at the lobby anymore. My heart stuttered, plummeted, or ached—time of day dependent—any time I saw a man in a well-tailored suit with brilliant auburn hair. Paisley didn't know what to do with me. I'd become a human zombie going through the motions of life but often forgetting exactly what I was doing when left to my own devices.

I'd told her to head home early. My meetings for the day were over, and my brain had become useless mush. If not for drinks with the Pitchfest girls, I'd have gone home as well. I debated multiple times doing just that. Sending some noncommittal text about having too much work and just cancelling.

I leaned against the window in my office, staring but not seeing. Usually the bustle of the city energized me or had me staring in awe at the bustling beauty of it all. However, today all I could do was stare, cradling a cup of coffee that had long since gone cold.

"Hi." There was a gentle rap at my office door. A woman with an oversized bundle of peonies, wearing an apron embroidered with an ivy-covered tree stood smiling at me.

For a moment I thought that Ellis had sent the flowers. I was about to tell her to send them back to him when she introduced herself.

"I'm Tennyson Auden—well, Tennie... you can call me Tennie. I'm your across the lobby neighbor! I own Auden and Ivy, the flower shop. I'm so glad we're both here at the same time. I keep missing you and wanted to just drop in and introduce myself and give you these."

She passed me the coral and deep pink peonies, some of my favorite variations of the flower. "Peonies." She told me, "Because your office reminds me of them. Beautiful and grounded. Peonies can be a little stubborn about when they decide to bloom, but once they do, they bathe your life in beauty. I hope you love it here."

I blinked, caught off guard by the perceptive assessment. It was happenstance of course that she'd brought me my favorite flower. Maybe my office did subconsciously evoke the suggestion of peonies.

"Thank you," I said, taking the flowers. I looked around my office again, taking in all of the inviting details. "I do love it. I just haven't had a moment to really enjoy it yet."

She nodded like she understood far more than I'd said. "You will."

"Thank you." I examined the precious petals before taking in their sweet scent. "I keep meaning to come over as well. Your shop is so cute, and *busy*!"

"Well," Tennie started to back up toward my door, "Now that we've met—just know you're always welcome to stop by. Even if it's just to get a few minutes away from your screen. I love having company!"

After she left, I placed the peonies on the small table near the window. Their delicate scent clung to the air, making everything feel a little less cold.

My phone buzzed, startling me out of my daydreaming. Then it buzzed again. And a third time.

> Lyris: Where are you?
>
> Hollis: Pitchfest is short one redhead. We need balance sis. There are way too many brunettes here.
>
> Greer: We ordered sangria. The red one that you like. Hollis is already throwing them back like she's getting paid to do so.
>
> Hollis: I've had TWO GLASSES.
>
> Greer: Don't make us drink by ourselves.
>
> Lyris: Just come. Even if you want to sit and babysit one glass the whole night, it will be good for you to get out.

I stared at the screen watching the texts roll in. Going home seemed a much more palatable option. Sweats, my comfy couch, maybe a sad movie to help me exorcise all of these feelings I didn't want to feel anymore.

Just the thought of having to put on a face, pretend I was fine, or even worse, have to cut myself open and bleed for them—it was all too much. Overwhelming even. I didn't have answers, and the thought of fielding questions when I didn't know myself? That did not sound like a fun night.

> Me: I don't want to talk about Ellis.

They weren't just friends though. They'd been my entire support system for years. No one knew better than them the struggles and triumphs. Because they'd been down in the trenches with me, struggling and celebrating next to me, with me, and concurrent to me.

> Greer: We just want to see you. You can sit here in total silence for the whole night and no one will judge you. Come. Please?
>
> Hollis: I'll share the famous coconut cake Beckett gave me from his sister-in-law's diner. 😌
>
> Me: Fine. But just know, I'm only coming for the cake.

The moment I slid into the booth, it was like coming home. Lyris pulled me into a fierce hug. It felt as if she held together every broken piece of me. Greer reached across the booth and took hold of my hand. "We weren't going to let you hole up. Withdrawing to hide your pain isn't how we work, hon."

"But we're not going to say anything," Hollis cut her with a sharp sideways glance that broadcast her displeasure with Greer's opening line. "Unless of course you want us to. No pressure. We'll follow your lead."

I stared down at the glass that Lyris placed in front of me. I swirled its contents, picked out a cherry and ate it, took a long sip and let it settle before I even opened my mouth.

"I'm all over the place." I began. "I don't even know what I want. Sometimes I wake up mad and I desperately want to shoot off a text to Ellis and really get into an *argument* with him. But I also know he wouldn't do that. He wouldn't fight back. Not in the way I need him to that would make me feel better. It's not his style. Then other times I feel numb. Mostly though, I'm humiliated."

The table fell silent. Lyris filled my drink back up, signaling the waitress for another pitcher. Hollis put some appetizers on a plate and pushed it in front of me. I took two bites of a street taco, barely tasting it.

"I feel like I was the only one who didn't know I was just an extra in someone else's reality show."

No one said anything. I saw them sending messages to one another with just tilts of their head and overly expressive gazes. Hollis reached into her bag and brought out a tiny yellow box with an *Ito Eats* logo emblazoned across the front.

"Cake makes everything better." She handed me a fork and opened the top of the box.

"How did you get cake from Texas?" I asked.

"Beckett had Priscilla FedEx one up here so that the team—well—you know so that people knew how good it was."

I'd been so caught up in my own shit, I forget the rest of the world orbited, even the pieces of orbit that were part of my friend group and bled into Ellis's world.

Greer forked into the slice, taking a moment to savor the dessert before saying, ""You don't have to forgive him. But you also don't have to decide anything right now. You get to be confused. You get to be mad. He broke your trust. And that isn't something that can easily be won back."

"I just can't make sense of it." I told them. "It felt *so* incredibly real. I can't figure out why he'd go through the whole theater of our relationship and make me believe it too."

"Have you talked to him?" Lyris asked.

"No. Not since I found out. I asked him to give me some space, and he's doing a bang-up job following that request to the letter."

"Oh...oh, shit." Hollis was hyper focused on something beyond my shoulder.

"Is that who I think it is?" Greer's voice didn't sound any better than Hollis's did. A combination of unfettered shock and awe.

I turned around to follow their gaze. The last person on earth I expected to be walking toward us as we sat and gaped at him.

"Keats?" Hollis asked, "What in the hell are you doing here?"

He lifted his hands in peace as he reached the table. "I'm Switzerland. I come in peace. I bring no secrets, no apologies, and definitely no brotherly manipulation."

"Did you *invite* him?" I asked Hollis, my voice practically apoplectic.

"I didn't," she said. "He asked me if Pitchfest got rescheduled, that's all. He was worried about you and checked in to make sure you were okay."

"I can get security over here." Green stood trying to find one of the waitstaff over the din of patrons.

"It's fine," I said with a resigned sign, passing Keats a sangria glass. "He can stay. But I don't want to hear about your brother."

He nodded and accepted the glass without saying anything.

"I'm not here to defend him," he said after a beat.

"Sounds a lot like the beginning of a defense." Lyris pursued. "Which is exactly what she just asked you not to do."

"Look." He placed both hands on top of the table as if he were submitting to a polygraph test. "You know Ellis, the guy is a walking binder of contingency plans. He's always thinking of eleven possible outcomes to every situation. He went on those awful dates, and he realized as he sat having dinner with each one of them that he had been subconsciously weighing them against you. You were real. Genuine. And he wanted to keep seeing you."

"Keats, seriously, would you look at her?" Greer pointed at me, anger painting her cheeks in strawberry hues. "She looks like she's about to split in half. Just stop. If you can't abide by her request, then leave."

"It wasn't about manipulation Rowan." He continued, ignoring Greer's request. "If you hear nothing else, please just hear that. He wanted to give you the chance to see how real it was between the two of you. He thought, if he had the picture he could buy some time with my dad. That's it."

"Staging a photo so that a person believes its romance is the very definition of manipulation, Keats."

Raze was unusually packed. Typically there were only a handful of people in the bar at the same time we had Pitchfest. Of course, we weren't meeting on our normal night, either. There was no path that took me to the bathroom unimpeded. But I didn't want to keep listening to

Keats defend his brother either. Because just the tiniest piece of me said his version of events made at least a little bit of sense. I wasn't ready in the slightest to start thinking with my head. My heart still called dibs on righteous anger.

"He thought he was going to lose you." He repeated again. "The picture was to give him enough time to win you the real way. By showing up. Showing *you* that nothing about being with you was about optics. It was about finally being able to genuinely love someone without any ulterior motivation."

"He had plenty of opportunity Keats. Why not fess up when the photo went viral? That seemed like the perfect time for truth telling."

Keats hesitated. "He thought if you saw it too soon, you'd never believe that what was growing between you wasn't fake."

The words gutted me. They were too close to what I'd hoped was the truth. Hearing them from someone other than Ellis cut me to the quick. It didn't make them feel any less like betrayal. In fact, it made that blade an even sharper cut.

"Instead of speaking for him," I said softly, looking away. "Maybe suggest to him that he stop managing a message behind his firewall of brothers. Tell him to sack up and tell me himself."

Keats nodded, finally leaning back in his chair. "Fair enough. Just know he's miserable."

Good. I thought. *So was I.*

I didn't know what tomorrow would bring, or what version of me would show up to face it. But tonight? I'd let the wine numb the edge. I'd let my friends hold me up. And I'd let Ellis Hawthorne sweat.

THE WEIGHT OF THE UNWRITTEN ENDING

ELLIS

Rowan didn't block me. Not that I expected a woman of Rowan's stature to engage in such immature antics, but she hadn't even disconnected our shared calendar. That was intended for project management. Silence though, was worse than her angrily taking a Ginsu knife to our interwoven lives. It was too passive. It said things like *I don't have time to give you*. It felt strategic. As if she wanted me to think she didn't care at all.

Unfortunately for her, I knew her all too well. Her silence meant she'd backed into a corner somewhere to tend to her wounds. I worried that she would withdraw from everything, even her friends. At least Keats confirmed she'd been out for drinks with the *Pitchfest group*. That was good.

That day in my office continued to haunt me. The look on her face, a mix of disbelief and pain was something I'd never seen on Rowan. She didn't crumble though. That is what terrified me. It was the stone faced determination she'd left my office with.

That spoke of endings, of severing the maggot riddled infection to save the rest of the body. I was terrified that this was how things would end. Silent, festering, and overflowing with assumptions and supposition.

I'd built this stupid house of cards based on *optics* instead of building a castle with the one woman I wanted the most. I'd just let her walk out. What kind of chicken shit doesn't even fight to keep her? She told me to leave her alone and that's exactly what I did. Instead of bringing food to our starving relationship, I fed it sand.

I went down to the Pivot offices, hoping to catch Rowan at a time when she wasn't meeting a client. Even if she told me to fuck off and that she hated my guts, it would be communication. A starting point.

The office nearly empty except for Paisley and Rowan's book keeper, Mei Lin. Paisley, deep in conversation with someone, barely paid me the time of day.

"Yes, I understand the penalty," Paisley said to whomever was on the phone. "I need to speak to the owner. Fine, then someone from the leasing firm." She continued. "I have questions about the language around subletting."

Paisley didn't even glance at me. She just circled something on her tablet with her stylus, sighed heavily, and said, "Are you sure? Oh, okay. We'll, he's standing right here. Thank you."

"Is she really trying to break the lease?" I asked.

"Is that a real question?" Paisley replied back, turning to her computer.

"Paisley." My voice came out sharper than I intended. "Why?"

"Why do you think?" She finally looked at me with a tone as icy as her stare. "No woman wants to build her future in a place built on a platform of lies."

I crossed my arms. "She signed a long-term lease."

"With a company she didn't know was yours." Paisley

fired back. "And to be honest, I don't even want to have to tell her. It will crush her. Just another layer of the tangled web of lies and dishonestly from Mister Mega Bucks who thinks everything is solved with a check and megalomaniacal obsession with control."

I exhaled. "It's not technically mine. It's a shell company—"

"Whatever, it still comes back to you, Ellis." Paisley cut in. "Why wouldn't you own the building? It only makes sense. I just can't believe I willingly walked right into your bullshit, and I didn't see it. God I was so blind. And then, me believing you meant I lied to Rowan. So now, on top of not being able to trust you, my trustworthiness is called into question too. All because I was so blind to the obvious, I willingly to ate the lies I was fed."

She didn't even bother with a dismissal. Not an angry finger pointing toward the door, or a threat to call security. Instead, Paisley simply turned back to her computer and began furiously typing without a second glance my way.

I left with my tail between my legs, being knocked down multiple pegs from one very protective assistant—I spotted the flower shop across the way and popped in.

"We deliver all over the Chicagoland area." The woman behind the counter told me. "Within the loop, I can have it delivered same day. Suburbs will be at least day, potentially two depending on where you're sending them."

"It's local." I tell her unsure if flowers are even the wise choice.

"If she's mad, don't send her favorite. Otherwise every time she gets them, she'll remember how much you hurt her, instead of how much you love her."

"Is it that obvious?" I asked with a derisive laugh.

"You're standing in front of a flower wall like it's going

to give you relationship advice. So… yeah." She walked up next to me, surveying the display.

"What would you suggest I send?"

"Forget the showy stuff. No red roses. No apology orchids. You want something grounded. Solid. Something that says, 'I'm not going anywhere.' Try a mix with camellias. Depending on what you did—pink is for longing, white is for devotion, blue and purple hyacinth for sincerity and regret, respectively."

I was so turned inside out I stood frozen, unable to even make a decision on what to get.

"Which one says, 'man I royally fucked up, I'm lost without you, and I'll do anything to make it up to you." I half joked.

"That kind of apology needs to be made in person, not through flowers, my friend."

"We're friends?" I asked, smiling as I joked. "I promise you don't want to be my friend. I've got a habit of hurting the people I most want to protect. Doesn't make for great friendship credentials."

"You may not be the first man to mistake control for care," she said, "But maybe you'll be someone who wants to get it right. Either way, screw ups kind of keep me in business because they're repeat customers."

Her laugh was throaty and full, like it took up every inch of space in the small shop. But she managed to get me to smile. These days that was a feat all on its own.

It was Dash's turn to host all of us. My house tended to be the gathering place. I lived most central and had a house that didn't feel cold or claustrophobic.

He lived in Lakeview, on Belmont in a gorgeous penthouse loft building that used to be a library. The massive building took up a full city block, and there were only three units in the building. However, even with his house being a loft, there were minimal places to sit like normal people. We typically ended up gathering around his television with one of us on his sofa, and the rest of us either on the floor or on stools we pulled over from his kitchen. Not the most comfortable place for hanging out.

"I don't know why you sent Keats to play Cupid anyway." Whit launched the first volley within minutes of arriving and getting settled with a drink.

"*I* didn't send him. He went on his own accord."

As if I'd ever send him to play messenger. Though of all my brothers, he was the most dialed into Rowan and her friends. Despite being annoyed by that fact—he may have collected some worthwhile reconnaissance.

"I know where they go for drinks and thought an unbiased Hawthorne might help the situation. Instead, she basically told me to tell Ellis to sack up and don't send your brother as your firewall."

I pointed at him. "He wanted to help yet ended up digging me even deeper into this shit pile."

"Your mistake was thinking you could you plan and control emotions." Dash said. "It's fucking love not a goddamned merger. And yet that's exactly what you expected. A contract negotiation with some sex thrown in. Either you want love, or you want a business arrangement. You can't have both."

The truth was, I didn't want both. Not now. I'd gotten

to taste what *love* felt like in its most pure form. When I'd picked Rowan, it wasn't because I thought she'd be my wife. I picked her because she always saw me. She was a thoughtful adviser, a most trusted partner, and when I needed her to—she never pulled a punch. Other than my brothers, she was the only one who held me, unwaveringly, to a standard that I had to work to maintain.

"I didn't plan for her." I told them, pushing off the sofa to Dash's fridge. I wasn't even hungry but I couldn't sit still. "I planned to just find someone who was equally as career driven as I was. That way we could just negotiate this thing and be on with our lives."

"But you picked Rowan." Keats said, quietly. "Someone who told you the truth. Who made you laugh. Who didn't care about the Hawthorne name."

"I didn't pick her! She wasn't supposed to be the plan." I blurt, raising my hands to emphasize my point and nearly causing my beer to spill over. "I called her because I knew she'd tell me what I needed to hear and help pick the perfect partner."

"Except," Keats continued to push, "maybe you called her, because somewhere deep down that you haven't even acknowledged exists yet—you called her after *five years* because *she* was always the perfect partner."

I nodded. "I don't care about optics anymore. I don't even care about Father and this stupid ultimatum. I just want her back."

Whit leaned forward, elbows on his knees. "Then you need to stop trying to manage the story like all you care about *is* optics. You've done it your whole life—crafting perception. If you want her back, you're going to have to be seen. Not curated. Not refined. Just seen. Even if it's messy."

"She never turned in her badge." Whit added. "She left a door open, even if she doesn't realize she did."

"Which means, since you clearly need things spelled out for you," Keats smiled, slapping my shoulder. "You start with her. Start at the beginning, tell her the truth."

Dash leaned back in his chair, running a hand across his jaw as he studied us. "I think though, you may need to start with yourself, Ellis. What *is* your truth? Do you even know? You've lived such a curated existence for so long now—do you know who you are? Because if you don't have the freedom of being unabashedly yourself and loving every minute of it—you'll never be able to love anyone thoroughly. And, someone like Rowan? The lioness of the pride, needs someone equally as strong and sure as she is."

I didn't know what Rowan would say when I finally got the words out. But for once, I wasn't thinking six steps ahead. I was just thinking of her.

32

TRUTH UNFILTERED

Rowan

> Ellis: I hate mushrooms. There's something about the texture. No matter who prepares them and in what style, I just can't get past their slimy coating.

HE TEXTED ME INTERMITTENTLY. There was no rhyme or reason to them. They never came with any preamble, and he never followed up with anything else. But each revealed something about Ellis.

At first it was in hours that I suffered, trying not to think about Ellis. Then eventually it moved to days. I wasn't sure what Ellis and I were. The door was open on both sides apparently, according to Keats; but no one walked through.

> Ellis: Hawthornes weren't allowed birthday parties growing up.

His revelations ran the gamut from small, insignificant things like personal preferences on food, like mushrooms. And sometimes achingly sad, like how Nathan Hawthorne didn't allow his sons to have birthday parties as kids. They'd celebrate with family and occasionally were allowed to have a friend or two over but blown out birthday to-dos with themes and cake and an avalanche of presents were verboten.

I got the full backstory from Keats, who randomly kept popping up at our Pitchfest. I didn't reply to that revelatory text from Ellis. So far, I hadn't replied to a single one. But they kept coming.

> Ellis: I grew up learning love was earned by being useful. That I needed to be irreplaceable or people left. I don't know how to be someone who doesn't have to prove their value.

That one hit me like a gut punch. He never asked for anything in return. He just patiently placed these tiny, breadcrumbs sometimes funny and sometimes heartbreaking but always so blindly honest.

The worst part of it all, as I came to depend on them. For a small second in my day I could breathe again. A full breath. And feel as if the sunshine had retuned.

Not because I'd forgiven him, mind you. He'd knocked me so far off my game, I'd begun to doubt my own abilities. Had I become so good at "the spin" that even I couldn't determine reality from performance? When had I become so blind?

The next text came Friday morning, just as I walked in to work. Paisley had the week off, and I'd been working from home so much that I'd gotten to the place where I didn't even bother matching my clothes anymore.

> Ellis: You asked me once what my truth was. I'd never been able to answer it before. But I'm starting to figure it out. What I know more than anything else is that I love you Rowan Sloane. Not because of how you make me look. Not because when put on a vetting sheet you align as a perfect partner. You saw me when I was still trying to figure out who I was.

The text chimed just as I'd turned on the lights and grabbed water for coffee. I figured that was the end of the text, but a second chime came minutes later.

> Ellis: I want to be real with you. 100%. No bullshit no façade.
>
> Ellis: I want to deserve you. No pretense, no ulterior motives. Just me. Ellis Hawthorne, showing you, Rowan Sloane, exactly how much I treasure you.

I didn't respond. Couldn't. My eyes had sprung a leak that had no hope of repairing.

Once I taken a few deep breaths and collected a mug of coffee, I made my way to my office to attempt to make it through a workday without thinking about him and his stupid gorgeous face just a short elevator ride up.

On my desk was a box, wrapped in silver paper. Inside it was an average, unmemorable black frame—the tag on the back read Macy's. The note read:

While Cinderella's castle is still my favorite memory from the day—I understand it may be tied to that ugly word I don't ever want to use again: optics. There was nothing about this moment that was fake or staged. It was me, shouting to the world, that I was in love and I'd chosen you. Given the recent events that may call that into question, I want you to have this. Me and you.
No filters, no fanfare. -E

The frame held a picture of the two of us, sitting on the patio at the Disney resort. We'd spent the day walking around, riding rollercoasters, eating crap food, and when we finally made it back to the resort, we were exhausted but content. He'd taken his phone out and snapped a photo of us so quickly, it had barely registered. But we looked happy. Genuine, bliss-filled happiness lit our eyes and pulled at our cheeks. Not just me. Us.

In a rare moment, Ellis was unguarded. No sunglasses to cover his eyes, no business suit to serve as armor. Just him in his Vineyard Vines polo shirt, his sunglasses resting atop his shock of autumn sunset hair. And me, in a "Belle & Boujee" shirt I couldn't resist getting as we walked the shops. He was right. Of course. This was the most unguarded, unfiltered version of us. And there was no lie in the contented peace I could see in both of us. And I hated how badly I wanted to believe that photo wasn't just a memory, but a promise.

I wasn't ready to talk. Not yet. I had my own sorting out to do. This scandal shook me to my core. I'd built a business on gut instincts and learning how to navigate bad messaging and find a way to help fix bad optics. But this thing with Ellis showed me even *optics* could be manipulated. And I didn't know what was worse, creating them in the first place, or manipulating the manipulation. It seemed so sneaky. So underhanded. I could still feel the breath stealing shame when Whit asked about the invoice. I'd been played by the biggest player in Chicago. Not just played, totally fooled.

"You look like someone just told you that your dog died."

I don't know what possessed me to walk across the hall to Tennie's store. We'd barely said more than good morning and exchanged pleasantries about the weather or traffic.

"I want to send a flower." I heard myself saying. "Just one."

It was an open door. Or, it was the same door, but I pushed it open just a hairsbreadth wider. I wanted it to say, "I hear you; we're making strides but we're not there yet."

"You two are killing me with this conversation via flowers." Tennie flipped the towel she'd been using to spot clean the flower fridges, over her shoulder. "When are the two of you just going to sit down and hash this out? What is this, the tenth round of flowers?"

I had zero idea what she was talking about. Other than the casual conversation I'd never purchased a single item from her shop. Tennie circled around her counter and pulled out and order pad, pen at the ready.

"This is the first time I'm buying flowers from you." I clarified, worried that in my zombie like haze over the last month that I'd been sleep-shopping.

"I just figured you were getting them from one of the dot coms. Every week he comes in here, still looking like you told him there was no such thing as Santa. It's always a bouquet—but never peonies. Let's see—Monday it was cherry blossoms, the Wednesday before stargazer lilies, a bouquet of white roses and amaryllis set with eucalyptus. God that was a gorgeous bouquet. I thought for sure you'd be back to walking with an arm around each other's waists, heads tipped conspiratorially after that one. And still no dice."

She rapped her pen against her order pad, flipping through Ellis orders.

"I've never received a single bouquet from him." I told her. "He must have moved on. A new girlfriend maybe."

"No way." She insisted, tucking her pen into her messy bun, shaking her mouse to wake up her computer. "We talk every time he is in here. There's not another girlfriend. He knows he fucked up, I promise. But I wonder where the flowers are going if not to you?"

Tennie's brows pulled together as she scanned her screen, then leaned against the counter, eyes narrowing thoughtfully. "You know... he always carries them out. Never asks for a delivery. Just pays in cash, thanks me, and walks out with them."

"So he's sending them... to no one?"

She shrugged. "Maybe he's not ready to let go yet? Perhaps buying them is his way to forgive himself while he waits for you to."

I swallowed hard, something sharp and unspoken catching in my throat. "Or maybe he's just decorating his apartment."

"Sure." Tennie said with a knowing smile. "That too."

33

ECHOES OF THE INVISIBLE

ELLIS

MY HOUSE SMELLED like a funeral home. Not because anyone had died, but because I'd been mourning something I didn't know how to bury. Every time I thought of Rowan, I bought her a bouquet that fit the apology I couldn't say. Tiger lilies. Eucalyptus. Stargazer lilies. Never peonies because Tennie said I would ruin those for her if I tied them to heartbreak.

Dash said I was a coward. That real men didn't send flowers, they sent truth. But I wasn't sending anything. I just kept collecting them like confessions I wasn't ready to mail.

"Jesus. Did your cleaning lady quit?" Keats stood in the doorway, taking in the bloom-cluttered living room. "You look like shit."

"Tell me something I don't know." I'd barely seen the light of day all weekend. Unusual for me, given my social calendar tended to be jam packed, but I had no desire to play pretend. The days of *optics* were over for Ellis Hawthorne.

Keats ordered food, gathered half-dead bouquets and

muttered something about staging an intervention. I didn't argue. Maybe I needed one. By the time Whit showed up, the three of us were eating Chinese and pretending I was salvageable.

"Just call her," Whit said. "Say you're sorry. Say something real for once."

I passed him my phone. "Tried that."

He scrolled. "You told her our parents didn't throw us birthday parties?"

"It was honest." I shrugged, passing Keats the fried rice he signaled for.

"Try a different flavor of honesty." He handed the phone back. "Tell her you didn't mean for the photo to define her. That you never meant to use her."

He dialed. Put her on speaker. I heard her voicemail and it gutted me. Her voice sounded the same. I felt like Kafka's fucking cockroach trapped in a body unable to articulate its own grief. I was frayed at the edges, and the only person who could pull me back had stopped answering my calls.

"Even if I wanted to say something, how the hell do I get her to listen?"

Keats leaned forward. "You don't beg. You show her. You make a gesture so honest she *has* to listen. Something that says, 'I see you. I'm not hiding anymore.'"

And just like that, I knew what I had to do. Ice men don't mourn. They didn't buy apology bouquets, and they sure as hell don't fall in love with women who see straight through them. But I did."

34

TENDER IS THE TRUTH

Rowan

I COULDN'T WAIT for Paisley to return from vacation. Between final preparations for Green Tie Ball, my client list who got crazier every day, and of course my constantly bleeding heart, I was one more phone call away from a total nervous breakdown. Being this close to Ellis every day was a quiet, constant demolition. I was holding the line by sheer muscle memory.

I'd told Ellis I needed space. That I needed to think about things, us. But I'd been "thinking" for nearly a month and was still stuck in the same whirlpool I had been a month ago. Did I love him? Absolutely. Was I sure he felt the same? No. And not because he hadn't spoken the words a million different ways over the last month.

How could I be sure this wasn't all just to save face? To keep up with the farce that he'd sold to the press. That this wasn't just the next episode in the *Find a Fiancée* reality show.

I took the elevator up from the parking garage, unlocking the door to our offices and flipping on the lights. A few things caught my attention at once. First the overwhelming smell of flowers. And not just the ambient smell that would sometimes waft across the lobby from Tennie's shop. This smelled as if *we* were the flower shop, not just neighbors.

As I walked toward the front of the offices, where our lobby entrance was, I saw them. Everywhere. Vases of flowers on practically every surface. One in particular said "read me first."

It was a basket of ranunculus, brilliant apricot and blush colored. The blooms were full and weightless, as if the card tucked inside would cause them to collapse beneath the weight. It was a linen note with EOH monogrammed along the top left corner. Why did his handwriting have to be so devastatingly elegant.

> I remember the first day you walked into my office. You wore a deep green dress and boots with gold hardware. You smiled when you thought no one saw you. I did. You were nervous. I was drowning. You didn't know it, but you were the only person who made me feel like maybe I wasn't completely failing. I never forgot that. It wasn't just your resume or the way you handled logistics. It was the way you made eye contact—unflinching, unwavering, like you weren't intimidated by me or the empire. I didn't know it then, but that kind of presence was rare. Priceless.

I couldn't catch my breath. It felt as if I'd run all the way there from Ukrainian Village. We'd worked together for so long, of course he'd have memories of me. But seeing them written down, staring me in the face. This wasn't just a PR move. It couldn't be, could it?

The second arrangement was in the kitchen. Eucalyptus and white lilies, somehow calming and bracing all at once. I opened the next card with trembling fingers:

> *I remember those weeks you took off. Keats reminded me of it when we were in Los Angeles. It was when you and Danny broke up. I didn't know it then. I just remember thinking how out of character it was for you to suddenly take off. You—who sends a binder full of instructions and contingency plans and cc'd every executive assistant in the office—every time you had a cold. I planned to ask when you got back, but I didn't. My father had just moved me into the executive seat, and I was terrified. Sixteen-hour days trying to prove I deserved the job—trying to outrun the whispers that I didn't. Your pain got buried under my panic. I'm older now. I've been in your orbit long enough to learn this: pain is meant to be shared. Yours. Mine. I feel it all now. And I will never be the reason you hurt again.*

How did he remember? How on earth did he know all

of this? I held on to the kitchen counter to try to steady the body that wanted to tilt in line with the earth's orbit. I refused to cry. It was just surprising. The emotions I felt were simply a result of being stunned silent so early in the morning.

I found the third bouquet—anemones—on the windowsill near the whiteboard in our collaborative space. I didn't open the note immediately. I just stood there, heart stammering against my ribs, like it already knew what he'd written. My chest ached like someone had shoved a fist between my ribs and pressed down hard.

> The day you left HMB, I told myself it was for the best. That holding you back would've been selfish. But I mourned you. Not the loss of the role—I mourned the loss of your presence. The bright, sharp, breathtaking woman who made everything feel lighter. You were a rocket though, Rowan. You needed to break free of our ozone and go out and explore your own solar system. I knew it then; I know it now. And even still, knowing all I know, I wished you hadn't flown so far away.

I pressed the heel of my palm to my sternum. A stupid, instinctual move—like I could quiet the ache just by applying pressure. There was another bouquet sitting on my desk in an old cracked white pitcher I used to collect pens and other random crap I didn't want cluttering my desk. I wanted to leave it there. To turn around and go home and wait for Paisley to return so *she* could read the note for me. I didn't think I was physically capable of reading another one.

> When my father gave his ultimatum, I didn't think. I picked up the phone and immediately called you. You see through the noise, you always have. You were the only person I knew would tell me the truth, even if it cut. I trusted you with something personal and ridiculous because I knew you'd commit. You're incapable of doing anything halfway. You don't spin. You sharpen. And I've always loved you for that.
> For seeing me. The real me. For never treating the cracks like signs to abandon the project.

I didn't realize I was crying until I saw the words on the note blur. Could I even do it though. Was I even ready? I needed time, to think, to figure out where the line was between lie and truth. I didn't want to fall again only to find out our beautiful story was simply another headline I hadn't written.

I brought the cards home with me, read them and reread them until they were burned in my memory. And still, the weight of them provided no comfort. Ellis's words didn't anchor me. They drifted. Beautiful, weightless—like balloons without ribbons, destined to slip away.

My phone buzzed, starling me. I tried to ignore it. Whatever was on that phone wasn't nearly as important as the gravity of Ellis's notes.

It buzzed again.

> Ellis: I'm here. Waiting. No matter how long it takes.

Panicked, my fingers moved across my keyboard and hit send faster than my brain could clock what I wrote.

> Me: Where?

35

THE LOUDEST SILENCE

ELLIS

THE TEXT CAME in just after midnight. Five letters. One word.

> Rowan: Where?

I sat up so fast the whiskey on my nightstand rattled. For a full minute, I didn't move. I was afraid to even breathe. Petrified that the singular act of releasing carbon dioxide into the air would somehow change the trajectory of our story, or of Rowan's emotional state.

I stared at the screen like it might vanish if I blinked. Feared even that maybe I'd imagined it. I hadn't. It was there, in plain sight, as sharp as a surgeon's scalpel at the ready for an incision.

Where? She'd sent. Not what. Or, why. Not even I'm ready. Just one word. Where.

The silence that had stretched between us for weeks cracked down the middle like ice on a winter lake. She'd read the notes; I assumed every single word. At least I had the audacity to hope she had.

As desperately as I wanted to shoot off an immediate reply, I knew better. Old Ellis would have done that. Would have changed the rotation of the earth if she'd asked. I would have sent a car, offered a plan, bent over backward to ensure she wanted for nothing, not even the inconvenience of determining a place.

But she never asked for a destination. She asked a question that I was certain meant something else entirely. She wanted to know where I was in my emotional journey. Was I ready to meet her. Could I truly stand next to her, keep her steady, bury my roots and have her depend on my strength. Those were the things I needed her to know. To understand. That if she took the risk and stepped forward, she would know it was real, and strong—and would never be affected by life's storms again. I had to be worthy of answering.

Earlier that week, I'd stood in the empty Pivot offices for nearly an hour, waiting for Tennie to finish arranging the last of the flowers. They weren't just bouquets. They were timestamps. Breadcrumbs. Every one of them anchored to something I should've said when I had the chance.

The first day you walked into my office...

The week you disappeared, and I didn't ask why...

The moment you left and I swallowed the ache like it was deserved...

Each note had its own life. An inhale, an exhale, a conversation all its own. They each were truths I'd carried in silence too long.

I didn't know if she'd read them, but I hoped. Until I saw her, I couldn't be certain if she'd kept them or torn them into tiny shreds and thrown them in the garbage. But if she had, I'd be okay with that too. Because the cards were not truly about getting her back. They were providing her the security of knowing that she never had to wonder if I'd seen her. Truly seen her for the amazing, bright, talented woman that she was.

I had. Every damn day. I'd been too much of a coward to give it voice back then. But now, I would shout it from the rooftops for the rest of my life. At first, I thought the loudest silence had been not knowing if Rowan would ever take me back and suffering through those weeks of not knowing. Now, I'd come to understand the loudest silence I would ever know would be the loss of Rowan in my life, forever.

She was still working downstairs. Technically, she was my tenant. She continued to run her business, send invoices, solve problems and attend planning meetings for Gateway Green and their big 30th Green Tie Ball. Our lives still occasionally intersected. But the life had been sucked from those interactions. They were brief. Cold. Lacking depth.

This version of Rowan wasn't her. Not really. Her laughter never reached the lobby. Her perfume didn't linger in the elevator. Her eyes didn't meet mine unless she had to, and when they did, it was transitory; brutally clean and emotionless. I would've preferred a slap.

Three days after I sent the flowers, I saw her. She was standing in her office talking to Tennie, smiling politely. She looked tired, worn thin but still standing. She glanced at me through the glass wall, and for a second, I thought she might come out.

She didn't. She turned back toward Tennie. Said something, I couldn't hear and then walked away. And I went home and sat in the dark, surrounded by all the unsent things I'd written her.

When I sent the text about waiting no matter how long it took, I meant it. I hadn't expected a response. But her message back split something inside me open. Not in pain. In *hope*. It was the first time I'd felt her reaching back.

I opened our thread. Typed a dozen different replies. Deleted all of them. Ater that day with Tennie, I sent the only one that mattered.

> Me: Wherever you need me to be.

36

CHAMPAGNE PROBLEMS

Rowan

WITH THE GREEN Tie Ball less than a week away, when the Pitchfest girls stole me away for a spa day, I definitely did not put up a fight. I felt wrung out. I had no more tears to cry or energy to expel trying to find right-side up again.

I squinted through my sunglasses at the spa entrance. Glass walls, rain-curved fountains, the soothing sounds of water chasing rocks along tiny brooks. The smell of eucalyptus with a hefty side of privilege wafted through the air.

"Did they see us pull up in your Jeep?" Greer asked Hollis. "I feel like just knowing we drove here in an American car is the first strike against us."

"I'm almost ashamed to give them my average, non-elite credit card for services." Hollis joked. "Will they even take something that isn't an Amex Black?"

We stood at reception, Lyris randomly sniffing the display bottles, Hollis practically breaking her neck scoping out the facilities, and Greer standing nervously next to me waiting to check in.

"How did you guys hear about this place anyway?" I

asked. None of them answered me. Lyris immediately ducked around the corner, pretending to need a cup of their special fruit infused water. Greer paled and looked to Hollis who rolled her eyes in my direction before finally admitting on a huff, "Keats, okay."

"You two are spending an awful lot of time together," I teased.

"Cooking show, remember? I think Keats is planning to move to Los Angeles soon. As soon as they get the greenlight from Ell—Oh, hey, check out these robes."

We were led to the dressing room, assigned lockers and given the usual rundown of undressing and putting on the heavenly robes before meeting in the relaxation room to begin our day with champagne.

"So, are we purposely *not* mentioning Ellis's name?" I asked calling out the elephant in the room. "You can talk about him; I won't fall apart."

"We just didn't know." Lyris rubbed my shoulder, before taking a seat next to me.

"You're awfully broken up over a fake relationship." Hollis asked with pointed accuracy so sharp she may as well thrown a dart at me.

"Hollis." Our friends name came out of both Lyris's and Greer's mouths simultaneously.

"It wasn't fake." I told them, waving off my friends upset. "At least not for me. Sure we said it was for the press —because he had those dates with all those women—but it never felt that way to me. But again—who knows where Ellis's head was or is."

"The man sent you a botanical thesis." Lyris's voice jumped an octave, garnering us pointed looks from the other women relaxing in the ready room. "We know where his head is. You're just too afraid to take the leap and believe it."

"Has he said anything since those notes?" Greer asked.

"He'd told me that he would wait, for as long as I needed. I replied back *Where*, and then he replied, *wherever I needed him to be*."

They all looked at me the same way—like I'd crack. I could tell in the weird, sideways lean they each had in their oversized massage chairs that they were all silently preparing to jump to my assistance the moment emotions began to spill out of me.

I was stuck between not wanting to talk about it anymore, and wanting to dump every unspoken thing onto the floor like a puzzle someone else could put together. I didn't need judgment. I didn't need advice. I just wanted someone to *see* me and help me figure out my next steps.

Lyris slid a chocolate-covered strawberry onto my plate and topped off my champagne. "You don't have to figure it all out today. You just have to let yourself feel it."

Greer clinked her glass against mine. "To feeling it."

Hollis leaned back in her chair, stretching like a satisfied cat. "And to soft girls with sharp instincts. We don't cry often, but at least when we do, we remember our journalistic training and make it a pretty cry."

Her comment caught me completely off guard, yanking a laugh right out of me. The sound felt like a cleansing. It provided me the smallest semblance of room in my chest to breathe. The ache didn't vanish, but for the first time in weeks, it wasn't the only thing I felt. Because maybe I didn't need to untangle everything today. I just needed to remember I wasn't doing it alone.

By the end of the day we were happily loose, unbelievably buoyant from the champagne, and for me at least, relaxed enough that I looked forward to my bed. The receptionist approached me with their signature sage green billfold, tab tucked discreetly inside.

"Everything has been taken care of Miss Sloane, even gratuities. I just need you to sign on the line and take the quick survey on your satisfaction with our services."

"Hey, did one of you pay for this already?" I asked the group as they lingered over the various products the spa sold to take home.

"No, remember I thought they'd give me side eye for trying to pay with a normal credit card." Hollis laughed. "A credit card which certainly would balk in a very loud and embarrassing way, if I tried to charge *four* all day treatments on it."

I opened up the billfold scanning the receipt. *Tendered: E. Hawthorne*

Even on a day when he wasn't supposed to be there, he was. Present. Quiet. Constant. Whenever or however I needed him. Just like he'd promised.

37

THE UNBEARABLE WEIGHT OF LEGACY

ELLIS

MOTHER INSISTED we all get together at the house. They'd be off to Martha's Vineyard soon, as was their habit for the end of summer every year. When they came back at the end of September, it would be full speed ahead planning for Father's retirement at the end of the year, and his party in November.

Based on the general less than enthusiastic attitudes of the rest of my brothers as we sat around the dinner table, I'd say that no one really wanted be part of the theater of family for the night. I'd been the only one who arrived on time. Keats showed up barefoot, pulling a pair of Birkenstocks out of the back of his SUV, claiming he'd been *hanging out* at the beach. Keats Hawthorne did not hang out at the beach. When I'd grilled him about it, he refused to expand any further.

Whit came thirty minutes late. In the Hawthorne house that was worse than an actual slap in the face. Even work was not allowed to come before family dinner, especially when it was scheduled on a Sunday afternoon. My father waved off his excuse of a "work emergency" that required him to go in first thing, with a terse expletive. Dash had come in right behind me and had been throwing back glasses of Father's very expensive bourbon like it was water. The Hawthorne men all seemed to be handling Father's looming deadline quite well.

"So, how is everyone tracking?" Father asked once dinner had been cleared and we were having drinks and cigars on the patio. Well, he was having drinks and cigars. Dash was still doing shots like a college girl, Whit couldn't take his attention off his phone, and Keats impatiently looked at his watch every five minutes.

"Oh, we're finally talking about our love it or lose everything clause?" Whit asked, his voice full of venom. "Just peachy, Dad. The women are lining up, desperate for a chance to marry a billionaire. It is so incredibly ironic that you spent our entire lives telling us to watch out for the women who would try to use us, abuse us, and back us into corners to steal our money, and yet here you are—basically forcing us to go vampire hunting just so the board has good optics, and you have a waiting line of progeny. Because I'm sure that will be next year's breaking ball."

Dash stared at Whit as if he questioned whether they were related, despite looking nearly identical. He shifted in his chair, clearly uncomfortable with Whit's outburst. As the youngest though, he tended to wait in the wings until one of us called on him to tap in to whatever slugfest we endured with Father.

"Do you really think this is still a good idea, Dad?" Keats asked, "Have you looked at your oldest son lately? Really *looked* at him? He's miserable. All because he's so desperate to follow your orders to the letter just to earn the role he's been groomed since adolescence to take. Never mind that he has essentially been filling it for years now, and yet you *still* won't give him the satisfaction of telling him what an amazing fucking job he's doing. Or god forbid tell him how lucky you are to have a son like him to crush beneath the weight of your ridiculous expectations."

Keats rarely got mad. Not like that. Vitriol and poison tipped arrows were not the things Keats Hawthorne dealt in. He preferred daisy chains and mediating for middle ground. This whole evening had taken a surreal turn.

Nathan didn't respond. He simply stood up, wiped his hands on his pants, turned on his heel and walked back inside.

After what felt like hours, Dash finally asked, "So do you think this means that the great fiancée find is over?"

"Not a chance," I said just before I heard Father's terse voice from inside, summoning me with a single *Ellison*.

I found him in his study. The door was open, he sat at his desk, lighting another cigar. Smoking inside? If mother saw him, she'd have his hide. If he risked her wrath, I was in for something huge.

Father's home study was exactly like him: ornate, stately, slightly out of date. The oversized windows behind his desk looked out over the expansive acreage of our childhood suburban home. With the amount of light he must get every day, it spoke of a time when sunshine streaming in meant nothing more than warmth on your back and not making it nearly impossible to see a computer screen and do business.

"You look awful." Father took a seat next to me, handing me a glass. Probably bourbon, and if I had to guess it was that trendy Lakshmi Bourbon that Whit was such a fan of.

"You should call her." He continued after a meditative sip from his glass.

"She won't answer my calls." I told him. "Believe me, I've tried, Whit has tried, Keats has tied."

It was because of him that the best thing that had happened in my life, called into question every sincere word and action over the few months.

"Unfortunately, thanks to your *requirements*," I valiantly tried not to spit out the word. To hold the same level of decorum and respect that we'd all been raised to treat Father with. But I couldn't. The realization that I lost the one thing that felt real and genuine, all because of him, decorum was the only thing holding me back from cold clocking him.

"Thanks to this mess." I pivoted after a deep breath, "all my sincerity has been clouded beneath the veil of requirement."

Father nodded. He took another sip of his bourbon, staring out at the infinite grounds of the Hawthorne compound.

"You were always going to be CEO Ellis. There has never been a doubt as to who would take the reins when I stepped down. My request that you find someone to love wasn't out of the need for optics, it was because I realized as I sat here one night with your mother, that I had unknowingly robbed from all four of you, precious years of *living*. Of having someone by your side, of watching your kids grow up and sit next to your partner with this kind of wild fascination that your children were *so* like you but also so different from you. You, most of all."

The fledgling five-year aged bourbon must have been stronger than I gave it credit. Of all the things I expected from Father not a single sentence of what he'd just said would have been in any realm of possibility. If I was the Ice Man, Nathan Hawthorne was the South Pole. Stoic, barren, bereft of life to bring any warmth to an interaction.

"When I started at Hawthorne, your mother and I were already married. Back then you pinned your love interest by junior year of university. You planned weddings right after graduation and were expected to announce the arrival of your first baby by the next spring. So we had you, and Whitman, Keats, and Dashiel, and eventually Brontë, long before I was sitting with my father in board meetings and discussing the time when I would take over.

"We were still just newspapers and television when I did. They were simpler to manage. Each was basically the same. It had expected outcomes and metrics. You were just starting graduate school, your brothers at various stages in their academic development, but you all pretty much were well on your way to adulthood. And then the world exploded into an information superhighway. Everyone struggled to get their hands around. But you,"

He laughed and pointed his bony finger at me. It had been a long time since I saw any kind of entertained delight from him. It felt foreign. Like I'd been thrown into one of those fun house mirrors at the carnival and was looking at life through a manipulated reflection.

"You took on every new development with enthusiastic inquiry. None of it befuddled you, and you were able to work seamlessly with print, terrestrial radio, then the internet, streaming. And as each new technological advancement popped up, there you were with ideas on how to capitalize on it and develop it for Hawthorne's benefit. You became a CEO at twenty-two without even realizing you'd taken on the role. And I'm blame myself. I robbed you of two decades that you should have been finding your life partner. Getting married, buying a house, having kids, and getting lost in the magical, wonderful, chaos of raising your kids.

"I leaned way too hard on the four of you. You made me so proud and you were all so desperate to prove how much you knew. How capable you were of making a significant contribution to the family legacy. And Hawthorne got so big so fast, that I gluttonously fed from your enthusiasm. Leading was so overwhelming that I had to offload to the four of you just to keep from drowning."

I wanted to say something. To tell him that it wasn't a burden. That he didn't need to bleed for me in the name of salvation. But my whole life was Hawthorne. And it had been for as long as I could remember.

"I realized as I started talking about retirement, and over drinks with friends who are similarly stepping down from their legacies, that I'm not like them. Their kids went off and lived their lives and maybe eventually returned to the family business. But their kids all have balance. Families and the business. The four of you have nothing but oversized bank accounts and bankrupt hearts.

"Your forties will probably be your best decade. You're at the top of your physical game, top of your professional game. Everything feels like picking the ripest fruit. That's why I put this whole requirement together. Because I don't want to steal one more second of your *life* from you. A life with laughter, and love, shitty handmade presents and *World's Greatest Dad* mugs. The stuff that fills your soul instead of your bank accounts.

"Dash and Keats, thankfully, they get to be a little bit ahead of the game. But you and Whit, unfortunately are just cresting into the last decade that you still *feel* young and invincible. By fifty the check engine soon light starts to give its warnings.

"First it will be a knee that just doesn't move as smoothly as it used to. Then you'll be playing with the kids in the backyard and you'll be clutching the bottle of pain killers like they were your lifeblood for all of the following day.

"I'm rambling now." He laughed, relaxing into his chair and crossing his leg over the other. "Bottom line, I want you to run toward Rowan. Without any fear or doubt. Second guessing has never gotten you anywhere in business and it certainly will not ever get you anywhere in love. And you love her. I know that without a doubt.

"Work? It will always be here. There are four of you to share in that burden. There's no need to run for professional responsibilities. They never end and there will always be more. But love? Life? Personal fulfillment. It's fleeting. A ticking clock counting down your expiration. You need to sprint toward love and once you have it, hold on to it and cherish it like you're afraid it will be ripped from your arms. Because one day, it will."

For the first time, I saw Nathan Hawthorne not as the man who built the empire—but as the father who built it hoping we'd have someone to share it with. He hadn't forged this legacy to suffocate us. He'd built it hoping we'd find something—*someone*—worth keeping it for.

38

IN THE COMPANY OF GIANTS

Rowan

I'D WORKED all summer like my career depended on this one night. In some ways, I kind of did. Of course, I still had Pivot. But being accepted into this inner circle could open a lot of doors.

Every pitch deck, planning meeting, vendor contract and committee meeting came down to the event of the season. The Green Tie Ball was a venerable who's who of Chicago's elite—mixed with those in media and the outer ring. People like me who could afford the ticket cost but weren't *in the orbit*. Until today.

I needed to prove to the Sweenie VanMeter's of the world that I belonged, even if my bank accounts weren't in the ten and eleven-figure range. Hell, they were barely treading water in the six-figure range.

I had value. I was the strategy. It was my vision that catapulted our success. My grit that found new avenues of funding, doubled the donation amounts from year's previous, negotiated a change of venue, and managed to do it all while tumbling endlessly in personal strife.

It wasn't lost on me that the only reason I was in the

room was because of the very man standing at the step-and-repeat looking devastating in his forest green, crushed velvet tux. That had it not been for him suggesting to Sweenie she reach out, I never would have had this opportunity.

I thought back to the small white lie I'd told Ellis. Solely because I wanted him to think I'd become a well-connected mover and shaker since I left Hawthorne. I'd said it so quickly, too casually, like my way of saying *look, I matter too*. Because I'd been so desperate for someone to validate me. My hard work. The drive that propelled me every day.

Ellis never called me on it. That lie. He looked at me with that infuriatingly sexy half-smile, and a raised eyebrow that broadcast interest not condescension. Instead he'd quietly moved the chess pieces in the background to create reality where I'd spun fairytales.

Now I stood in the lobby of the Adler Planetarium, in my floor length, emerald, green ball gown that I'd bought off-the-rack at Nordstrom. A $700 Mac Duggal. Ellis's bow tie probably cost more, or the delicate floral clutch that Sweenie VanMeter carried with her as she worked the room.

I'd chosen my dress carefully. It declared ownership of the room. Paisley said it looked stunning, Romanesque, with its strategic draping, peek-a-boo slits, and delicate florals that draped down the side and into a train that followed behind me.

If my heart had to spend all night in a blender of emotions seeing Ellis Hawthorne again, I wanted to make sure I at least *looked* put together. Even if my world had been slowly falling apart. I'd been too chicken shit to ever reply back to his text. His willingness to meet me, wherever I was, whenever I was ready. What did ready look like?

How did you know when it was time to take a deep breath and jump?

I watched as all four of the Hawthorne brothers stood at the step-and-repeat. Flashbulbs exploding like a Fourth of July finale, desperate to collect the perfect shot of Chicago's royalty. They all carried on and joked with each other and the people taking their picture. None of them appeared to have come with a date. Their father's deadline was fast approaching. Had the firestorm of attention on Ellis and I caused the brothers to all throw their middle fingers up at the requirement?'

Whit was the first one to notice me staring. He smiled and winked in my direction, before turning to head toward the registration desk. Keats was next, knocking his brother's chest and pointing at me. I'd been preparing myself all week for this moment. The very second that I felt Ellis Hawthorne's attention on me again.

The pair approached me before I could turn and find something to pretend pulled away my attention. My heart. It had been beating steadily as it always did. But as soon as Ellis got close enough to get lost in his *Après Ski* scent, it stuttered and then rushed into a frenetic beat as if I'd just mainlined speed.

I wanted to be unmoved. I'd spent the last month rehearsing for this very moment.

Telling myself I could look him in the eye and feel nothing. But the truth was, I felt everything. Everything I'd tried to bury under ambition, and stubborn pride, all those long nights building something that mattered. The magic *thing* between us that I'd foolishly pretended wasn't love. He looked at me like I was still his, and I hated how badly I wanted to believe it.

His mouth curled at the corner like it always did when

he was about to say something low and dangerous. Something that would leave me rattled for days. But before he could speak, the lights dimmed. The orchestra struck the first note. And Sweenie stood at the podium, directing everyone to take their seats.

"Gorgeous," he said, his lips grazing against my cheek as he brushed past.

That was it. Nothing more.

FEAR IS THE SIBLING TO AMBITION

ELLIS

I saw her before she saw me. Of course I did. I'd been scanning the room since the second I walked in, hoping to get a glimpse of her.

Ever the hostess, she stood near the step-and-repeat, wearing green as was the custom at the Green Tie Ball. Hers, however, was the kind of green that made every other dress in the room look like background noise. She'd swept her hair up and to the side, like a regal braided crown. Her dress, with its floral draping, trailed behind her like a comet made of silk and ceremony.

My breath caught. Actually *caught*. Lungs that had dependably provided my body with air for nearly forty years, suddenly ceased to function. She looked like the future I hadn't let myself plan for. The future that ever since welcoming her back into my life, I dreamed of.

She was here.

If not for Dash and his compulsive preening, we would've arrived during cocktails. There should have been plenty of time. For us. For the moment where I could pull her aside and say something. *Anything* that would have mattered before I had to become the man behind the podium again.

The only thing I could do was kiss her cheek and compliment her dress before they handed me a mic and ushered me to the stage. Sweenie gushed into the microphone talking about all that I helped the accomplish. Finally, pointing at me she said: "Ladies and gentlemen, please welcome this year's Legacy Benefactor and CEO of Hawthorne Media Group, Mr. Ellis Hawthorne."

The screens behind me lit up with my name, title, company and the words: *Legacy Benefactor*. As if the people in this room didn't know who I was. Like the last six weeks of press scandals hadn't made me a household name.

"Good evening, everyone. Thank you once again for coming out to the thirtieth anniversary of the Green Tie Ball. I speak for all at Hawthorne Media Group, that we continue to support Gateway Greens and all the work they do expanding green spaces across the city, once again as the legacy benefactor. In a world where concrete moves faster than compassion, your enthusiastic support means more than you know.

"Green spaces matter. They slow us down. Remind us to breathe. Tell us that what's cultivated with care has the power to last."

I scanned the room, as much as I could under the heat of the spotlights. I was searching. Not for applause. Not for approval. Just for her.

"In my role at Hawthorne, I give a lot of speeches. Some are for events like this. Others are for awards, or investor calls, or to light a fire under executive teams. But many years ago, I gave one that stuck. I was young, just starting my rise, and I said something I thought was profound at the time: 'Fear is the sibling to ambition. They co-exist. Fear guides you to the choices you most need to make.'

"At the time, it sounded good. Sharp. Confident. I'm sure it read well in an article, centered next to a glossy photo of a man in a Brioni suit."

The audience laughed. I let it carry for a beat; let it buy me time. She still wasn't at her table. Next to Sweenie, there was an empty chair. My stomach dropped. Had she left? Had she intentionally avoided sitting front-row at the event she helped plan just to avoid seeing me?

"Over the past ten or so years, I've learned a thing or two. Especially regarding fear. Something I wish I understood when I was younger. Fear is a compass, yes. But it's not just meant to push us toward ambition. It's meant to point us toward *truth*. Toward the things that terrify us *because they matter*. Starting something. Building something. Loving someone.

"The real fear isn't failure. It's *staying stuck*. It's hiding behind titles and polished answers. It's realizing—too late—that you never let yourself want what you actually needed."

I finally spotted her, near the back of the room. Regal and radiant in her gown, surveying the space with the sharp assessment I'd come to depend on. The kind of look that said she already had seventeen contingency plans locked and loaded.

"I've built a legacy on strategy. On knowing the next move before the board shifts. But green spaces—like love, like courage—aren't built through control. They're built through presence. Patience. Trust."

I paused. Just long enough to look at her. Just long enough to be sure she saw me seeing her.

"Tonight, I'm not speaking as a benefactor or CEO. I'm speaking as someone who understands fear isn't the thing to beat. It's the thing to face, hand and hand with the person who reminds you what's worth building in the first place. Thank you to Sweenie and to tonight's rising star of Gateway Green, Ms. Rowan Sloane. The two of you are the dynamic duo of making Chicago even more beautiful than it's ever been."

There was applause. Heads turned to search for her. Rowan simply lifted her chin and gave a small wave from the back of the room. One day, I hoped, I'd be able to bring her into the spotlight and keep her there. Because someone as phosphorescent as she was deserved to dazzle beneath the lights she helped create.

"Thank you again to all of you for supporting this cause. For helping to create space where beautiful things can grow. It's because of you, that we can all walk away tonight remembering that to create lasting beauty sometimes you have to step back, have patience, and watch it take root before it can bloom. In that waiting we know that something beautiful will come from it. Courage doesn't roar, and fear doesn't hide. Sometimes both exist in the quiet whispering: *I'm ready to begin whenever you are.*"

40

THE TRUTH IN THE QUIET

Rowan

Ellis Hawthorne had always been good with words. That was a given. You don't ascend the Hawthorne legacy without being able to rally the troops in any number of situations. But this hadn't been a rally. It wasn't performative or polished for *optics* and legacy headlines.

It was him. *Ellis.* Speaking directly to me, in a language only I would recognize.

His voice had trembled just slightly when he said *love*. He'd looked for me in the room, repeatedly. I watched as he unsuccessfully scanned blinded by the spotlights. But he'd named me. In a room full of his peers, he'd called me by name and associated me into this event in a way that ensured I was a partner and not a polished accessory. Not only for everyone in the room—but for him. His equal.

Fear is the sibling to ambition. He'd said, transporting back to that ballroom in Las Vegas so many years ago. The speech that watered the seed that became Pivot. He'd been listening when I told him. He'd taken it, digested it, and helped to keep me both grounded and blooming, while also building enough scaffolding that I could bloom toward the sun.

He cracked me open with the possibility of forever. Held himself up as an example that it was okay to fear the fall, because faith said someone would be there to catch you. On instinct I pulled my phone out of my clutch, scanning for his name. My thumb hovered. I saw the unanswered reply he'd given me. *Wherever you need me to be.*

Wherever. That looked like so many things since that fated phone call so many months ago. It was in quiet conference rooms, making connections for me behind the scenes instead of exposing my lie. And showing up in my office with sandwiches because he knew I'd worked through lunch. In diverting the burning heat of the media's attention away from me, while also creating professional havoc for a person that harmed me. It was sending me on a spa retreat when he knew I'd be burned out. *Wherever* turned out to be everywhere, without it feeling like everything.

I headed into the melee of the ballroom. Toward the lights. Toward him. Because I didn't want a speech. I didn't want apologies or drawn out conversations of wrong doing. I just wanted him. And I was finally ready to say something back.

A RING BETWEEN THE LINES

ELLIS

I felt Rowan long before I saw her. I stood with Whit chatting to one of our clients, wishing that for one night I didn't have to be Ellis the CEO. Initially before everything went to shit with her, I'd pushed for Whit to give the speech. Telling him it had to be more than just me as the face of HMG.

The shift was subtle, as if the air separated in acknowledgment of her regality. One minute I was offering to buy old what's-his-name a drink and the next, a sea of people in varying shades of green broke apart, and she stood there, just watching me.

For weeks I'd lived on the razor's edge of suffering and silence. I tried to respect the space she'd requested. Forced myself to believe that if I held on for long enough, she would find her way back to me.

And there she was. Looking like the leprechaun offering me its gold, with a flame of copper hair and a bright green dress.

We weren't running anymore. Not away. Not toward.

Just forward, with intent, toward the one truth that had always been waiting for us.

Rather than speak, I held out my hand. She placed hers in mine without hesitation. A shy smile pulled at her lips; cheeks tinged with pink. The orchestra shifted into something slow, timeless. As if the universe had sent a song right on cue.

We began to sway in time to the music, and I allowed myself to become lost on a sea of sensation. The feel of her soft skin against my cheek, the sweet smell of her perfume, the luxurious texture of the satin of her dress against my hand resting protectively on her back.

"I love you." I whispered in her ear. "Over these weeks, I wondered if I told you that enough. If in that oversight, I'd allowed you to exist in a place where you doubted just how important to me you were. Have always been."

She turned her head, eyes focusing on mine, shifting ever so slightly across my face, as if looking for the lie. I kissed her. Long and slow, hopefully signaling to her how heartfelt and true they were.

"Thank you," she said, running her hand along my jaw. "For being everywhere, even when I didn't know where I needed you to be."

Her mouth trembled. Her eyes misted. But tonight wasn't for tears. Not for reliving what we'd lost. Tonight was for standing in awe of everything we'd planted. The bloom of something we thought might not survive.

I pulled her closer, placing a kiss against her temple. I held her for long minutes, simply losing myself in the feel of having her in my arms again. There'd been times over the last month I'd feared I wouldn't ever have that opportunity again. So I would take my time and savor it.

"Put your hand in my pocket." I told her, eventually. "Outside jacket pocket, left side."

Her nose wrinkled and she tilted her head in that cute way she did when she couldn't tell if I was joking. But instead of challenging me, she simply slid her hand beneath the flap, finding the cool circle of metal adorned with a single, peony pink diamond. One of the rarest of the lot, just like her.

"What?" She just gaped at me, blinking rapidly.

"Just trust me." I replied, kissing the question from her mouth.

Her fingers stilled in my pocket, but she kept it there as we wound around the dance floor.

"I'm not asking tonight." I whispered. "I wouldn't. Because tonight is about you in a spotlight. And what is in my pocket, and the question that comes with it is just for us. You and me, in the quiet. Real. I don't want it to be under the bright lights or in front of cameras. It will be on a morning where you warm your hands around a coffee cup, your hair is falling out of the messy bun you slept in, and I'll look at you with your sleepy smile and be able to finally tell you what I've always known."

Rowan buried her face in my neck. I heard the quietest exhale of breath that sounded too much like a sob. I pulled her tighter, allowing us to relish in the quiet of the moment until she was able to collect herself.

"Sweetheart, it's always been you," I said, rubbing her back and pressing another kiss to her temple. "Even when I didn't see it. When I was too afraid to say it out loud. You're it for me Rowan. I'll choose you every day for the rest of my life, whenever you are ready to take my hand and jump into the unknown."

The music kept playing. We continued to dance. Neither of us let go. She never took the ring out of my pocket, but her hand never left it either.

42

THE MAGICAL FOREVER

Rowan

By the time the band packed up and the caterers started break down the tables and packing away the china, I was barely held together. My feet throbbed and the only thing I wanted to do was go home eat something and spend some time with Ellis before passing out cold.

Ellis Hawthorne was a man that ascended the carpet laden steps and stopped for pictures. He was green rooms and hordes of assistants falling over him to make him comfortable. His kind didn't park in the employee lot and carry bags of knick knacks packed for any number of potential emergencies.

Yet he'd stayed. Despite the sideways glances from clients and associates, the suggestive winks and hoots from his brothers, and the wide berth and questioning looks from the waitstaff, Ellis sat at the bar, watching for any moment to provide assistance while we closed the party down.

The moment the last bag was packed up, he gathered me in his arms and carried me out to my car. We drove back to his place—him driving my car—with just the music on the radio station and our thoughts to keep us company.

He had a ring in his pocket. I tried not to think about it. Tried to remember that he'd said *when the time was right* not at that very moment. I knew though, the moment he brought it out what my answer would be, without hesitation.

My hand felt right in his. Where it had been through the entire ride back home. His thumb swept gently across my knuckles, lulling me into a contented silence that eventually lulled me into sleep. When he pulled into his driveway, I was out cold, the events of the day exhausting me deep in my bones.

He collected me from the passenger seat; my heels pinched between my fingers even in sleep.

"I can walk." I protested, the moment feeling achingly familiar.

"I know you can. You are Rowan Sloane, the most amazing woman I've ever known. But I want to carry you. Love doing it in fact."

Cradled against him, I melted into his hold. My head tucked beneath his chin, felt like the most natural place for it to me. As if when he'd been created, they'd melded that space to the specifications of my head. The soft cashmere of his tuxedo caressed my cheek as he ascended the stairs to his bedroom.

I should've insisted that I walked. Laughed, or said something to break the tension winding itself tight between us. But I realized it wasn't tension; it was a sense of rightness that wrapped my body in a subtle awareness of his.

He pulled back the covers on his bed, placing me on the mattress before turning just enough to access the back of my dress. He removed it slowly, reverently kissing each piece of exposed skin the descending zipper exposed.

As I stood and the dress pooled at my feet, he pulled me against his chest, gathering my lips against his. He kissed me reverently. So gentle had my eyes not been open, I wouldn't have known he'd done it at all.

His jacket came next, along with his bowtie and suspenders. Once those were off my bra followed, the hooks trembling beneath his gentle hands. Each of us dealing an article in a game of strip poker where the stakes were nothing more than mutual pleasure.

We moved together in an unhurried dance. Like we had all the time in the world. As if the universe had finally given us permission to feel every moment and take in each gasp or sigh as if the actions alone weaved our individual existences together.

He kissed me like a prayer. Gentle, eyes full of worship, and hands moving slow, exuding love and passion with each pass across my gooseflesh riddled skin. When he reached across me to grab a condom from his nightstand, I stilled his hand.

"No barriers," I said, "I want all of you."

He froze, mid-reach. Not because I'd scared him, but because we both understood the weight of what I said. No more pretending anything between us was temporary. Because it wouldn't be ever again. The ring in his pocket promised that, but even more than that, we'd said as much to one another through our actions over the last few months. We were it. The end of the line for one another.

He dropped his head against mine, taking in my earnest request. His warm cocoa eyes full of a hope-filled question, and my amber ones assured in my declaration. This was what reconciliation and renewal looked like for us. Our first joining with all of our barriers dropped. Both the emotional ones and the physical.

He kissed me again, lips hot against my skin as they took a topographical journey to map my skin. My fingers did the same, slow and deliberate. As if to document everything we'd nearly lost. My desire rewound everything my heart had unspooled through the course of the evening.

Ellis took his cock in hand, gently running it through the slick that had gathered between my legs. He stilled before pressing in, looking at me as if he needed to be assured that yes, I did in fact want him to enter me unsheathed.

"Please Ellis. I need this."

It was all the permission he needed. When he slid inside me, it was with a gasp and a groan, like he'd just stepped into something holy. Like he'd found home. We moved together, focused and slow. There wasn't any reason to rush. We were simply heated skin and desire coiling and desperate for release.

"Ellis." His name on my lips as I came wasn't rushed. I didn't scream or cry out when I called him. It was soft, reverent, like a promise. A vow of forever.

His lips found my shoulder, my collarbone, the hollow of my throat. He whispered words I couldn't understand, half-formed declarations lost against my skin. But I felt them. Felt everything. Because, this time was different.

MORNING CAME with sunny warmth streaming through the windows we'd neglected to close the night before. Six in the morning was way too early for anyone to be awake, after having only gone to bed a few hours previous. Just beyond

Ellis's windows, I could hear the bustle of a city just beginning to wake.

So much had happened the night before. There were questions, explanations, things that needed to be addressed. But at the heart of it all: I was in love with Ellis Hawthorne.

"I can hear your brain moving a million miles a minute, again." I heard Ellis's sleep graveled voice from beneath a pillow behind me.

It was de ja vu, bringing back to that first night when we'd done this at my house. When everything was uncertain. Ellis arm snaked around my waist, pulling me against his chest. His fingers tickled down my shoulder, along my arm, until he stopped at my hand.

I hadn't even noticed what sat on my finger. Not until Ellis wiggled it back and forth where it sat, catching the morning light and spraying rainbow patterns against the wall. Cool. Smooth. A gentle circle of metal hugging my left hand. My heart paused—only for a beat—and then restarted. Slow and steady, assured. There was no panic, or anxiety, nothing to weigh me down other than the soothing comfort of Ellis's arm.

The ring was delicate, unmistakably me. A peony pink diamond, brilliantly cushion cut and proudly sitting alone, so it could be seen and admired without the competition of other sparkling stones.

His hand came to rest against my jaw, thumb brushing the corner of my mouth. "I didn't want a spotlight. Not a photographer. Not a crowd. I just wanted you to wake up and know you were mine."

I nodded, tears slipping free despite my best efforts. "I am," I told him. "I do."

He smiled his signature smile, "No, that part is for later, with white dresses and tuxes and a minister that asks if you'll have me forever. For this part, your answer should just be yes or no but wait for my question."

I turned so I could face him. He propped his head on his hand, tracing my lips with his fingers. He kissed me slowly one last time before pulling away.

"I should have at least gotten breakfast or let you get dressed. But last night after you fell asleep, I grabbed it from my jacket so it wouldn't get lost. And I just couldn't wait. I needed to see it on your hand, to know that you would be mine forever.

"I used to see a man in the mirror who measured worth by control, precision, legacy. But then you walked back into my life and wrecked all my careful definitions. You challenged me, every day, to want more—not in power, but in character. And now, when I look at you, I see the man I want to become reflected in your eyes. That's the version of me I will spend the rest of my life becoming if you'll let me. And after all the spreadsheets, background checks, and personality matrixes we built to find me the perfect partner—turns out, none of them even came close to you."

I wasn't able to locate my voice. I used it regularly, every day in fact. Suddenly the one time I needed it more than ever, emotion had taken it hostage and locked it away beneath a chest-full of emotion.

"If it's too soon, I'll wait forever." He clarified, misunderstanding my pause. "If that's what it takes, I can spend my entire fortune sending you daily flowers to tell you how much you mean to me."

I traced his jaw, pulling his beautiful face closer to mine so I could kiss his soft lips. My emotional levee broke, tears overflowing and soaking into the sheets. He kissed me again, through my tears. There wasn't an urgency, any attempt to shut off the tears to arrive at an answer. He gave me the space I needed. The same peace I found in quiet mornings, or golden afternoons, with him.

"The only flowers I need are the ones for my bouquet—when I say *I do*." I giggled, nodding like a besotted school girl.

"There is one thing we need to figure out though." I schooled my features with mock concern.

"What?" Ellis looked panicked, every ounce of joy that had just rained across his face had suddenly been schooled beneath the CEO mask.

"Whose house are we selling? Because the cross-city commute is an absolute drag."

He licked at his lips; I saw his brain working to volley something back at me. I'd expected something sensual or quippy. Like "you're a billionaire now, we can keep both." Once again, he surprised me by choosing none of the above.

"Whichever one doesn't have you in it—because that one's already worthless."

"Then let's build one together," I whispered, losing myself all over again in his heated kisses and quiet promises of forever. "One that only has room for us."

For so long, I believed I had to prove I belonged in the room. But maybe I just hadn't found the right one to build—with someone who already saw me as enough. I didn't need to beg for a seat at the table. Ellis showed me that any table worth sitting at had a chair pulled out, already waiting for me.

He taught me that being seen—truly seen—by someone who understands you, challenges you, and loves you without condition... will always be the most valuable place to belong.

43

WHAT THE LIGHT REVEALED

ELLIS

FOUR MONTHS Later

My parent's estate had a warm, ethereal glow about it. While winter threatened just on the horizon, somehow it stayed at bay. We were all gathered: Whit, Keats, Dash was running late as usual but promised he'd be in attendance. Even Brontë had somehow made her way back from Mexico or wherever she'd presently taken her little van and YouTube channel and graced us with her presence.

Rowan sat around the outdoor fire pit with Whit and Keats's women, the three of them having formed an instant, familial bond. That settled something deep inside me. Knowing that my soon-to-be wife had insinuated herself not just into my heart but had become the figurative head of the next generation of Hawthornes. They all looked to her for guidance, not just the women, but my brothers as well.

She kept Pivot—I hadn't expected her not to—and with the rousing success of the Green Tie Ball, had more offers than her tiny staff of five could handle. Good thing she had four exceptionally astute businessmen to help guide her expansion. Even Father offered to act as consultant, now that he was retiring.

From somewhere inside my mother's laughter, a rarity in the Hawthorne household, rang out as Father snagged an early helping of whatever dinner was being laid out for the celebration. Not just his official retirement from HMG, but his seventieth birthday. A milestone. The kind of moment when you gather the people who know you best and remind them who you were, who you became, and what you're still holding onto.

We all assembled, taking our seats at our assigned places around their ballroom ready to enjoy the dinner and dancing my mother had arranged. Whit, clinked his knife against his glass, standing to draw everyone's attention. Before we start, my brother's and I want to pay tribute to the man we're here to celebrate.

"To the man who led the charge," Whit said. "Who ran the empire like a tactician and raised four sons who all thought they had to live like emperors to keep up."

Keats went next, winking at me as he raised his glass, "To Dad. Who demanded excellence, withheld praise like it was a finite resource, and somehow still made us desperately want to impress him every day. We all hope we've earned your respect, and our places at the table."

Both of my brothers, and basically the entirety of the ballroom, turned to me. I stood, kissing Rowan as I did. No matter the reason, without his ridiculous demand, I would have never been forced to face my fears or jump into the promise of forever.

"Father, you once told me that in your desire for us to help you build the Hawthorne legacy, you neglected to give us the space to learn about what was most important in life. However, I disagree. You taught us love: for one another, for our family, for what it means to be a Hawthorne and to love the story that this family has been building for over a century. You taught us words like honor, respect, decency, social responsibility and telling the truth, unflinchingly and without bias. You built us, not just as sons that reflected your values, as leaders who keep your legacy, but as men who know true legacy isn't in paychecks, buildings, or the stories people will tell when you are gone. Legacy is love. It's family. It's falling without fear into the all-encompassing nature of finding a partner who reflects your soul's greatest desires and holds your dreams as reverently as they hold yours. It's what we carry forward when the lights are off and the cameras are capturing someone else's story. To Nathan." I held up my glass and the room toasted his honor.

My father stood, his face reddened from more than the bourbon. "I leave the company in competent and capable hands. My sons," he turned and looked at us, raising his glass singularly to each one of us, "your work matters—of course it does. It always will. But you are not married to HMG or the legacy of our company. These women, the ones holding your hands, looking at you as if you were personally responsible for the sun that wakes them every day—they are your future. Guard it like it's the most precious thing in the world, because it is. I love you all and am so incredibly proud of who you have become."

The applause and well wishes drowned out the sound of the front door opening and closing. One moment we were all toasting Father, hugging him as he passed by, and the next Dash stood in front of us, looking just as his named described, *dashing* in his black on black tux.

"Mom, Dad, Brontë...guys...I'd like you to meet my wife."

PRE-ORDER WHIT'S STORY!

💍 A fake engagement. A billionaire CFO with a legacy to uphold. A florist one missed payment away from losing everything.

Whitman Hawthorne doesn't make messes—he solves them. But when his father demands he settle down to secure his place in the family empire, Whit makes the most efficient decision of his life: a fake engagement.

Tennie Auden is colorful chaos, tenacity in a flower crown—and months behind on rent. Partnering with the most emotionally unavailable man in Chicago wasn't her Plan A... but it might be her only shot at saving her business.

But what starts as a contract becomes something far

messier: shared dinners, tangled routines, and a little girl with friendship bracelets who thinks he hung the moon.

🔥 For fans of Ali Hazelwood, Lucy Score, and Lauren Layne

🏷️ Tropes: Fake Engagement, Grumpy/Sunshine, Found Family, He Falls First

💚 Featuring: Emotional intimacy, hot tub tension, soft touch moments, and a single mom with a spine of steel

WILLOW'S MEA CULPA

HELLO I'M Mea Culpa

For those who have read me before, you know that I use my mea culpa to admit/acknowledge/accept all of the shit that I took serious creative license on in my book. As a reminder this is a literal last minute brain dump thrown into the back of the book just before I hit publish—so there's probably going to be typos. No one sees this but me.

First before I get into the Mea Culpas, I'm not sure if anyone but my own nerdy little literary heart will catch the chapter titles, but they are all a nod to Ralph Ellison, whom Ellison is named after. You'll notice that in all four books (well, there might be more, we'll see) but definitely with the four brothers. Each will have chapter titles dedicated to their namesakes.

I have such a huge sign for the universe for Whit's story which is like 40% written right now. But as much as I'm dying to talk about it, it should really go in his Mea Culpa and not this one.

Also, I realized that I now have Ellis (Ellison) Hawthorne and Bryce Ellis (Date and Switch) and Penn Ellis (Bed of Roses). I just finished casting etc the audiobook for Date & Switch so maybe that is why I had Ellis on the brain—not sure.

When I started this book and was looking for names, I just googled "Literary male names" and Ellison was one of the ones that popped up that I liked the sound of- probably because I'd been elbow deep in Bryce Ellis. So Mea Culpa for the name confusion now that will happen going forward. I'll try not to let the Ellis's cross paths with the Hawthorne's haha.

Also my editor and I were laughing at the fact that I've suddenly become obsessed with people's names that end in S — and she's ready to kill me for falling back on old grammar habits using an S' to show possession instead of an S's ... like there is probably a stress doll she's torn to shreds because of me. I actually got a very formal sounding paragraph in my word document about grammar rules, cited from the Chicago Manual of Style hahahah.

Alright, I think that's everything from my brain dump. On to the Mea Culpas

1 I haven't lived in Chicago for about eight years. I was unaware that the Signature Room closed until I looked it up for this book. Mea Culpa. It was a good restaurant in its heyday. Im pretty sure I celebrated at least three anniversaries there.

2 Also its been ages since I lived in Chicago. Back in my

day Ukranian Village was an up and coming hipster neighborhood where all the newly graduated from college kids who couldn't afford to live in the holy trinity of the north side (Wrigleyville, Lincoln Park/Lakeview & Old Town).

    3 My apologies to the Astor club. Its a new club. My eyeballs nearly fell out when I saw how much it costs to join. I'm sure its not all new money. As if new money is something to be ashamed of. I don't have new or old money so you're a step ahead of me

    4 Did you catch the Annie Templeton reference? I wanted poor jealous Ellis to have one, one up on Beckett. Sure Beckett may have known Rowan first... but he could only pine after Annie Templeton... Ellis has her VCard.

    5 One time when I worked in radio we had Dennis Miller (the comedian who also hosted a radio show syndicate) in town for this huge event we had with all our radio syndicators. He was flying on the private plane of another of the radio hosts- Im not going to say his name because he's quite polarizing. Anyhow they flew in together on a private plane. Dennis's "Set" went over or someone else went over and made Dennis late I don't remember the whole story but long story short, apparently because of that the plane missed its takeoff window at O'Hare and was fined $15,000. So that is actually a legitimate thing. Who knew you got fined if you didn't take off as planned.

    6 No shade at sorority girls. I never was one. My dad wanted me desperately to join Delta Delta Delta just so he could call and re-enact the SNL sketch. But they were expensive. I did watch sorority life on MTV. Sadly as I was thinking about it, I realized I can still sing the opening song. Great. I can't remember my password five seconds after I

have to switch it, but I remember the theme song of a show from the nineties that lasted all of one season– or maybe it was two. I feel like there was one season at UCSD or USD and then another season no one watched. I just googled it was Cal Davis, not San Diego. And it was on for three seasons...the more you know *rainbow*

7 There have been so many signs from the universe lately. Abundant signs from the universe. Which, given I was laid off from my regular job two months ago and desperately trying to stay positive, keep writing, push through-it's a struggle. Every day. You'll hear more signs from the universe in Whitman's book which is next because they are overflowing with that one.

8 If you've read me all the way to the way back machine– starting with Dirty Little Secret and Secrets of the Heart (dont worry if you havent the books are dinosaurs). But you get glimpses of Ivy and Hillary in more recent books [my Love on the Air series, and most recently in Date and Switch). Anyhow, Ivy Hursch, son of Lucas Hursch, got his start in Chicago as a beat writer, I can't remember which newspaper or magazine I had him working at. But in Secrets of the Heart he tells Ivy about the day he met her mother–it was a New Year's Eve party thrown by the Heffners. I can't remember anymore under the fog of deadlines and my note for this Mea Culpa just said "Dont forget to mention the Playboy connection." I hate when I write notes to myself and dont understand what I meant. I'm so inconsiderate sometimes, haha.

9 When I picked the name Rowan it was simply because it was literary and Ellison themed (I think he has a poem named Rowan?) Anyhow–I googled good last names for Rowan and Sloane came up – of course having Hillary Sloane as my character from a million years ago, I thought

what a fantastic connection because Hillary still lives in Chicago and helps run Hursch Media– great connection and perfect excuse as to why Rowan couldn't stay with HMG (also IDK why I have two media empires in Chicago both with H names.)

10 I know in Redhead in Bed, you get a peek at all of the Murray brothers when Priscilla has Ella, and there is talk of Beckett at that moment trying to get Priscilla on a cooking show. That would have happened *before* the pitch here since Beckett and Lane are already expecting baby #2. The timeline is like barely incongruous. Mea Culpa. For all we know he was talking about it as a hope and not a fact – let's just go with that, Haha

11 I really love crossing over worlds. It happened totally accidentally with this one. I'm not even sure which scene it was, I think the boardroom scene when they're talking about tattoos and whatnot. And I think whatever university I intended for her to go to didnt have a Delta Gamma chapter. And I know nothing about sororities other than the few my friends were in. And a LOT of them were Delta Gamma (at different universities, which was why I picked it because they were nice people so *shrugs* I assume its a "nice person" sorority) I knew they were at Iowa because an old friend of mine's younger sister went to Iowa ad we went to sister weekend so that's how it got picked. I still am not a fan of Iowa–just to keep that straight.

12 If you've read the Murray brothers, you know that Beckett went to Iowa because they like to think they're a huge powerhouse swimming school (*whispers* they're not) and like to claim the invention of the butterfly as being "invented" at Iowa. So when I wrote that she went to Iowa I was like Oh my god! Beckett went to Iowa, that would make so much sense. And of course since her friend Hollis is a

sports journalist and went to Iowa with her, naturally they would have also known Beckett if Hollis was also a member of Iowa's swim team.

13 In case anyone in Chicago goes looking for Ike's – sorry, it's a Phoenix sandwich shop. Literally my favorite place like hands down better than Subway, Jimmy Johns, Jersey Mikes etc. It has the longest vegetarian menu known to man and every sandwich is freaking amazing. They have meat eater sandwiches as well, but as someone who has been a vegetarian since high school to have a "cheap" (as in the cost of the food not the level of taste) sandwich place make a zillion considerations for people who don't eat meat is just the absolute tits. Especially considering you're lucky at the other places to even get something with protein for your sandwich (like the veggie patty at Subway) versus just bread and lettuce (I'm over simplifying but you get the point).

14 So just as a taste thing, I personally hate ketchup, always have. But it's simply a personal preference not my Chicago showing. So when I saw this little mini documentary on YouTube about the history of ketchup and why Chicago was so anti-ketchup as a city, I was like WOWWWW 😳. That little interlude between the brothers is a hundred percent true. People used ketchup to cover up the taste of bad meat and given Chicago was a slaughterhouse and meat-packing city, they prided themselves on quality. The more you know!

15 The Green Tie Ball and Chicago Gateway Green are legit things. Though I have no idea who runs it. Back in the day pre pre-pandemic, getting an invite to the Green Tie Ball was like height of "cool." Having worked in radio back then, I attended ... once. I had a poor just out of just-out-of-college working girl's salary back then and could

barely afford the table fee (I'm pretty sure I charged it to a bloated credit card). But just *being there* was the coolest experience. The actual ball isn't around anymore– for anyone in Chicago who yelled at me as they read it, Mea Culpa. The Gateway Green still has fundraisers, just not that one.

16 I hope people catch my easter eggs. My editor, Amy, called me the "Taylor Swift" of interconnected stories. High praise. I'm still shimmering from that compliment haha. Anyhow, there are so many worlds and references in here for the readers who have been through all of my stories. If you haven't, no worries.

a. The references to Beckett Murray, Presley and Priscilla Murray, and Harris Murray begin with Beckett's story, Thirst Trap. This story would occur *after* Harris's story (Redhead in Bed).

b. It also would have occurred after all of the Barren Hill stories (Gemini Tate). Beard on Tap is her story. I drop references to Lakshmi Bourbon a lot in this story. That is Jasper Raj's story–Whiskey Business (also part of the Barren Hill series but like everything else is an interconnected standalone).

c. The Hursch origin stories start with my very first published books: Dirty Little Secret and Secrets of the Heart. They're written in 3rd person and aren't nearly as dirty as I write now.. So forewarned. But that will give you the Hursch backstory. If you want the more up-to-date Hursch backstory, you'll see them first in Independence Bae, and then again in Date and Switch. They may be in someone else's book too, but all of the stories are fuzzy, hahah.

Alright, I say every time "I can't believe I had this much

to say" like suddenly Im surprised that, as a writer, I could be so verbose 😅🫠🙈

Anyhow, as always thank you to the Unicorn Squad, Amy- my editor turned friend, Anna & Andi Lynne. You all have the most special places in my heart. Thank you for showing me what true friendship looks like. I love you each to infinity.

PAY A VISIT TO WILLOW'S WORLDS!

Heir Agreement: The Hawthorne Brothers

None of the Above (Ellis & Rowan)

Good on Paper (Whit & Tennie)

No Comment (Keats & ... 😏)

Terms & Conditions (Dash & ... 😏)

Love on the Air Series

Screwg'd (Bear & Marley)

Bed of Roses (Raven & Penn)

Independence Bae (Bear & Marley, Raven & Penn and some old friends from Dirty Little Secret & Secrets of the Heart)

The Miller Sisters (Love on the Air Spinoff)

Date & Switch (Sera Miller & Bryce Ellis (Penn's Brother)

Rental Clause (Felicity Miller & Klaus Baer)

Under a Starlit Sky (Date & Switch Spin Off) – Appeared in Christmas Anthology will release soon

Enemies in Ernest (Acacia & Edwin (Klaus' Cousin)

Salve (Rex Miller & Regina Cole - Felicity & Sera's brother) Coming soon!

The Murray Brothers

Thirst Trap (Beckett & Lane)

Flirt Like a Champ (Cash Murray & Harlow Prince)

Secret Santa (Priscilla King & Presley Murray)

Redhead in Bed (Harris Murray and Lorelei Donnegan)

King of the Cul De Sac -*Murray Brothers Spin Off*- (Lennox Shaw & Jesse King) Harlow's Sister & Priscilla's Brother

The Barren Hill Series

Beard on Tap (Finn & Gemini)

Codename: Dustoff (Emmett & Amelia)

Whiskey Business - *A Barren Hill Spinoff*- (Jasper & Remle)

A Whole New World (*A Whiskey Business Spinoff*, Coming Eventually)

The Jones Brothers (Coming Soon!)

Capivate Me (Sterling Cooper Jones)

Titillate Me   (Sullivan Carter Jones)

Extracurricular Academics

Booking Dr. Wrong (Dr. Patrick Ryan & Tabitha Spence)

Witch Please (Dr. Sebastian Doyle & Dr. Imogen Pilar)

Missed Connections (Dr. Phoebe Wagner & Anders Larochette)

The Royals - An Extracurricular Academics Spin Off

Mile High Monarch (A Missed Connections Spin Off)

The Expireship (A Mile High Monarch Spin Off) Coming Soon!

Deck Pic (Sawyer & Wren)

The Power of Two (Soon)

Romantic Suspense

I Will Always Find You & Found (The Jefe Duet)

Contemporary New Adult

Dirty Little Secret

Secrets of the Heart

ABOUT THE AUTHOR

willowwriting.com